A Gorgeous Excitement

A Gorgeous Excitement

A Novel

Cynthia Weiner

CROWN
NEW YORK

Crown

An imprint of the Crown Publishing Group

A division of Penguin Random House LLC

crownpublishing.com

Library of Congress Cataloging-in-Publication Data

Names: Weiner, Cynthia, author. Title: A gorgeous excitement : a novel / Cynthia Weiner. Identifiers: LCCN 2023052963 | ISBN 9780593798843 (hardback ; acid-free paper) | ISBN 9780593798850 (ebook) Subjects: LCGFT: Thrillers (Fiction) | Novels. Classification: LCC PS3623.E432434 G67 2025 | DDC 813/.6—dc23/eng/20231113 LC record available at https://lccn.loc.gov/2023052963

Hardcover ISBN 978-0-593-79884-3
Ebook ISBN 978-0-593-79885-0

Editor: Amy Einhorn
Editorial assistant: Lori Kusatzky
Production editor: Terry Deal
Text designer: Andrea Lau
Production manager: Heather Williamson
Managing editor: Chris Tanigawa
Copy editor: Rachelle Mandik
Proofreaders: Michael Fedison, Monika Dziamka, and Tess Rossi
Publicists: Mary Moates and Josie McRoberts
Marketer: Kimberly Lew

Manufactured in the United States of America

9 8 7 6 5 4 3 2 1

First Edition

In memory of my parents

. . . a gorgeous excitement and a maniacal compulsion to move.

—Sigmund Freud, *Über Coca*, on the effects of cocaine

A NOTE FROM THE AUTHOR

A Gorgeous Excitement is inspired by my teenage years in Manhattan in the 1980s, and the horrific death of a young woman in the summer of 1986 that would come to be known as the "Preppy Murder." I've always wanted to write about those years and that terrible event, not journalistically but fictionally, to try to capture the frenzied psyche of the era and the illusory sense of invulnerability my girlfriends and I shared. In an age before cell phones, social media, or contemporary notions of parental supervision to keep track of us, we ran rampant through the city streets, did cocaine with strangers at nightclubs, and traipsed through Central Park in the middle of the night. We were invincible, without limitations or consequences—or so we believed until the morning of August 26, when we heard about the dead girl in the park.

Like Nina, I grew up Jewish on the Upper East Side, near my grandparents. I also knew the guy who would be charged with murdering the girl in the park and spent many nights drinking with him and his friends at Dorrian's (the model for Flanagan's bar). But this is a work of fiction. Stephanie is an amalgam of girls I have known and adored. Alison was fabricated as a foil to Nina's insecurities and competitiveness for the affections of Gardner Reed. And Gardner is a fictional redrawing of the exceedingly handsome, charismatic guy every girl wanted and every guy revered, but who, it turns out, no one truly knew.

A Gorgeous Excitement

Chapter One

It was the summer of 1986 when the girl was found dead in Central Park behind the Metropolitan Museum—half-naked, legs splayed, arms flung over her head. Larynx crushed.

There was a matchbook in her pocket from Flanagan's, the preppy hangout on Eighty-Fourth Street. Police learned she'd left the bar with him at four a.m. Unbelievably handsome guy, charismatic, popular Flanagan's mainstay. By nightfall, they had him under arrest. She'd coaxed him into going to the park to have sex, he told the police. Her death had been a terrible accident.

PREPPY SEXCAPADE TURNS DEADLY! screamed the cover of the *New York Post*.

Of course it had been an accident. Horrible, unthinkable, but an accident. "I liked her very much," he'd tell police. "She was easy to get along with. Easy to talk to." Why would a guy like him suddenly decide to kill a girl he liked? It made no sense.

Everyone had known him forever. Buckley, Surf Club, Gold & Silver committee. Remember that time he went down Ajax Mountain on one ski? That epic backgammon game in Palm Beach?

And her? Nice enough, the Flanagan's regulars said, if a little annoying. She'd been after him all summer. That night, she'd hung around Flanagan's until closing time, trying to get his attention. Kept going to the bathroom so she could parade by his table in the back where he sat drinking whiskey and playing cards. Outwaited all the other girls—Campbell Hughes, Minnie Potter, Brooke Limbocker. Waylaid him at the door and said, "Wherever you're going, I'm going too."

An hour later, she was dead.

Not that it was her fault. But that didn't make it his.

"She forced my pants down," he'd tell police, "without my consent," straddled him, squeezed his balls—made it hurt. He'd yelled for her to stop, yanked her off him. She landed at the base of the tree and didn't move. He thought she was kidding, but she was dead.

ROUGH SEX GONE WRONG! said the *Daily News*.

A freak accident, everyone decided. She hadn't known when to quit.

"She was a very nice person," he'd say. "She was just too pushy."

But that wouldn't be until August. It was still early June, and a different girl was on the cover of all the city tabloids, a young, beautiful model with an ugly gash down her cheek. A pair of lowlifes with razor blades had slashed her face outside a West Side bar the night before, hired by the girl's landlord after she turned down his repeated advances.

BEAUTY AND THE CREEP, the cover of the *Post* proclaimed.

Nina Jacobs bent over the doorman's console to study the photos, wincing at the girl's 150 black stitches. The model was twenty-four, six years older than Nina, but she looked years younger: round cheeks, angelic smile—in the pre-attack photo anyway. She was from Wisconsin. Nina pictured apple orchards and open country roads, log rafts drifting down the river, picnics on its banks with your neighbors. No wonder she looked so good-natured and gracious, even with the Frankenstein stitches. No wonder she'd felt safe meeting the landlord at a bar to get back her security deposit, despite the beard on him that looked like a layer of dirt. Nina wouldn't have met that beard in Grand Central Station during rush hour. You knew better when you grew up in the city.

She glanced at herself in the lobby mirror. She was headed out to Flanagan's to celebrate graduation with her Bancroft friends and, while she was at it, scout a candidate to please God take her virginity this summer before her apparatus rusted shut. She'd aimed for the opposite of her usual plain-Jane look: moussed-up hair and thick, dark eyeliner, Spandex skirt, and a satin camisole under a denim jacket. But now, with the model's wholesomeness in mind, it seemed she'd swung too far in the other direction. "Smile," she ordered her reflection. "This isn't a lineup." She rubbed off half the eyeliner and pushed down her hair.

True, it hadn't been a banner day, starting with her mother showing up late to Nina's graduation after the graduates had already marched down the aisle and up onto the stage in their floor-length white dresses, where they sat in rows of folding chairs, looking, she imagined, like a choir of virgin sacrifices—as if she needed another reminder of her status. For weeks, her mother's depression had been heavier and angrier than usual, with Nina and her father taking turns as targets. They hadn't been sure she'd show up today at all, and Nina couldn't say she was happy she had, watching the commotion of her entrance, Frances bumping her way down the row where Ira had saved her a seat just in case, inexplicably dressed in an argyle sweater and gray flannel skirt even though it was ninety degrees outside. People craned their necks as she kicked a man's leg and hissed that he'd tried to trip her.

"Who *is* that?" Polly Jessup, seated beside Nina, had asked, but Nina just shrugged, so tense her shoulders got stuck up by her ears.

During the headmistress's speech, her mother had squatted with her camera in the aisle, hollering Nina's name like a crazed paparazza

(*Ohhh*, Polly said, inching away) until, lightheaded from Nardil or Darvon, she lost her balance and toppled backward onto her butt. At the reception, she'd raged at the bartender over too many ice cubes in her cranberry juice and then threw one at Ira when he tried to shush her. When Nina tried to intervene, her mother slung what was left of her drink at her, splashing the white commencement dress scarlet.

But at least razor-blade-wielding thugs hadn't ambushed Nina on the way home from the reception. She could walk into Flanagan's tonight without a face full of stitches. And in even better news: eighty-six days, ten hours, and twenty-eight minutes until she finally, blessedly, left for Vanderbilt. Not her first choice, but her top picks had rejected her, maybe because she'd mistakenly checked "Native American" as her ethnicity on the applications. For some reason—she couldn't rule out the shots of her father's vodka she'd consumed while she filled them out—she'd honestly thought Native American meant "born in America," and "Caucasian" somewhere in Asia. The applications were already in the mail to Brown and Georgetown before she realized her mistake. But the silver lining was that Vanderbilt wouldn't be crawling with New Yorkers: she hoped to bask in the prestige surely afforded a girl from Manhattan at a college in the Deep South.

As she crossed the lobby toward the door, she heard what sounded like belly-dancing music—cymbals and sitars and a man's tremulous wail—coming from the doorman's transistor radio. The doormen weren't supposed to play music while on duty, but she secretly liked the idea of his music seeping into the walls of her uptight apartment building, the echo of thrusting hips and hookah pipes rattling the sugar scions and Daughters of the Revolution who'd barely let the Jacobs family past the co-op board ten years before. Nina still wasn't sure why her parents so badly wanted to live here. Yes, it was an elegant building in a desirable neighborhood, but how elegant and desirable could Ira and Frances feel when, even now, the co-op board president, Carter Lorillard, insisted on greeting them in the lobby as "the Jewish Jacobses," as in, "Always good to see the Jewish Jacobses," or "How are the Jewish Jacobses this evening?" Nina had yet to hear him greet "the Episcopalian Sloanes," or ask "the Catholic Ryans" how they were doing.

The doorman came back inside from fetching a taxi for a tenant. Freddie was in his thirties, lived in a basement apartment in the Bronx, and dreamed about opening a car wash one day. He gave her a wet-lipped grin as he approached. Nina's father had once told her that Freddie had escaped some godforsaken country where half his family was still locked away in the bowels of a medieval government prison. His history made her stomach clench, but so did he.

"Black stockings very pretty against Miss Nina's white, white skin," he said.

She'd cut the feet off a pair of lace tights to resemble Madonna's, although now she saw she might have chopped too much since in the lobby mirror they looked more like knickers.

"Leggings," she corrected him. Her voice was stern, but that didn't stop him from closing the space between them to embrace her. The doormen also weren't supposed to touch the residents, but she submitted to his hug for the usual count of five, her unspoken quid pro quo for Freddie not ratting her out to her parents for various transgressions, like the time she and her friends tossed raw eggs out the bathroom window and a pissed-off casualty called the police. Or six weeks ago, over spring break, when she came home drunk from Walker Pierson's after a humiliating effort to shed her virginity, with bits of her own vomit still caked in her hair.

The first time Freddie had surprised her with an embrace, she figured maybe it was a customary greeting in his country. She later noticed he didn't hug any of the other residents—or leer at them or comment on their clothing or their figures—but it seemed too late to renegotiate the terms of their tacit agreement.

Freddie clutched the back of her shirt, fingers digging into her spine. *Four, three, two,* she counted silently, averting her head to avoid inhaling his garlicky sweat and loneliness. No big deal, she told herself as she pulled free. Let it lie. He grinned at her again and tipped his gold-braided hat as she hurried past him out the door.

Outside was a sapphire sky, a moon as round and translucent as an onion. She shook off Freddie's grope, and the model's cut-up face, and the Walker Pierson fiasco, and even her raging mother, for now safely ensconced upstairs in a Halcion fog, and practically galloped to Third Avenue.

Most nights, Flanagan's was a drowsy hangout for divorced lawyers and neighborhood alcoholics, indistinguishable from the scores of other pubs that lined Second Avenue: red-and-white checkered tablecloths, pressed-tin ceiling, potted plants in the windows. But on weekends it transformed into a preppy spectacle, with throngs of kids who'd known each other forever from boarding school or the Maidstone Club or Fishers Island. The girls had stork legs and satin hair. The guys exuded the cocky nonchalance of the chosen. Everyone glowed with crazy good luck and yellow brick road futures. It was thrilling to walk among them, but intimidating, too, if you lacked the bona fides. Bancroft was a prestigious all-girls private school, but Nina's father, originally from St. Louis, was a tax lawyer with a mid-tier firm, and while the Grossbergs on her mother's side had done well in construction, they were from Queens, where in fact Nina was born and lived until she was two. She'd bet no one else at Flanagan's tonight had spent childhood summers in Rockaway, where the ocean was a cold stew of seaweed and sewage, and the beach in the morning often spattered with blood from a late-night gang fight. Or went out for dim sum and a movie on Christmas Day. Or got *Zuckerman Unbound* as a graduation gift.

The handful of times she'd been to Flanagan's, she'd gone mute with self-consciousness and spent the night with her head ducked, making towers out of coasters and bracelets out of straws. Tonight she was better prepared: she'd snuck one of her mother's Klonopin and washed it down with two shots of her father's Belvedere, a concoction that had gotten her through dinners at her grandmother Pearl's and dozens of her mother's explosions. She'd thrown in some Midol and Dexatrim for good measure. She'd also rewatched Kathleen Turner's hair maneuver in *Body Heat*. "You're not too smart, are you?" she says to William Hurt as she gathers her hair in a fist above her head. "I like that in a man"—then drops it in a cascade over her shoulders, which Nina practiced as she approached Eighty-Third Street.

Inside the bar, clouds of smoke mixed with Anaïs Anaïs perfume made her eyes burn. She pushed through the crowd, past the long bar and huge brick fireplace and the black-and-white photographs hung all over the walls. Leigh and Meredith were drinking sangria at a round table wedged between two wood pillars. Nina had been friends with them since first grade at Bancroft, although neither had turned out to be a true-blue kindred spirit. It had always been a loose trio of shifting alliances, but the connections had felt especially frayed this past year, the banter off a beat, so half the time you couldn't tell when someone was kidding. Maybe their impatience to start the next part of their lives turned them all a little tone-deaf. Or maybe it went deeper than that, but Nina hadn't really wanted to investigate. Turn over the boulder of friendship and who knew what might be wriggling underneath.

Newports and Parliaments littered the table. Nina still craved the whirl of smoke in her lungs, but six weeks ago she'd stopped cold turkey, the morning she learned Pearl had died.

"How's your mom?" Leigh asked when Nina arrived at the table. She giggled and apologized. "I know it's not funny, but wow did she wipe out today."

Nina plastered on a breezy smile. "It *was* kind of funny." It wasn't. It was humiliating, and galling of Leigh to bring it up. Even thinking about it now, twelve hours later, Nina felt the weight of it pressing down on her, threatening to crack her Klonopin-and-vodka cocoon.

But no one wanted a killjoy at a celebration. She forced a laugh as she sat. "Her ass will probably be black and blue tomorrow."

Everyone complained about their parents, but Nina kept the grimmer details about Frances to herself. It had always been understood in her family that her mother's condition was not to be publicly discussed, or even acknowledged: it was no one else's business, and no one else really wanted to know anyway. The times Nina had ventured into forbidden territory with her friends, mentioned her mother flying off the handle over an empty sugar bowl or not leaving her bed for a week, she'd been met with uncomfortable silence and a swift change of subject.

"I was telling Meredith that I saw my gyno the other day," Leigh said. "To start on the pill."

Nina squirmed. She was the only virgin at the table, the only one inadvertently abiding by Bancroft's motto—*Honor Virutis Praemium*. Was virtue rewarded with honor when one's virtue was unintentional, not to mention unwanted? She was desperate to join the ranks of the dishonored: Leigh had lost it to her deb ball escort, Meredith to some guy she met at Danceteria. Even Polly Jessup, with her ribbon headbands, Fair Isle sweaters, and A. A. Milne quotes on her yearbook page, had done it in a Pompei alley with an Italian tour guide over spring break. Like, three feet from a cluster of ash-entombed corpses, apparently, but Nina still envied her. Who cared how imperfect or unpleasant the first time was? The Danceteria guy, who they now called the Hypnotist, had pulled out Meredith's tampon and swung it back and forth like a pocket watch on a chain. Leigh's escort couldn't figure out how to work the condom. Perfect wasn't the point. The point was the leap to the other side.

"It was so embarrassing," Leigh added. "He delivered me, and now he's asking me how often I have 'relations.'" She took a Newport out of a gold-embossed cigarette case from Tiffany, testament to her obsession with all things Jackie Kennedy, who had the same one according to the most recent unauthorized bio.

"I've heard you can gain ten pounds on the pill," Meredith said.

Leigh reached for the pitcher of sangria. "I need to *lose* ten. Who wants to do SlimFast with me?"

"Blech," Meredith said, her mouth in a sour twist. "Those shakes taste like dog poo." She took a sip of sangria, making another face. "This doesn't taste much better." Never hugely cheerful anyway, she'd been even crabbier than usual since getting rejected by every Ivy besides Penn, which she called Jap City even in front of Nina but was resigned to starting in the fall. The fact that Leigh was going to Princeton didn't make things easier.

Nina pinched some excess skin at her waist. "I might start drinking Rum and Tabs."

"I read in *Glamour* that even Tab is fattening," said Meredith, who always gave her own thoughts the credence of written text. Leigh, who always gave credence to Meredith, nodded.

"Doesn't the commercial say 'Just One Calorie'?" Nina asked.

Meredith gave her a sudden, sly smile. "I wonder how many calories there are in semen."

Something was up. Nina shifted in her chair.

"I can't believe people swallow it," Leigh said. "Talk about blech."

Nina tried to push aside the image of Walker Pierson's thing in her mouth, jabbing the inside of her cheek. The first blowjob of her life and she tried to give it cross-eyed drunk. What had she been thinking?

"What's the difference between sperm and semen, anyway?" Leigh mused.

Sepia vomit puddling on the bedspread. Walker's livid eyes.

"You know, Nina," Meredith laughed, "you might be the only girl in Bancroft history to *lose* weight giving head."

Leigh turned red. Nina hadn't told anyone other than her, since she was the one who'd introduced her to Walker that night.

"I'm sorry," she said. "But I only told Meredith, I swear."

Nina tried to change the subject: "Did you guys hear about that model whose face got slashed to ribbons?"

But Meredith was undeterred. "Did she give an even worse blow-job than you?"

Nina felt her expression go stony. Then she pictured her mother's face at graduation, contorted with fury, eyes on fire, snakes for hair that rattled and spit. She reapplied her smile. "I don't know, Meredith," she said as she poured herself another glass of sangria. "But maybe you ought to worry about the guys at Danceteria. I hear they want their money back."

By eleven o'clock, Leigh and Meredith were seriously drunk, screeching along to the jukebox and slurring suspicions about their teachers' sex lives. Nina tried to grab on to the collective buzz like the tail of a kite, but she was lead. Her mouth tasted like stale lemons and apples gone to rot. Clearly, sangria wasn't her drink. She wove through the crowd to get to the bar.

Girls in short silk dresses danced to Yaz while the guys watched them, slit-eyed. The air was humid with endorphins, the windows blurred with steam. In the corner, a girl in striped pants backed into a guy with gel-spiked hair, her hand reaching behind her to toy with the zipper of his jeans. A guy in another corner held his cigarette to a girl's red-lipsticked mouth, watching intently as she let the smoke seep out through parted lips, then drew it up her nose in smutty, silvery whirls.

God, Nina missed smoking. It was all she could do not to grab the cigarette from the girl's mouth for a drag.

Up at the packed bar, she managed to get the bartender's attention to order a sloe gin fizz. For the longest time she'd thought s-l-o-e was s-l-o-w, but even knowing the difference, she still felt languid drinking it. Catching sight of her face in the mirror behind the bar, disappointed as always that she wasn't Flanagan's pretty—blond, blue-eyed, cute-nosed—she reminded herself of the cashier at Brentano's last week who'd called her sexy. Maybe she was becoming something as good as pretty. Or better? Because pretty was for girls, who put together top-ten lists during French class (*prettiest hair, prettiest smile, prettiest overall face*). Sexy was for guys, the way their eyes moved over your body, what they said under their breath. Pretty was nice to look at; sexy was desire.

Although did you have to actually have sex at some point to qualify as sexy? It was a concern.

Behind her, a voice called for a martini. It had a familiar edge that sliced through her. *I think you've done enough for one night* was the last thing that voice had said to her when she offered to pull the puke-sodden sheets off the bed and wash them.

She ducked her head to try to go invisible. The sudden motion set off a shower of sparkles in her brain—she was drunker than she'd realized. The crowd surged and Walker Pierson stumbled into her. He leaned around her to apologize, but the instant he recognized her, his eyes went arctic.

"Hello!" she said, and immediately regretted it. Humiliation made her voice boom, and judging by his wince, the moldy taste in her mouth had infiltrated her breath.

"Hello." Walker looked around, anywhere but in her direction. The nostrils of his aristocratic nose flared. The night they met, she'd been mesmerized by its slender, elegant line; hers was wide with a bump at the top, the nose of her non-*Mayflower* forebears.

"Listen," she said, although he obviously didn't want to, "I can't say how sorry—"

"It's fine."

She recalled the model's graciousness. "Can I at least pay for the dry cleaning?"

Why had she brought that up? Disgust darkened his eyes. She could see he was remembering the clotted mess dripping down his torso onto the lavender quilt, stray curds spattered on the coral silk headboard. His parents had been away for the weekend. Using their king-sized bed was guess whose genius idea.

"Not necessary," he said stiffly. He put up his hand to ward her off, then turned to greet a friend with a slap on the back.

She stood motionless, incinerated. As if she'd gone home with him just to throw up on his parents' bed. As if he hadn't seen how plastered she was at Trader Vic's. How she'd gotten lost on the way from the bathroom to the table, inexplicably carried out a stack of menus, tripped into the taxi and landed face down on his khaki-covered knee, and then kissed his pants as if she'd flung herself there for that purpose. Mr. Manners, Mr. Yale. He'd been perfectly happy to squash her boobs in his know-nothing palms. What did he expect?

She'd never be this mean to someone for getting sick, especially when they'd been trying to do something nice.

When her drink came, she bolted it down so fast she burped, loud as a frog's croak. Now Walker did look at her, sneering as he backed away. Did he think she was going to puke right here? Without a word, he turned and shoved his way through the crowd.

"Don't worry!" she shouted after him. "I only throw up on dicks when they're in my mouth."

Was that model-gracious? Walker didn't look back, but others glanced her way, wide-eyed and snickering.

"Good to know," a voice behind her said. Nina turned in its direction and froze. Gardner Reed. Tall and lanky, with thick eyebrows, a jutting chin, and a deep indentation above his lip. Eyes a cobalt blue she didn't know eyes could be. For years, she'd observed him from a distance, playing Hacky Sack in Sheeps Meadow or eating a slice of pizza at Mimi's on Eighty-Fourth Street, but she'd never been this close. This close, he was dizzying.

She covered her face with her hands.

"Hey." He peeked around her fingers until she couldn't help laughing. "Walker *is* a dick," he said.

Dizzying, and an Upper East Side legend. Famous for calling in a bomb scare to Spence to get the senior girls out of their calculus exam. For sneaking home a pound of pot from Jamaica by hiding it in a flight attendant's overnight bag. For snatching a fur coat from the Plaza checkroom last winter and giving it to the stunned homeless woman outside after he'd heard the coat's owner complain about her to the manager.

He took out a pack of Marlboros and a Surf Club matchbook from his back pocket. He put a cigarette between his lips, then held the pack out to Nina.

She shook her head. "Last time I smoked," she blurted, "it might have killed my grandmother." She knew this wasn't literally true, and what kind of sicko used their dead grandmother to flirt, but here she was, winding her hair in her hand and holding it for a Kathleen Turner second before letting it fall over her shoulders.

He raised his eyebrows. "Okay, I'll bite." He lit his cigarette with a match and blew out a stream of smoke to extinguish the flame. She thought of all the guys she'd seen shake a match out, how excessive and clumsy that now seemed. She told him how her grandmother Pearl had despised smoking, always lecturing people, coughing hysterically, waving their smoke away. "She said it showed poor breeding."

"She sounds delightful," Gardner said.

Nina laughed. "So six weeks ago I was walking home, smoking a cigarette, and I realized I was right across the street from her building. I looked up to one of her apartment windows and I saw the curtain move, and—I'm pretty sure—a woman's face. I thought, Oh shit, she'll have a stroke if she just saw me smoking."

"And?"

"She did. Have a stroke, I mean. That night, I swear. She died in her sleep. I've been too freaked out to smoke since."

"Huh." He dipped his head as he inhaled from his Marlboro, tilting it back to blow a column of smoke up toward the ceiling. "I mean, obviously it's just a coincidence, and you don't even know if she was at the window. But I get why it spooked you." He took another cigarette out of his pack and placed it on the bar, parallel to her pinkie finger. "One thing's for sure," he said. "You can't kill her twice."

A shadow bloomed between them that Nina itched to step into. He watched her contemplate the cigarette on the bar, the crisp white paper and gold-flecked filter. Little chills of electricity ran down the back of her neck. But she shook her head. She knew she hadn't actually killed her grandmother, she wasn't a superstitious crackpot, but since that night, her mother's depression was the blackest it had ever been. Most days she stayed in bed, matted hair, dull stare at the ceiling, in the same dingy velour tracksuit she'd worn for a month and a half. And Nina's grandfather, already a bit senile, was more and more befuddled, often forgetting Pearl was dead. Smoking was the least Nina could sacrifice.

He picked up two drinks from the bar that appeared there like magic—Gardner Reed didn't have to ask for what he wanted. His eyes moved down her legs, lingering at the rough edge where she'd cut the lace tights. "I'll be seeing you around, Madonna," he said as he walked away.

She turned in a daze. All around the room, girls were sneaking looks in her direction. Paige Waterbury, Cricket Hutchinson, Mimi Foxwell. Alison Bloch, who didn't bother to sneak but flat-out stared, lip in a jealous curl. What a rush, to be the object of envy. Nina started back to her table to tell her friends what had just happened. But how could she possibly capture the significance, how their words, while ordinary on the surface, tangled underground in intricate designs like the roots of trees? Why dig them up and expose them to Meredith's derision? Because obviously Gardner Reed was out of Nina's league. Not to mention he was dating the stunning and very blond Holland Nichols: debutante, Duke Kappa, recently featured in *Town & Country* jumping a show horse over a hedge. The horse would probably have a better chance with Gardner; Nina doubted that *sexy* would even get her out of the stable.

Still, something had passed between them.

When she reached the table, she said good night with a counterfeit yawn and an excuse about the excitement of graduation finally catching up to her. Gardner was still around, but better to slip away and leave a little mystery. Pushy never got you anywhere with guys, a lesson she'd first learned in kindergarten when a boy she'd literally chased around the classroom for a kiss slammed into the wall, and his nose erupted in blood.

Leigh said to wait ten minutes and they'd all share a cab. But Nina just waved, pretending not to hear, and made her way to the door. Even if the *something* with Gardner didn't mean anything, she wanted a few more minutes alone to savor it.

She decided to walk for a while instead of going straight home. It was only a little past midnight, and Freddie was still on duty until one a.m., when Jimmy's shift started; she'd rather avoid another grope and blast of garlic. And it wouldn't hurt to give her mother more time to burrow into sleep. Nina could do without a tirade about her self-centeredness, or the insomniac roaming that would invariably follow, Frances's white nightgown billowing over her tracksuit like an agitated ghost.

She walked for a mile down Third Avenue and another up Lexington, listening to the Talking Heads on her Walkman. "*Watch out,*" David Byrne sang, "*you might get what you're after.*" She couldn't think of a single time she'd gotten what she was after, or even gone after anything for that matter, and hoped at least once in her life she'd have the chance to find out why this could possibly be a problem.

She considered heading to the Yorkville dive she'd liked to frequent after school—"Debate Club" if her parents happened to ask where she'd been. Debate Club reeked of Winstons and stale beer. The ossified patrons didn't give a shit if your family was listed in the Social Register: you were practically a celebrity if you weren't on dialysis. But now she saw it through Gardner's eyes, stools held together with duct tape, floors that buckled underneath, Nina downing shots with World War II vets in a sea of wheelchairs and oxygen tanks. Holland Nichols wouldn't set foot in a place like that.

At 12:50 she stopped in a deli for a pack of Yodels. She waited at the counter while a guy in a yellow satin jacket bought a lottery ticket. He had a face full of acne scars, which she studied until she remembered the name for them: ice pick scars. He met her eye and she looked away. She must have been staring. But when she glanced back to check if she'd offended him, he winked and said, "Wanna be my good-luck charm and choose the last number?"

"Give it a rest, Anthony," the guy behind the counter said, but he was smiling as he handed over the lottery ticket.

Nina's face burned. It was embarrassing to be flirted with in public, mainly because she knew she shouldn't be flattered and yet she couldn't help it.

To avoid him, she stared down at a stack of *New York Post*s, the cover photo of the model with her stitched-up cheek. Had the girl had a clue how vicious her landlord was? Could that degree of menace be concealed? Nina was sure it would betray itself if you paid attention, a trace of cruelty in a smile, a coldheartedness that would give you chills if you stood too close.

The bell jangled as the door opened and a pretty woman with long black hair came in and grabbed a Milky Way. She had a gold chain around one ankle, long tanned legs, tiny white dress. Anthony with the ice pick scars lasered in, blinking like her ass emitted light. Nina couldn't believe she cared, but her stomach knotted with the disappointment of being cast aside. She stared more directly at him, competitiveness rising. Before she realized what she was doing, she'd shrugged open her jacket to reveal the skimpy camisole underneath, the ledge of her too-big breasts. That did it. His eyes veered to Nina's chest. She never displayed her body this way, an object to be leered at, but she pretended it was Gardner's eyes on her, his gaze as palpable as warm hands cupping her breasts.

For the second time that night, she silently counted down *five* . . .

four . . . three seconds until she lost her nerve and clutched her jacket closed. She booked out the door and ran to the subway entrance, down the stairs and back up the opposite side across the street. Not that she thought he'd come after her, but better safe than sorry in the city—something the model hadn't lived here long enough to know.

Kind, ancient Jimmy greeted her at the door with a pleasant "Good evening," and then shut it firmly behind her. Home safe, Yodels in hand, even though she'd forgotten to pay for them.

Chapter Two

Eight o'clock Monday morning, Nina switched on her radio as she got dressed for her first summer temp job, a weeklong stint at the Midtown headquarters of a mid-tier hotel chain. Bryan Adams coming to the Garden, the DJ said. First caller wins two tickets! Update on the model: her former landlord, who'd hired the thugs to ambush her, used to let himself into her apartment when she and her roommates were "in a state of undress." Nina, herself in a state of undress, glanced at her bedroom door. Her father always knocked first, and anyway, he usually left for his office at seven thirty. Her mother, who didn't knock first, and whose habit of banging open the insult of a shut door had left a deep gouge in the wall, was presumably still in bed, having lain there most of the weekend. Before Nina left for work, she'd have to check if Frances needed anything, a glass of water or a tissue, even though Nina's very presence seemed to annoy her. Last night, she'd merely glanced at her grandmother's cashew-shaped hearing aids in a porcelain bowl on Frances's bedside table. "Those are mine," her mother snarled as if Nina were plotting to steal them.

She pulled on one of the linen skirts she'd bought for temping, trying to imagine the model's bedroom—chrome lamps, glass brick walls, flowing white silk curtains—compared to her own pink-

and-green wallpaper and Laura Ashley bedspread, a visual reminder of Nina's failure to blossom into the demure, sweet-natured girl her mother had outfitted the room for. Even her bookshelf was decoupaged with little pink petunias, although the tatty Steinbecks and Updikes dirtied things up a little, along with three volumes of *The Book of Lists* that she'd found used at the Strand and spent many weekends poring over. Two of her favorites: Famous Phobics (Salvador Dalí—fear of grasshoppers), and Famous Virgins (Adolf Hitler, who "shook with rage" when a woman kissed him under the mistletoe).

Gardner Reed was no virgin. She imagined herself shaking when he kissed her, though obviously with something other than rage.

She walked quietly down the dark hallway that led from her room to the front door, pausing at her parents' bedroom to look inside. The shades were down, the air murky. Stacks of newspapers filled every corner, so old their headlines screamed about Watergate—her mother insisted on keeping them for "research." Frances lay on her back in bed under the covers, her face a vacant gray. On the bedside table, beside the bottles of Xanax and Klonopin and Halcion and the bowl with her dead mother's hearing aids, was a small orange notebook of graph paper she used as a kind of journal. She'd write something, rip out the page, fold it as tiny as she could, and stick it in some crevice in the apartment, as if it were one big Wailing Wall. *Everything is hideous and black* was a note Nina had found jammed under the salad plates in the kitchen cabinet. Stuffed inside a little wooden box of paper clips: *I used to be a nice person, now I am worthless bitchy lousy ugly.* The words themselves were awful enough, but their fevered scrawl made them even worse, the way the letters ran roughshod over the little printed squares. Why bother with graph paper then? It made it all twice as chaotic.

"Mom." She leaned her head inside the room but kept the rest of herself in the doorway, in case of a sudden eruption. Interesting fact: there were names for the fear of one's mother-in-law (pentheraphobia), and of motherhood (tokophobia), and even of becoming *like* one's mother (matrophobia). But nothing for the plain old fear of one's mother, which seemed like quite an omission.

"Should I open the shades?"

A vague head movement that Nina read as no.

"Do you want some of your breakfast?" Every morning before he left for work, Nina's father set a tray on the bed for Frances with a soft-boiled egg in an egg cup, a saltshaker, and a cloth napkin. His life's mission, for which he'd enlisted Nina, was keeping Frances on an even keel, whatever it took. When she lay limp and crying in bed, they canceled plans, brought her tea, and rubbed her neck. When she overturned chairs or hurled books, they bit their tongues and cleaned up. Unless of course Nina had somehow provoked the explosion, in which case she and her father were no longer on the same team, and Ira would rebuke her for disturbing the calm. Just losing her bus pass or drinking the last of the milk could do it. She'd hide in her room and weep over the injustice, but she was never surprised.

Beside the egg cup was Ira's daily handwritten love note for Frances, on his embossed stationery. Today's said,

June 9, 1986

High 74, low 69

Israel declines to congratulate Kurt Waldheim on Austrian election victory. Celtics win 16th NBA Championship.

My darling, courageous F. I hope today is brighter than yesterday. I'll call at lunchtime.

Nina never stopped marveling at his devotion, whether Frances was in a blazing rage or like today, cold gray ashes. He held on to the memory of the Frances he married, the one who inhaled spy novels and encyclopedias, the etymology fanatic who loved saltwater taffy and dressing up in chiffon and gold sandals for holiday parties at the Amity Club. In Ira's mind, this was the real Frances, although this seemed to Nina like wishful thinking. She might be the *best* Frances, but they saw her the least—so who could say which was real?

"How about I turn on the TV before I go?"

Finally, a verbal response: "Fine." The syllable was caked in dust, but at least she'd stated a preference. Nina found the remote at the foot of the bed and clicked through the channels. "Wheel. Of. Fortune!" SE_ON_ TO NONE. No answer from the contestant. "Second to none, Mom?" No answer from Frances. Screechy exercise guy with a perm, singing cartoon vines, sportscaster with the highlights of a baseball game: "Red Sox pound the Indians for eight runs," he said.

"Shouldn't that be pound the Native Americans?" Nina asked Frances.

No answer. Next channel, a woman with very high hair interviewing Gene Kelly in a studio. "When I was a teenager, dance was a form of courtship," he said. "It was how you got your arms around a girl."

Now Frances stirred. "Grandma always liked him."

"She did?" Nina tried to imagine dour Pearl, bleach-stained housedress and drooping compression socks, enjoying Gene Kelly's twinkly charm. Exuberance had revolted her: showy makeup was for hookers; bright clothing was a sign of conceit. When Nina once showed up to dinner wearing red lipstick and flowered pants, Pearl glared at her from soup to nuts. In fact, all Nina ever knew of her were glares and admonishments. Nina was selfish, spoiled, uncouth, and always tracking dirt inside the house like an unruly mutt. Frances was lazy, a disappointment, self-pitying, and unable to properly iron a shirt to save her life.

"I miss her." Frances's eyes filled with tears.

"Me too," Nina lied. She'd never heard her mother speak affectionately of Pearl, yet here she was, bedbound, depleted, nearly catatonic, crying for her. Nina couldn't believe how backward she'd gotten it, so sure Frances would be happier with Pearl no longer around to torment her.

Although shouldn't she be a *little* happier?

Gene Kelly leaped from his chair and performed a winsome slide step. Frances squeezed her eyes shut and moaned. Nina started toward the bed. Her mother usually couldn't tolerate people around when she was down, but this wasn't ordinary down, this was anguish. Fuck the temp job. Her mother needed her. She'd spend the day brushing her hair and coaxing her to eat. She'd call the video store to deliver candy and movies. When her father returned, he'd find them curled up together, devouring Jujubes and watching *Splash*.

"I'm staying home with you today," she said. But as she came close, her mother raised her arm to block her. Her eyes were narrowed and bloodshot. "Christ, you're like a noose around my neck. Didn't you say you had a job? Go do that." She gritted her teeth so hard you could hear the scrape.

Walking fast to the subway station, head down, heart clattering, Nina made a vow: this would be a summer of icy dignity. In another Strand find called *Closing Remarks*, she'd read that Marie Antoinette's last words, on her way to the guillotine, were "Pardonnez-moi, monsieur," when she'd accidentally stepped on her executioner's foot. Talk about dignity. When the subway lurched and Nina accidentally fell against a guy reading his paper, instead of OH MY GOD I'M SO SORRY!, she mouthed a cool "Pardonnez-moi." In the elevator up to her temp job, instead of her usual THANK YOU SO MUCH! when another passenger pressed her floor for her, she merely nodded.

There'd be no more THANK YOUs! No more HIs! And

PLEASEs! And HAVE A GOOD DAYs! No more flashing her tits at some random guy in a deli for approval.

Remembering the little speech she'd planned for the office manager this morning made her cringe (*so excited, my first job, what a beautiful view, I want to learn so much, have you worked here long?*). She'd say the least she could get away with. Which worked out fine, since as soon as she got off the elevator, the guy launched into a canned orientation as he guzzled coffee from an oversized New York Jets mug.

Her desk was down a bunch of corridors. There were none of the photographs or knickknacks she'd seen on other desks they passed, only a silver barrette wedged between the edge and the wall.

"If anyone calls for Marjorie," said the office manager, "don't say she's not here. But don't say she'll call back either. And whatever you do, don't say the F word." Why would she say *fuck* just because Marjorie got a phone call? He handed her a stack of handwritten pages. "These are reports from our undercovers. They stay at our hotels posing as guests and report on their experiences. We need you to input them in our system so the higher-ups can take a gander."

"Input," she repeated.

"Type?" He looked at her doubtfully. "You've worked on a Wang before?"

"Of course."

"Good. Can you believe they send us temps who don't know Wangs?"

"I can't," she said, although obviously she could, since she was one of them. He delivered a disquisition on a temp who cracked an entire box of floppy discs trying to jam them in upside down, then he hustled back down the corridor. It dawned on her that the F word was "fired."

Once she figured out the computer, she started inputting the undercovers' reports. Most were dry and matter-of-fact. A dirty towel in the Pittsburgh hotel's junior suite. Too much chlorine in the

Hartford swimming pool. She stifled a yawn. She'd have thought the icy part of icy dignity would mean crisp alertness, but instead she felt flattened out, low on oxygen. Since she didn't like the sludgy taste of coffee, she considered picking up a bottle of Vivarin when she went out for lunch, but she worried all the caffeine might make her too convivial. She imagined a big, freakish grin stretched across her face as she asked her coworkers, HOW'S YOUR DAY GOING? WANT TO BE FRIENDS? She remembered her mother's look of revulsion as she warded her off this morning and felt black, slimy shame on her skin like a layer of oil.

All the undercovers signed their complete names except one, who went by E. B. Jinks. Nina perked up when she got to E. B.'s reports. In Little Rock, E. B. was beset by a *grisly spider* and *obscenely slow room service*. In San Jose, *an offensive lack of hangers*. A Raleigh hotel bathroom *reeked of feculence*. A New Orleans pillow was *lumpy* and *injurious*: attached to the report was a bill from E. B.'s chiropractor. She tried to guess what the "E. B." stood for. Embittered Bachelor? The pages were smudged and wrinkled like they'd been gripped by sweaty fingers.

The rest of the day, Nina mostly stuffed envelopes and Xeroxed memos. A batch of reports finally landed on her desk at four thirty. E. B. had saved the best for last. This time the insult was a Houston concierge's belt buckle—an *ornate brass eagle* that had forced E. B.'s gaze *crotchward*. Nina input happily: the *avian accouterment* had *gleamed like the desert sun*, its wingspan *the length of a forearm*. The description went on for another half a page. The eagle's *knife-sharp beak*. Its *canny claws*. Its *challenging stare*.

She finally stopped and stared at the screen. How long, exactly, had E. B.'s gaze been directed crotchward?

It dawned on her that all this outrage was probably sexual frustration. E. B. just needed to get laid. Then she rolled her eyes at her own smugness. Considering she'd just read *My Secret Garden* for the thousandth time, not to mention the countless rewinds of the make-out scenes in *Valley Girl* and *Roman Holiday*, maybe she ought to dial back the judgments.

One advantage of working office hours was that when she got home, Freddie was busy with the door and couldn't corner her for an embrace. The disadvantage was that the other residents in the building weren't especially fun to engage with either, like DeeDee Elkin and her daughter Kassidy, a bratty fifteen-year-old, who Nina was now stuck riding with in the elevator while they bickered.

They didn't interrupt their skirmish to say hello. DeeDee pulled at the hem of Kassidy's plaid skirt, which barely skimmed the tops of her thighs. Kassidy slapped her hand away. Nina kept her eyes fixed on the lighted panel, watching the floors tick up, filled with a mix of distaste and covetousness. How obnoxious to treat your own mother like that. How enviable to be able to.

"I can see your underwear," DeeDee said. She had a perennially stiff face and a pinched, aggrieved expression. "This isn't the Playboy Club."

"You're my biggest nightmare," Kassidy hissed back, although even the hiss had a babyish whine to it.

Didn't Kassidy know you changed into a longer skirt before you got home? But like most Upper East Side girls, Nina thought, she was too coddled to be wily.

Upstairs, her father was at the kitchen counter eating Ritz crackers, dropping crumbs all over his suit. He had on a blue-and-lavender striped tie and a pocket handkerchief in matching shades, dressed up for a concert at Carnegie Hall—but "Mom doesn't feel like going," he said. His face was drawn and bewildered. Frances's moods seemed to sideswipe him every time, as if he'd never encountered them before.

His hurt pained her almost as much as her mother's depression and sometimes filled her with just as much anger. It was wonderful, a man so devoted to his wife for better or worse, in sickness and in health. Except maybe if he loved her a little less, he wouldn't be so besieged by her moods.

There was some current of longing in her father Nina sensed but didn't quite understand, her mother's aloofness and his ceaseless efforts to please her. Hanging above the kitchen doorway was a framed *Carousel* Playbill from the night they met. It was a sketch of two horses on opposite sides of a carousel, facing away from each other, which always made Nina feel slightly bereft. One horse had a perplexed tilt to his head—she imagined this one as Ira, sensing the Frances horse nearby but never able to see her or catch up as the carousel went around. An endless, yearning loop. Did the Frances horse even know the Ira horse was there? Did she even give him a thought?

They'd met in the lobby during intermission. Ira was finishing his law degree at NYU, Frances a year out of college. He'd turned to her, expecting a pleasant exchange about the talented cast or exceptional orchestra, but instead she'd launched into a spirited critique of one of the male chorus dancers who kept kicking so ridiculously high she was sure he was going to split his pants. After the intermission, Ira had gone back into the theater holding his breath for the high-kicker to show off, and when he did, could hardly stop himself from shouting, "Look! He's doing it again!" By the end of the second act, he'd decided to turn down the job waiting for him at his uncle's law firm in St. Louis. He'd lingered outside the theater until Frances emerged, insisting she join him for coffee.

Nina had seen photographs of her mother from that time, black eyes on fire and graceful Audrey Hepburn neck. In one photo she leaned over a birthday cake, staring into the camera with her eyebrows arched high and her mouth puckered to blow out a circle of blurry-flamed candles. In another she lay in a lounge chair at the beach in a purple bikini and radiant tan, a flowered scarf around her hair, gazing dreamily at the ocean. She was bewitching; how could Nina blame her father for being bewitched?

He stopped chewing and pushed the box of crackers away. "How does Mom seem to you?"

"Not . . . great?" His tone made Nina uneasy. "How about you?"

"I've never seen her so inert."

They stood there for a few seconds, staring at each other. His eyes looked bleak, as she guessed hers did too. Trying to lighten the moment, she brushed the crumbs off his jacket and said, "You've got almost a whole cracker there."

He smiled distractedly, then blinked several times, a nervous habit that set off warning bells. "I had a long talk with Vladimir this morning," he said. Louder bells: Vladimir was Frances's psychiatrist. Nina always pictured him with fangs and a Dracula cape, although the one time she'd picked up her mother at his office, she saw that his waiting room was filled not with silver goblets and wrought-iron candelabras but cactuses and cowhide pillows, and a steer's skull on the wall. A New York shrink with a vampire name and a Santa Fe waiting room. She'd thought psychiatrists were supposed to care about clarity.

"He's considering ECT," Ira said.

She looked back in confusion. Another medication?

"Electroshock," he said.

The word was loud and terrible in their quiet kitchen, a baseball shattering the window. Her brain scrambled. She pictured the electroshock scene from the movie *Frances* with Jessica Lange, a rubber stopper shoved between her teeth. Her mother, electrodes stuck to her temples. Frances Jacobs and Frances Farmer, held down by orderlies as their bodies convulsed.

"You can't do that," she blurted.

"We don't want to," he answered sharply. "But this can't go on."

"You said she's still mourning Grandma."

"Yes, but there's no sign of it lifting."

"But people can mourn for years."

"Not like this." He crossed his arms.

"That can't be the only thing left to do."

"Vlad's got one last medication to try." He sighed and let his arms fall. "Please don't tell Mom about this, not until he thinks it's time. I don't want her to worry." Then he asked her to pick up dinner for her grandfather and bring it to his apartment on Seventy-First Street. The aide was sick and had gone home early.

Before Nina left, she looked in on her mother. The shades were still down. The air smelled like sweat and old teabags. Her mother lay facing away from Nina, under a comforter though the room was stifling, only the back of her head and one pale foot visible. Nina thought uneasily of her father and Vlad deciding Frances's fate; an image came to her mind of the helpless model ambushed by the landlord's hired thugs. On the other hand, Frances's toes were bruised and swollen, like maybe she'd kicked a wall, and her hair was matted and clumped as a feral animal. Imagine waking up to that rage and pain every day, your brain polluted with black smoke. Maybe she *would* be better off with the darkness cooked out.

Frances coughed and kicked at the comforter. Nina got out of the room before she could be lambasted for hovering again.

She picked up dinner for Seymour at David's Chicken, then stopped at the supermarket for the pistachio cookies he liked, the ones that looked like green leaves with chocolate in the center. She waved to his doorman on her way to the elevator, and he gave her a friendly wave back. She toyed with telling him about Freddie, to reconfirm it wasn't normal doorman behavior, except she already knew that, so what was the point. Upstairs, a country song roared through Seymour's front door out into the fifth-floor hallway. He had his radio on all the time lately, at full volume, but didn't seem to care what he listened to: news, country music, sports, a local call-in show with people arguing about whether the Mets should trade Dwight Gooden over drug rumors or yelling about the feds' inability to nail John Gotti for the Sparks Steak House hit. It was a miracle he heard the doorbell. It was a miracle he could even get to the door to answer it, with all the hulking furniture from his and Pearl's house in Rockaway crammed inside this small apartment, claw-foot tables, breakfront, TV console. The mahogany obstacle course Pearl had insisted on keeping intact, even though it had been two years since they moved to the city so Nina's parents—well, Ira and Nina—could look after them.

Nina went straight to the radio sitting on top of an enormous brass-edged credenza and switched it off.

"Where's Pearl?" her grandfather asked. He was wearing pajamas and black dress shoes with the laces undone. His eyes were filmy, heavy pouches beneath.

"Visiting Mrs. Messing." Mrs. Messing was their years-ago neighbor in Rockaway. Nina worried it was cruel to keep him in a state of endless anticipation for Pearl's return, but Ira said it was kinder than breaking her death to him over and over.

And his face did relax. Honesty wasn't always the best policy, Nina thought—in fact, when was it ever? Seymour nodded and said, "Very good." Never too talkative to begin with, he now relied on a few stock phrases and pleasantries: "Okay," or "Very good," or "What can I tell you?" He might throw in a little Yiddish here and there, which made Nina nostalgic. When she was little, he'd make her laugh by whispering Yiddish words in her ear while Pearl went on about some friend or relative. Nothing mean, really, just some silliness about Mrs. Lieberman's constant kvetching, or Pearl's shmendrik cousin Henry, always with a hand out. But *that* Seymour had been fading since before Pearl died. Her departure had only hastened his disappearance.

She set the bags of food on the kitchen counter, then went into the bathroom to check under the sink in case Pearl's bottle of Miltown had magically reappeared. It had been there the day of her funeral, and Nina had taken one even though they were months expired, but the next time she checked, the bottle was gone. Nina blamed Seymour's aide for the efficiency.

Still gone. Although she spotted a few dusty bobby pins trapped in the cabinet's crevices, which provoked an unpleasant memory of a summer out in Rockaway when she'd bobby-pinned her hair in little waves like Molly Ringwald's, and Pearl, with the sneer of a playground bully, said, *You think you're so cute.*

Nina went out to the kitchen and placed the chicken on a platter and the asparagus in a bowl, then set two places at one end of the dining-room table. Then she went to the living-room window and lifted the curtain like she did every time she came over. If she squinted into the darkness outside, she could just make out faces and shoes on the sidewalk below, the red tip of a cigarette. *Had* Pearl seen Nina smoking? Considering the suffering Pearl's death had caused, Nina wished she could go back to that night when she'd looked up to the window. Grandma will have a *headache* if she sees me smoking, she'd say this time, or a *fit*—anything but a *stroke.* She let the curtain fall. Not for the first time, she entertained the suspicion that her grandmother had died on purpose, out of spite, so Nina would feel guilty the rest of her life.

"Mom says hello," she told her grandfather. Not true, although what could it hurt. "We're having lunch Sunday at the Amity Club for Father's Day." Hopefully true, although veering toward unlikely. They'd skipped Mother's Day last month since it fell so soon after Pearl's death, with Frances in no shape to celebrate anything. It was hard to imagine her summoning the requisite verve by this Sunday. Although maybe if she knew what lay in store if she didn't rally soon, it would scare her out of bed.

She pulled out her grandfather's chair and got him settled at the dining table. He said something in Yiddish that sounded like "zart" and grabbed a chicken breast with his hands. She picked up his fork to pass to him but then put it back down: he was eighty years old, let him eat the way he wanted. She tried to imagine her mother as a young girl, watching him tear into dinner, though presumably with a fork and knife back then.

"What was Mom like when she was my age?" she asked. She knew a few things: Frances had played the clarinet. She'd slept with her hair in metal curlers. She'd tried unsuccessfully to get people to call her Frankie after she read *The Member of the Wedding*. She wore a Band-Aid around her pinkie for all of sixth grade to cover the fuchsia birthmark that squiggled around her nail after some boy called it the mark of a witch. Nina had always thought the birthmark was beautiful and, as a kid, had often drawn a similar squiggle around her own nail with a pink magic marker.

"Who?" Seymour asked.

"Your daughter. Frances." She wished she'd thought to ask when Pearl was still around. "What'd you talk about at the dinner table?"

He paused from eating to look at her. Her heart jumped like he might have some singular, vivid memory to illuminate the past. Then he shrugged, and his eyes went back to blank. "What can I tell you?" he said. In other words, bupkis.

She bit into a piece of asparagus that tasted like soap.

After dinner, he switched the radio back on and sat on the couch to listen. Nina settled in beside him. A preacher was screaming about the assaulted model and the wages of vanity. "She was a harlot who tempted the flesh! Pride cometh before the fall, my friends." Nina slid her hand under her grandfather's. It was automatic, how his fingers closed around hers. She was pretty sure he didn't know who she was; he might even think she was Pearl. White lies were one thing, but was it immoral to hold hands under false pretenses? Except it felt so deeply comforting. With her other hand, she flipped through the copy of *The Bell Jar* she'd brought with her, searching for one of the electroshock scenes. A sentence she'd highlighted in yellow caught her eye: "Ever since I'd learned about the corruption of Buddy Willard, my virginity weighed like a millstone around my neck." She told herself it was okay that this was her main takeaway from a story about a girl's descent into madness.

The radio played an ad for a wedding hall in Brooklyn, classical music blasting in the background and nearly drowning out the owners' promise to "make your dreams come true." Nina thought of Frances on the long-ago days when she was out of bed and feeling okay, putting one of her records on the stereo and humming along as she got dressed or straightened a room. If Nina was around, she'd explain what a nocturne was or enthuse about Dean Martin's "liquid baritone." When Nina gave her a little pillow for her birthday last year, embroidered with black velvet musical notes, her face had lit with surprise and pleasure—a look that seemed to say *Oh! You were listening.* The musical knowledge, that occasional flare of connection with Nina: the electroshock would incinerate it all.

Fuck the temp job, she thought for the second time today. But unlike this morning, she now understood that Frances needed to get *out* of bed. First thing tomorrow morning, Nina would put one of her favorite Mozart concertos on the stereo, the buoyant piano one with the chirpy violins. She'd coax her to the kitchen for orange juice and scrambled eggs, then they'd go outside for a walk through the park. By the end of the day, Frances would have color in her cheeks, and she'd be smiling, or at least not grimacing.

Nina allowed herself a brief, corny fantasy of her mother thanking her. *No big deal, Frankie,* Nina would say.

"I'll take care of her," she told Seymour, and squeezed his hand.

"Ekht," he answered. Which meant either "thank you" or "too expensive," she could never remember.

———

She brought home the extra pistachio leaf cookies, since her mother liked them too. In the kitchen, she arranged four of them on a plate in an inviting little circle, then knocked on her parents' half-open door. When she didn't hear an answer, she peeked inside. They lay in bed under the covers, her mother in her tracksuit, her father in blue pajamas. He was watching a woman in a red gown sing opera on TV while Frances lay corpse-like with her hands folded on her chest. A vein bulged at her temple.

She turned her head and squinted at Nina in the doorway. "What do you want?" Her tone said, *Your existence tortures me.*

"I thought you might like a treat." *Mozart concerto,* Nina reminded herself. *Dean Martin.* As she entered the room, she noticed the plate was shaking and ordered her hand to grow up. She held out the plate so Frances could see the cookies. "Tomorrow's supposed to be a beautiful day. I thought we could go to the park after breakfast."

"What are you talking about?" her mother asked incredulously, her mouth twisted with contempt.

"The park, walk around, get some fresh sun."

Her mother stared at her, as if suspicious of Nina's garbled words. Her narrowed eyes were dark and fevered. Behind them, you could sense sparking wires and shards of glass.

Nina kept her face blank to signal *I am not a threat. I am barely here.* The way you freeze when you come upon a coiled snake. She took a small step forward to set the plate on the bed, but nerves made her clumsy, and her foot caught the edge of the rug. Two cookies slid onto the bedspread, smearing chocolate on the duvet cover.

Frances recoiled as if they were water bugs. "Get her out of here!" she said to Ira.

He sat up quickly, blinking and shooing Nina with his hand toward the door. "Just go," he said urgently.

She went back to her room. A fist clenched in her stomach. She swallowed a Xanax to stop her ugly thoughts. But they ran on anyway. Frances—not the movie Frances—strapped to a gurney, a rubber stopper forced between her teeth, electrodes stuck to her temples. Orderlies held down her shoulders. Nina stood in the doorway while Ira stayed outside in the hall. Vlad had his hand on the machine's dial, awaiting Nina's decision.

Let her burn, she said.

Chapter Three

She brought bagels to her temp job the next day, plus the leftover pistachio cookies, trying to compensate for her stone heart. She'd had only Mylanta for breakfast. She wanted to blame her indigestion on last night's soapy asparagus, but she knew what it really was: an acid splash of shame over last night's ugly fantasy. Her mother was ill. What was Nina's excuse? She kept her head down the rest of the week and stayed out of their room.

Seventy-nine days, five hours, and forty-nine minutes till she left for college.

Friday night, armed with Tums and Valium, she went to Flanagan's to meet up with Leigh and Meredith. At the door, Brian Flanagan, the owner's son, gave Nina his usual friendly welcome, which he probably gave everyone but felt warmly specific to her. She nodded back, for a moment feeling a little less bleak.

She checked the bar for Walker Pierson, thankfully absent, then ordered a sloe gin fizz. On the way to the tables in the back, she slowed to look at some of the photographs on the brick walls: Marilyn Monroe on the subway grate, two bare-knuckled fighters in a boxing ring, a group of women in long skirts and high-necked blouses sitting around a picnic bench, a naked Rita Hayworth veiled in a shimmery scarf. Nina recognized this last picture as a still from *Pal Joey*, which she'd watched on TV with her grandparents a few years back. She still remembered the misery of sitting between them on their itchy tweed sofa as devious, sexy, shifty-eyed Frank Sinatra seduced a naïve chorus girl and derided women as *mice* and *gassers*. What shadowy piece of her was excited by his crassness? Her groin had glowed hot as if someone put a match to it.

At their table, Leigh and Meredith were debating the flavors at a new Columbus Avenue gelato shop.

"The vanilla tastes like lima beans," Meredith said. "So not worth the calories." She grimaced and pulled on some flesh below her chin, although she looked the same weight as always. Twenty tons more preppy, though: khaki skirt, pink ribbon belt embroidered with lobsters, Bermuda bag, and gold shrimp earrings, as if to double down before she hit Jap City in September. On her pinkie was a new signet ring engraved with her initials, M.W.B., for Meredith Winthrop Bakewell. Winthrop was her mother's maiden name. Leigh's middle name, Coolidge, was also her mother's maiden name. Nina was grateful her parents hadn't tried this out on her. Nina Grossberg Jacobs didn't exactly have the same panache.

"The amaretto gave me the runs," Leigh said.

"Shh," Meredith hissed as she fluttered her fingers at someone approaching. Gardner's girlfriend, Holland, was gliding by their table, Delft-blue eyes and an iridescent satin halter top that left her tiny shoulders bare.

Why couldn't Nina be named for a country? Except her parents would probably have picked someplace weird and dank like Latvia.

Meredith asked Holland how her summer was going.

"Fantastic."

Meredith beamed back at her. It didn't seem to bother her that Holland didn't ask how *her* summer was going. No doubt Holland had forgotten all their names, if she ever knew them, even though she'd only been a year ahead of them at Bancroft. Holland Nichols had the self-absorption of a toddler. She'd brush her hair in the cafeteria while everyone at the table was eating, switch off lights when she left a room—never mind who else might still be in there—and gossip about people two feet away, mumbling out of the corner of her mouth like a Mafia don.

"I'm doing a deep dive on Gorbachev for Peter," she said. "He absolutely loves my work."

She assumed they'd know that Peter was Peter Jennings of ABC News, where Holland had a summer internship, procured by a family friend they referred to simply as "the senator."

"Are you going to Southampton this weekend?" Meredith asked her.

"Grand-Mère opened the house in May."

"I saw her at Schmidt's the other day," Meredith chimed flirtatiously. "Please tell her I hope she enjoyed her Caesar salad."

Holland's face betrayed not one iota of interest. She lit her cigarette with a gold lighter, *H.H.N.* engraved in script across the front, which Nina knew stood for Holland Harkness Nichols, just as she'd known Peter was Peter Jennings. She wished that knowledge hadn't lodged itself in her brain.

Meredith and Leigh continued to fire questions, desperate to keep Holland from drifting away.

"Is that the ring you got in Florence?"

"Do you get to drive your dad's Jag this summer?"

"Did Grand-Mère's Caesar have anchovies?"

"No," Holland said blandly. "Yes. Uh-huh."

Nina had always been scornful of Holland, self-righteous about her own warmth and good manners, but admittedly her scorn was shot through with envy. If you didn't think for a second about anyone else, you wouldn't be plagued wondering what they thought of you, if they'd taken note of the way you hunched your shoulders or crossed your arms and were repelled by your self-consciousness.

"Who wants a whiskey sour?" Holland asked. A question! An

offer, even! Except she turned and headed to the bar without waiting for an answer.

Leigh made an apple-sized circle with her fingers as she watched her walk away. "How is her butt so small? Does she have her own StairMaster?"

"She has her own boyfriend," Meredith said. "I bet sex with Gardner burns a ton of calories."

"Huh," Nina said as if this were an idea that had never crossed her mind: Sex with who? Gardner Reed? Meredith shot her a look of amusement. Sometimes it was hard to remember her sweetness as a kid when she and Nina made up dances to Blondie songs and scratched each other's backs and gave each other manicures: Nina could still feel her fingers cradled in Meredith's palm as she painted each nail, so gentle the tenderness had made her shiver.

Nina excused herself and went to the ladies' room to sneak a Valium. Inside the stall, someone had written *I'M DRUNK AGAIN BECAUSE* . . . Beneath it was a stack of answers in various pens and handwriting: *Chip Wainwright's a cheater, Cuervo rules, I didn't get into Bowdoin.*

Amateurs, Nina thought. Who needed a reason?

On her way back to the table, Brian called to her from the jukebox. The first time she came to Flanagan's, she'd thought she might have a little crush on him and got the sense it could be mutual. He was good-looking, with thick russet hair, intelligent, and friendly eyes. He was a few inches taller than her, but when they talked he stood with his legs apart so their eyes were even, which struck her as respectful. Except she soon realized that she felt too relaxed around him, more sisterly than sexy. Nothing like the buzzy euphoria she'd felt around Gardner.

"Do you like the Ramones?" he asked her. "I added them to the jukebox. The Clash and U2 too."

"Isn't it just one 2?"

He laughed, kindly, at her dumb joke. "What are you doing this summer?"

"Here for the duration, just temping. You?"

"Working." A lurch of the jukebox caught his attention. "Hey, don't abuse the privilege," he said to someone squatting behind it. "There's a lever in the back," he told Nina. "Five free songs if you jiggle it right."

The guy behind the jukebox emerged and straightened up. For the second Friday in a row, Nina was face-to-face with Gardner Reed. Broad shoulders in a green Lacoste shirt—not a newly purchased, oversaturated green, but a worn-in olive he must have had forever, the collar rumpled, a careless tear by his shoulder.

"Ladies first." Brian swept his arm toward Nina.

Gardner looked her over. "You're back." He gave her a private little smile as he tapped the jukebox glass. "Go ahead. Five free ones."

The song titles went in and out of focus as he stood behind her, looking over her shoulder. Her taste in music was pure pop, nothing he'd respect. She stared at the smudge of his fingerprint on the glass. He was closer than she'd realized, his breath on the back of her neck. Here was the buzz and the euphoria. Here was her groin glowing hot.

The Clash she knew from that music video with the sheik and the rabbi. She pressed 1-7-2 and watched the mechanical arm grab the record, remembering the rumor that Gardner had fingered that famous Romanian gymnast at a Clash concert. Another version had him fingering her and her teammate, one with his left hand and one with his right.

"Should I Stay or Should I Go" came pounding out of the speakers.

"*It's always tease, tease, tease,*" Gardner murmured in her ear. She could practically feel his fingers between her legs. In a daze, she spotted the Cure and pressed the numbers for "Let's Go to Bed."

"Nice one, Madonna," he said. A cigarette appeared before her eyes. "Grandma still spying on you?"

She turned to face him. "Probably. I doubt a little thing like not being alive would stop her."

Brian cleared his throat. Nina came back to herself. She'd forgotten he was there, an appalling way to treat a nice guy who was probably a regular victim of the spotlight's swerve to Gardner. She turned her attention on him full blast, pointing in the air to where the last notes of the Clash song hung. "They're the best," she gushed. "And you're the best for adding them."

Brian smiled. "I aim to please."

Gardner held a match to his cigarette, watching them over the flame. "You coming by the bandshell this week?" he asked Brian.

"Do I get to wear a fancy orange jumpsuit?"

Gardner snorted. "Careful what you wish for. You'd have to haul around seventy-pound bags of topsoil all day."

Nina glanced at the muscles in Gardner's arm, a brief, involuntary flick of her eyes, but she saw him notice. "Haul what where?" she asked.

"Whatever and wherever the Parks Department tells me." Gardner shrugged. "Community service."

Now Nina remembered: "Tavern on the Green," she said. Another Gardner Reed legend. Stoned on a bitter-cold night last winter, he'd picked the lock, rummaged through the walk-in fridge, and fallen asleep under a table with a pile of restaurant napkins for a pillow. A security guard found him there in the morning, snoring.

"Yeah, the food was good but the service sucked," he said.

She laughed. "What's it like in the park at night?"

"Pitch-black except for the streetlamps. They make the sky this trippy, blurry white. And it's dead quiet. I like it. I can hear myself think."

She wondered why anyone would want that. Her own thoughts were deafening. *Let her burn* still scalded her ears. "Is it scary?"

"There's nobody for miles, so it's only scary if you scare yourself, I guess."

Brian looked puzzled and a little skeptical. Nina nodded as if she knew what he meant, although she suspected she'd spend hours this weekend pondering the statement's hidden depths.

"What's scary?" asked Holland, who'd appeared next to Gardner.

"My dad, when he sees what songs I've put on the jukebox," Brian said, and laughed.

Holland looked through him and held her hand out to Gardner with two fingers in a V. I'm Vacant? Vapid? I have VD? He wedged a cigarette between them, snapping Nina out of her trance. They were together. He knew what her gestures meant. He lit her cigarette and she inhaled and blew out the match's flame. Then she launched into a soliloquy about her family's Father's Day brunch this Sunday at their house in Southampton. "Aunt Edith's in charge of sides, Aunt Liddy the steaks, and Mom the desserts. We have a table for thirty on the lawn. Did I tell you we had a miniature golf course installed with a replica of the Montauk Point lighthouse? Grand-Mère will supervise from the pergola. She can't wait to see you."

Gardner raised his eyebrows, which Nina hoped meant, *Any chance the place will burn to the ground before Sunday?* Someone who craved pitch-black solitude shouldn't be hanging out in a pergola, whatever that was, making Grand-Mère giddy.

"Is Flanagan's busy for Father's Day?" Nina asked Brian, to change the subject.

"Booked solid. Dads get a free Bloody Mary with brunch." He had such an upstanding face. She wished she wanted his tongue in her mouth.

"How about you?" he asked.

"We have this dumb club we go to," she said. "The Amity. I call it Amityville Horror." She noticed Holland staring at her with a confused look.

"Is her name Miriam?" she mumbled to Gardner out of the corner of her mouth.

Nina blushed. Of course Holland would pick the Jewiest name

she could think of. She waited, breath held, for Gardner to answer. Although obviously he didn't know her name. Why would he? There'd be no reason. For all she knew, he thought her name really was Madonna.

"Nina," he said to Holland. But he was looking at *her*.

Due to her rotten sense of direction, Nina rarely went to Central Park by herself. She was always winding up behind a maintenance building, or in a transverse where crosstown buses flew by streaming diesel exhaust. But a few days after Father's Day, after a new temp gig at an Upper West Side public relations firm, she decided to risk it. The sky was crystal blue and the park had that mid-June calm now that summer was well under way and half the population was out in the Hamptons. And not that she was here to see him, but Gardner could be working at the bandshell today for his community service. If she happened by—admittedly a long shot, considering she was already lost—would she seem too pushy?

She wasn't exactly in a hurry to get home anyway. Her mother was still yo-yoing between catatonia and fury. On Father's Day, instead of lunch at the Amity Club, Nina had wound up taking her grandfather to Stark's while Ira stayed home with Frances. Vlad's last-ditch medication would likely take two weeks to kick in—Frances had started on it a week ago—and even then there was no guarantee. So far the only change was headaches and a vicious dry mouth. Ira had added a bowl of butterscotch candies to her already crowded nightstand.

Nina's own head hurt and her mouth was the Sahara. As she skirted the baseball fields, she tried to remember the word for sympathy symptoms, like when an expectant father got morning sickness. She dug a box of cinnamon Dynamints out of her tote bag and shook a bunch onto her tongue.

She wanted to save her mother from ECT. Except it might help her. But it could also wreck her. Look at Mr. Finch, the father of a girl in her class at Bancroft, who several years ago had stepped on a buried power line at a construction site where he was the architect. Before the accident, he was a monster, crazy eruptions of rage if someone dropped a fork at dinner, fireworks if the toilet paper hung the wrong way. Everyone was terrified of him. But his electrocuted brain left him sweet and docile. When Nina went to dinner at their house months after the accident, Mr. Finch sat at the table with a placid, blurry smile. Dinner felt practically festive, and Nina couldn't help a blip of envy.

Although later, Jenny Finch told her that half the time, her father didn't remember who she or her mother were, couldn't judge distances, and sometimes walked into doors and walls. Every night, someone had to put his toothbrush in his fingers, instruct him to spit in the sink, wipe toothpaste off his chin. He couldn't read or tell time or remember the name of the street he grew up on. His intricate personhood had been charred to ash.

Nina walked up a little hill and nearly tripped over the thick roots of an elm to avoid a guy stomping around an overflowing trash can while screaming multiplication tables. He stopped dead and scrutinized her. He had puffy ocher eyes and wet lips, and a bald patch over his ear the size and shape of an electrode.

"Are you laughing at me?" His voice was shrill. "Did I say something funny?" He slapped himself hard across the face and shouted, "Idiot! You missed the joke again."

Nina stared at the ground and walked faster. Besides her abysmal sense of direction, this was another problem with the park: unhinged inhabitants seemed always drawn her way, perfectly comfortable interacting with her—accosting her, actually—as if she'd been invited to their Mad Hatter tea party. The baby-faced guy next to her on a bench who'd muttered, "Hasn't anyone informed you that big tits are rude?" The guy on the Great Lawn who came and stood directly over her head when she was sunbathing, unzipped his pants, and waved his dick around like he was conducting an orchestra. There was no fast escape route in the park: no subway stations to cross through or taxis to hail or stores to hang out in until the insanity passed.

The guy from the trash can was now jogging alongside her, his cheek splotched red where he'd slapped himself. She picked up her pace, but he maneuvered himself in front of her, running backward. Nina swerved left past a jagged hunk of rock, but he stuck by her. "I'm talking to you!" She was walking so fast, her shins were knotting up, her feet rubbed raw in her temp-job heels and starting to blister.

"You think I'm vomit, Ms. Fuck?" People walking by glanced at them with mild interest, but Nina was too embarrassed to make a scene; at some point he'd grow bored or tired and leave her alone. Wouldn't he? She tried an abrupt stop to throw him off, but the ground was spongy from the rain this morning, and when she slid a little, he stopped and slid, too, in a weirdly exaggerated way. When she stepped left, he did the same, blocking her escape.

"Stop it," she bleated, embarrassed how afraid she sounded, except she was afraid.

"Stop it," he said in a high, mocking voice. His face was contorted, nostrils flaring, mouth hanging open—*her* face, she realized. He was mimicking her.

"You think I'm manure, Ms. Bitch?"

Behind them a girl's voice shouted, "A steaming pile of it, you crazy freak." He turned toward the voice just as a stream of water hit his eye. The girl had shot him with a large plastic water gun. A bead of black liquid trailed down the side of his face.

"Oh my God, is that hair dye?" she said, laughing.

His face went red. He turned and flounced away. Was that all it took to stop him, an insult to his vanity?

"*Ms.* Bitch, huh?" the girl asked. "At least he's a feminist."

Now Nina laughed, but then she saw her chicken face in the girl's mirrored sunglasses, her mouth still hanging open in fear. She snapped it shut.

"Are you okay?" The girl took off the sunglasses. She was Nina's age, wearing a bikini top and denim miniskirt, wide hips, skinny legs, dark blond hair clipped in a spout that erupted off the top of her head. She was a little shorter than Nina but the hair spout and the shoulders-back posture made her seem taller.

"I've got to get a water gun." Nina was still out of breath and her voice was shaky.

"Here." She passed her the sunglasses. "Put these on for a minute. They'll make you feel calm."

Through the lenses, the sky glowed silver, the clouds edged in mercury. A charcoal plane droned by.

"Next time I'll bring a machete," the girl said. She had green-gray eyes made up like a tropical sunset, streaks of magenta and coral and lilac up to her eyebrows. "If I see him again, I'll cut his fucking balls off."

A woman jogging by frowned at her.

"What," said Nina's new pal, "you can't say 'balls' in Central Park?" She opened her mouth and squirted in a stream of water. For all that swagger, she had a sweet smile, with a tiny gap between her front teeth that made Nina wish her own weren't so boringly uniform. She studied Nina for a second, then asked, "Do you know where to get pot around here?"

She was flattered that she looked knowledgeable about drugs, even in her office blazer and skirt. She'd actually never liked pot—it made her paranoid, and ravenous for Burger King. But Leigh's older sister had filled them in on where to buy it in the park: ask one of the '60s throwbacks at the bandshell.

The bandshell—talk about serendipity.

"I do know, actually," she said. "It's not far from here." She hoped not anyway. Now if she ran into Gardner, how perfect to say: *Just showing my friend here where to buy pot,* like an old hand.

"Let me go grab my stuff. Don't leave without me!"

Nina took the opportunity to stop another passing jogger for directions. When the girl returned, she had on a T-shirt with a drawing of a red apple, BITE ME in black letters above it, and a leopard handbag with the water gun and a pack of Eve cigarettes sticking out the open zipper. All Nina had was the Dynamints and a copy of *The Bell Jar*, in which she'd found the ECT passage she'd been looking for: *I thought my bones would break*, Esther Greenwood said. *I wondered what terrible thing it was that I had done.*

"Cool shirt," Nina said.

"My dad hates it, so I wear it every day." She sniffed one of her underarms. "It's starting to stink."

"My dad made me throw away a T-shirt that had this snarling tiger's face," Nina said. Which wasn't exactly true. The one time Nina had put it on, he'd flinched as if she were the one snarling, and she'd guiltily shoved it back in her drawer.

The girl sniffed her other underarm, making the stack of bracelets halfway up her elbow jangle. They were gold bangles studded with rhinestones the size of postage stamps. It would be nice to carry that weight on your arm, Nina thought, a reminder of your strength.

Without thinking, she stuck out her hand to shake. "I'm Nina, by the way."

"Stephanie." They awkwardly grasped each other's hands.

"I don't know why I just did that," Nina said. "I'm temping this summer and the corporate thing's seeping in."

"No, I'm impressed," Stephanie said. "It's very *Who's the Boss.* Where'd you work today?"

"This PR company on Columbus. Their biggest client makes high-end cameras. I almost mailed out two hundred press packs for their newest model before anyone realized they hadn't included a picture of the thing."

"Ironic," Stephanie said.

"That's what I said. Although no one seemed to appreciate my take." They started down a tree-shaded path. "How about you?"

"Speaking of unironic. Do you know Maison Rouge on Seventieth and Third? Silk potholders, gold-plated cheese graters?"

"Uh-huh." Nina stepped out of the way of a rollerblader with a boom box on his shoulder blaring Gloria Gaynor. Then she spotted the volleyball courts and allowed herself to relax. They were headed in the right direction.

"Gold-plated cheese graters?" Nina prodded.

"I direct people to the correct aisle for all the crap they don't need. Either that or I ring up the crap they don't need. My new hobby's counting how many Platinum American Express cards I get. Double points if the customer slips 'My Hamptons beach house' into the transaction."

They walked past rows of crowded benches. A bearded man with a red towel around his neck eyed them, tensing as if he might lunge off the bench, but he settled back in his seat when Stephanie flashed her water gun. The towel around his neck uncoiled, revealing itself to be a snake, and flicked its rubbery tongue.

"Holy shit!" they said, clutching each other's arms.

The snake's owner flicked his tongue at them, too, as they passed him.

"I bet that's his entire personality," Stephanie said.

"You're so right. He can't leave his cave without it. Nobody would recognize him."

"My neighbor back home had a pet snake," Stephanie said. "I used to watch him through binoculars feeding it live mice."

"Back home where?" Nina was surprised. Stephanie seemed too at ease, too New York, to be a tourist.

"Hewlett." She smiled at Nina's blank face. "Long Island. It's one of the Five Towns?"

"Oh, right," Nina said. She had no idea.

"It's barely twenty-five miles outside the city, but to city people, it might as well be Bumfuck Egypt. Another reason my boyfriend hates Manhattan." Stephanie shrugged. "You're from here?"

Nina nodded and tried not to look smug like all native New Yorkers were over an accident of birth.

"My father's got an apartment here," Stephanie said. "Well, his girlfriend does, actually, and they're living together as of last month. That's where I'm staying."

"Sounds . . . complicated."

Stephanie nodded. After a long pause, she added, "She was a cheerleader at the University of Tennessee a thousand years ago, which is bad enough. But everything in the apartment is this radioactive Tennessee orange."

"Like living in a pumpkin," Nina said.

"Exactly."

"Coincidentally, I'm going to college in Tennessee, but to Vanderbilt. Its colors are black and gold."

"Like living in a bumble bee," Stephanie said.

The bandshell came into view and Nina shouted, "There it is!" realizing she sounded way too excited for a blasé native New Yorker, but relieved to have found it. "The bandshell, I mean," she said less exuberantly. The grandeur always caught her by surprise, the marble columns, the swooping concave dome, and the stage you could walk right onto like you were a major performer. Two guys at the side of the stage filled a wheelbarrow with loose twigs and branches. Both wore gray shirts and pants: community service uniform?

"Let's scope it out from here," she said, stopping at a tree about a hundred feet back. Now that Gardner might be near, nerves made her voice shake. No way she'd pull off some nonchalant line about buying pot. She took off Stephanie's sunglasses and the day rushed back in with startling intensity.

"Keep them. They were a dollar off the street."

Was that him raking leaves? She almost stabbed herself in the eye putting the sunglasses back on.

"You okay?" Stephanie stared at her.

This was the second time Stephanie had to ask her that in what—ten minutes? Nina must be the biggest wuss she'd ever met. "I know a guy who works here," Nina said quickly. "I don't want him to think I'm stalking him."

"Are you kidding me?" Stephanie said. "Look at you. You look like you walked out of a Mötley Crüe video. What guy wouldn't fall to his knees if you showed up?"

"Yeah, right. Anyway, Gardner probably has twenty girls an hour dropping by to flirt with him."

"Oh, he's a gardener?"

"No, that's his name. And his girlfriend's name is Holland."

"Really? I know a guy named Dutch. I could set them up. Problem solved." Stephanie twisted her hair back in the clip. "You think he's got pot?"

"For his sake, I hope not." She pointed at the wheelbarrow. "That's his community service." She told Stephanie about the Tavern on the Green escapade.

"I hope he trashed the place. We wanted to hold our prom after-party there and they were like, *Fuck you, plebians.*"

"I heard he ate himself into a lobster-bisque coma."

"Cool. Let's go say hi."

They went a few yards forward and stopped at another tree. She focused on the guy crouched at the base of a bench close to the stage fiddling with a pair of pliers. Broad shoulders, knife-sharp jaw, black hair falling in his eyes.

She yanked Stephanie behind the tree. "That's him," she whispered.

Stephanie snuck a look around the trunk. "Holy *shit,*" she whispered back. "He's sex on a stick." She gaped at Nina with admiration, which Nina allowed herself to bask in, as if she and Gardner had a relationship consisting of more than two minuscule interactions.

"Is he a model?" Stephanie asked. "Actor? He looks like that guy on *The Edge of Night*."

Nina peered out. Gardner pushed down on the slats of the bench with one hand while he tightened a bolt with the other. God, the muscles up and down his arms. "He's a normal guy," she said. "I mean, he goes to Boston University." It occurred to her that only private-school city snobs considered college *normal*. "Are you in school?" she asked.

To her relief, Stephanie nodded. "I will be after the summer. I'm going to Pratt to study design."

Nina eyed her BITE ME shirt. "You should do a line of T-shirts. Like SUCK ON THIS with a picture of a lemon."

Stephanie laughed. "Not fashion. Structural and interior." She pointed at the bandshell dome. "See those geometric indentations?"

The dome's interior was inlaid with rows of hexagons. "What are they for?" Nina asked.

"No idea. That's why I'm going to school."

What Nina would give for such a clear sense of purpose. She did a quick self-inspection for any curiosity about the hexagons but came up empty. Why kid herself? What she was really curious about was why Gardner had on a black leather belt while the guy he was talking to now—half a foot shorter, hay-colored hair pulled back in a frizzy ponytail—had on a tan one. Did it say something about their status, as in karate? She pressed against the tree and watched them squat at the base of the bandshell stairs, shoulder to shoulder, tensed like racers waiting for a starter's pistol.

Stephanie lit a cigarette, its filter wreathed in flowers. She exhaled a cloud of smoke.

"Nice. It smells like burnt sugar," Nina said.

"It tastes a little like caramel, although my boyfriend says it's more like prunes."

"That's funny. I always thought Marlboro Lights taste like raisins."

"I'll have to tell him. He loves raisins."

Nina made a face.

"Right?" Stephanie said. "I can't even stand Raisinets, and I'm a chocolate fiend." She took another drag. "Want one?"

"You have no idea," Nina said. "But I can't. I quit." She was about to tell her why when she noticed Gardner and the other guy racing up the stairs of the amphitheater stage at full speed. Gardner overtook him and leaped up the top steps three at a time. He raised his fists and hollered "Adrian!"

Nina laughed. Suddenly, he turned in their direction. Had he heard her? She spun around, hoping her shoulders and hips didn't jut out the sides of the tree. Hiding made you a hundred times more stalkerish.

"Do you think he can see the smoke?" she asked, then winced and apologized as Stephanie ground out the cig against the bottom of her shoe. "Did that sound like I was blaming you? I'm sorry, I'm being a child. Is he coming? Will you check?" She sounded like one of those dolls that spewed out a torrent of words when you pulled their string.

"It's fine," Stephanie said soothingly. "My lungs thank you." She glanced around the tree. "The coast is clear. He's headed to the dumpster over there." She pointed to the far side of the bandshell, then smiled at Nina. "I'm sure he didn't see you. You want to just go and say hi? Plant a seed, in case he and the girl from Holland break up?"

Nina's forehead was sweating. Her makeup had probably oxidized to orange streaks, and she was still dizzy from the spin around the tree. "I'm not up to it," she sighed.

Stephanie shrugged. "Life is long. He's not going anywhere."

Nina had never heard that. *Life is long.* As philosophies went, it had a nice, laissez-faire ring she appreciated. She pointed out a guy on the stage with stringy hair and tie-dye as a likely dealer.

"Thanks." Stephanie relit her cigarette and exhaled a stream of the sugary smoke. "I've got this. Come see me at Maison Rouge this week. Sundays to Thursdays, ten to six."

"Well, I could use a mink dishrag for my Hamptons beach house."

Stephanie laughed loudly, more than the dumb joke deserved, and Nina smiled back, with a little rush of gratitude. Then she walked quickly away before Gardner could spot her, so fast she set the Dyna-mints rattling. Worry flooded back—dry mouth, butterscotch candies, ECT, her mother's mind in cinders. It all awaited her at home. Still, it was nice to have forgotten for a while.

Chapter Four

That Friday night, Nina stayed at Flanagan's past midnight, but Gardner never showed. Had he spotted her at the bandshell behind the tree and clocked her as a stalker? She wished she'd just gone up and said hello. A little pushy had to be better than a lot creepy.

But he was there the next Friday, playing cards with Benji Peterson. She made sure to look down at her cocktail napkin when he walked by to get a drink, so as not to get caught staring at him. At her table, Leigh was busy administering a personality test: Write your favorite color on the napkin along with three adjectives to describe it. Leigh loved personality tests: Are you a leader or a follower? Which TV detective are you? Nina wrote "jade," although it wasn't her favorite color. Did she even have a favorite color? Jade was the girl in *Endless Love*, whose unabashed smuttiness had driven the guy obsessed with her to sign a love letter in his own blood. Nina had read the novel this week, then immediately reread the raunchiest parts, but now the stalker aspect of the story hit a little too close to home. Maybe she ought to change her answer, especially since the guy ended up setting fire to Jade's house with her family inside.

But her head was swimming with her father's tennis-elbow codeine, and no other color broke through.

"Sexy, dirty, neurotic," she wrote for the "jade" adjectives, then folded the napkin over so her answers didn't show. You had to reserve the option to change them on the sly once Leigh let on what they were saying about you. Nina wouldn't mention *that* Jade, not just because of the arson but also because Jade was played by Brooke Shields in the sappy movie version of the book, and she was on Leigh's shit list for defiling Princeton with bodyguards and paparazzi.

"Oh my God," Meredith said. "Is that the Hypnotist?"

She motioned with her head to the bar. A short, sunburned guy was ordering drinks for himself and a girl who barely looked old enough to be in high school. It was the Danceteria guy Meredith had lost it to, who'd pulled out her tampon and swung it in her face.

"Jesus," Meredith said. "Has that girl even *gotten* her period yet?"

Nina laughed, but Leigh was all business when it came to personality tests. She tapped Nina's cocktail napkin. "Favorite animal, plus three adjectives to describe it."

"Ant," she finally wrote, then quickly scratched through it. Whose favorite animal was an ant? She'd only thought of it because the codeine itch felt like red ants gnawing at her skin. The two Benadryls she'd also taken from her father's medicine cabinet, along with a Darvon from her mother's, weren't making much difference. A Flock of Seagulls song clattered from the jukebox. "Bird," she wrote. "Delicate, chirping, winged."

She looked at Leigh for further instruction, but right then Meredith's eyes went wide and she caught her breath. "Look who else is here." Her voice was euphoric with gossip. "That guy Craig from Rex's party last weekend. Did you guys hear about him and Clea Glass?"

Nina sat up straighter. Rex Parrish was Gardner's best friend. News about Rex could be news about Gardner.

"I heard about the party," Leigh sniffed, twisting her strand of pearls—the color of bone because quality pearls, she liked to remind everyone, should never be whiter than your teeth. "First of all, you're not supposed to hold an event on the beach without Town Board approval."

"It was amazing," Meredith said. "A bunch of Rex's Dartmouth friends came out, including—" She gestured with her chin toward the clump of clones in khakis moving toward the bar.

Leigh squinted in their direction. "Craig Bishop? That Craig? He went to Andover with my cousin. What was he doing with Clea?"

Clea Glass went to LaGuardia High School, but they knew her from various parties she was notorious for crashing. She was also notorious for her aggressive yet highly successful baby-voiced flirting. Nina used to join in the collective derision, until one night at a party, Clea had cheerfully offered to let Nina try her Kissing Potion lip gloss while they waited on line for the bathroom—the toffee flavor they only sold in Dublin, sent to her, she said, by an Irish guy she met at Limelight.

"She was totally coming on to Craig," Meredith continued, "showing him her tan lines, asking if he liked skinny-dipping. Then she goes"—Meredith made her voice an octave higher—"*Have you ever skinny-dipped in the ocean at night?*" She nodded meaningfully. "Well, now he has. The next morning, Clea called Rex all hysterical and said Craig had tried to drown her, that they were splashing around in the water and Craig put his hand on her head and shoved her under and wouldn't let her up for like three minutes."

Leigh snorted and drank down half her martini. "Wouldn't you be dead after *two* minutes?"

It was true that Clea was a drama queen: at the Kissing Potion party, she'd gotten in a fight with another girl and emptied her handbag out the kitchen window, makeup and hair ties raining fifteen flights down to the sidewalk. But why would she tell Rex a huge lie about Craig? On the other hand, the guys congregated at the bar looked . . . like regular guys. None had the ferret eyes of the model's landlord or the deranged intensity of the guy who'd menaced Nina in the park that day with Stephanie.

"Maybe some salt water got in Craig's eyes when Clea splashed him," Nina said, although not with a lot of force. She was muffled by the codeine, and besides, she wasn't going to start an argument in the middle of Flanagan's to defend Clea Glass just because she'd once shared her lip gloss. "Maybe he was, like, groping around to get his bearings and accidentally pushed on her head."

"Right." Leigh shrugged. "And now she's Natalie Wood."

"There are two sides to every story," Nina said, wishing she had the courage of her convictions—or at least some convictions to be courageous about.

Leigh waved her hand to dispel further talk of Clea and Craig and faux drownings. No doubt the instant she saw it was Craig Bishop from Andover, her mind was made up: Clea Glass went to a performing arts school, which didn't even have Latin or a squash team. "Next question." She pointed to Nina's napkin. "Favorite body of water."

Ironic, she heard Stephanie say. She shifted uncomfortably and dug her nails into the itchy skin on her back. It was easy to make fun of Leigh's snobbishness, but what about her own blank face in the park when Stephanie mentioned Hewlett? Were her native-New-Yorker blinders any less ludicrous? She wrote down "bath," even though there was nothing viler than sitting in a swamp of your own dead skin. Stepping out of the tub onto a cashmere bathmat might be nice, though. She'd been meaning to go by Maison Rouge to see Stephanie, but fear of coming off needy—BE MY FRIEND? PLEASE?—kept stopping her.

Leigh drummed her nails on the table, impatient for Nina to finish the question.

Frowning, Nina said, "Who has a favorite body of water anyway?" as she searched her slowed brain for bath adjectives besides "unsanitary," "swampy," and "putrid."

Leigh and Meredith met her frown with incandescent grins.

"What?" Nina wiped her nose and patted around her face. "Do I have something weird going on?"

But they were beaming over her shoulder, at Gardner. He pulled out the chair beside Nina and sat in one fluid motion as if *he* were submerged in a body of water. He tilted the chair back and stuck out his legs. Nina thought of what her mother used to say when Nina showed up late to the dinner table—*You've decided to grace us with your presence, Your Highness?* Here was real grace. She felt—what was the word for it? Exalted. Better yet, anointed.

"I have a favorite," he said. "Car wash."

"Adjectives for a car wash," Meredith said, leaning forward on her elbows and propping her face in her fists so her cheekbones jutted out.

"Hey!" Leigh admonished. She glanced at Gardner and played with her pearls. "Three adjectives, please."

"Flappy. Wet." He lifted Nina's glass to his mouth, pushed aside the skinny red straw with his tongue, and drank. A shard of ice cracked between his teeth.

"Third adjective!" Meredith said urgently, like Gardner would leave if they didn't pin him down with this dumb quiz.

Brian appeared on Nina's other side. "Mind if I join you guys?"

Gardner laughed. "You own this place. You can sit wherever you want."

"*I* don't own it." He dragged an empty chair out from the table beside theirs, pulling too hard on one side so it tipped and almost fell over. He righted it with a clumsiness that Nina empathized with. Then he brought out a flyer for next week's July Fourth party at the bar: PRESIDENTIAL TRIVIA! RED, WHITE, AND BLUE MARGARITAS! As he held it up to show them, Gardner turned to Nina with a cigarette.

She shook her head. "Not yet."

"Better than *never,* anyway."

She realized she was sweating. *Had* he spotted her and Stephanie behind the tree? Prophylactically, she said, "I was at the bandshell last week. I didn't see you. Are you still doing community service?"

"As of five o'clock today, I'm officially a free man. At least for now. What were you doing there?"

"Buying pot with a friend," she practically whispered, so Meredith and Leigh wouldn't overhear and hammer her with questions. (*What friend? Since when do you like pot?*)

"You think Grandma would approve of that?" He lit his cigarette with a match and exhaled smoke to extinguish the flame. She thought, I would swallow a lit match if you asked me to.

His eyes dropped to the loose threads at the hem of her cutoff shorts. His hand brushed her thigh as he wound one of the longer strings around his finger and pulled.

"They're supposed to be like that," she said, trying to hold her breath to stop any mortifying gasping sounds from leaking out. He rolled the string between his thumb and middle finger. *Sex on a stick* suddenly made sense. Everything about him made her feel skewered.

The string snapped off. He stuck it in the pocket of his jeans.

"Nina," Meredith called across the table. She was watching them with a curiosity that verged on suspicion. "Who was the first president born in a hospital?" Brian had been quizzing her and Leigh on presidential trivia.

She made a wild guess. "Kennedy?"

"Carter," Brian said. "But you were a lot closer than I was. You should be on my team. My brothers destroy me every year."

Meredith, keeping her eyes on Nina, asked Gardner if he'd be in Southampton for July Fourth. "With Holland," she emphasized.

I *know*, Nina thought irritably. But when he said "Yup," her heart still sank.

"Hey," Meredith continued, "we missed you at Rex's party last weekend."

Brian directed a tiny, tense shake of his head at Meredith.

"Fuck Rex," Gardner said, and ground out his cigarette in the tin ashtray, smashing the filter to bits. "He's a piece of shit."

Meredith looked confused. "Is this about Craig?"

"Who's Craig?" Gardner's voice was sharp.

"My favorite body of water's a river," Brian said.

But Meredith had Gardner's full attention: no way she'd be diverted. "Craig Bishop. I thought you knew him. He goes to Dartmouth with Rex. Clea Glass said he tried to drown her at Rex's party last weekend."

"What?" Brian asked.

"Show me who you mean," Gardner told Meredith.

"We doubt it's true," Leigh said. "Clea's a walking soap opera."

Gardner's jaw was tight. "I wouldn't put anything past a friend of Rex's." A category that apparently no longer included him. He pushed back his chair.

"Where are you going," Brian said, more warning than question.

"I just want to check it out." Gardner's smile said *no big deal.* "I know Clea. She's a cool girl." He asked Meredith: "Craig, right?"

She nodded, looking worried, and Gardner got up and went to the bar. Nina craned her neck to watch his progress through the crowd.

"You shouldn't have said anything," Leigh said to Meredith, gulping down the last of her martini.

Meredith crossed her arms. "I heard he and Rex made up. I wouldn't have mentioned it otherwise."

"They're not friends anymore?" Nina asked. She hadn't heard, but it was good news to her. She'd disliked Rex Parrish since that day last winter when she saw him on line for *Spies Like Us* and, recognizing him from Flanagan's—thin lips, pointy nose—gave a timid smile. He'd stared back dead-eyed with his mouth in a slit, as in, *What makes you think you get to smile at me?*

"I heard he hit on Holland," Leigh said.

"I heard Gardner fucked up his car," Meredith said.

Brian shook his head. "You guys should write for *People.*"

"What *did* happen?" Nina asked.

"Long story." He half-stood for a better look. Gardner was approaching the herd of khakis at the bar. They were too far away for Nina to hear over the music, but he must have said Craig's name. A stocky guy turned, dirty blond hair and round, dopey eyes. The guy smiled, maybe recognizing Gardner in connection to Rex, and extended his hand to shake.

Very *Who's the Boss,* Stephanie had said about Nina's handshake in the park. Nina decided to get over herself and stop by Maison Rouge this weekend.

Suddenly Brian bolted from his chair. Gardner had twisted Craig's arm behind his back and pushed him down against the bar. He leaned over him, saying something in his ear while Craig struggled. Nina was so shocked, she thought they were kidding around. She'd never witnessed an actual flesh-and-blood fight. In the moment it took her brain to catch up, Craig managed to shake free, yelling, "What the fuck?" He shoved an ashtray off the bar and butts went flying. Gardner lunged at him, but when Brian stepped in and extended his arm, he backed off.

Nina and her friends exchanged stunned looks.

"Mr. Flanagan is not going to be happy," Leigh said finally.

Brian didn't look happy either. He stood stone-faced at the door as Craig and his friends stormed out. Gardner squatted to pick up the ashtray and the cigarette butts. His head hung in what looked to Nina like contrition. After a minute, Brian shrugged and called for a broom, then slung his arm around Gardner's shoulder. Someone played "Eye of the Tiger" on the jukebox and a few of the guys threw joking fake punches in Gardner's direction.

"Craig *did* look like an asshole," Leigh mused. "I'll ask my cousin what his story was at Andover."

"What do you think Rex will do when he hears about this?" Meredith asked, and Nina entertained a quick fantasy of his face crumpled with shame when he heard how Gardner had vanquished his buddy in public.

Three adjectives for what she'd just witnessed: "violent," "alarming," "exhilarating." She lifted her glass and placed her lips over the faint imprint of Gardner's before downing the rest of her drink.

In the ladies' room stall, there were some new responses beneath *I'M DRUNK AGAIN BECAUSE . . . I will always love Mark. Another yeast infection.* She was formulating her own answer for tonight—*Why not?*—when a voice called from the next stall: "Goddammit. Have you got a cork? I just got my period."

The voice was Alison Bloch's, the girl who'd stared disbelievingly at Nina that first night she'd talked with Gardner at the bar. As if she were any more Gardner's type than Nina. Although she was, admittedly, a better flirt, always fluttering around him, coming up from behind him to cup her hands over his eyes—*Guess who?*—or challenging him to thumb wrestle. None of which Gardner seemed to mind, now that she thought of it.

But what she wasn't was a blue-blooded Upper East Side girl. (Pre-Holland girlfriends were Calista Cooke, Nightingale class president, and Marina Delafield, star of one of Jill Kcode Krementz's *A Very Young* books.) Before this summer, Nina had never seen Alison here. She had no idea where she was from, except it was somewhere the girls wore jeans so tight you could see the impression of their underwear and slithery blouses that glowed in the dark. Her hair was teased into sticky whirls and she was tanned to deep walnut on the front of her body but not her back (a Jap tan, Nina had heard it called, procured by sunbathing rather than from tennis or sailing).

"Sorry, fresh out of corks," Nina answered, trying not to visualize the charming image of a bloody cork on a string. When she came out of her stall, Alison was at the sink. She towered over Nina in white patent stiletto sandals. Her bottom half was thick, encased in those skintight jeans, but her chest and back were slim and she wore a sheer tank top that ended just below her bra, which was black lace with slim straps and just one back hook, as opposed to Nina's off-white, nylon, saddle-sized bra.

"How could I not have a single tampon?" Alison said. Pinned to the straps of her Sportsac was an array of buttons with various sayings: SEX HAS NO CALORIES. RUDE GIRL. YOU BET SIZE MATTERS. She pulled out a tube of mascara and tossed it on the counter, followed by four lipsticks, a small brush with her dark hair tangled in its bristles, and a pink plastic retainer case. Then she looked up into the mirror. Her eyes widened for an instant as they met Nina's, then quickly narrowed again. She grabbed the pink case.

"Maybe I should just stick this up there."

"Your retainer?"

Alison's jaw dropped. She stared gleefully at Nina's reflection, then burst out laughing. The door opened and another girl came in, red feather earrings and a mole on her neck, who Nina recognized as Alison's friend Jill. Alison pointed at Nina and said, "She thought my diaphragm was a retainer!"

Jill cackled along.

Alison bent over, heaving with laughter. "She thinks a retainer goes up your twat."

"You know I didn't say that," Nina said. "I didn't even see it." But no point trying to have a normal conversation with someone in hysterics at your expense. She shook her head and headed back to her table, annoyed and embarrassed. Although later, as she walked home, she thought of Alison's initial glance in the bathroom mirror, that flare of recognition, the momentary crumble of the facade when you're unexpectedly face-to-face with your competition. Or at least she hoped that's what it was, that Alison had seen Gardner sitting beside Nina earlier, drinking from her glass, brushing his hand against her thigh, pocketing the thread he'd pulled from her cutoffs.

When she got home, she stood at the entrance to her parents' room to listen at their half-open door. The sounds of Frances's sleep—or non-sleep—had always helped Nina know what to expect the next morning. Shallow, fidgety sleep meant Frances would rise at dawn with droopy eyes, calling for a Librium. Raspy muttering ("get off the ice," "let me go") meant bad dreams, Frances looking haunted the next day, and easily provoked. Dry coughs meant she'd be up for a glass of water and Nina better make sure the hall was clear, so her mother wouldn't trip on an errant shoe and lose her shit. Dead silence, like now, was rare. This had to be Halcion sleep: black, heavy, and narcotic. Sleep you couldn't help but be grateful for.

Had anyone ever known so much about their mother's sleep? Nina had even considered writing her college application essay about it, though in the end she'd gone with how much she'd allegedly learned about the human condition handing out dinner rolls in a Bowery soup kitchen, which she'd only experienced a single Sunday morning when she was hungover from Debate Club.

Now, standing here in the dark, her ears ringing with silence, she cautiously stuck her head in to confirm the Halcion bottle on her mother's bedside table. But Frances's side of the bed was empty, just a rumpled silhouette in the sheets where she'd been, like a chalk outline at a crime scene. No Halcion bottle either. Her father lay on his back, out cold. This could be another state of sleep entirely, or non-sleep: Frances in the kitchen, foraging for cookies and ice cream, then retching in the bathroom.

Nina checked the bathroom, also empty, then spotted a light on in the kitchen. She steeled herself for the unleashing of her mother's temper when she pried away the Oreos and tried to coax her back to bed. But when she peeked in, there was Frances sitting at the kitchen table with a rag and a bottle of silver polish, scrubbing the tarnish off one of Pearl's old-fashioned filigreed trays. Instead of the velour tracksuit, she wore a satin robe and slippers with marabou feathers at the toe. Her hands were streaked with tarnish and the air stank of polish fumes, but her expression was tranquil. Not tranquilizer tranquil. Just plain contentedness, which was why it took a minute to identify.

Nina stayed out of sight in the doorway and watched her mother work the rag into the corners of the tray with a competent flick of her wrist. This had to be Vlad's new medication kicking in. She quietly backed away, so as not to startle Frances out of her trance. As she crept to her room, she tried to temper her hopefulness. There'd been other promising starts with other medications, good stretches when Frances brushed her hair and washed her face, bought groceries, and picked up the dry cleaning, only to sink back to baseline, or below, within a matter of days. Hope made the disappointment twice as shitty.

In her room, she undressed, her leg still tingling where Gardner had touched her. What would go through his mind when he found the string in his pocket? She dug out her jewelry box from under a pile of sweatshirts in her dresser drawer and lifted out the bracelet compartment stuffed with Actifeds and Dexatrims to get to the ring tray, where she'd made a rainbow out of Xanaxes, Valiums, Klonopins, and a small handful of emergency Halcions. The itching had mostly subsided but, along with a Xanax, she took a last Benadryl, then got into bed with her copy of *Endless Love* and reread the ending, when David tells Jade he imagines himself in an otherwise empty theater in the middle of the night. "I see your face, I see you, you; I see you in every seat," he says. How amazingly lucky, to be seen like that.

She hoped the book would inspire a dream about Gardner. But instead it was her parents driving her to Vanderbilt, which turned out not to be a college but an abandoned farm in the middle of nowhere. An old farmer appeared and said, "You're hundreds of miles in the wrong direction." He looked like Henry Fonda in *On Golden Pond*, except the sky wasn't blue and peaceful but a tin gray with dark clouds like in *The Shining*. They got back in the car, which was now a horse-drawn buggy, and rode another hour to a tall, windowless office building made of black marble that a guard told them was a glue factory. Another long ride, a clump of buildings that looked like a college campus but was actually a Hawaiian village. She started to panic. She wouldn't be going to college. It didn't exist.

Somehow they wound up outside Flanagan's, standing in the rain. Her parents, unaccountably uneasy, insisted Nina not go in but instead come home with them. Which was when Craig Bishop grabbed her breasts and said, "These tits don't look like they want to go home." He ran off when Gardner came out. "You can't even get me to college," she said to her parents. "Why would I go home with you?" and took Gardner's hand. As they headed into Flanagan's, she saw her parents dissolve into a puddle of silver polish and get washed down a grate.

Benadryl always gave her the strangest dreams.

Chapter Five

Her grandfather liked to take long walks around the city, but as his mind had begun to splinter, he kept getting into trouble. He'd wandered into St. Patrick's Cathedral and lit a cigar with a prayer candle. He'd tried on a pair of wingtips at Lord & Taylor and walked out wearing them. Two weeks after Pearl died, he boarded a bus to Atlantic City, even though he'd never gambled a day in his life, and lost $4,000 at the roulette table. Since then, Ira saw to it that his aide stuck by his side during the week.

Nina took a walk with him most Sundays. She'd pick him up at his apartment and then they'd go slowly up one block and down another, past the castle-like armory on Sixty-Seventh, the rich grays and pewters of the old apartment buildings, the yellow marigolds planted beside the curb, the apothecary on Lexington so ancient it once sold leeches and opium.

Today she inched them toward Third Avenue, in the direction of Maison Rouge, where Stephanie worked, a glass box that took up most of Seventieth Street. "What do you think? Are we in the market for a gold-plated cheese grater?"

He nodded. "Very good."

They stopped outside the door to the store so she could fasten a button he'd missed on his shirt and help him re-tuck the tail that had pulled loose from his waistband. She wondered if any part of him missed, or even remembered, the pinstripe suits he wore to his office before he retired. Maybe that was the best thing about aging, relinquishing vanity. Although as she straightened his shirt collar, she got a familiar whiff of lime that soothed her: he still combed his hair, thick and pure white, with the same tonic.

Inside, Maison Rouge was aisle after aisle of expensive knick-knacks. Enamel boxes, onyx coasters, pastel soaps wrapped in parchment and tied with silk cord. She looked around for Stephanie in her BITE ME T-shirt, then realized that of course they wouldn't let her wear it here. All the salesgirls had on the same puff-shouldered, cherry-red blouse. Nina tugged Seymour's hand to steer him around a corner, but the space was tight, and her elbow knocked a crystal owl off a shelf. It shattered against the hard floor. Great, she thought. Two minutes and I've already wrecked her store.

A salesgirl appeared beside them with a broom and a dustpan and promptly swept up the pieces of broken owl. Her rainbow eye shadow—striations of ruby, pink, and rose—was the first thing Nina recognized. Today her long hair was pulled back with a red bow, and Nina noticed a bunch of piercings up both ears, filled with tiny moon and star earrings. Nina hadn't been allowed to pierce her ears even once until her eighteenth birthday, this past March. Frances didn't have pierced ears. Pearl thought making holes in your body was barbaric.

"Nina—it's you! I can't believe it!" Stephanie hugged her, accidentally smacking the back of her head with the broom handle, not that Nina minded. "I was hoping you'd come."

They stood there smiling at each other. Until that moment, Nina hadn't realized she'd brought her grandfather here as a kind of prop, so she'd feel less exposed if Stephanie wasn't glad to see her. Now she squeezed his hand to communicate an apology. Then she pointed to the dustpan in Stephanie's hand and apologized to her, too: "I make a mess wherever I go. Can I pay for it?"

Between her birthday, allowance, graduation, and last week's temp job, she'd amassed $500.

"Oh, please. With all this breakable stuff, you'd think they'd carpet the place." She smiled at Seymour, who was looking off into the distance, then stepped into his field of vision to include him in the conversation. "Who's this handsome gentleman?" she asked.

Nina introduced them.

"Hello, Seymour," Stephanie said cheerfully. "You have a very smart and special granddaughter."

"What can I tell you."

"Nothing I don't already know." She was more hyper than Nina remembered, tapping her tongue against the roof of her mouth, her fingers against her legs. After dumping the broken glass into a bin in the corner, she led them on a tour of the store, pointing in various directions. "Those lamps are made of agate from a beach in California. This obelisk is malachite. Russian tsars would panel the walls of their castles with it—it's supposed to protect against the Evil Eye." She was talking too fast for Nina to absorb most of it, but her delight in the details gave everything a glow.

"That seahorse is mother-of-pearl. Did you know it comes from the shells of mollusks?"

"Equinophobia is fear of horses," Nina said—she could at least contribute something—"so maybe fear of seahorses would be aqua-equinophobia."

Stephanie turned to Seymour: "Like I said: smart. And special."

Nina bit her lip to stifle a dopey smile.

Down another aisle for disquisitions on Art Deco decanters and Guadalajaran vases. Finally Nina had to stop her. "This place is a workout," she joked, although actually, Seymour was struggling to catch his breath. She was meant to take him for a walk, not run him into the ground. "I think he could use a break."

Stephanie studied Nina for a second. "Follow me. Just a tiny bit farther, I swear." They walked to the rear of the shop, where they came to a door with a sign that said EMPLOYEES ONLY. By the door was a scruffy armchair and beside it a boxy black leather recliner with a rip down its side that Nina guessed was awaiting repairs. Stephanie asked Seymour if he wanted to take a load off. Nina couldn't imagine how he knew what she meant, but he went straight for the recliner.

"You look like Captain Kirk." Stephanie smiled at him. "Can I borrow your granddaughter for a minute? I want to take her to the stockroom and show her the new waffle irons we just got in."

He nodded. "Very good."

Nina didn't really like waffles, the way the syrup got stuck in the craters, but Stephanie looked so eager.

"Where's Pearl?" Seymour added.

"She'll be here in a few minutes," Nina told him. "Don't go anywhere or she won't be able to find us."

"Ekht," he said, and waved her off.

She followed Stephanie through the door and down a dimly lit corridor to another closed door. Behind it was the stockroom, with floor-to-ceiling shelves crammed with jars and bottles and boxes, stacks of throw pillows, dishes, and candlestick holders. In the middle of the room was a long steel table with mismatched chairs around it and a half-eaten tuna sandwich wrapped in plastic. Strewn across one end were a bunch of travel brochures for Fort Lauderdale.

"Are you going to Florida?" Nina asked.

"Not if I can help it. My mother just moved there. She's trying to get me there, too, but no way I'm leaving the city." She went to a row of lockers on the back wall and turned the dial on one of the locks. "Is Pearl your grandmother?"

It took Nina a second. "Oh. Yeah. But no. I mean, she died. She had a stroke."

"I'm sorry."

"It's okay. She wasn't the nicest. But my grandfather keeps forgetting she's gone. My father says it's kinder not to keep reminding him."

"Wow, that's sad. I'm going to hate old age, with everyone lying to me even more than usual." She got the lock open and pulled it off. Inside hung a neon-green dress and a red handbag. She rifled through the bag, asking over her shoulder, "Want to get high?"

Nina laughed. Only she would fall for the waffle-iron ruse. "I can't go back out there smelling like pot," she said.

"Not that kind of high." She pulled out a small baggie filled with white powder. Nina had never seen cocaine in real life, but she recognized it from a term paper she wrote in ninth grade for a drug education class. She'd pored over glitzy photos of Studio 54, learned that Thomas Edison drank a cocaine-laced Bordeaux called Vin Mariani to help him work through the night, and read Freud's description of a cocaine high: "a gorgeous excitement." She'd also watched *Scarface*, mesmerized by Michelle Pfeiffer's crystal-handled coke spoon. Was there ever a more glamorous accessory? Maybe Bancroft ought to rethink that drug class.

Now that the real thing was actually in front of her, she hesitated. Her nose started to twitch as if hit by a sharp wind.

Stephanie swept aside the travel brochures. "We'll just do a little. My boss is here today. Did you see her out there, black hair and cat-eye glasses? If she catches me wired, I'm dead."

Nina's mind went to the news last week about the college basketball player who really *was* dead. Something Bias. His heart had short-circuited from a cocaine overdose. The *Daily News* headline that day: GAME OVER. Don't be a pussy, she told herself. He'd just gotten drafted by the Celtics and probably ingested a barrel of coke to celebrate. The tiny bit Stephanie tipped out onto the steel table wouldn't fill a sugar packet.

"My friend Damian gave me an eight ball for my birthday," she said.

Was there ever a more glamorous sentence? She took out a credit card from her wallet and sliced the powder into lines. Nina saw that the card had Stephanie's name on it, not her mother's or father's like the one Nina had to use, and even then she often had to show a signed permission slip from her parents as if she were ten years old.

Stephanie snorted one of the lines through a rolled-up dollar bill and handed it to Nina, who brought it to her nose. It smelled like ink and sweaty palms. She leaned down and sniffed half a line, pausing to see how it went. A slight sting but nothing dire.

"If it hurts, I have Vaseline," Stephanie said.

Nina shook her head. She sniffed the second half. Within seconds, her brain switched to its highest voltage ever, like one of Edison's lightbulbs on overload, and she was hit hard by a wave of—yes, Dr. Freud: *gorgeous excitement*. Suddenly the need to speak was as urgent as the need to breathe. "What an amazing birthday present," she said. "What a fantastic friend! For my last birthday, my friend Meredith gave me a Jane Fonda video." Did cocaine make you verbalize every thought? But why not, when every thought was so enchantingly profound?

"Why do Jane's leotards have belts?" Stephanie asked.

"Right? The last thing that should need a belt is a leotard."

"Did you know maxi pads used to have belts? Like wearing an upside-down bra around your waist."

"Do you get cramps?" Nina asked. "I have a thing called mittelschmerz. My stomach kills when I'm ovulating." She gestured vaguely to where her ovaries might reside.

"Oh!" Stephanie said. "Some old guy at the mall the other day complimented me on my hüftgold. Do you know what that means?"

"I think hüfts are hips?"

"Hip gold?" Stephanie said.

"As in your hips are so beautiful they're made of gold."

Stephanie shimmied her hips and Nina envied her pride in them. She wasn't the straight up and down of the Flanagan's girls, either, which to Nina had always seemed the right way to look. But Stephanie carried herself like she was right, too. For the first time, Nina truly got the word "aplomb."

"Hey, want to come to my July Fourth party?" Stephanie asked. "My dad and his girlfriend are going away, but they said I could have a 'small patriotic gathering' to celebrate the Reagans. His girlfriend campaigned for Ronnie." She stuck her finger in her mouth, as in *gag me*. "You can meet Patrick, show him not every city girl's an annoying snob."

"Patrick's your boyfriend . . . ?" Although Nina had already guessed, based on the way Stephanie lingered over his name, like saying it made her mouth feel good.

She nodded, smiling as she scrawled her address on the back of an Everglades airboat brochure. "Want to bring that hot gardener from the park?"

Nina filled her in on what had happened at Flanagan's Friday night: Clea Glass, and Gardner going after Craig Bishop.

"Of course no one believes the girl," Stephanie said.

"Clea can be kind of dramatic. Although Craig did look like a prick." If she waffled any more, she really would need a waffle iron.

Stephanie laid out two more lines on the table. "Sounds like Gardner showed incredible restraint. Patrick would have just beat the crap out of that asshole if he'd done that to me. No questions asked." She bent over the table, then handed the dollar to Nina.

As Nina snorted her next line, all at once this time, she felt the last of her worries evaporate. Gardner hadn't really hurt Craig, but he'd made his point. Even if Clea had exaggerated a little, the prick would think twice before manhandling another girl.

"Anyway," she told Stephanie, "Gardner's still with his perfect girlfriend."

"There'll be a lot of guys at my party." Stephanie touched her finger to a trace of powder, then ran it over her gums. Nina did the same, feeling them go pleasantly numb.

"I'll find someone for you," Stephanie said. "I'm a really good matchmaker."

"Want to hear something funny? My grandfather's neighbors met in Auschwitz and used to say Hitler was their matchmaker."

"Yikes." Stephanie twisted the baggie closed. There was a ghost of residue on the table that Nina wiped off with her sleeve. Then kept wiping, admiring the grace of her movement, like a one-armed breaststroke. "Anything else in here need cleaning? I've got so much energy."

"Speaking of your grandfather: we should get back to him."

It took Nina a second. "Holy shit. How long have we been in here?" She yanked open the door to the stockroom and rushed down the corridor. She threw open the door to the store. The black leather recliner was empty.

Stephanie appeared at her side. "Don't worry. He's here some-where." She pointed to the front of the store. "I'll take those aisles, you take these."

Nina zipped down the curtains aisle and up the lamps, down the bath towels and up the sheets. She turned in circles, craning her neck. How far could he have gone? Her head was spinning and her neck felt like a Slinky, and she still hadn't caught sight of him.

Stephanie reappeared, shaking her head. "I promise, he didn't just disappear. Let's keep circling." She'd have been more reassuring if her eyes weren't so glassy, the pupils huge black caves thinly ringed in green.

Nina avoided her own eyes in the mirror above a marble side-board. Worry ballooned to dread. She'd not only dragged Seymour here so she could make a friend, she'd ditched him to do cocaine. "If I've lost him," she told Stephanie when they intersected at the pil-lows aisle, "I honestly think my parents will send me to prison."

"I'll go ask the other salesgirls if they've seen him. I'll check the restrooms too."

Nina continued her march up and down the aisles. She couldn't stop clicking her teeth together, which sounded like chattering and made her shiver. Every scenario sent her mind reeling. She saw Sey-mour hoisting himself off the recliner, no idea where Nina was, prob-ably no idea where *he* was. What if he'd had a stroke? What if he'd fallen and hit his head? She'd have killed off a second grandparent, this time for real.

She was starting to give up hope of finding him in the store. Could he have wandered outside? Tried to make his way home on his own? She prayed he hadn't been hit by a bus. The ghastly spectacle at the visitation the night before Pearl's funeral replayed in her mind: Pearl in her coffin, thick undertaker's makeup troweled onto her face, here and there a patch of gray skin showing through; and the next morning, as they closed the coffin's lid before the funeral started, Frances squatting farther and farther down for a final peek at her mother's face. Nina ran toward the store's exit, keeping her eye out for older men with white hair. She passed one in the kitchenware aisle, studying a set of napkin rings topped by jeweled flamingos. Right build, but not Seymour. An elderly man checking the price on a gilt-edged creamer: also not Seymour. A man with his finger in the spout of a copper tea kettle. Not him either. A white-haired man gazing at pepper mills. Not Seymour. No, wait. Seymour!

Looking none the worse for wear. She had to stop herself from startling him by throwing her arms around his neck. She tried to slow her haywire breathing.

"Would you like one of these?" she asked. She was still out of breath and choking back tears.

His expression didn't change. "Where's Pearl?"

"She'll be right back. She went to look at rugs." She leaned closer and sniffed his lime scent. How could she have left him alone? She grabbed a pepper mill to buy for him, a silver-and-ebony one that cost half of last week's salary, but too bad, she was lucky to get off this easy. While she was at it, she grabbed a second one for her parents.

Stephanie caught up with them at the cash register. "She found you," she said happily.

Nina gave her a small headshake. He didn't know he'd been missing. No point clueing him in and risking it getting back to her parents, who were always going on about Nina's carelessness and ir-responsibility: lost jackets, lost bus passes, her head if it weren't at-tached to her shoulders. Lost grandfather? No thanks.

"You found each other," Stephanie amended. She told the girl behind the register to give Nina the employee discount, then got back there herself to wrap the pepper mills in a blizzard of bows and tissue.

"See you on the Fourth," she said as they were leaving.

"That girl's got shpilkes," Seymour said, back out on the sidewalk.

"She does have a lot of zip," Nina said. Shpilkes, she remembered, meant ants in your pants.

"Like your cousin Esther," he said, chuckling. Nina didn't have a cousin named Esther. Pearl had, but she didn't correct him.

Nina's father looked puzzled when he opened the gift box with the pepper mill nestled in the jumble of tissue paper. "Is it someone's birthday?"

"I saw it in the window at Maison Rouge," she explained, "when Grandpa and I walked by today." She snuck a look at Seymour, seated next to her at the dinner table. He remained mercifully neutral, but that didn't stop the bone-chilling visions of what could have happened if he'd really been lost. Visions so vivid, there was dialogue and blood.

"Well then," Ira said. "We should christen its maiden voyage with this magnificent brisket your mother made for us." He beamed as he passed the pepper mill to Frances. "Here, dear, give it a whirl."

It was already surprising that Frances had joined them at the dinner table. Even more surprising was that she'd found the energy to make a meal after months of Nina and Ira making frozen pizza and TV dinners. More surprising still was her enthusiasm for the pepper mill. She gave it a few twists over her salad: "It grinds so beautifully." She turned a little knob at the bottom, exclaiming, "Look, you can adjust the size!" and vigorously ground pepper over her brisket. She had on a peppy new shirt with a pair of embroidered eyes across the chest, the right one wide open with a clump of aqua beads for an iris, the other closed in a wink with some loose black fringe for lashes that fluttered as she brandished the pepper mill.

"Want to take it for a ride?" Ira asked Nina.

"No thanks."

"It really livens up the taste. You sure?"

Frances waved him off. "Stop peppering her with questions." Her voice had the teasing flirtation of her shirt's winking eye.

Ira glanced at Nina with a smile that said, *How about this!* He was so heartbreakingly incautious; he always forgot that the good stretches ended. She raised her eyebrows back to say, *We'll see.* One silly joke didn't mean happily ever after.

Although, with *happily ever after* in her head, she absently scratched her nose and wondered what exactly had become of Michelle Pfeiffer's character in *Scarface.* You never saw her again after she threw the glass of wine in Al Pacino's face and stormed out of the restaurant. Nina had always assumed she'd suffered some off-camera gruesome death, or, at best, a miserable existence on the streets of Miami. But why the pessimism? Maybe *she* got a happily ever after, living a perfectly nice life in a suburb somewhere, head of the PTA— the coke spoon tucked away in a drawer with the good silver, a souvenir of a long-ago adventure.

Frances jumped up from the table and went through the door to the kitchen, then reappeared holding a miniature tape recorder. She pressed the Record button and a tiny red light switched on. "Dried basil," she said into it. "Eggplant lasagna." She clicked the Stop button. "Isn't this ingenious? It's from Sharper Image. So much more efficient than hunting around for a pen."

And so much less disturbing than chaotic graph-paper scrawl, Nina thought.

Frances pressed Record again and laid it on the table next to Seymour. He glanced at it then back to his plate, stabbing at the brisket with his fork, globs of sauce spattering his shirt.

"Daddy, let me help you," Frances said. Usually around her father she was frowning and grim—Nina had once seen her punch the crown of the fedora he'd left at their apartment until it looked like a collapsed cake. But now her voice rang girlishly as she addressed the recorder while slicing his food: "What's it called when the salt and pepper say hello? Seasons' greetings."

Seymour smiled. Ira threw back his head and laughed. Even Nina let out a little snort: Frances's lightheartedness was hard to resist. "Good one, Mom," she said as she allowed her mother's mood to wash over her. Why not? Her grandfather was safe and sound, tossing back green beans like a champ. Stephanie thought she was great, and Nina was going to a July Fourth party next week, and even though Gardner would be away with Holland, there'd be a crew of new guys to flirt with, and if she were lucky, more gorgeous excitement.

Chapter Six

Her parents left that Friday afternoon for a last-minute trip out to Montauk, giving Nina time before Stephanie's party to indulge in one of her favorite activities: drinking alone in her bedroom. She mixed vodka and Diet Coke in a tall glass, put Chaka Khan on the stereo, sat on the floor with her back against her bed, and relaxed. Just her and her music and the waves of warmth rippling through her body. She serenaded her glass: *Ain't nobody loves me better*, accompanied by the distant booms of early Fourth of July fireworks.

How would she steal these moments when she was at college? Would she ever get to be alone? Meredith's sister at Georgetown had a roommate named Casey who wore a puppet on her hand, and whenever Meredith's sister returned to the room, the puppet would say, "Casey wondered where you were," or "Casey missed you," although Casey herself never said a word. With that in mind, Nina had pleaded for a single on the Vanderbilt housing questionnaire. She'd never shared a room with anyone, one of the benefits of being an only child. For all she knew, she made weird faces when she studied or passed gas in her sleep. Who wanted to be observed that closely? It made her think of something she'd once read in an Annie Dillard book, about the first cataract surgeries for people who'd been blind since birth. There was joy at the flood of light and color and shapes, but there was also horror that they'd been visible to others their whole lives, not always so winningly. Maybe with some food in their teeth or a hairy mole or thinning hair. The book didn't supply these examples, but Nina called them up in an instant.

She finished her drink, the reassuring solitude of it.

Stephanie answered the door wearing a red leather skirt, a cropped white tank top, and a bunch of blue beaded necklaces. Oh, of course. Pretty much everyone here, what looked like fifty or sixty people, had on some combination of red, white, and blue. It hadn't occurred to Nina to dress up for the Fourth of July. She didn't have the flair for costumes. Even for Halloween parties, she always came, lamely, as "night"—navy shirt and jeans—and now she felt just as hopelessly bland in her black tank dress and espadrilles.

AC/DC was cranked so high, she had to shout for Stephanie to hear her. "I'm sorry my outfit's so unpatriotic."

"Well, *un*-patriotic would be, like, a KGB uniform." Stephanie looked her up and down. "You should let people know."

"Know what?" The music and the noise of the crowd made her miss the first part.

"Your figure!" Stephanie shouted in her ear. "It's killer."

"What people?"

Stephanie laughed. "Well, since you asked, let me show you a few of tonight's options." She led Nina to the low-ceilinged living room behind her. AC/DC ended and a slower Led Zeppelin song started up. The lights were dimmed, but Nina made out two long orange couches, a couple of goldfish-colored armchairs, a poppy-splattered rug, and a huge painting of an orange-hued sunset. Stephanie hadn't been kidding about all the Tennessee orange. Who knew lampshades came in carrot?

"Adam's single," Stephanie said. She pointed to a guy with massive shoulders who'd slashed his Islanders jersey down both sides for a view of his furry pectorals. "So's Ritchie." Red face, thick neck, combing his hair with long, loving strokes. Nina had vowed to make out with somebody tonight, to distract from thoughts of Gardner and Holland watching fireworks together. But it wouldn't work if she didn't feel at least a quiver.

"Maybe the Islanders guy," she said to be polite, remembering Stephanie's pride in her matchmaking skills.

"Out of cups in here!" a voice called from the kitchen, so while Stephanie went to find some, Nina wove around a group of guys in Mets shirts reenacting Darryl Strawberry's homer in last night's game. She made her way through a cluster of couples slow dancing and making out, to the windowsill, where bottles of orange liqueurs sat on a tray between the tangerine curtains. A pretty girl with shrewd eyes and a skirt printed with American flags stood there watching red-faced Ritchie comb his hair.

"Seven," she said to Nina.

"Really? I'd give him maybe a six."

"No, *number* seven. The seventh guy I slept with. I'm shooting for twenty by my twentieth birthday. I'm holding at twelve, last week in the bathroom at Mother Kelly's." She smiled breezily. "You know how they're always so worried you like them too much? I say, 'No problem. Call or don't call, I don't care. But if you do, say your number because I won't remember your name.'"

"Wow." Could Nina pull that off? She'd need to work on her breeziness.

A guy wearing a green foam Statue of Liberty crown joined them. He had interesting bags under his eyes, which could mean a smart, restless mind that kept him up at night.

"I like your costume," he told the girl.

She looked up at him from under her lashes. "Last time I was on the Staten Island ferry, some guy flashed a hundred-dollar bill at me. He thought I was a hooker."

"Cool." He drew out the word with admiration. So maybe the eye bags weren't from insomnia.

The girl gave him a meaningful smile. *Thirteen, your table is ready.*

Nina wandered over to the fireplace to check out the photos on the mantel, arranged around a bowl of nectarines. Stephanie, ten or so, sundress and flip-flops, standing next to a man with the same high forehead and wide-set eyes—her father, Nina guessed. Both were beaming. A willow tree bowed sweetly behind them. Next to that one, a photo of her father, arm in arm with a woman younger than him though not embarrassingly so: big curls, peach blush, self-satisfied expression. This had to be Kay, his girlfriend and curator of this house of orange horrors. At some point between photos, Stephanie's father had grown a Tom Selleck mustache. It was thick and optimistic. It said, *This is my second act, and I am living it.*

Nina mixed herself a drink, strong enough so she could float around unselfconsciously, but not so strong she'd slur her words or trip over the edge of a candy corn–colored rug. She cruised the living room, eavesdropping on conversations: "Scotty bought a keg for Saturday," "Did you hear Meryl's mom got a DUI?" "Bon Jovi's playing Binghamton September ninth." She wondered if Damian was here, the guy who'd given Stephanie the birthday cocaine. Her nose prickled as she remembered the chemical exhilaration. Something about the good-looking guy sitting on the couch by himself made him a Damian candidate, his watchful eyes and taut shoulders. Not that Nina would march up and ask him for coke, but he was nice to look at anyway. Messy hair with bangs falling into narrow eyes, Champion T-shirt, sinewy arms, lightning bolt tattooed on his bicep. No discernible July Fourth getup either. Nina allowed herself to reframe her lack of costume as cool and unconcerned. He was playing air drums to "Fool in the Rain." *Where'd you get that radical tattoo,* would be her opener. She was practicing it in her head when Stephanie appeared out of nowhere and dove into his lap, kicking cups and an ashtray off the coffee table. She wound her arms around his neck and he lifted her butt so she was straddling him. They started masticating—there was really no other word for it—each other's mouths.

Oh. So this was *Patrick*.

"Get a room!" people yelled fondly, obviously used to the PDA. Stephanie gave them the finger without breaking the kiss. When she finally emerged for air, she spotted Nina and her face lit up. "Come here!" She rolled off Patrick's lap and patted the couch on her other side. "I want to introduce you guys."

"The girl from the park," Nina heard her tell Patrick as she came over. What was the wary look that flashed across his face? Get a grip, she told herself. Although once she sat down, he regarded her with what she could only describe as distrust.

"You're the one with a thing for the gardener."

"You're the one with the raisin fetish."

He raised his eyebrows. She got the feeling he was used to intimidating people and was pleased to have met him halfway. Stephanie leaned back so they could talk over her. Her stomach was dusted with red glitter that caught the light and made her skin shimmer in a way that Nina immediately coveted.

Patrick circled his finger around Stephanie's belly button. "Do you piss in public bathrooms?" he asked Nina.

Before she could respond, Stephanie said, "We know this girl from the city who won't pee in public, even at a restaurant."

Patrick rolled his eyes as he took a pack of Juicy Fruit gum out of the pocket of his jeans. "Typical New York princess."

Stephanie squeezed Patrick's leg. "He's worried the longer I stay here, the more of a pussy I'll become."

"I pee anywhere," Nina said. "In fact, I'm peeing right now."

Stephanie laughed, but Patrick just tilted his head as he kept his eyes on her. "Ever been to Hewlett?" He shoved two sticks of Juicy Fruit in his mouth.

Nina shook her head.

"You probably don't even know where it is."

Now she raised her eyebrows. "It's one of the Five Towns."

He still looked skeptical.

"Fine, I confess." She laughed. "Stephanie filled me in." Who are you, she thought, to make me jump through fifty hoops? But if Stephanie liked him, there must be something appealing beneath the abrasive surface.

"If you're ever lost and wind up there," he said, "stop by Paddy McGee's. That's probably where we'll be." Was this his idea of a gracious invitation?

"Oh, come on," Stephanie said. "She's too cool for that shithole." Patrick looked annoyed, but she didn't seem to notice. She brought a cigarette to her lips. Her pinkie fingernail was a little longer than the others and painted bright red while the rest were bare. She tried puffing on her cigarette, giggling when she realized it wasn't lit. Patrick pulled out a matchbook with a picture of a horse with STALLIONS arched over it.

Stephanie abruptly sat straight up. "When were you there?"

"Steph," he said. He closed his hand around the matchbook.

The air was suddenly sharp with tension. Nina's stomach knotted, like mittelschmerz had hit a week early.

"No, seriously, when?" Stephanie said, her voice tight with fake nonchalance. Nina looked away to give them privacy, to an orange pillow embroidered with T's and V's. She'd never realized how antagonistic a color orange was. Who would decorate their whole house with such hostility?

Stephanie turned to her. "You know Stallions by any chance? Italian place on Jericho Turnpike? Skanky whore named Raquel used to bartend there?"

Nina shook her head with the least motion possible, keeping her face still, hoping it might help dissipate whatever was going on here.

Patrick winced. "She kept calling *me*. It wasn't my fault."

"It *was* your fault she had your number in the first place. Or what, she dialed numbers at random and hit the jackpot?"

They glared at each other for a long moment. Then Stephanie sighed. "I'm sorry. You know how I am when I drink tequila. And anyway, she got what she deserved." She took the matches from his hand and lit her cigarette. In a low voice, she told Nina: "I got the bitch fired, and made sure she knew it was me. I had everyone tell the owner she was stealing, which happened to be true. Fuck with me"— she shrugged—"and I'll fuck you back harder."

She exhaled a stream of sweet-smelling smoke that went straight to Nina's lungs. Nina coughed and thought she ought to mind, except she didn't. Same with Stephanie's vengefulness, which was also harsh but didn't faze her either. She could use some of that ferocity herself, that sense of entitlement. Fuck with Nina and—what? Not much. Live long and prosper.

Patrick got up from the couch and asked if anyone needed a refill. She saw now that the lightning bolt on his bicep was drawn on in ballpoint.

"I'm too wasted," Stephanie said. She leaned back and sang along to Culture Club on the stereo. Nina's brain was starting to feel soggy from the alcohol—no wonder "sloshed" was one of the words for "drunk"—but Patrick's eyes stayed on hers like a dare until she asked for another vodka and tonic.

He gave her an approving nod.

"He likes you," Stephanie said when he was gone. "Maybe he won't be such a dick about me living here if he knows I'm with you."

"Happy to help," Nina said, even happier that Stephanie saw them spending more time together. "I like him too." It wouldn't have passed a lie detector, but Stephanie looked pleased.

When he came back, Nina leaned forward to reach for her drink and almost fell over. She told herself to slow down but soon her glass was empty again and her bladder full. She spotted a line of three people outside a closed door and asked Stephanie if that was the bathroom.

"Ugh, these animals have probably pissed all over the seat," Stephanie said.

Nina shrugged and glanced at Patrick. "That's fine, I pee standing anyway."

He laughed and she decided he was perfectly fine. She reminded herself that she always got hypersensitive at parties, among other places.

Stephanie pointed to a hallway behind them. "Use mine," she said. "In my room, down there on the left."

Nina walked carefully down the dim hallway, careful not to trip on the rug and wipe out on her drunken ass. The walls in Stephanie's bedroom were the same awful orange as the rest of the apartment, but she'd covered them with so much stuff you hardly noticed. A poster that said, MY FAVORITE DRUG IS *MORE*. Sketches of butterflies and spiders. A bulletin board spray-painted magenta, pinned with a postcard from Niagara Falls, a rabbit's foot, a pair of filmy lilac underwear. A block of driftwood with "IT" spelled out in screws. Nina laughed when she figured it out: *Screw it*. Where could she get one? A zebra-striped bedspread, a mirrored dresser covered with nail-polish bottles, tiny bud vases full of iridescent beads, a black enamel bowl of Starbursts. On her nightstand was a photo of a young Stephanie on ice skates, in a pink down jacket and pom-pom hat, looking rickety but overjoyed, with her father on one side and a woman Nina guessed was her mother on the other, based on the resemblance and proprietary hand on Stephanie's elbow.

Nina imagined Kay's vexation whenever she entered this room.

In the bathroom, towels were splotched with blue and red makeup. An open jar of Dippity-Do was on the windowsill, along with an open plastic case *not* for a retainer. In the mirror, she noticed the pale expanse of skin between the top of her dress and her chin, like a field of snow. Why hadn't she worn a necklace? She spotted a jar of red glitter gel on the edge of the sink, what Stephanie had on her stomach. Nina remembered the easy gift of her sunglasses the day they met in the park and guessed she wasn't possessive about her things, as opposed to, for instance, Leigh, who kept the name of her perfume secret, or Meredith, who wouldn't let anyone try on her rings. One of Nina's life goals was to have some signature accessory that everyone wanted to copy. She dabbed the red gel across her collarbone, watching it gleam in her reflection.

When she went back out to the bedroom, Patrick was sitting on the edge of the bed, bent over the night table. He glanced up briefly from the small pile of cocaine he was cutting up with a razor blade.

"Don't mind me," he said. "This is my usual spot."

"No problem." Cocaine had been on her mind tonight, but the sudden blast of craving surprised her.

"Want to do a line?"

"Where's Stephanie?"

"She'll be here in a minute." He tapped the blade against the table. "She's dealing with Dawn. The dummy's out there blubbering over some chucklehead."

She liked that he assumed she knew who Dawn was, like Nina was already a member of their crew. He tore the cover off the Stallions matchbook and rolled it up inside out. Good, now Stephanie wouldn't have to be reminded.

He leaned over the table and snorted a line, then danced the cardboard tube in her direction. "Going once, going twice . . ." he said. When she nodded, he shifted closer to the headboard to make space. Was she supposed to sit next to him? She told herself it wasn't a bed in this context, just a surface to sit on. Here she went making a big deal out of nothing again. But she kneeled on the carpet anyway, beside the night table. He handed her the rolled-up matchbook cover and she sniffed one of the lines. A few seconds later, she felt the switch in her brain, the accelerated voltage. The torrent of words rushing out of her mouth the second she opened it.

"All this orange is going to give me a stroke."

"Go Vols," he said.

"I'm starting Vanderbilt in September. Have you been to Graceland? Did you know Elvis Presley's last words were 'I'm going to the can'? Wouldn't that be crazy, if that's the last thing you ever said?" She clamped her hand over her mouth to stop the babbling. Only a neophyte would get this coke-addled from a couple of lines. Although Patrick was pretty revved up himself, playing air drums up and down his legs. She noticed his fingertips were peeling, like he'd rubbed them with sandpaper.

"Elvis blows," he said.

"Oh, really? Who do you like, then," she kidded him. "Quiet Riot? Twisted Sister? Ratt?"

"Right, like you know any Ratt songs."

Whipping her hair in her face, she sang a few lines of "Round and Round" that her brain on hyperdrive recalled from an MTV video.

He winced like he was injured. "I think my ears are bleeding."

She laughed as she sat on her heels. A major disadvantage of an all-girls school was that she didn't have any male friends. It would be nice to have a guy to talk to without an unspoken *Where is this going?* storm cloud hanging over them.

"I've got it," she teased. "You like Rainbow."

"Nice try."

"Cinderella?"

"You know what I like?" he asked.

"Iron Maiden?"

He leaned forward and brushed his finger across a spot on her collarbone, where she'd spread Stephanie's red shimmer stuff. "I like that glitter," he said, then lowered his gaze, down to her breasts. Shit. Instinctively she crossed her arms, but at the same time tried to look casual and unaware, so they could pretend this wasn't happening.

He dragged his gaze back up to meet her square in the eyes as if seeking some kind of acknowledgment.

Get a clue, dipstick. She jumped to her feet. "Thanks for the coke!" She waved a big, stupid wave.

A muscle jumped in his jaw. He resumed the drumbeat on his thighs. "Anytime," he said.

In the living room, people were gathered around the TV to watch the fireworks, extra spectacular for the Statue of Liberty's Centennial. Nina hung back, holding tight to the couch. She tried to breathe normally. Her head spun, a mix of vodka, cocaine, confusion, and guilt. What had just happened? Why had she waved and *thanked* him instead of shoving him backward and telling him off? Had her band chatter and awful singing come across as flirtation?

The TV cameras panned to the Reagans gazing up at the rainbow flares. Stephanie gave them the finger and shouted, "You suck!" But for all of Stephanie's bravado, Nina already felt protective of her. Didn't she deserve to know her boyfriend was coming on to other girls? Except what if Nina had misread the whole thing, or been partly responsible? What if it were nothing but a coke-fueled one-off? She couldn't win. Telling Stephanie meant she'd never see her again. No new friendship could bear that weight.

Patrick appeared in the doorway, walked up behind Stephanie, and slid his arms around her bare midriff. Look at her face: she was crazy about him. She laid her hands over his and leaned back against him. Nina remembered the empty diaphragm case in the bathroom. They were connected in a way she'd never been with anyone.

The sky on the TV lit up again and again. "The fluffy ones look like dandelions," the girl in the flag skirt said to Number Thirteen in the green foam crown. They were holding hands. Stephanie lit a cigarette and blew three perfect smoke rings that hung quivering in the air. Suddenly Nina wanted to fill her lungs with billows and billows of smoke. Her guilt about her grandmother was obviously a nutty delusion—as if she'd held any sway over the blood vessels in Pearl's brain.

She asked Stephanie for an Eve.

As soon as the smoke hit her lungs, she moaned. The nicotine made her vision go black for a second, but then she was enclosed in a soft, gauzy halo, and everything else fell away.

"Paradise," she said. She hoped she had enough cash with her to buy a pack of Marlboros on the way home.

Stephanie smiled. "Welcome back to the dark side."

"You don't think it tastes like prunes?" Patrick asked.

"Not like any prunes I've smoked," Nina said. She gave him a long look that said, I won't tell her, because I'm too selfish to sacrifice our friendship, but if it happens again, I won't hesitate. It was a lot to communicate in one look, but judging by the nervous twist of his mouth, he seemed to get the message.

Chapter Seven

A few days later, after work, Nina waited outside Maison Rouge for Stephanie to finish up so they could go for a drink at the Lighthouse, a new bar on Ninety-Third and Madison that Steph had read about in *Details*. Nina had changed out of her temp outfit in the ladies' room at the lifeless life-insurance company where she'd spent the day typing letters denying customers' claims, into a striped Benetton dress and a dozen neon rubber bracelets. How naïve of her to have thought that a summer of temp jobs would help her figure out what to do with the rest of her life, or at least what to major in at college, or even what to take for a freshman elective. So far, the only thing she'd learned was to hope for someone odd enough at the next cubicle to keep things interesting. At a medical supplies company last week, it was a woman who constructed tiny people out of Play-Doh. At an accounting firm, a guy who spent most of the day leaving messages for various women: "Hello, my delectable Meghan," "my beguiling Katherine," "my pulchritudinous Christine." Today the streak continued with the woman at the next desk over, reading aloud and unprompted from a book called *Dianetics*. Nina misheard the title as *Diabetics* and wondered how asking yourself questions like *Are you making life or is life making you?* helped control your blood sugar. When the woman went to lunch, Nina snuck over to her desk for a quick look, realized her mistake about the title, and searched for "sex" in the index, which led her to a baffling passage about "coital engrams."

"Patrick's mom is diabetic," Stephanie said as they walked over to Madison. She stopped to look in the window of an art gallery at a blurry watercolor on an easel. "She eats spoonfuls of grape jelly when her blood sugar falls. Patrick calls her 'Sweet'N Low.'"

Nina laughed. In the days since the party, she'd prodded herself toward a Patrick reappraisal. So he'd touched her collarbone. It wasn't like he'd lunged at her with his tongue out. Stop with the hysterics, she told herself. And stop reading *Lady Chatterley's Lover*, where every fleeting glance pulses with sexual significance and lasts three pages.

Stephanie paused at a store window, this one with safari-ready mannequins decked out like Isak Dinesen in khaki jackets and pith helmets. To Nina it all looked a little ridiculous—where were these savannas on the Upper East Side?—but Stephanie stared and nodded like she'd received whatever message it was meant to convey. Then again, Stephanie was wearing her belt backward, so the gold serpent buckle rested at the base of her spine. Nina had never thought to wear an article of clothing in any way except how everyone else wore it. She pulled half the bracelets off her wrist and stopped midblock to stretch them over her right foot onto her ankle.

"Nice," Stephanie said.

"You've inspired me," Nina said shyly.

"Ditto," Stephanie said, which couldn't possibly be true, but Nina let it pass. They continued walking.

"So how was the rest of your weekend?" Nina asked.

"Good, until Patrick came by the store on Sunday to pick me up. His first time there, and my boss spots him, gives him the side eye, and I shit you not, starts dusting the SHOPLIFTERS WILL BE PROSE-CUTED sign."

"Seriously?" Nina stepped over a torn paper American flag in the crosswalk, streaked with mud. It was always depressing to see holiday decorations turned to street trash.

"Like he's a derelict or something because he's wearing Pumas. I just wish the shrew hadn't given him more anti-city ammunition."

Reappraisal or not, Nina was glad for whatever kept Patrick out in Hewlett, where he lived with his mother. Stephanie stayed with them most weekends—his mother didn't mind, so long as Stephanie promised not to get pregnant. Patrick only came to the city if Kay and Stephanie's father were out of town.

"You're so lucky you don't have the same boss all summer," Stephanie said. "Why does mine have to be such a cunt?"

A man walking by frowned at them. *I* didn't say it, Nina thought, followed by a stab of annoyance at her reflexive good-girl disavowal. Stephanie seemed completely oblivious, or maybe she noticed and didn't care. Why did Nina? Even Frances, who used to lose her mind if anyone so much as looked at her sideways, didn't seem to care anymore. The other day at the florist, she'd mashed her face into a vase of tulips and said, "This vase is a good kisser because it's got *two lips.*" The saleswoman's catty laugh didn't even make a dent, although Nina would have liked to smash the vase over her head. She'd pulled Frances out the door before something worse happened that might set her off.

Although her new mood was so far proving pretty durable. For the past couple of weeks, she'd been singing along to her opera records. She washed her hair and threw the velour tracksuit down the incinerator. She stuck a barrage of Post-it notes in Nina's college catalog to mark all the courses she wished *she* could sign up for, like Physics and the Universe—"If we took that one together, they'd call us the Family Joules." Was punning a sign of improving mental health? Nina was beginning to believe this might be who her mother really was, out from under Pearl's storm cloud. Maybe she was a little slap-happy, but who wouldn't be, after such unrelenting misery?

Stephanie stopped on the corner of Eighty-Second to light a cigarette. Nina lit one too. She'd been trying to restrict herself to two a day with lectures about discipline and cancer, but the sterner the lecture, the stronger the craving. Two a day had quickly become two an hour.

"*Then,* my mother calls." As they continued up the block, Stephanie blew three perfect smoke rings. Nina made a mental note to ask for a lesson.

"She's obsessed with Kay. She makes me feed her info on what she eats, the magazines she reads, who sleeps on which side of the bed. Sunday night, she has me go through Kay's underwear drawer and describe her bras."

"What?" Nina coughed out a mouthful of smoke.

"Down to the little bow between the cups. Thank God I didn't have a heart attack and drop dead clutching one of the bras like some kind of pervert. Knowing my mother, she'd have hung up the second I hit the floor, then acted all horrified at what I'd been up to."

"I'll tell everyone it was her idea, if that ever happens," Nina swore.

Stephanie laughed, a little hollowly. "She keeps hammering away until it's just easier to do what she wants." They peered into the window of the fancy meat store near the corner, where huge carcasses hung like trophies.

"Plus I feel guilty," Stephanie added. "My dad did kind of dick her over, and now here I am living with him and Mary Kay."

Nina smiled at *Mary Kay.*

"My nickname for her. All the makeup and that bubbly fucking personality." She took a drag of her cigarette. "You'd probably just tell your mother to go fuck herself."

Ha. If Nina ever told her mother to go fuck herself, it would be *her* carcass hanging in the butcher-shop window. But she liked Stephanie's misreading. She considered the possibility that some new grit, invisible to herself, was nonetheless showing on her face.

She took a long drag of her cigarette as they continued up the block. She was about to say the thing about the carcass but found herself surprisingly disinclined toward maternal shit-talking. "The thing is," she said instead, "things can change when you least expect it. My mother's been psycho forever, but this morning on my way out the door, she stops me all giddy to tell me that *daughter* is *laughter* with a *d*, and *mom* is *wow* upside down. How weirdly sweet is that?" She left out the looming specter of ECT, since that wasn't the point.

Your mother could shed her old skin for a new one at any time: *that* was the point. You had to hold out hope.

"Huh," Stephanie said, exhaling more smoke rings. "I never realized that about 'laughter' and 'daughter,' or 'mom.' Wow."

"Upside down," Nina said, then asked for smoke-ring instruction.

Stephanie tapped the back of her jaw. "Think blowjob mouth, but the motion's from here."

Nina inhaled and made a tiny *o* with her lips.

"Not a blowjob for a guppy."

"Hey, girls," a guy yelled from the synagogue doorway across the street, "wanna practice on me?"

"That's where I had my bat mitzvah!" Nina laughed. "Mazel tov, minnow dick!" she screamed back at him. You could only shout at strangers on the street like that if you were with a friend, or maybe only with a friend like Stephanie, who yelped with delight at *minnow dick,* as if it were the cleverest retort she'd ever heard, and also didn't mind when Nina grabbed her arm and made them run until the guy was two blocks behind.

They stopped at the corner of Eighty-Ninth to catch their breath. "I went to a bar mitzvah once," Stephanie said. "That's for guys, right? *Bat* is girls?"

Nina nodded, pleased that Stephanie cared enough to want to get it right.

"Michael Eisenstadt. His voice kept cracking and I've never seen a face that red. Did you have to sing at yours?"

"Yup. My voice made people's ears bleed." Too late, she recalled Patrick's critique of her singing at the July Fourth party, in Stephanie's bedroom. Her skin prickled with guilt. She asked herself for the hundredth time if it was wrong to not tell Stephanie. She answered herself for the hundredth time: Tell her what, exactly? Stephanie knew that she and Patrick had done lines in her bedroom. Anything beyond that was a matter of interpretation—and hadn't Nina been drunk anyway? And high on coke? Don't be a shit-stirrer, she reminded herself.

"Bleeding's my terrain," Stephanie said. "Catholics have a blood fetish: Christ nailed to the cross, crown of thorns, curse of a woman's period, et cetera. Church wine's supposed to be Jesus's blood, but it's really just shitty wine."

"Kosher wine is bad too," Nina said. "Manischewitz is Jewish cough medicine." That didn't stop the ladies of her synagogue's Sisterhood from guzzling gallons of the stuff at her bat mitzvah reception in the temple basement, she remembered—thick Jewish women in Suntan pantyhose, with clunky sandals and clunky names like Yarkona and Batya, washing down bricks of bone-dry marble cake. Then she remembered, with a wave of shame, how glad she'd been to get back upstairs into the daylight with her Bancroft friends in their Lilly Pulitzer dresses for lunch at the Amity Club, everyone making fun of the rabbi's accent in the taxi.

Nina and Stephanie headed north, past a bank and then a grocery store called Gentile's Market.

"Remind me not to ask for matzoh there," Nina said.

Stephanie looked at her. "Are people weird about you being Jewish? It seems like there's a ton of Jewish people in the city."

"The Upper East Side is super WASPy. Everyone I know knows how to sail. My high school had a Prayers assembly three mornings a week, where we had to recite Bible verses and sing hymns. I always feel a little, like, darker."

"You're the palest person I know," Stephanie joked. "Your skin's like porcelain."

"My hair, then."

"What do you mean?"

"Your hair has different colors in it. Everyone's does. But mine's this dark, opaque curtain."

Stephanie gave her a doubtful look. "I see chestnut, and auburn . . ."

"Okay, it's not really that," Nina conceded. "It's more, dark as in I'm in the shadows, skulking or maybe sulking." She heard herself and stopped abruptly, embarrassed. She'd never said this out loud before. "Honestly, it's fine. I don't really care."

"Of course not," Stephanie said. "But a little?"

It was a relief to admit: "Maybe a little."

"I think it's better to be on the outside," Stephanie said, absently touching the serpent buckle at the small of her back, "watching instead of being watched. It makes you more interesting."

At Ninety-First Street, Nina squinted at a building halfway down the block made of limestone, two columns on either side of the tall red doors, unsure why it seemed familiar until she recognized it as Spence, another one of the Upper East Side's all-girls schools. She'd gone to one of Leigh's volleyball matches there; she'd been a star player for Bancroft until she started worrying about bulking up her arms with muscle and quit. Nina's pulse suddenly amplified. She remembered hearing that Gardner lived on this block, and that the Spence girls used to gather on his stoop at three o'clock to wait for him to get home from school.

"I think one of those buildings is Gardner's," she told Stephanie, pointing down the street.

"Let's see if he's home."

"Right. Just knock on every door and ask, 'Is this where Gardner Reed lives?'"

But at least she could walk on the pavement he walked on every day, absorb the sights and sounds of his psyche. Maybe she'd learn something secret about him from scrutinizing his house, if she could figure out which one it was. She decided on the three-story brick townhouse with the whitest shutters and the pristine flower boxes filled with tiny purple violets in regimented rows. She envisioned his mother as cool and aristocratic, a Babe Paley type. She'd read that Babe was so meticulous, she'd trim the perforations off stamps before affixing them to her party invitations. On her deathbed, she'd planned the food and wine for her funeral luncheon. Babe would have those violets. And the lanterns, too, with the candlesticks in them, flanking the glossy black door with the lion's-head knocker.

She ducked into a doorway across the street, motioning for Stephanie to join her in case Gardner suddenly showed up and spotted them. They had no good reason to be on this block.

"I'm having déjà vu," Stephanie said. She stationed herself behind Nina and peered over her shoulder. "Which one do you think it is?"

"That one." Nina pointed to the townhouse she'd settled on.

They lit cigarettes, contemplating the shutters and violets through their smoke rings.

"You're a natural," Stephanie said. She looked across the street. "You think his parents own the whole place?"

"I wouldn't be surprised." Nina had no idea what Gardner's father did for a living, but *Reed* sounded so austere, one of those families where money cascaded down the generations. This past spring, Gardner was on the junior committees for the Red Cross Gala *and* the Bronx Zoo dinner dance. Ordinary people weren't tapped for those committees.

Which window was his bedroom's? All the curtains were drawn and she couldn't make out anything or anyone inside.

"When I have my own house," Stephanie said, "I'm going to have translucent floors with fish swimming underneath, and a white mink blanket on every bed." She took a film canister out of her handbag and uncapped it. Nina's heart raced when she saw the powder-filled baggie inside. She watched Stephanie dip in her long pinkie nail.

"I know," Stephanie said, "it's so tacky. But"—she sniffed out of it—"necessity is the mother of the coke nail." She waved her pinkie at Nina. "Bend down like you're looking at my watch."

Nina did, then straightened up, wondering how long it took a nail to grow that long; she'd always cut or bit hers. A woman in white sponge-soled nurse shoes came out of a building two doors down from the spiffy brick one. This one had lopsided paper shades in the windows, and the stoop was splattered with pigeon droppings. The nurse was in her fifties, with a sharp, thin-lipped face and short, bristly gray hair. She walked down a couple of steps, then bent to pick up a beer can with a disgusted, "Christ, these *animals,*" in a strong Irish accent.

"Nurse Ratched needs an enema," Stephanie said.

A man came around from a side door that led to the basement. The nurse shot him a chilly look from the steps and held up the beer can. "How many times have we talked about this, Armando?" She said his name like you'd say *dimwit.* "These steps are supposed to be cleaned off regularly." She thrust the can at him. Then she stepped down to the sidewalk and picked up a cigarette butt, which she handed to him, too, her lips bunched with distaste.

"Need I remind you that my rent pays your salary?" she said. "Don't think I won't call the office again if I have to."

"Oh," Stephanie said. "She lives there."

"That would explain the shitty attitude." Nina wiped her nose, which stung lightly, in a not-unpleasant way. "I thought nurses are supposed to be so kind."

The woman continued to scold Armando: "When do you intend to fix the leak in our bathroom? The Dunnes have called me *twice* to complain about water damage."

"Mrs. Reed," he said patiently.

That had to be a coincidence.

"I told Gardner to give me a good day and time to come by," Armando said. "We need someone at home while we do the repairs."

Holy shit. Nina stepped out on the sidewalk, so shocked she forgot she was hiding. There was no trace of Gardner's grace or charm or lake-blue eyes. This was no Babe Paley. This was Babe Paley's nightmare.

"Monday at three," Mrs. Reed said snippily. "I'll make sure Gardner's home." She turned and stomped down the block and disappeared around the corner, while Armando gritted his teeth and headed back to the basement, presumably to toss the trash she'd handed him.

"She is so not 'wow' upside down," Stephanie said as they started toward the corner.

Nina nodded as empathy washed through her. How could she have gotten it so wrong? She'd never questioned that Gardner came from the same ease as everyone at Flanagan's, the same peppy, preppy parents. She suddenly remembered a night she saw him at Flanagan's last month, leaning against the wall beside the bar. His hair fell in his eyes as he surveyed the room. Above his head was a framed advertisement for a Spanish bullfight. The bull stamped the ground, a mass of pent-up energy, his eyes fixed on the shuddering crimson cape. Gardner's lean was casual but his eyes were sharp. They moved restlessly from one person to the next. Now she better understood that intensity, the darkness she'd sensed in him. No wonder he walked alone in the park at night.

She and Stephanie continued up to Ninety-Third Street, but when they got to the Lighthouse, the bartender took one look at Nina's ID and said she had to be kidding. She and Leigh had made fake IDs last December when the drinking age went up to twenty-one, then got them laminated at Woolworths.

Back outside, Stephanie bent over laughing as she looked at the crooked photo and fuzzy print. "Does that say NYYU?" Hers was her actual driver's license, altered with an X-Acto knife.

"I know. It looks like a *Ghostbusters* diploma. They don't card at Flanagan's."

They decided to call it a day, but as Stephanie hailed a cab, she suggested they go to Playland in Times Square to get Nina a passable fake ID.

"You'll need it anyway, for bars at college," Stephanie said as she got in a taxi to Penn Station. "Let's go next week."

The next night, as Nina was leaving for Flanagan's, her mother leaped out of her bedroom with a bottle of Opium in her right hand and a bottle of Poison in her left.

"Every woman needs a signature scent," she said as she blasted Nina with Opium. "A man should recognize you even if he's blind-folded."

"Those are my choices? Drug the guy or kill him?"

"Fragrance is the essence of desire," Frances said, with a mortify-ing emphasis on *desire*. Nina's face burned. They never talked about anything in the neighborhood of sex. You couldn't even say they tip-toed around—or alluded to, hinted at, or skirted—it, since that im-plied an acknowledged *it*. Nina had hidden *Forever* in a *Brave New World* book jacket. She bought her bras herself. She didn't even have the guts to tell Frances when she got her first period. No wonder she was still a virgin. Even the mention of that word around her parents, no matter the context—wool, Islands, olive oil—made her squirm.

Now Frances sprayed her neck with Poison.

"Not both, Mom." Nina coughed. Her sinuses stung, but Frances gazed at her with bright eyes. Nina pictured Gardner's mother's face from the day before, that glacial disdain, and held out her wrists for more Poison. Things can change, she'd told Stephanie, when you least expect it.

Well, maybe not everything. In the lobby, Freddie intercepted her for a hug and sniffed her neck.

"Miss Nina smell very good tonight."

"It's bug spray," she said.

He clutched her waist. "You are funny girl."

The crowd was thick at Flanagan's, everyone here but Gardner. Nina tried to bite back her disappointment. It had been a week since the Fourth of July; surely he wasn't still out in Southampton with Holland. She didn't want to ask Brian, who'd just sat down beside her, since he was probably asked a hundred times a night where Gardner was; or Meredith, sitting across the table in her usual foul mood and full of complaints: "If that girl doesn't stop screaming about Judd Nelson, I'm going to wring her neck." Or Leigh, who'd just come back from the bar with two Negronis, which she'd recently read was Jackie Kennedy's favorite cocktail. *Why would* you *want to know where Gardner is?* she'd probably ask, tilting her head in her innocent way, as if Gardner's and Nina's presence in even the same sentence was utterly incomprehensible.

"Guess who's here?" Leigh actually did say, and Nina momentarily brightened.

"The Hypnotist, with an even younger girl than last time!"

Oh.

"I want to see!" Meredith jumped up from the table and pulled Leigh back to the bar.

"What's that all about?" Brian asked.

Nina explained.

"Did she cluck like a chicken?"

"In a manner of speaking."

Brian laughed as Nina sat back and lit a cigarette, reminding herself that it was already July and *she* still hadn't made the leap. She surveyed the bar. What about that guy with the cleft chin? Or the one with the tortoiseshell glasses? Or the one at the bar with the dopey eyes waving a fifty-dollar bill to get the bartender's attention—

"Hey." She nudged Brian. "Is that Craig Bishop over there?"

"Who?" Brian looked toward the bar.

"The guy—" She almost said *whose arm Gardner nearly wrenched off.* "The guy who pushed Clea's head underwater. Rex's friend?"

"Better not be." Brian squinted, standing halfway out of his chair. Then he sat back down. "Nope, not him." He sounded relieved. "You ought to get your eyes checked before you start school. My sister failed Rocks for Jocks because she couldn't see the blackboard."

"I'm probably just drunk on Pepsi." Nina took a sip from her glass. The rush of sugar and caffeine—she'd already swallowed three Vivarin tonight—had lately become more appealing than the spacey blur of alcohol and tranquilizers. Not as fun as cocaine, but still a pretty good zip.

The guy who wasn't Craig Bishop balled up the fifty and threw it at the bartender. Nina turned to Brian. "So what's the story with Gardner and Rex?"

He frowned, as though reluctant to say anything. "Just between us, okay?"

Nina nodded.

"Rex got caught with a ton of pot in his room at Dartmouth back in March, like enough to sell. Campus police got involved, and the administration was threatening to expel him."

"Wow."

"It all went down a few days after Gardner visited. Rex said he didn't know anything about it, and he and his father pointed the finger at Gardner."

"What, as if Gardner just left it there without telling him?" Nina saw herself invading Rex's pointy nose with a very, very sharp knife.

"Exactly." Brian shook his head. "I mean, maybe Gardner was in on it, but Rex definitely was. It was his room. On top of all that, Gardner was supposed to work at Rex's dad's brokerage firm this summer, but Mr. Parrish froze him out and won't even return his calls."

It was enraging, the sanctimonious old guard making sure the castle doors stayed barred. And Nina could only guess how Gardner's mother had reacted when she learned about the pot situation. This stunning boy she'd produced and sent out into the world, surely with the highest expectations: Nina pictured her icy eyes as Gardner protested his innocence, her crooked witch-finger aimed at the door as she threw him out. Was that the night he broke into Tavern on the Green, to have somewhere to regroup while she cooled off?

On the jukebox, Prince's synthesized voice intoned, "*Dearly beloved.*" Then the drums kicked in, and, like magic, Gardner appeared in the center of the room. Where had he come from? How had she missed him? How satisfying to see him so flushed and happy, especially with all the crap that had gotten thrown his way. He raised his arms like Prince's in the video, slice of tan skin above his waistband. People gathered to cheer him on. Benji Peterson handed him a bottle of Heineken and Gardner held it up like a microphone, singing, "*Oh no, let's go.*" The bass banged in Nina's chest, the wailing guitar nearly splitting her ears. Gardner's shirt was streaked with sweat. She wanted to pull it off and drape it over her face. He stuck out the bottle for people to sing along. "*Let's go crazy, let's get nuts.*" He played air guitar to Prince's solo, then held up a finger as the final notes of the song spooled out and climbed to the squalling crescendo. At the concluding *whomp*, he punched the air. Everyone did go nuts, clapping and screaming. He drained the rest of the beer in one swallow.

Leigh and Meredith came back in hysterics over the Hypnotist's date—"You think she's even potty-trained yet?"—while Brian got up at his father's summons to deal with a refrigerator problem. Leigh took his chair, setting down two more Negronis.

"Guess Gardner's okay about the breakup," she said.

With Rex? Nina's mind was still half at Dartmouth.

"They broke up?" Meredith asked.

"Whoops," Leigh said. "Maybe it's not supposed to be public knowledge."

Nina held her breath. The breakup with Rex *was* public knowledge.

Leigh, drunk with Negronis and gossip, continued: "Holland's sister told me. Big, ugly fireworks in Southampton last weekend."

For a second it seemed that Flanagan's had gone silent. But it was just that Nina couldn't hear anything over the blood pounding in her ears. "Really," she said blandly, as in *That's . . . mildly interesting.*

"I don't exactly know what this fight was about," Leigh said, "but apparently, it's been building for a while. Holland thinks Gardner drinks too much."

Nina was offended on Gardner's behalf: define *too much.* Leigh finished her (fourth? fifth?) Negroni in two quick gulps, her eyes already at half-mast. Meredith grabbed for the pitcher of sangria, nearly elbowing Nina in the cheek. Just last week, Nina had watched Holland knock back an entire bottle of Taittinger she'd brought to Flanagan's, slurring about how *pickled* she was.

"And," Leigh added, "apparently some of Grand-Mère's Nembutals were missing from her medicine cabinet after Holland and Gardner left. Not for the first time, I might add."

Grand-Mère's Nembutals! Nina ducked her head to hide her smile. *Great name for a band,* she imagined saying to Gardner. She felt giddy and speedy and clever. What had been an ordinary night now sparkled with promise. Good riddance to Holland, who had the soul of a python. Gardner's mother probably worshipped her.

Meredith's eyes lit up as she looked in Gardner's direction. Nina would have liked to clamp her hand over them and tell her to keep it in her pants. In fact, over every girl's eyes in the bar, because as news of the Gardner-Holland breakup got around, girls began to swarm him, rubbing up like cats, giggling idiotically. Alison Bloch gave him a sloppy lap dance. Pippa Deloitte made him try on her preposterous cowboy hat from spring break in Ft. Lauderdale. Gardner laughed along and bought them drinks.

How could Nina possibly hope to stand out? She lit a cigarette to ponder what Stephanie might do and unthinkingly hitched her jaw for a smoke ring. Well, none of the other girls had thought to make a blowjob mouth. She waited for him to break away to order a drink, then went up to the crowded bar, got as close as she could get, and sailed four flawless rings in his direction.

"Hey, chirping bird," he said.

"Hey, flappy car wash." She wished she weren't so surprised he remembered her.

"You look good smoking." He snatched the cigarette from her fingers for a drag. She forced herself not to stare at his mouth. She wanted to put her finger between his lips. She imagined him biting down on the tendon.

"And you smell good too."

"Really? New perfume."

He stepped close and lifted her hair off her neck. Sniffing behind her ear, he said, "Plums. You smell juicy."

Whatever those *Dianetics* engrams were, hers were going wild. "It's called Poison."

He gave her an assessing look. "Are you going to off me in my sleep?"

Who's going to be sleeping? she thought.

He smiled as if he'd heard her. Then he pulled a square card out of his back pocket, with a picture of the French flag and *Fête Nationale* printed down the side. He laid it on the bar. "Bastille Day party at Palladium Monday night. You should come."

"Mais oui," she said like an idiot, although at least she hadn't said, *Monday's leak-repair day at your apartment. Three o'clock. Don't forget!*

His eyes were so blue, his cheekbones so sharp. His mother's drabness still so hard to fathom.

"See you there?" he said.

Had he just asked her out? She rolled her eyes at herself: Get a grip. He'd probably showed this thing to every feline in the colony. As if on cue, two girls in sundresses and pearls bore down on them, yowling Gardner's name, fire in their eyes. Nina grabbed the invite off the bar before they shoved her out of the way, then brought her hand to her mouth for a drag before realizing he still had her cig. The whiff of plummy perfume off her wrist made her feel succulent. She ordered a real drink from the bartender and he smiled at her with a gleam in his eye. She ran the corner of the Palladium card down the side of her leg. Monday night. She'd trail a cloud of Poison from room to room around the club, Gardner in pursuit. Behind her someone cleared her throat. The plum fantasy was displaced by hairspray and tanning-oil fumes.

"Don't flatter yourself." They were Alison's fumes. "He's been handing out those invites all night."

"Oh, really?" She kept her face blank to betray no sign of believing her, even if she wasn't sure. "Then where's yours?"

Alison shrugged. "In my bag." Pinned to her tube top, right between her boobs, was a button that said EAT MY CHICKEN, I'LL BLOW YOUR MIND.

"What does that even mean?" Nina demanded.

"Do I seriously need to explain it to you?"

"In other words, you have no idea." It felt surprisingly good to loosen her grip on herself and unleash her annoyance. They glared at each other. Finally, Alison broke the stare-down.

"So what do you think? Who does him first, me or you?"

"I assume by *does*, you mean has sex with him." Nina made her tone so arch, it practically bent back on itself.

"Is that what you assume?" Alison smiled thinly. "You private-school harpies have the biggest sticks up your asses." She flounced away, Nina mentally mocking her acid-washed microskirt, but once again acknowledging the obvious: the summer was half over and Nina was still, *still,* so ludicrously and shamefully a virgin.

Chapter Eight

The Palladium bouncer snorted at Nina's pitiful NYYU ID and motioned her out of the line with a bored flick of his hand. She mentally kicked herself. Why hadn't she just gone to Playland over the weekend, instead of waiting for Stephanie? Yet another frustratingly bad decision. She started to back away, but Stephanie took a step forward and gazed up at him beseechingly.

"Gardner personally invited us. He'd be so disappointed."

The bouncer clearly had no clue who she was talking about, but he eyed her red tank top, which said L'AMOUR in sequins across her breasts. Nina's instinct was to let Stephanie handle it, but then she imagined Alison Bloch somewhere in the crowd with her usual derisive look, watching Nina cower, and she took a step forward next to Stephanie, catching the bouncer's attention. Without a word, she opened her blue cotton Esprit jacket—a grudging nod to Bastille Day, with a white lace tee beneath—and gave him a long look. He ping-ponged back and forth between her and Stephanie's chests for a minute, then shrugged and unhooked the rope.

Light spilled out the door as a tall guy in a tutu and fishnets emerged, and they ran in before the bouncer could change his mind.

"Playland for an ID this week?" she asked Stephanie.

"Absolutely, you shameless slut." Stephanie had to shout over the music, which pounded like jackhammers. *You are an obsession, I cannot sleep. Gardner, Gardner,* Nina's mind sang. *Gardner, Gardner, Gardner, Gardner.* They climbed a long staircase with hundreds of bulbs embedded in the steps. Ascending was like leaping on beams of light. An enormous glowing grid, blinking gold, cyan, and orange, soared four stories above the titanic dance floor.

"I read that this place was an old movie palace." Stephanie pointed to the domed ceiling and gilded cornices as they moved deeper into the club, through throngs of people dancing in place, lights flashing over bodies painted silver or gold or neon yellow, draped in sequins or beads. When they reached the bar with the wall-to-wall Basquiat mural—black skeletons and squiggly white sketches on a fire-red background—Stephanie sighed. Nina envied her innate appreciation of art and architecture. The closest she ever got to that feeling was when she came across a thrillingly apt misspelling, like last week at work in a memo she was proofreading—"defunked" for defunct and "hay day" for heyday.

They ordered drinks, and as Nina rummaged around her bag for cash, she pulled out the miniature tape recorder her mother had bought for her at Sharper Image. A gray-haired man with a cane and an eye patch rushed over.

"Are you a journalist?" His accent was a jumble of British and drunk. "I was badly misquoted in *Details* last month. You must allow me to set the record straight."

"Of course." She'd been carrying the recorder around for a week, too self-conscious to take it out and do anything with it. But who better for a first taping than an inebriated pirate? She pushed the Record button.

"I did not say that Area is *over.*" His red-veined eye glared at her. "Merely that their disco theme was derivative."

A woman with a shaved head wearing a mesh, breast-baring shirt leaned against the bar, nipples poking out. "Are we discussing Area?"

Stephanie reached over and directed Nina's recorder toward the woman.

"What did *you* think of its disco theme?" Nina asked her.

She shrugged. "If we're talking disco, I saw Chic last year and it was life-changing. Nile Rodgers is a god."

It was like a superpower. You could talk to anyone.

Nina and Stephanie took their drinks up another long staircase, this one made of steel and painted royal blue, to a balcony overlooking the dance floor. People were in groups or sprawled out alone on rows of black-lacquered tiered seating, blowing smoke at the ceiling where it hung in pearly clouds, illuminated by the grid's flashing lights. They went to the front and leaned over the edge to scan the dance floor.

"Do you see Gardner anywhere?" Stephanie asked.

Nina pointed vaguely into the massive crowd below. "I think he's that speck."

Stephanie laughed. "Should we go look?"

The sight was exhilarating, the dance floor ringed with giant video screens flashing tree branches and sparklers and marbled human faces. It made Nina's head spin a little. "Let's drink some more first. I'm too nervous."

As they climbed to a middle row, Stephanie winced and massaged her shoulder.

"Have you ever had sex in a car? My head was hanging back over the seat and now I'm all twisted up."

"I don't even know how to drive," Nina said, dodging the question. She ordered herself to come clean about her unfortunate chastity, since the longer she waited, the odder it would be when she fessed up.

"Let me teach you! I bet Patrick would let us use his car."

"You think?" Nina coughed to cover her reflexive flinch at his name.

"He taught me. That's how we got together: he was just a friend giving me driving lessons. But by lesson three, I was so distracted I almost crashed into a tree."

Nina nodded, smiling with all her teeth.

"Finally one day I pulled over on Avalon Road and said, 'I think I need some hands-on instruction.'"

Nina tried not to picture Patrick's ragged fingertips scouring Stephanie's bare flesh. "Was he your first?"

"Nope." Violet and silver lights swooped over her face, but her fingers around her glass went bone white. It was a few more seconds before she spoke. "When I was fifteen, I crashed this LIU frat party. I went upstairs with this guy I met there, to his room. I was so drunk I passed out, which he took as an opportunity to pull up my dress and stick his dick in."

Fuck.

"By the time I came to, he'd splooged all over me." She tipped her glass side to side, watching the ice cubes clunk against each other. "On my favorite Betsey Johnson dress, which at the time seemed like the worst part. At least he pulled out. I cut off the top half to wear as a blouse, but it kept unraveling."

"Did you report him?" She imagined Stephanie screaming bloody murder until everyone came running.

She shrugged. "To who? You pass out with a guy on top of you, how shocked can you be when he goes the distance?"

"I know, but—"

"I probably would've slept with him anyway, if I'd been conscious."

"But—"

Stephanie's set jaw said, *Stop.* Nina clamped her mouth shut, embarrassed at overstepping. It wasn't *her* experience to interpret—she hadn't been the one pinned beneath the guy, wet globs trickling down her collarbone onto her dress. She pictured the dress chopped in two, jagged edges and a snarl of torn threads, and was filled with a sympathy she didn't know how to put in words. "I have a Betsey Johnson dress that would look gorgeous on you," she said, feeling like a blockhead. "I'll bring it next time I see you."

Stephanie's face relaxed. "Yes! Thank you! God, I miss that dress." She bumped her shoulder against Nina's and took a deep breath. Nina did too. Even if it wasn't what she wanted to say, she'd somehow managed to say the right thing.

"Your turn," Stephanie said. "You were at least semi-conscious, I hope?"

Easier to come clean now that Stephanie had been so honest. "It hasn't happened yet."

"Oh!" Stephanie's eyes widened.

"Pathetic, right?"

"Not at all. I shouldn't have assumed."

"No, it's all right." She so rarely confessed anything that embarrassed her, it was always a surprise when she didn't combust. "It isn't for lack of trying," she said, and told Stephanie about Walker Pierson.

"First-class prick with a second-class dick."

"Did you just make that up?"

Stephanie laughed and lit a cigarette.

"Can I bum one of those?" called a voice behind them. It was a man sitting by himself, in his thirties, Nina guessed: high, shiny forehead, receding hairline, spiky Adam's apple, striped green-and-yellow tie pulled crooked.

"Sure!" Stephanie called back. To Nina, she said, "He looks wired, right? You think he's holding?"

"Holding what?" She'd have liked to stay right where they were, just the two of them, talking; she didn't much feel like engaging with some guy right now, especially this one, with his aggressive, jumpy energy, dancing in his seat to the Donna Summer song that thundered over the speakers.

Stephanie pulled Nina up.

"Isn't he a little old?"

"The older the guy, the better the coke."

"I don't remember Nancy Reagan saying that."

"Let's check it out." Stephanie climbed to the seat beside him. She handed him a cigarette. Nina followed reluctantly, taking the seat on her other side. "Bad Girls" blared from every speaker.

The guy wiped his nose with the back of his wrist and, not that they asked, launched into an analysis of the song: "*Toot-toot, beep-beep* is the call and response between johns and hookers," he shouted. His eyes bore so urgently into theirs he might have been instructing them how to defuse a bomb in the center of the dance floor.

"Huh," Nina said. No wonder he was sitting by himself. She tried not to stare at the insides of his large nostrils, which were speckled with tiny white crumbs.

He huffed the Eve like his lungs were starving. "Get it? The men give their cash, and the girls give their bodies?"

Nina continued to pantomime interest, hoping a friendly rapport would make him want to share his coke, but it wasn't until Stephanie sniffed pointedly that he produced a glass vial with a tiny spoon attached by a chain. Nina had a lot to learn. He sniffed his own spoonful of powder, then loaded it for each of them. God, cocaine was pretty, the crystals like microscopic rock candy. They went around twice. Nina tapped her foot to the music as she felt a wave of possibility lifting her. This weird guy now jabbering about a Pet Shop Boys song—"West End Girls" had overtaken "Bad Girls"- could actually be a mad genius, and he was leaning so close to Stephanie, he was practically in her lap. A Patrick replacement? Thirty wasn't ancient. If they got together, Stephanie would be in the city full-time.

She caught Stephanie's eye and they beamed at each other. This hum between them, this emerald field of warmth and connection—may it last forever and ever, until they were old ladies on their porches in rocking chairs, amen.

Meanwhile, the cokehead/amateur music critic was literally foaming at the mouth as he deconstructed "West End Girls." "He's trapped in the gang life of London's East End. The West End's the affluent part of the city and the East End the poorer. And yet the West End is the dead-end world. 'He's got no future, he's got no past—'"

"Wow," Nina said, impressed, "you should be on MTV." She pulled the tape recorder out of her bag. "Let's make a VJ audition tape."

His nostrils twitched ominously as she pressed Record, but she was still riding the optimistic wave, oblivious to the sharks circling just beneath the surface. "What's the line about Finland Station mean?"

His eyes were slits. He grabbed her arm, fingers digging into the bone. "Are you a cop?"

She stared back, dragged under now, ocean water filling her lungs. He squeezed so hard her fingers went numb and dropped the recorder. It clattered to the ground.

"Who sent you?" He gripped the edges of his seat and started to stand, face red and fists clenched, looming over them before he was even out of the chair. "How'd you bitches know where to find me?"

Nina felt the breath leave her body.

Suddenly his face was dripping wet. He fell back into his seat and clawed at his eyes. "What the fuck. You—vile—"

Stephanie put her water gun back in her bag and said, "The bitches will always know where to find you."

Nina yanked Stephanie up, pulling so hard they both spun off balance and almost fell off the bleachers. But they managed to stay upright and reach the aisle. Nina heard heavy breathing behind her, although that might have been the start of a Cure song. She kept running, leading Stephanie down two flights of stairs to the Basquiat room, where they stood panting in the corner, checking the doorway to make sure he hadn't followed.

"That was insane," Stephanie said, keyed up and laughing. She looked like she belonged inside the mural, hair wild, eyes surreal green, swooping klieg lights illuminating her face.

"Imagine caring that much about the Pet Shop Boys," Nina said, trying to remain cool even as her hot breath rushed back into her lungs and her forehead broke out in sweat. "I always thought that song was about West End and East End *Avenues*. I used to sing it to my friend who lived on Ninety-Third and West—"

"Open up," Stephanie said, pointing to her mouth. Nina opened and Stephanie squirted in a stream from the water gun, hitting her right in the back of the throat.

"Vodka?" Nina said.

Stephanie nodded and squirted a stream into her own mouth. "You need heavier ammo at night." She looked closely at Nina. "Be careful with that tape recorder, okay? Coke paranoia's no joke. Patrick punched out a guy at the mall once he was sure was DEA."

"Was he?"

"Nah, just a salesguy at the Wiz."

They stayed in the Basquiat bar until their pulses slowed to normal, or at least to cocaine-normal. Once they were sure the guy hadn't followed them, they went out to circle the dance floor and look for Gardner. After a few minutes, Stephanie singsonged, "Look who's here," and pointed a few feet ahead, where Gardner was talking to a guy with a frizzy ponytail who Nina recognized as the other community-service guy from the bandshell, tonight wearing a Bastille Day beret. There was something vaguely disquieting about him that took Nina a minute to put her finger on: his tense, ropy neck reminded her of the landlord who'd hired the thugs to attack that model. Gardner, no deference to Bastille Day, had on a yellow Lacoste shirt and jeans. Nina's memory of his face never prepared her for the wallop of the genuine article, his thick eyebrows and square, Clark Kent chin, his hot energy like lava you wanted to rush over you.

The ponytailed guy stalked away and Gardner looked irritated, but he smiled when he saw them. "Having a good time?" he yelled over the music.

"Totally," Nina said, "except for the nutjob we just met on the balcony." She introduced him and Stephanie, and they told him what had happened upstairs.

"You two have a death wish? Never mess with a guy who's been doing blow all night. The paranoia's a killer."

"Right?" Stephanie laughed. "One time at work I flushed a gram down the toilet when I convinced myself a customer was a narc."

Gardner laughed also. "I flushed two when I thought the FBI was staking out my dorm room."

Nina felt a spasm of jealousy. She'd have liked to contribute her own paranoia story, like the time she was so stoned at Burger King, she was sure she'd spotted her gym teacher at a table and begged the guy at the fries station to let her hide in the kitchen. But that was bush league, just a couple of bong hits.

"I was just telling Nina how my boyfriend punched out a guy in the mall he thought was DEA," Stephanie said.

"Turned out he worked at the Wiz," Nina provided, but Gardner's gaze lingered on Stephanie.

"He didn't want to come tonight?"

"He wasn't invited," Stephanie said. She gave Gardner a twinkly smile. A *we share a secret* smile? Or just a friendly one? Speaking of paranoid, Nina chastised herself. But even if Stephanie didn't mean to flirt, she was bound to appeal to Gardner, her wild blond hair, flashing eyes, sequined boobs. Nina could feel herself diminishing, plain and dull, one of those little nothing birds the color of dead leaves, pecking the ground for scraps.

"Not like he would have gotten in," Nina blurted, picturing Patrick's Champion T-shirt and feathered '70s hair.

Stephanie gave her a look. "What's that supposed to mean?"

Too late, Nina realized how snotty she'd sounded. Face burning, she tried to recalibrate. "Wouldn't he hate it here? You're always saying how much he hates the city."

"But you didn't say he wouldn't have wanted to come. You said he wouldn't have gotten in if he had."

We barely got in, Nina wanted to say, but couldn't make herself in front of Gardner, who was studying them, head swiveling back and forth.

"You two need a moment?" he asked.

"I'm going to dance," Stephanie announced, although she looked irritated enough to fight.

"You're the one who didn't invite him!" Nina said. What was wrong with her? Why was she being so combative? "I'm sorry!" she called as Stephanie started to walk away. "I didn't mean it."

"Whatever." Stephanie waved her hand over her shoulder, although she still seemed miffed as she pushed through a swarm of bodies to the dance floor. Nina started to follow, until she felt a hand close around her waist.

"I'd let her cool down a minute," Gardner said.

Stephanie had disappeared into the thrashing mass on the dance floor that blinked bright then dark in the strobe lights. Maybe Gardner was right. Instead of chasing and smothering, give people a moment to cool off. Not that Nina could have gone very far, anyway, with Gardner's hand tightening around her, and her legs going weak.

The bouncy opening chords of "Our Lips Are Sealed" thrummed over the sound system. Beside them, a guy in black leather pants ground against a girl in a white leotard splattered with her sweat.

"Her lips won't be sealed for long," Gardner said, laughing, with a glance at the girl.

"So true." Nina laughed along while trying to push away the odious image of Walker unzipping his khakis. She stopped laughing as Gardner slipped his hand under the hem of her shirt to touch the bare skin at her hip, his fingers lightly stroking the curve. Every cell whooshed to that inch of territory because no other part of her existed any longer.

She watched the dance floor through a blur of pleasure. Gold confetti cascaded from the ceiling and a circle of girls raised their hands to catch it. The strobes blinked faster. One of the girls danced into the middle of the circle and her friends tossed handfuls of confetti at her, like rice at a bride. Her blond hair skimmed her back. Her dress was cut low and her tanned shoulders gleamed. She was thrown into darkness, then opalescent light. She twirled with her arms extended so everyone else had to keep dancing backward or get swatted. Not that she noticed or cared—of course not, because she was Holland Nichols.

The song ended and the dance floor went dark. Nina kept herself as still as possible, no hint of anything wrong. Had Gardner seen her? He'd seemed completely fine the other night at Flanagan's, euphoric even, belting out Prince, but who knew how he'd react to seeing Holland whooping it up in public so soon after their breakup.

The dance floor lit back up as a new song started. A couple of guys danced near the circle of girls ringing Holland, cracking each other up with their asinine robot moves. Nina half recognized one of them, robot-chopping his way into the circle. Bent at the waist, he butted Holland with his head. She stopped spinning and swayed in place with her eyes closed, arm curled around his neck. Was that her hand winding through his hair? Was that his tongue in her ear?

Nina stared at his pointy nose until her vision gelled: Rex Parrish. What the hell?

Did Gardner know? She turned to face him. His face was blank, but it was hard to discern in the dizzying lights if it was hadn't-seen-a-thing blank or ice-angry blank.

"Let's go get a drink," she said to distract him.

"Let's see if that guy's still up on the balcony." He smiled—hadn't-seen-a-thing blank, evidently—then gave the same meaningful sniff that Stephanie had earlier.

Speaking of Stephanie. Nina peered around the dance floor but couldn't spot her. Hopefully she'd understand once Nina explained. She led Gardner up the royal-blue staircase, briefly worried how the guy might react when he saw her. But what was there to fear? Gardner was tall and strong and more than a little intimidating.

"Which one is he?"

She scanned the rows of seats, now occupied by a trio of mimes. No striped tie and shiny forehead. She even looked under the seats in case he was hiding but saw only clusters of empty glasses and cigarette butts, and a small pile of plastic rubble that may or may not have been her broken tape recorder.

"He's not here," she told Gardner. "I'm so sorry."

"Fuck," he muttered.

Was there any way to salvage this? "Maybe he went to the bathroom or something. Let's go look for him."

Gardner shook his head, eyes going flat. He looked so defeated. Was this about cocaine or something else? *Did* he know about Holland and Rex?

"Do you want to talk?" she asked. "Sit down, I'll get us drinks. I'll be back in two minutes." While she was at it, she'd run and find Stephanie to tell her where she was.

"It's okay," he said. He was standing close enough to kiss her. She could smell the plum Poison scent in her sweat. The air jumped briefly with a flicker of voltage, but then went dead. "I'm going to find Victor and get out of here."

"Who?"

He looked closely at her. "When you get your hands on something, let me know."

"Of course. Flanagan's Friday?"

He shook his head. "I've got to go to Newark with my mom to a reception at the church for this priest she's friends with."

She tried to keep the disappointment from yanking her down. "Cool."

He rolled his eyes. "Hardly. I wouldn't go anywhere near those cocksuckers if she wasn't making me. It's a big deal to her. The guy's going to be the new archbishop."

"I went to the Vatican once, " Nina said, "on a trip to Rome with my parents."

But his attention had fallen away. He turned and headed back down the staircase, moving so fast she couldn't keep up.

She pushed past dozens of sweaty, reeling bodies on the dance floor before she realized Stephanie wasn't there. Had she left too? Nina had insulted and then abandoned her: Why *would* she stick around? Nina's skull throbbed with a headache and her mouth filled with a sour shame. All around her, people were dancing and laughing, but their joyous faces suddenly struck her as desperate, like they'd burst into tears if they stopped moving.

At least she didn't see Holland and Rex on the dance floor, flaunting their hideous new love for everyone to admire. Shame ought to be filling their mouths, but they were probably too full of each other's tongues. She searched the club until she came upon Stephanie in a connecting hallway, its walls and cathedral ceiling awash in swirls of coral and rose. Nina started to apologize, but Stephanie stopped her. "I got bored dancing, so I came out here to look around. Francesco Clemente," she said, pointing to the birds and bears painted on the ceiling. "Where's Gardner?"

"He had to leave."

"I should probably head home too," Stephanie said.

There was a coolness to her tone that made Nina feel as desperate as the dancers she'd just seen. "Listen. What I said about Patrick—"

"It's okay," Stephanie said, unconvincingly. She studied the tangerine shells and flowers painted on one of the walls. "These murals are so mind-bending."

"I know I sounded like a snob."

Stephanie said nothing, just pulled her hair back in her fist and fanned the nape of her neck. Her rhinestone bracelets clanked against each other.

"Maybe I was just jealous of you and Gardner," Nina said.

"Me and *Gardner*?"

"The way he was looking at you. Talk about paranoid: I like him so much I can't think straight."

"I would never do that to you."

"I know you wouldn't."

Stephanie cocked her head and stared at Nina for a moment before sighing. "I can't stay mad at you. Just don't be an asshole, okay? Don't make me send you back up to that balcony for another round with coked-up Casey Kasem."

A pinprick of guilt. She couldn't tell Stephanie she'd just gone up to the balcony with Gardner—how selfish she'd look, ditching her to run off with him. Let it lie, she told herself, no pun intended. But the image of Gardner's downcast eyes reminded her: "Speaking of coke. How would I go about getting more?"

"Damian's stopping by Maison Rouge this week. I'll get you a couple of grams."

They started pushing their way through the writhing crowd, making glacial progress toward the exit. Stephanie smiled as she slung her arm around Nina's shoulder. "My little baby bird, sprouting her wings."

Chapter Nine

On her rare visits to Times Square, Nina had always kept her head down around the adult movie theaters, the ones that showed *Girls in Cages* or *Girls in Trouble* or *Hot Nasty Girls* or *Super Big Busty Girls*. The lit-up marquees made her own *Girl*-ness feel fluorescent, as if she were a walking X-ray for public consumption. But on her way down Forty-Second Street to meet Stephanie at Playland, she made herself slow down to check out the poster for *Frisky Nymphos* outside the Venus Theater. See, not so bad: four plump girls in garters, hands crossed coyly over their chests, standing back-to-back in a circle. At the Grand Pussycat, the *Blazing Babes* poster was a girl in sunglasses looking over her bare shoulder, flames from an unseen fire reflected in each lens. Also no big deal. The *Shanghai Sluts* poster at Circus Cinema: a circle of Asian girls on their knees, surrounding three sets of men's hairy legs. Okay, bigger deal. Still, there was something to be said for inhabiting a body so central to all this lust. So much power in a pair of breasts, the sway of hips and ass. She was suddenly aware of a sex energy just below the pavement, its current flowing through the electric grid. Plugged into it now, she continued toward Broadway with a little charge in her step.

The line for fake IDs outside Playland stretched halfway down the block. Stephanie was close to the end, cigarette in one hand and her snakeskin sandals in the other, because why not go barefoot in the middle of Times Square.

"Hello, my frisky nympho," Nina said.

"Is that what's playing at the Venus?" Stephanie asked.

"Only you would know a porn theater by name."

Stephanie smiled, although her mouth was tight. Nina forced herself not to pry. On the phone these past few days since the Palladium, everything had seemed back to normal; if Stephanie was still pissed at her over the Patrick comment, wouldn't she say? *Let it lie.*

"A bunch of us went there after the SATs," Stephanie said. "It's the unsexiest place you can imagine. The bleach fumes are like tear gas." At Nina's blank look, Stephanie pistoned her half-closed fist in front of her crotch. "They have to mop after every showing. It was so gross, we didn't even make it to the first cum shot."

The guy in line ahead of them, leather blazer, cross earring, hair slicked up into a glistening peak, turned and eyeballed them.

"Oh, I'm sorry." Stephanie's voice dripped fake remorse. "Did we offend you? Is that Venus jizz in your hair?"

Nina felt a stab of empathy for the guy, imagining him at home in front of the mirror, carefully crafting his look, but she was more concerned about Stephanie, who seemed to be trying to dig cement out of a sidewalk crack with her toe.

"Are you okay?" Nina asked carefully, still worried Stephanie's foul mood was her fault.

Stephanie shrugged. "I was on the phone with Patrick before I left for work, and his call waiting kept clicking. I was like, 'Shouldn't you get that?' and he's like, 'Get what?' Like I don't know what call waiting sounds like and I'm delusional." She blew a mangled smoke ring and frowned at it. "He says living in the city is making me paranoid."

Dirtbag, Nina thought. But she only said, "Remind him that paranoia isn't location dependent. Wasn't the Wiz guy he punched out in Hewlett?"

"He totally encouraged me to live here this summer, but now it's like I've betrayed him. Every time I come home, it's all, 'Where'd you get that jacket, why have I never seen those earrings, what's going on with your hair?' He makes fun of everything I say, like I'm this pretentious *city girl*. I told him I went to the Village with my dad to see a movie, and he's like, 'Oh, the *Village*.'"

"What are you supposed to call it?"

"'Oh, the *bodega*. Oh, Eighty-First and *Lex*.' Like I think I'm better than him."

"Because you say 'bodega'?"

"When I told him about the Palladium, his head practically exploded."

"He's probably just jealous you're having fun without him."

"He's out partying at Cartoons till three every morning! Am I supposed to sit home and watch *Dynasty*?" She sighed. "It's not just Patrick. Guess what I found in Mary Kay's underwear drawer?"

At least now they were back to more neutral ground. "Your mother made you spy again?"

Stephanie held an imaginary phone to her ear. "'Okay, Mom. There's a pink pair. There's a lacy, orange pair.'" She pulled the imaginary phone away: "Holy shit. There's a velvet box with a diamond ring inside."

Nina's jaw dropped. "In Mary Kay's underwear drawer?"

"Maybe they're waiting to tell me before she starts wearing it."

"Did you tell your mom?"

Stephanie shook her head. "I hustled her off the phone. She'd have found a way to blame me."

Nina wanted to offer Stephanie one of Frances's transgressions as commiseration, but didn't want her to think she was trying to one-up her. And things continued to improve on the Frances front. Last night at dinner, Nina had expelled a tiny belch, which in the past would have been treated as a capital offense. But her mother had smiled sunnily and said, *Well, hello, Burp Lancaster!*

"I can't believe my father's going to marry someone so awful." Stephanie threw her cigarette down to the sidewalk and went to grind it out with her bare big toe.

Nina yanked her back. "That would not feel good."

At least Stephanie dropped her shoes to the ground and stepped into them. She was clearly exasperated, but Nina told herself not to take it personally.

"She calls Woody Allen 'that funny little Jewish fellow,'" Stephanie said.

"At least she thinks he's funny."

The sky suddenly turned silver, and gray clouds gathered. Soon the sidewalk was speckled with pin-sized raindrops. She already felt guilty that Stephanie was doing her a favor while she felt so down. "Let's go get a drink then come back. The sign says they're open till midnight. And I doubt anyone in porn land will card us."

"You sure?" Stephanie crossed her arms around herself. "I could really use a shot."

"No shit, Sherlock," said the guy with the hair.

Nina tensed, waiting for Stephanie's retort, but her temper seemed to have loosened its grip.

"I'm sorry," she told him. "I'm in a crap mood. And I'm sorry what I said about your hair, which is actually pretty fucking awesome. What do you use on it?"

"Dep," he said.

"Huh. Not Dippity-Do?"

"Ugh, please, that toothpaste smell." Evidently warmed by Stephanie's interest, he came closer. "But the spray, not the gel. The gel is way too gloppy."

"I know!" Stephanie laughed. "It's like slime; you can't get it off your hands."

"Try scrubbing with sugar."

They traded more hair-sculpting tips as the rain fell even harder. Half the line had scattered. Nina started to worry that the Betsey Johnson dress she'd brought for Stephanie, rolled up in her bag, would get drenched. Not to mention the cash she'd brought for some Damian cocaine. She invited the Dep guy to come with them for a drink, but he had a blind date at Boy Bar later and couldn't chance not getting a fake ID.

There were a hundred peep shows in Times Square, but they couldn't find a single bar. "Everybody just comes and goes," Stephanie shouted over the pelting rain. They ran through puddles in the crosswalks until they came to an awning of a boarded-up electronics store where they could wait it out.

After they caught their breath, Nina took the Betsey Johnson dress out of her bag, only slightly damp. It was ultra-short and buttoned up the back, a high-pitched magenta that drowned Nina out. But it made Stephanie glow. She hugged Nina, her eyes bright with surprise. She unbuttoned all the buttons and deliberately put it on backward, like a long vest. It was clearly how it ought to be worn, even if Betsey hadn't planned it that way.

"And I have something for *you*," Stephanie said. She rummaged through her handbag while Nina imagined Gardner's delight—and appreciation—when she let him know she'd gotten her *hands on something*.

Stephanie took out two green brocade coin purses with royal blue snaps. "One for each of us." She looked so pleased with herself that Nina pushed down her dismay. She'd put her damp cash in it. "That's so thoughtful. Friendship purses!"

"Open it, you spaz."

Nina took it from Stephanie. Something was inside; when she

pressed it, her fingers squished together. Powder. This must be what it felt like to get the keys to your own car.

She passed the cash to Stephanie—two weeks' worth of temp salary, which her parents said was hers to use as she wished—and gazed at the coin purse in her palm, admiring its deceptive granny-ness, the emphatic clack of the snap. "Let's inaugurate it." She'd planned to save it all for Friday night, when she knew Gardner would be at Flanagan's, but now that it was right here in her hand, and she and Stephanie in this private bubble shielded from the pouring rain, she couldn't resist.

"We don't have to do yours," Stephanie said. "I have some too."

"We always do yours. My turn." She showed Stephanie her pinkie nail, which she was letting grow.

Stephanie laughed. "I couldn't be prouder."

Sniffing out of the nail felt gloriously tacky, Michelle Pfeiffer in her satin *Scarface* slip. Stephanie dug in her own nail, and they went back and forth a couple of times, until Stephanie suddenly said, "Damn." Blood was trickling out of her nose. She blotted it with the back of her hand and then pinched the bridge. "For future reference, this is the best way to make it stop bleeding. Hold it at least two minutes."

For future reference—Nina liked the sound of that. Her own nosebleed, this glamorous mix of vice and vulnerability.

As Stephanie continued pinching her nose, something across the street caught her attention: Nina followed her gaze to a place called Le Sex Shoppe, with hand-lettered signs obscuring the windows. ADULT NOVELTIES, MARITAL AIDS. XXX VIDEOS partially blocked another sign so all you could see of it was IZZLERS.

"Twizzlers?" Nina said.

"I'm guessing sizzlers?" Stephanie said. "Like really hot movies."

"Too bad," Nina said, suddenly craving sugar.

"We should get a sex toy for you and Gardner."

Nina laughed uneasily. "Kind of putting the cart before the horse?" Which was still, she reminded herself, in the stable.

"We could start you off with something cute like edible underwear. Ask him this weekend what's his favorite flavor."

"He'll be away. Some reception in Newark for the new archbishop."

"Wow. That's almost like the pope." Stephanie touched her finger to her nose to check for blood. All clear. "Anyway, edible underwear won't spoil. It's got the half-life of plutonium. Let's go." She headed out from under the awning.

"Wait. You weren't kidding?" Nina asked. "In there?" She pictured a grim space, lighting like the bottom of a well. Men huddled in corners with frantic hands in their pants.

"We can't stay out *here* forever," Stephanie wheedled.

Presumably there was some middle ground between there and here. On the other hand, didn't she want out of the middle? The summer was halfway over and she and Gardner hadn't even kissed.

"Okay," she said, and they ran through the rain across the street.

Inside the store, an old guy sat at the cash register, fringed black leather vest, clunky silver skull rings. He flipped through a magazine called *Beaver Hunt*: Nina got a glimpse of a pair of boobs the size and shape of soccer balls, so plastic-looking they'd click if you tapped them with your fingernail. She'd have thought he'd appreciate the female flesh and blood right in front of him, their shirts drenched and clinging, but instead he seemed annoyed at the interruption.

"Yeah?"

"Where do we find the edible underwear?" Stephanie asked.

He gave an impatient snort as he pointed to the center aisle.

"How about whips?" she asked. But it made no difference: he jerked his thumb over his shoulder with a look like, *Who let you out of Barbie's Dreamhouse?*

"Why's he so pissed?" Nina whispered.

"My guess is he never gets to bag the beaver," Stephanie whispered back.

Nina covered her mouth to stifle her laughter. She was glad for something to laugh about in here. The first aisle they turned down had shelves and shelves of candy-colored vibrators on one side, and dozens of paddles hung from the walls on the other, unbashed as a display of spatulas at Macy's. How crazy to see this stuff out in public. How unexpected her arousal. For the first time, she remembered the minutes before the disastrous Walker Pierson blowjob—his tongue in her mouth, her fingers in his hair, their bodies grinding together. She'd felt primitive and a little deranged. She'd shocked herself with her panting.

Stephanie darted ahead to a display of corsets, but Nina stayed put, her attention captured by a TV mounted to the ceiling, on which a sizzler played soundlessly. A girl in a white bikini thrashed around in a pool like she didn't know how to swim, the camera moving in as she gulped water and called for help. The lifeguard dove in and dragged her out of the pool, onto a towel conveniently spread out at the water's edge. He started doing CPR on her. The chest thrusts just happened to undo her bikini top. A perfect breast popped out, a vertical globe of ivory against her tanned skin. No way would Nina's first time be outdoors, in the blinding sunlight, with Gardner getting an eyeful of her pastiness and floppy breasts. The girl did some stagy coughing, the mouth-to-mouth morphed into a make-out, and she pulled off the guy's bathing suit. Nina tried to recall the word for fear of the sun, but her brain was short-circuiting. Because despite the hammy acting and the guy's disconcertingly massive edifice, she was riveted. The girl reclined with her legs raised in an open V. They were supposed to be up in the air like that? The lifeguard hovered above her in a plank, then lowered himself and rammed inside.

Nina flinched. The space between her legs felt open and animate. Over the years, to see what sex might feel like, she'd filled it with various objects: her fingers, a Revlon Hot Coral lipstick—even, once, a zucchini, a skinny one, its skin coarse and warty. Each time the sensation had been startlingly pleasurable, even the zucchini, the gather of atoms and climb of desire, but it had been a solitary pleasure. It was hard to imagine being relaxed enough to lose herself with someone else there.

"*That*," Stephanie said, pointing to the TV screen, "is a recipe for serious sunburn." Her teeth tapped together in a deliberate rhythm that must have matched a song in her head. "One time my friend and her boyfriend fell asleep on the beach, and when she woke up she had a bright red stomach with two white handprints." She watched the screen for a few seconds. "Holy shit. That's not a dick, that's a baseball bat."

Nina laughed. "How does it even fit inside her?"

She must have sounded more anxious than she realized because Stephanie looked at her closely. "You know, there's no rush," she said. "Don't do it until you really want to."

"Of course I want to!" Nina tried to rein in her defensiveness. "I want to. And honestly, I am in kind of a rush. I have to do it before college."

Stephanie stopped tapping her teeth. "How come?"

"I can't start college as the same old me."

"What's wrong with the same old you? The same old you is awesome."

It was nice to hear, even if it wasn't what she'd meant. "If by 'awesome' you mean uptight and prissy."

"We're high on cocaine in a sex shop." Stephanie swept her arm like a game-show model toward what looked like a field of cactuses.

"That's different." On closer inspection, the display of cactuses was actually many, many dildos. "Sex is chemical. I think it changes you cellularly. Or maybe neurologically. It puts an awareness in your eyes that other people can see."

Stephanie pointed at a shimmering purple dildo. "This would make you pretty fucking aware. And at least it doesn't smell like boy sweat and Clearasil."

Nina laughed and gingerly petted the tip. "Gardner doesn't have acne."

They continued down the aisle, Stephanie fiddling with the buttons of the Betsey Johnson dress as she contemplated the merchandise. After a minute, she asked, "Remember I told you about that frat party?"

Nina nodded, although she tried not to picture it, Stephanie unconscious, pinned beneath that grunting dickweed.

"I found out his mom's address and sent her a huge, veiny dildo on Mother's Day, with a card from him that said, 'To the greatest mom, from your not-so-little boy.'" She laughed. "I have to say, it felt good to get even."

"That's brilliant." But was it really getting *even*? And even with whom?

Stephanie fished her coin purse out of her bag, and they each sniffed a reinvigorating nailful. Then they flew from aisle to aisle, played tug-of-war with a studded leash, threw bottles of lube at each other, then took turns reading aloud off the boxes of inflatable dolls.

"'Gretchen has three warm and inviting love holes.'"

"'Just fill Juanita with air and her body responds to your loving touch.'"

The face and breasts of each doll were visible through the cellophane, their red mouths open in big, fat O's.

"'Created of strong, lasting vinyl, Kiki feels smooth and almost too human.' Yeah, God forbid."

"I should get one of these for Patrick," Stephanie said. "He's always saying he wants a threesome."

"Perfect." Nina laughed. "No new jacket or earrings for him to freak out over." She examined the empty space on either side of Kiki's balloon head. "No ears, even. She couldn't even hear his call waiting."

Stephanie froze. Blood rushed to Nina's face. She'd stepped in the quicksand despite herself.

"Hold on," Stephanie said. "Do you think some girl *was* calling Patrick?"

"Of course not," she lied. Why couldn't she pay more attention to what was in her brain before her mouth got involved? "Don't listen to me. I was making a dumb joke."

Stephanie clutched the box with Gretchen to her chest, which somehow made her distress twice as piercing.

"Maybe he couldn't hear the clicks from his end," Nina added. "And even if someone *was* calling him, that doesn't mean he asked them to or even knows them. Sales calls, wrong number, could be anything."

"I guess you're right." Stephanie took a breath. Then she laughed ruefully, turning the box to address Gretchen's plastic face: "Does coke turn *you* into a paranoid nutjob?"

Past a row of chastity belts was a rack of plastic-wrapped beaded bracelets marked $3.99. The beads were pink and white and lavender, the size and iridescence of pearls. Leigh would disapprove of the obvious cheapness, but Nina had to have one. Make that two: one for her and one for Stephanie, friendship bracelets to go with their friendship coin purses, and make up for yet another Patrick misstep.

And if anyone asked where it was from, she could answer, "A Times Square sex shop," like, *duh*.

The guy at the register, though. He'd curl his lip at the dumb virgin tourist who'd left a sex shop with nothing but a couple of lame plastic bracelets. Maybe she should throw in a riding crop. Or here was a thought: avoid him altogether by just dropping the bracelets in her handbag.

She scanned the store. No guards, no cameras. No mirrors on the ceiling, just the TV playing the same porno, a group of naked revelers now going at it in the pool. Nina hadn't shoplifted since third grade when she got caught in Mary Arnold's with a yo-yo in her pocket, but her hands moved deftly as she plucked two bracelets off the rack and let them fall into her open handbag.

"Let's go," she whispered to Stephanie, who'd come back to see what she was up to.

"So, no edible underwear?"

Nina opened her handbag just enough for Stephanie to see inside, pleased when her eyes widened. Nina continued toward the exit with an extra snap in her walk, a bit of showmanship to make Stephanie laugh. The guy at the register was still reading his magazine and paid them no attention. They could easily have slipped out the door, no problem, but Nina deliberately cleared her throat to get his attention, wanting him to see her smug smile, so he'd remember her when he figured out the missing bracelets. Her tame version of getting even: a message about customer service.

He looked up and held her eye. For a second she thought he might be on to her, but he said nothing. Instead he pointedly laid the open magazine on the counter. Photos of a woman, naked, lashed to a wooden pole, coils of rope around her neck, breasts, thighs, and ankles. Her nose yanked into a snout by metal hooks, a lit cigarette wedged into each nostril. Tears and makeup ran down her cheeks.

"That's—" Cocaine tried to push out words, but revulsion made her speechless.

"A waste of two perfectly good cigarettes," Stephanie finished for her as she hustled her outside.

The rain had let up, but the sidewalks were still damp. Stephanie took off her shoes again, but Nina was too disheartened to police her. She couldn't stop picturing the metal hooks snouting the woman's nose, hearing "squeal like a pig" from that horrible scene in *Deliverance*. An infuriating sense of humiliation gripped her. The absurdity of thinking she'd gotten even with the guy by swiping a couple of dumb plastic bracelets. He got the last word without saying a word: she was just a subhuman sex toy, a hanging carcass in the window of a butcher shop.

"Don't let it get to you," Stephanie said after they'd walked a block in silence. "Those magazines are for skeevy fuck-face losers." She sidestepped a grease-stained napkin. "And besides, you got out with free cock rings. That's quite a leap from edible underwear."

"Free what?"

"The cock rings. Are you going to use them with Gardner?"

Nina stepped in an ankle-deep puddle. Her shoes were drenched, but it didn't matter. She burst out laughing. What a rookie sex-shop mistake.

"I thought they were bracelets."

Stephanie laughed too. "Sometimes you're my favorite person in the world."

Nina's mood lifted. She took one of the—Jesus, cock rings—out of her bag and tossed it to Stephanie. "Here you go. My treat. Friend-ship cock rings."

Stephanie caught it high in the air. "Aw, you shouldn't have."

They walked back in the direction of Playland. Nina's feet squelched in her shoes. Fuck it: she pulled them off. The pavement was cool and sleek beneath her bare feet.

"We are so going as Kiki and Gretchen next Halloween," Nina said. Then the one thing too many despite herself: "Let Patrick get his own blow-up date."

Stephanie's face fell.

"I'm sorry," Nina said quickly, promptly stepping into another pothole, this one filled with what felt like warm sludge.

"No, it's okay." But now Stephanie was distracted; she didn't seem to notice Nina's slime-coated foot. "It's just he's probably having a heart attack wondering why I'm not home. I bet he's left, like, six messages on my answering machine. I should get back."

"Really?" Nina dragged her dirty foot against her other leg to rub off the muck. Off-balance, she listed to one side, grabbing onto Stephanie's shoulder to keep from falling. Stephanie absentmindedly squeezed her hand, then put up her own for a cab.

"Will you drop me off at home?" Nina asked as the taxi stopped. "I can go to Playland some other time."

"Don't be silly. You're right here."

She got in the cab and waved as it pulled away. Nina tried not to feel deflated. Patrick would always come between them, even when he wasn't physically there. Nina would always have to watch what she said when it came to him. She put her shoes back on and headed toward Playland, stopping every few seconds to scratch her feet, which had started to turn red and were itching like crazy. What had she stepped in? Back waiting on line for her fake ID, she concocted an elaborate cover story in case her parents noticed, although she already knew they wouldn't.

Chapter Ten

Frances burst into Nina's room with an ad she'd torn from the newspaper for a store in Soho called Think Big. It sold giant replicas of everyday objects: sunglasses as wide as a refrigerator, oar-sized crayons you could actually draw with. Wouldn't Nina like a tennis racket for her dorm room that was as tall as the door? Nina would not, thank you, but she didn't have a temp job today, so sure, let's go take a look.

Her mother stumbled a little as she got into the elevator. She had on high-heeled espadrilles even though she'd always warned Nina to never wear heels around the city unless she wanted a broken ankle. Nina, unaware of the rule change, had on Tretorns, her feet inside them dotted with cortisone cream, still itching from the toxic goo she'd managed to wade through in Times Square after chastising Steph for going barefoot.

She pressed the button for the lobby. Next to it was a button with a fireman's hat that would light up if the elevator got stuck, to let you know the fire department had been called. HELP IS ON THE WAY, it read, and for years Nina's answering thought had been: *I doubt it.* Riding down from her apartment, fists clenched from the tension of tiptoeing around her mother, or riding up in dry-mouthed dread, she'd known no help was coming. Things were stuck like this forever. Her life would keep filling with black clouds of smoke and no one would ever notice.

But help had come. Her mother's despair had magically evaporated: now she was giggling over the Think Big ad, expressing delight about a plastic Oreo the size of a manhole cover. And Nina had met Gardner. She patted the tote bag slung over her shoulder where she'd stashed the friendship coin purse. She wouldn't do any more before she saw him, but she didn't want to leave it at home today, not with the housekeeper coming to clean.

Freddie opened the lobby door for them, eyeing Nina as she dug the toe of her left shoe into the right one's instep. Behind her mother's back, he shot her a look that said, *I will add whatever this is to the tally.*

"Freddie is such a nice man," Frances said to Nina on the sidewalk. "It's such a pity what he's had to endure." Nina resisted the urge to say the same about herself.

They descended the stairs to the 6 train. Besides the espadrilles, Frances wore a necklace made of heavy gold links, even though she'd also said never to wear jewelry on the subway unless you wanted to get mugged. Also: never stand near the edge of the subway platform unless you wanted to get pushed in front of an oncoming train— another expired threat, apparently, because Frances teetered all the way up to it and leaned forward to peer down the tunnel.

"Careful!" Nina pulled her back.

"My daughter, the worrywart," Frances said jovially.

A man standing a few feet down the platform glanced in their direction. He wore Bermuda shorts embroidered with crabs and carried a Cheese Cellar shopping bag.

"You didn't get the chicken noodle soup, did you?" Frances called. "They use too much salt, and they skimp on the vegetables."

He blinked, and Nina saw her mother through his eyes: flamingo-pink lipstick, startling friendliness, voice a little loud. "*Mom,*" she said under her breath.

"Yes, my sweet?"

Nina gave her a look that suggested she take it down a notch.

"I'm just conversing with the nice gentleman," Frances said. "It's what civilized people do."

He smiled. "I like Wolf's," he said. "Very tasty."

Frances made a face. "Oh God, no. Those soggy noodles, all that fat floating around."

"How about Fine & Shapiro's, then?"

"I suppose, if you like stringy chicken," Frances said.

Nina looked down. She'd overreacted again. The guy was clearly enjoying the impromptu soup debate.

"If you want the real deal, try Carnegie Deli," Frances called over the arriving train. "It has the most heft."

"Will do!" He waved as the subway doors opened and stepped into the car ahead of theirs.

"You made his day," Nina told her mother as they got on their car.

Frances shrugged. "Goys know nothing about chicken soup."

"How do you know he's not Jewish?"

Her mother laughed. "Jews don't wear shorts with crabs on them."

The subway wasn't too crowded, so they got seats together. The train catapulted down Lexington with its usual clanking and shrieking. At Fifty-Ninth Street, a transit cop got on with an enormous police dog straining against a chain leash. They began a slow march up the aisle to where Nina and Frances sat. Hadn't Nina read somewhere that transit police dogs were trained in drug sniffing? She told herself to keep calm, even as she clutched the strap of her tote bag on her lap.

"I always tell your father he should take the train. He says it's dangerous, but look: we're perfectly fine. We even have a policeman and his puppy on board."

The dog's ears pricked up and its massive head swung in their direction, staring at them with affronted black eyes.

"Hello there, sweet thing," Frances said. She held out a hand to the dog, who pulled closer to sniff. "What kind of dog is this?" she asked the policeman, who now loomed over them.

"German shepherd, ma'am," he said in that bland, unreadable cop way Nina recognized from *Serpico*. She tried to shrink herself down to the size of a BB. Think small, she told herself, but the dog was straining in her direction, its slab of a tongue dripping saliva. She made herself breathe normally and gaze at an ad for Ivory Snow. Someone had drawn a dialogue bubble coming out from the baby's mouth: *Looking for a date?*

The dog pulled the cop even closer and started sniffing Nina's shoes.

"Did you put Alpo in your socks again?" Frances asked, then smiled at the cop.

"Cortisone cream." She tried to sound matter-of-fact. Her feet itched to high heaven, like an accusation, or maybe an admission of guilt. She held herself as still as she could so the dog would forget she was there. Or was that for a grizzly bear? She was too panicked to remember, and anyway, the dog didn't forget. It nosed around her crotch, exhaling heat.

She was eye-level with the cop's belt, the gun and the nightstick and the handcuffs. He'd probably already clocked her pinkie nail. Would a cop cuff you in front of your mother?

"You must have your period," Frances said to Nina. "Dogs love the pheromones."

"Mom!" Nina said under her breath.

"I'm embarrassing her," she said to the officer, who glanced at Nina's lap and his dog panting there. "Menstrual shame runs in our family. When I got my period, I didn't tell my mother for months, until she found the stained underwear under my mattress. She slapped me! Not because she was angry. It's a Jewish tradition."

Was Frances seriously telling him about her menstrual history? He had the round baby face of a Boy Scout, and a pimple on his chin, but that didn't cancel the handcuffs and the gun, and that nightstick wasn't for playing fetch. The dog was still nosing around Nina's crotch, making a damp spot at the base of her pants zipper. Her thighs trembled.

"A slap across the face tells a Jewish girl that from now on life will be full of pain," Frances told the cop, "so get used to it." She pointed to the dog, still standing guard at Nina's crotch. "Speaking of Germans, do you know how you get a Jewish girl's number?"

The baby-faced policeman stared back at her, looking confused.

"Roll up her sleeve."

"Mom!" Nina said. She felt her face flush.

The cop's eyes widened, but at least he finally tugged the dog away. "Sorry, ladies," he said politely. "Tank gets a little overexcited sometimes." He and the dog got off when the subway stopped at Thirty-Third Street.

"I'd like a dog named Tank," Frances said. "I'd call him Sherman."

Nina didn't have her period, but her stomach was cramping anyway. She was queasy with excess adrenaline, which for some reason made her want to confess.

"I did the same thing," she said. "I didn't tell you when I got my period."

"Blood under the bridge," her mother said with a dismissive wave, and Nina's eyes watered: it felt so good to be forgiven.

Everything in Soho was huge and shiny and in-your-face. Soon Nina was riding a wave of relief, plus a nailful of powder snuck behind her mother's back, which made things even shinier. One shop window had a chandelier on a spinning disk so the sun arced off the crystals in broken rainbows. Another had a nest of twigs and peacock feathers that turned out to be a $600 hat. Think Big's window had a hairbrush the height of an eight-year-old and a hand mirror for a giant.

"What's the point of a three-foot-tall hairbrush?" Nina asked, then answered herself: "There is no point. And *that's* the point, that there is no point." *Pipe down, Miss Gabby,* said the part of her brain that the coke hadn't permeated.

But her mother beamed at her. "When did you get so smart?"

Inside, they stopped in front of a mammoth harmonica suspended from the ceiling by thick cords.

"Should we try it out?" Frances asked.

"Are you allowed?" Nina glanced at the saleswoman on the other side of the store, showing a young couple how to twirl a jumbo cheerleader's baton.

Frances rolled her eyes. "What are they going to do, arrest me for playing without a license?"

Nina checked the front of her pants. The dog's saliva had evaporated.

A saleswoman came over and asked if they wanted to try the harmonica. "Bruce Springsteen came in last week and played 'Hungry Heart'!" Her earrings were fist-sized metal clovers that pulled down her earlobes. She'd probably come in one day with normal-sized clovers but was encouraged to think bigger.

Frances took out her tape recorder and pressed Record. Nina wondered if the coked-up guy who'd smashed hers at the Palladium was still holed up inside the club, cowering in a coat closet. Her mother puffed hard into the harmonica holes and a few random notes bellowed out. "That was 'You'll Never Walk Alone,'" she said. "The abridged version."

The saleswoman turned to Nina. "Want a try, hon?"

Nina blew once and produced a scrap of sound. "That was the last note of 'Material Girl.'"

"Isn't she terrific?" her mother asked the saleswoman, then paid for the harmonica and had it shipped to their apartment, along with the gargantuan hairbrush for Nina's dorm room. They left the store and went to Ad Hoc and bought coat hangers and tie racks since Frances was planning a redo of Ira's closet. Nina basked in *terrific*, all those chirpy consonants, as they compared various drawer pulls. They bought shirts at agnès b. and spicy sausage and Buffalo mozzarella at Dean & DeLuca. They stopped into Just Bulbs, where Frances asked if they sold Bic pens or tie tacks and the salesmen chorused, "Just bulbs!" and laughed as if no one else ever came in with that question, seeming so utterly charmed that Nina gave her mother a closer look. She sometimes forgot how pretty she was: high cheekbones, chestnut hair, dark, arched eyebrows, radiant skin. You didn't see it most of the time, her depression like a layer of wax that leeched the life from her face. They stopped at a café on Greene Street for a late lunch and ordered a vegetable omelet to share that they both just picked at—even the side of french fries didn't make Nina hungry. Loss of appetite was one of her favorite effects of cocaine. How refreshing to not feel so relentlessly needy every second of the day. She examined her own face in the mirrored wall behind their table. Her cheekbones, like her mother's, were definitely more prominent. She looked mysterious, maybe even a little exotic.

At dinner, Frances told Ira she'd played a giant harmonica that Bruce Springsteen had played the week before.

"Your cousin's kid?" Ira asked. "The bar mitzvah in Roslyn?" He gazed at Frances across the table. She'd changed into a silky pink dress Nina had never seen before that made her skin rosy.

"Bruce *Edelstein* was Roslyn," Frances said. "Howard and Marcia's son. The harmonica holes were as big as bricks. Wait until you see. It's coming this weekend."

"For the Edelstein kid? What's wrong with the kiddish cup we gave him?"

"Not that we ever got a thank-you note," Frances said.

Nina laughed. Her parents were such goobers.

"I played 'You'll Never Walk Alone' for you," Frances told Ira.

He paused mid-bite of mozzarella, his eyes going soft. Oh, right. Their first date at *Carousel*.

Hungry heart, Nina thought. Everybody's got one.

"I was thinking of calling Roger," her father said. Roger was her parents' travel agent. Nina couldn't remember the last time she'd heard his name mentioned. "What would you say to a week in Rome this September?" he asked Frances.

"You should go *now*!" Nina said, imagining the apartment to herself, her first time with Gardner on a real bed (the king in her parents' room—would that be tempting fate after the Walker Pierson debacle? but Nina's was only a twin, with a trundle better suited for slumber parties). No rush, no curfew, no one knocking on the door. Gardner would deal with Freddie in some man-to-man way that ensured his silence. They could hunker down all week with the TV and the liquor cabinet and Stouffer's French-bread pizzas. They'd do lines off her desk while she read the dirty parts out loud from *The Thorn Birds*.

Her parents were eyeing her sideways.

"Be spontaneous, I mean," she said lightly. "Strike while the iron is hot."

Ira shook his head. "The iron's too hot, is the problem. Italy's a thousand degrees in the summer. Your mother and I were there in *June* on our honeymoon, and it was like walking in fire. No one had air-conditioning then."

"Wouldn't they have it now?" Nina asked, but she could see she wasn't getting them on a plane that easily. How much privacy did Gardner have at his apartment? She imagined his mother in her nurse's uniform, listening at the door with a glass to her ear.

Frances speared a cube of cantaloupe with her fork, then steered it idly around her plate. "Daddy and I hardly left the hotel pool. We had chlorine in our hair for weeks. And terrible sunburns! All the Americans did. We didn't realize how strong the sun would be. However, some very smart man thought to bring Solarcaine."

She beamed at Ira. Was he blushing?

"All the women kept telling me, 'You've got one of the good ones.' As if I didn't know." She blew Ira a kiss from across the table. His face glowed with such pleasure that Nina felt like a Peeping Tom, but she couldn't look away. She'd been watching him love Frances one-sidedly for years. She hadn't known how much she'd longed to see her mother love him back.

Frances dabbed her lips with her napkin, although she hadn't eaten anything. "Do you think our hotel is still there?"

Ira raised his eyebrows. "Where would it have gone?"

"Iceland? To cool off?"

Ira laughed and Frances stood up, laughing too. "I'll be right back," she said. "Go ahead and clear, please." She rushed out of the room. Nina and her father carried the dirty plates and glasses to the kitchen. She rinsed the plates in the sink and he loaded them in the dishwasher.

"Well!" he said.

"I know!" Nina answered.

It felt funny to be standing in this exact same spot, rinsing and loading these exact same dishes, where they'd had hundreds of hushed conversations about Frances's misery and rage.

"The medication's working, isn't it?" Nina asked.

"It definitely seems to be." His voice was hopeful as crossed fingers.

"You think it will last?"

"So far, so good." He positioned three glasses in a careful row.

"You don't think she's a little . . . hyper?"

He thought for a second. "Well, your mother's always been quirky. It's part of her charm. We just haven't seen it for a while."

"But the puns?" Nina asked. "The shopping?"

"What do you mean?"

"She bought, like, a hundred coat hangers today."

"She has a lot of coats." Now his voice was a closed door. Nina considered pushing further—the five shoe racks from Ad Hoc, in addition to the hangers; "Just in case," her mother had said, the same thing she'd said last week when she bought a dozen tin flowerpots from Conran's, even though there hadn't been so much as a leaf in their apartment since Nina was a kid. Just in case *what*? But when Nina asked, Frances just shrugged and fluttered to a new subject.

"Damn." Ira's face was pinched. He was trying to fit a dinner plate in a salad plate slot. She took it from his hand and slotted it in the right spot.

Frances rushed into the kitchen out of breath, holding her mini tape recorder aloft. She pressed the Record button and a tiny red light switched on. "*Three coins in the fountain*," she sang into it, "*each one seeking happiness*." She clicked the Stop button. "Miei amori," she said, looking back and forth between Nina and Ira.

Her father brightened and Nina's heart turned over.

"Mine got broken," she told her mother. "Can you get me another one, next time you're at Sharper Image?"

Frances flashed her new girlish teeth-baring smile. "'We shall see,' said the blind man."

Chapter Eleven

Leigh lit a Newport. "Don't let me smoke anymore this weekend. I'm going to a new dentist on Monday. I heard he keeps a glass jar in his office with a cancerous tongue floating inside it, and if he smells smoke on you, he'll make you hold it on your lap for the whole exam."

"The tongue?" Nina asked. She was only half-paying attention as she fought to not stare at Gardner, who was playing poker a couple of tables away with four other guys. She still didn't know if he'd seen Rex and Holland together at the Palladium on Bastille Day, or heard about it, or if their skeevy cavorting had even meant anything. At least neither was here tonight. Gardner sipped from a shot glass between hands of poker, looking so relaxed that Nina let herself relax. If he was fine, she was fine.

Meredith rolled her eyes. "The *jar*, with the tongue inside. You really think a dentist would dump a severed tongue on a patient's lap?" She was, if possible, even pricklier tonight than usual. From the moment she got here, nothing was right, starting with too many Bridge-and-Tunnelers, the place "rancid with Drakkar Noir." It took half an hour to get a drink ("which is why I always get two at a time," Leigh said). There was a mile-long line for the ladies' room full of "outer-borough skanks doing drugs."

Which confirmed Nina's decision not to tell them she'd been doing cocaine. Drinking was fine with them, even a hit off a joint at a party, but serious drugs were trashy. They had no tolerance, much less appetite, for trouble. They weren't even curious, which Nina considered a lack of imagination. She thought of Stephanie gaping at the Palladium murals, transported, of her running barefoot in the rain. Funny how someone who dropped into your life from out of nowhere could make more sense than the people entrenched there from the start.

"The thing I don't understand," Leigh said, halfway through her second Negroni and looking a little woozy, "is how he can talk without a tongue."

"Do you seriously think it's *his* tongue?" Meredith squinted at Leigh as if to say, *And I'm the one who didn't get into Princeton?*

"I'll take three," Chip Wainwright told Gardner, who was dealing. "Give me *something* to work with, will you?"

Gardner passed Chip three cards, then brushed the hair out of his eyes, surveying the other players with panther watchfulness. Benji Peterson also wanted three cards, Dean Ehrenkranz two, Spencer Barrett one.

"Dealer takes two," Gardner said.

Nina petted her handbag, envisioning the coin purse inside. *Want to get paranoid?* was the line she'd rehearsed endlessly at home, until she recognized it made no sense out of context and amended it to *Want to get high?* Now she toyed with *Let's get high,* no question mark: more self-assured. Parsing these, she caught sight of Gardner sliding a card across his leg beneath the table. While his friends studied their poker hands, he brought the card up to the ones in his hand and let one fall to his lap. His expression didn't change except for what must have been a tenth of a second when he turned his head to look straight at Nina, as if he somehow sensed she was watching him. He lifted a corner of his mouth, and she gave a faint smile back.

An instant later, Leigh glanced in his direction. "Holland says Gardner got kicked out of BU, so he's going to Hunter this fall."

"Why is Holland gossiping about him if they're broken up?" Nina asked, certain his expulsion was fallout from Dartmouth and Rex. Either way, she was glad he was escaping New England and its uptight *Crucible* puritanism. He belonged in the city. She liked that she knew what his life would be like here. She liked that if she came home from Vanderbilt for the weekend, he wouldn't be four hours away.

"I think she's just worried about him," Leigh said.

Nina snorted. "She should worry about herself." Leigh and Meredith eyed her suspiciously, but getting into Holland and Rex at the Palladium would entail too much explanation, and why risk attaching herself to a piece of gossip that might wend its way back to Gardner?

Leigh downed the rest of her Negroni. "Did you see Walker?" she asked Nina. "He's back from Northeast Harbor."

"I'll go say hi later," Nina replied. As in *after I'm dead* later. Talk about someone with no tolerance for trouble. How had she allowed a guy that bland to get under her skin?

"Maybe he'll want another blowjob." Meredith smirked.

"I don't know," Nina said, irritation rising. "I'll ask him after he hypnotizes me with my tampon."

Meredith's face fell. Leigh gave Nina a death stare that caught her off-guard.

"What?" she asked Meredith. "Have you decided you like him? I thought he was just a onetime thing."

"*Like* him?" Meredith shot up from the table, shaking her head, mouth in a hard line, and Leigh followed her. Nina watched their retreating figures, bewildered. What had just happened? She considered following them, except she clearly wouldn't be welcome.

The stacks of cash were growing higher at Gardner's table. One by one the other guys folded until it was just him and Chip. "All in,"

Gardner said, pushing a mountain of bills into the middle of the table.

Chip laid down two kings and three nines. "This house is full," he gloated.

"Nice," Gardner said.

Chip started to reach for the cash, but Gardner stopped him: "Check out the Village People," he said, laying down four queens.

They all stared. "Unbelievable," Benji finally said.

"How the fuck—?" Chip stared skeptically at the cards, and Nina tensed. Chip glided through life on a boat of inherited money, with an ego like he'd built it, rigged it, and hoisted the sail. A little fleecing wouldn't kill him. She prepared herself to jump into the fray if he threw out an accusation and things got ugly, swear she saw Gardner draw two more queens fair and square.

But Gardner coolly shrugged him off and pocketed the cash. "Drinks on me," he announced.

Chip retreated. "Macallan 12, you lucky fuck."

"Luck's got nothing to do with it," Gardner said, then headed to the bar.

Leigh and Meredith came back to the table with a pitcher of sangria.

"Are you okay?" Nina asked Meredith. "I'm sorry if I said the wrong thing."

Meredith's face was slightly blotchy, but she seemed otherwise composed, although she didn't meet Nina's eye.

"No big deal," she snapped. "I'm just premenstrual."

In other words, no further questions.

"On behalf of humankind," Nina said to Gardner later, "thank you for wiping that smug look off Chip Wainwright's face."

He turned on the barstool to face her, drinking from a bottle of Heineken. "On behalf of myself, humankind is most welcome."

Nina laughed. "You should work on Wall Street. At this firm where I temped last week, there was a chalkboard in the kitchen that said 'Rules Are For . . .' and the traders wrote in their answers. Like, 'pussies,' 'cowards'—"

"Chumps and suckers," Gardner said. "They get it on Wall Street. The game's rigged. You've got to rig it back."

"They randomly dare each other all day, like, Eat a ghost pepper for five hundred dollars, lick the tire of a public bus for a thousand. Name your baby Blaze and I'll give you ten thousand dollars."

"For ten grand I'd name my kid Weasel," Gardner said. He picked at the Heineken label. "Speaking of weasels, did the paranoid coke fiend from the balcony ever show back up?"

"Nope." She lifted his beer to her lips, extending her pinkie to showcase the nail. "But he's not my only source."

His attention tightened. "You've got others?"

She nodded. For some reason, she wanted to prolong this.

He sat straighter and pressed his knee into hers. Oh, that was why: to see what he'd do to draw it out of her.

His hand hovered at the hem of her shirt. He moved his thumb underneath, brushing bare skin, that same spot he'd touched at the Palladium. Her vision blurred as if she were back with the lifeguard in the porn movie at the sex shop, staring into the blinding sun.

She was just barely as tall, standing, as he was sitting down. She stood up straighter, liking the upper-hand sensation.

He smiled and gripped her waist, hard. Her insides melted. Forget the upper hand.

"I fold," she said.

He leaned closer. "Meet me outside in five minutes."

———

She told her friends she was running down the street for some Dyna-mints, then grabbed her bag and headed for the door. Happiness filled her like helium. Outside, she floated around the corner to wait. He appeared a couple minutes later and led her past a row of dusty tenement buildings to a brownstone halfway down the block. Behind a long dumpster was a flight of iron steps. He unlatched the gate and they went down to a brick alcove below that had the sour smell of mulch. Sounds drifted from the sidewalk above, scraps of conversations and high heels striking the pavement, but they were muffled and made the rest of the world seem far away.

She rummaged in her bag for a smoke. "Shoot. I left my cigarettes inside."

He rested his beer on one of the steps then wedged his fingers in a crack between the bricks. He pulled out a half-crushed pack of Marlboros and a matchbook from the Border Café.

"Emergency pack." He lit a cigarette, took a drag, and handed it to her. When she brought it to her lips, it was like their mouths were touching.

"I just found out I have a single room at college," she blurted, then busied herself rummaging through her bag, a little embarrassed how much like an invitation it sounded.

"Cool," he said, though less committal than she'd have liked. "Where are you going?"

"Vanderbilt." She found the coin purse and fished out the baggie.

"Nashville," he said. "Jack Daniel's and Johnny Cash."

"Boston," she said. "Red Sox and Faneuil Hall." Maybe Holland was spreading false rumors.

"I transferred to Hunter." He plucked the baggie from her palm. "Boston sucked. Anyplace the bars close at midnight is not my scene."

So had he gotten kicked out or just chosen to leave? Either way, all this talk about college was reminding her that summer was expiring fast. She took a step closer to him, although she was careful not to disturb the small heap of powder he was shaking onto the ridge between his thumb and index finger. He sniffed it up, leaving a faint dusting on his skin she wished she had the nerve to lick off.

"Your turn," he said as he shook out some more. He held his hand level beneath her nose, his fingers skimming her cheek. She managed a relatively graceful sniff, even while holding her breath so she wouldn't wheeze all over him. When she was done, he moved his hand to cup her face, his eyes fixed on hers.

"Thank you. You've made a really shitty night better."

"My pleashuh," she said, calling up a Massachusetts accent in her nervousness and immediately regretting it. Simmer down, she told herself. Stop making your lips a moving target.

He continued to gaze at her. His eyes were glossy black, all pupil. He pulled her face closer and a sigh blossomed in her throat. Her nerves finally fell away. Their mouths were half an inch apart.

From the sidewalk above them, a girl shouted, "Gardner, are you down there?"

Holland. Nina would know that lockjaw anywhere. Obviously she knew about this spot.

"Jesus," Gardner hissed. "Why is she yelling?" He stepped back, dropping his hand. Nina looked up to the sidewalk and saw right up Holland's dress, a slice of white underwear glowing in the dark.

"Sorry. I've got to deal with this." He gently touched the edge of her ear and gave her a long, serious look she read as regret. "I'll see you later." He wiped his nose, grabbed his beer, and ran up the steps.

"Enough already," he told Holland.

"You haven't returned any of my calls."

"I've got nothing to say."

"We're worried about you." *We?* Holland's voice rang with over-the-top concern. She'd played Marmee in a senior production of *Little Women* and Nina remembered her voice ringing with the same faux concern as she tended to the wilting Beth.

Gardner snorted.

"He feels terrible," Holland said. Did she mean Rex? Were they official? Nina could almost hear Gardner gritting his teeth.

"You should talk to him," Holland said. "Meet him for a drink."

"Both of you stay far the fuck away from me."

"Gardner," she said in her Marmee voice, but Nina could hear his footsteps heading back down the block. She counted to sixty to give Holland time to clear out. She wondered briefly what *we* were so worried about, but there was too much buzzing in her brain for any single thought to stand out. Instead, as she climbed the steps, she stroked the edge of her ear, feeling Gardner's finger there. She zeroed in on that, the inscription of tenderness, and then the pain she'd heard in his voice and what she could do to ease it.

Back inside Flanagan's, the air was hot and smelled of sweat. Benji and Chip had another card game going with two other guys, shouting to each other over Cheap Trick. Alison Bloch and her friend Jill marched around polling any guy who'd answer what he liked better in a girl: long hair or short? Big boobs or small? Missionary or doggy-style?

Nina ordered a Pepsi at the crowded bar. She noticed Rex Parrish and Walker Pierson talking a couple feet away. It figured they were buddies. It was easy to eavesdrop, considering their booming voices; they obviously didn't care who heard them, or probably even notice anyone besides themselves. Rex had to be the terrible-feeling *he* Holland had mentioned. He ought to feel terrible about the madras pants he was wearing, not to mention those loafers, which had actual pennies in the slits. Hard to believe that Holland had gone from Gardner to him.

Rex gulped half his drink then slammed the glass down on the bar. "Did I tell you the big news in Mom's building?" he asked Walker. Of course he referred to his mother as "Mom"—not "my mother" or even "*my* Mom"—the same offhand way Holland called Peter Jennings *Peter.*

Brian appeared at Nina's side with a dishrag. He said hello as he blotted up a puddle of spilled beer at her elbow.

"I'm getting the story on Rex's building drama," she told him.

Brian nodded. "Another of his delightful anecdotes, I'm sure."

"This chick on the tenth floor's been screwing the super's son." Rex pursed his lips. "Puerto Rican punk, walks around with a ghetto blaster on his shoulder."

A few feet away, Alison collared a guy in a paisley bow tie: "*Playboy* or *Penthouse*? Spit or swallow?"

"Like we really need them ruining Sheeps Meadow every weekend with that 'music,'" Walker said. As he made those loathsome air quotes, Nina shuddered at the thought of his thing in her mouth. She imagined Gardner's—animate, ample, the color of cream—and felt herself blush, although she'd have to stop thinking of it as a thing if *their* thing progressed.

Rex continued his story. "So Puerto Rican shit-for-brains takes the girl to some squalid nightclub in Spanish Harlem." He had the arched black eyebrows of a cartoon villain. "And while he's in the bathroom, some other guy there 'assaults' her." Those air quotes again. "I don't know, asks her to dance, grabs her tits."

Brian made a disgusted face. Rex and Walker probably would have snickered at the *Beaver Hunt* photos, Nina thought, the girl trussed up like a pig, headed to slaughter. They'd probably have enclosed Stephanie's frat rape in those same sardonic air quotes.

"Bitch freaks out and suddenly it's this huge deal. They fired the super yesterday, and now Mom says he's threatening to sue the board for 'discrimination.'" Rex lit a cigarette with a gold lighter that Nina instantly recognized as Holland's. She squinted at the engraved *H.H.N.,* then glanced at Brian.

He nodded, frowning.

"Gardner knows?" she asked.

He nodded again.

Which would explain the gravel in Gardner's voice outside when he told Holland to stay away from him. Their pity must be so galling, she and Rex in such *agony* over fucking him over—and now literally fucking.

"Holland said the parents will probably figure out how to turn this into a buck too. Between them and the super, Mom's maintenance will go through the roof."

"What's a girl from 850 Park doing with a super's son anyway?" Walker asked. He ran his hand through his hair and Nina was pleased to see his scalp glinting through. She imagined him bald by Christmas, everyone mocking his comb-over attempts.

Rex shrugged. "Spoiled kike decided she wanted to go slumming."

Nina went hot with shock. She'd never heard anyone say "kike" out loud. She opened her mouth but no sound came out: there was no breath in her body to make one, not that her brain was supplying any words.

Brian started toward them, but Alison got there first. "Spoiled kike right here!" Her face was flushed crimson, her eyes black as bullets. "Say it to my face, you Nazi dickweeds."

Rex's eyebrows shot up, a twitch of surprise before the haughtiness returned to smooth over his features.

"*Gay kaken ofn yahm,*" Alison hissed. "That's kike for *go fuck yourself.*"

Walker smirked uncomfortably as Alison turned on her heel and stalked away.

Next to Nina, Brian bristled. "I should kick those guys out."

"Don't make a worse scene," Nina pleaded. "They probably have to leave soon for a Hitler Youth meeting, anyway." She signaled the bartender to order a real drink. There was too much crashing around inside her for just a Pepsi, the old interloper shame that came and went but never fully disappeared. Her humiliation that it had taken Alison Bloch, of all people—who knew she was Jewish?—to call out Rex and Walker while Nina stood mute. Although didn't Alison know they weren't supposed to call attention to themselves?

Leigh came up on Brian's other side, her eyes drooping. "Where'd you disappear to?" she slurred at Nina.

For a second, Nina couldn't remember anything before three minutes ago, but then her hand instinctively floated to her cheek, Gardner's touch there from the alcove. Happiness pulsed away the lingering shame and revulsion. Rex and Walker were two lowly slugs sliming a trail at Gardner's feet. She stomped on them in her mind, watching their guts smear the cement.

"I've been right here," she told Leigh, "behind my invisible shield."

"Cool." Leigh smiled fuzzily. "I'm gonna take off."

"Where's Meredith?" Leigh and Meredith usually went home together since they lived on the same block.

"She left already. Squash in the morning. Or tennis. Something with a racket." Leigh rummaged through her open handbag. A comb and a lipstick clattered to the floor. "Whoopsie."

Brian bent to pick them up. "How are you getting home?"

She looked back and forth between him and Nina. "Hey! You guys gonna get together? You should get together!"

Brian blushed as he handed her the lipstick. Oh. Damn. Nina realized she'd had an inkling, but without the knowledge quite breaking the surface. Why couldn't Leigh have kept it to herself? Once an unrequited crush was out in the open, the friendship was doomed, choked by guilt up one side and resentment down the other.

"We're barely two feet apart," Nina said awkwardly. She waved her hand between them and Leigh grabbed for it, nearly taking a nosedive before Brian caught her. No way she'd make it home on her own. Nina pictured her wandering drunk down Lexington, stumbling into a stream of buses and cars.

"I'm going to take her," she told Brian. She wouldn't mind some fresh air herself; she could still come back here afterward. She just had to let Gardner know she wasn't leaving for good. "Will you watch her for a minute?" she asked, and parked Leigh on a stool under Brian's watch.

A quick trip to the ladies' room for a hit out of the coin purse. *I'm drunk again because . . . John Lennon's still fucking dead,* said the wall. Nina was definitely glad to not be drunk, that undignified state of chaotic impulses. Cocaine kept you so much more sober and self-contained: another reason to be grateful to Stephanie. She clicked her tongue as she planned a little speech about the alacrity of a co-caine high versus the messiness of inebriation for the next time she saw her.

She found Gardner at a small table in the back with Brian's father, playing poker and smoking cigars. Mr. Flanagan always sat in one of those fatherly folding lawn chairs, with a cordial expression on his face, but she'd detected a hard gleam in his eye after Leigh mentioned that *his* father, Brian's grandfather, had been a hit man in the IRA. She envied Brian working here, the white-hot center of Upper East Side social life, although she also wondered if he had much choice.

"I have to take my friend home," she told Gardner, "but I'll be—"

"Sorry I left you outside," he interrupted. His face was drawn. "Things are kind of complicated right now." He tossed two cards on the table with a tense snap of his wrist that called to mind Rex flick-ing Holland's lighter. Sympathy coursed through her.

"It's fine," she assured him. *See how uncomplicated things are with me?*

Mr. Flanagan dealt two cards, politely looking the other way. She appreciated the discretion, although she hoped he hadn't witnessed this scene play out between Gardner and a dozen other girls this week.

"I'll give you a call," Gardner said.

She nodded casually, like he'd be lucky to get through with guys calling her night and day. But sure: Give it a try.

She and Leigh crept through the dark apartment, trying not to wake Leigh's parents. Or at least Nina tried; Leigh kept bumping into furniture and whispering, "Shit!" at the decibel level of a screech. Nina followed a straight line down the hallway parquet, savoring her alertness and perfect balance.

At the Bancroft graduation, when her mother fell in the aisle, Nina had seen Leigh's parents in the next row glance down at her sprawled there, shaking their heads as in *Frances Jacobs, what an embarrassment.* If one of them were to emerge right now, Nina would slip soundlessly out the front door. Let Leigh fend for herself.

But they made it safely to her room. Nina steered Leigh onto the bed and pulled off her shoes. She didn't hear any rumblings to signal a pending upchuck, but she put a trash can near her head just in case. She sat at the foot of the bed, waiting for Leigh to pass out and looking at the postcard taped to her mirror, a sepia image of a stately brick mansion on Princeton's campus labeled "Cottage Club."

Leigh opened her eyes and followed Nina's gaze. "They just started taking women. I can't wait to bicker with them."

"If you want in, shouldn't you try to get along?"

"Bicker's what the clubs call 'rushing.'"

In the corners of the mirror were photographs of Meredith, the invite to Meredith's sweet sixteen, and a pink heart-shaped pennant embroidered with Meredith's initials.

Leigh opened her eyes again. "She said I'd never have gotten into Princeton if I weren't a legacy."

"Why do you listen to her? Anyway, who cares. I only got into Vanderbilt because I said I'm Native American."

"I thought you were Jewish."

"Remember in second grade, when she told everyone you gave her lice?"

"She says you have a Semitic nose." Leigh sat halfway up. "Hey, did you hear Caroline Kennedy just married a Jewish guy?"

"Astounding, isn't it," Nina said dryly.

"You know, Meredith's going through a lot right now. She cried when she didn't get into Princeton." Leigh teared up herself. "People don't realize how sensitive she is."

"Her and Leona Helmsley."

"I can't imagine not seeing her every day." Now the tears streamed down her cheeks. She curled onto her side and sobbed into the pillow.

What was going on here? Was this the alcohol or something else? Nina patted Leigh's bare foot, murmuring, "It's okay," and "Thanksgiving's just around the corner," while she contemplated the secrets people kept to themselves, and maybe also from themselves. She didn't come to any brilliant conclusions, though.

"Anyway," Leigh said between sobs, "I *did* give her lice."

Nina laughed as she got up and headed to the door. "Go to sleep. I'll call you tomorrow to make sure you're surviving your hangover." When she said "call," she thought of Gardner dialing her number. No reason to go back to Flanagan's now and risk becoming a nuisance. Not to mention the Gestapo brothers, who she'd rather not have to face again tonight.

———

One last cigarette on the way home, before she walked quietly past a dozing Jimmy in the lobby. Her parents should be asleep by now; she planned to just head to her room, take a Halcion, and drift off reading *The Easter Parade*, which began with the promising line: "Neither of the Grimes sisters would have a happy life." Her favorite kind of book, the bleak end laid out at the start so you didn't have to worry about an unpleasant surprise.

But inside the apartment, the lights were blazing and *La Traviata* was on the stereo. Her mother bustled around the living room, carrying a squat, square vase crammed with pink roses. Nina quickly poured a quarter-box of Dynamints into her mouth. Frances would have a conniption if she smelled smoke: she hated cigarettes as much as Pearl had.

Although the scent of all these roses should take care of whatever got past the Dynamints. Besides the pink ones, there were dozens of others around the living room in pitchers, glasses, jars, and a teakettle. Had Nina forgotten a party? Was the florist down the block going out of business? She had that trippy, dreamlike sensation of unreality.

Frances beamed when she spotted Nina in the doorway. "Shh," she whispered, even as a throng of violins wailed from the stereo. "Daddy's asleep." She placed the vase on a mirrored table in a corner of the room, then spread out her arms. "How does it look?"

Like the Rose Bowl Parade, Nina didn't say. She still wasn't sure if Frances's new ebullience could withstand teasing.

"It's Grandma's birthday tomorrow," Frances informed her. She carried a jar of white roses from the coffee table to the windowsill, teetering in her feather-toed satin slippers. "She adored roses. Remember that beautiful rosebush outside our house in Rockaway? And Grandpa always gave her roses on their anniversary. As you know, I almost named you Rose."

"Really?" Nina had never heard this.

"Your father talked me out of it. He didn't want you to have Rose Kennedy's bad luck." She glanced at the clock on the mantel. "I guess it's already tomorrow." She waved at the ceiling and her robe sleeve fell back; there was a pink scratch down her arm where she must have snagged herself on a thorn.

"Do you need some Mercurochrome?" Nina asked.

Frances ignored her, still focused on the ceiling. "Happy birthday, Mom. I hope you like your roses."

Nina waved also, to keep her company, but if Pearl was looking down at all, it was with disapproval. *How much money did you waste on those flowers? Do you think I can smell them from here?*

She said good night and started for her room, but when she looked back, Frances was sweeping rose petals off the coffee table into her hand, squatting like she had in the aisle at graduation with her camera before she lost her balance. Nina remembered the wave of humiliation that had broken over her as she watched her mother struggle to stand, how much she'd despised her fragility. Maybe Nina's protectiveness of Frances came from wanting to shield her mother from her own revulsion.

"Actually, I think I just got my second wind." She stuck out her hand for her mother to grab on to and hauled her to her feet. "Want some help?"

"*Yes.*" She clasped Nina's hand between hers in what felt like a grateful hand hug.

"Be right back." Nina raced to her bathroom and spilled out some coke on the edge of the sink, three times what she'd meant to. "Waste not, want not," she said out loud, with an attempt at Rose Kennedy's accent, her second Boston accent of the night. "My word," she added, "*whom* did my Caroline marry?" Lifting her nail to her nose, she pictured the ridge of Gardner's hand, his fingers on her cheek. A twinge of panic as it dawned on her that he didn't have her phone number. But then the coke kicked in and she laughed at her worried face in the mirror. She stuck out her tongue, bright red from the cinnamon Dynamints. Of course she would just call *him*. She snorted the rest of the coke.

Back in the living room, she was entirely invigorated. *La Traviata* soared. The roses seemed to have blown open. They were carmine and amethyst and cream shot through with magenta. Her mother came from the kitchen with an armful of ruby dazzlers.

"Everything's coming up roses!" Nina said.

"Sing out, Louise!" Frances replied in an Ethel Merman boom.

She stuck the roses in a porcelain pitcher. "You sound stuffed up. Do you have a cold? Do you need Sudafed? A warm bath?"

"I'm good. I'm great!" Her mind was full of exclamation points. If my brain had fingers, she thought, they'd be snapping!

Frances took out the tape recorder from a pocket in her robe and pressed Record. "What do you call a spy in a bathtub?" she asked. "Bubble 07."

"Are you recording that joke for posterity?"

"For my autobiography." She held the recorder close to her mouth. "I was known for my sense of humor even in my teens, often inter-jecting wry quips to lift the mood at somber events. My mother called me Henrietta Youngman."

"Really?" This sounded unlikely. But Nina's mind was too coke-jumpy to stay in one place. Already it had leapt from Pearl's birthday to her funeral, and now to a documentary she once saw in history class about death rituals. "In Madagascar," she told Frances, "they take the bones from the graves and wrap them in silk, so the dead won't get cold. In China, they have this kind of tissue paper called Joss paper. They make little houses and cars out of it that they set on fire on their deceased loved ones' birthdays, so they'll have nice things in the afterlife."

Her mother stared at her intently. Stop yammering, Nina told herself, and for God's sake, stop grinding your teeth.

Frances addressed her recorder: "Knowing nothing of these other cultures' burial rituals, I put a hundred dollars in singles in my mother's coffin, for tips in the afterlife. And a flashlight, just in case some of the passageways weren't lit."

"Interesting," Nina said, at a loss.

"I want Grandma to have roses," Frances said. "Let's burn some roses for her, like the Chinese."

"I'll find some tissue paper." Nina pictured them together at the kitchen table, folding intricate paper petals. It could become a shared pastime. *Mom and I like to do origami at night,* she would tell people. *It's this thing we do together.*

Frances pulled a handful of yellow roses out of the teakettle and dropped them to the rug. "She should have dozens to show off to her friends up there. *Their* kids probably forgot all about them the instant the will was settled." She dropped an armful of peach ones to the floor beside the yellow. Beads of water darkened the rug. "Go get the matches from the kitchen."

Did she mean burn the *actual* roses? "That's not how they did it in the documentary," Nina said, like that was why her mother shouldn't start a fire in the middle of the living room.

Frances tossed more roses to the carpet. The morning of Pearl's funeral, Nina had been sent to the hardware store for batteries; her mother had collapsed in frustrated tears when Nina brought back the wrong size. They must have been for the flashlight. Why hadn't Frances told her?

But she was telling her now. Or, at least, telling her something about grief, if Nina could just hang in and pay attention. And it wasn't like they were going out to the cemetery to dig up Pearl's bones.

Nina grabbed a pair of white roses and let them fall.

Frances laughed. She was swaying from foot to foot like her delight was so huge, it was pressing on her bladder. "I've never liked this rug," she said into the tape recorder. "However, your father's mother gave it to us as a wedding present. Grandma Ruth hadn't even heard of *Meet Me in St. Louis* before I mentioned it. How can you live in St. Louis and not know *Meet Me in St. Louis*?"

"*Clang, clang, clang went the trolley,*" Nina sang. Oh, the marvel of cocaine. Her voice was as strong and sweet as Judy Garland's.

"I said to Ruth, 'Creve Coeur' means broken heart—did you know *that* when you moved there?' She said, 'It may mean that in French, but not in English.'" Frances twirled her finger around her temple, as in *cuckoo.*

"Grandma Ruth isn't good with the truth."

"You're a poet and you don't even know it!" Frances laughed. "Now, go get the matches."

Could Frances be sleepwalking? Except her eyes were wide open.

"We can't," Nina said, although the funny thing was, she wouldn't mind seeing a rose on fire, the petals' steamy unfurling. "Not a whole mass of them," she added sensibly, as if any of this made sense. "How about we burn just one, from both of us? That's what the Chinese did with the Joss paper, just one, so it was more special."

But not in the living room, where the flames could leap from the rug to the curtains and take the whole building down.

She coaxed her mother to the kitchen. The counters were heaped with mounds of crumpled florist's paper and wet rubber bands and grimy plastic. Better clean that up before morning!

"The women in this family are the adventurous ones," Nina said, sniffing the rich musk of the rose she was holding. Ira was probably dreaming about tax regulations and IRS opinions.

Frances set the tape recorder on the edge of the sink and pressed Record. Then she took a box of wooden matches from one of the cabinets. She struck one against the box, its spark reflected in the window over the kitchen sink, lighting up the blurred outline of their faces. She launched into the "Happy Birthday" song with a bunch of dips and trills.

But when she held the match to the rose, the outermost petal merely shriveled. Another match: a little charring. Three more matches, the kitchen starting to stink of sulfur but the flower still refusing to catch fire. Selfish rose, Nina thought, pinching the stem in her fingertips. Stubborn as Pearl. Frances's mouth quivered at the corners. She held the next match so long it would have burned her thumb if Nina hadn't blown it out.

Then Nina remembered Meredith's birthday dinner last year at Maxwell's Plum. For dessert, a waiter brought a baked Alaska to the table, sprinkled it with liquor, and set it on fire.

She went to the cabinet above the fridge and pulled out the bottle of Smirnoff.

Frances brightened. "You're a genius." She added, with a teasing look, "How did you know where Dad keeps the vodka?"

"Lucky guess?"

Frances looked closely at her as she returned to the sink. "The secret life of Nina Rachel Jacobs. A riddle wrapped in a mystery inside an enigma."

"Isn't that Russia?" Nina asked through the sudden knot in her throat. She didn't think her mother even remembered her middle name, much less was aware of another part of her in the shadows.

Frances uncapped the vodka bottle. Alcohol, like aged cheese and citrus fruits, was a bad mix with her antidepressants, so Nina had never seen her drink, let alone swig straight out of a bottle, which she did, shockingly, now—twice. She passed the bottle to Nina, who gulped a mouthful, then picked up a fresh red rose and sprinkled some vodka on its petals. She stepped back to admire how the droplets resembled dew.

"More!" Frances windshield-wiped her arm to pantomime pouring. Nina tipped the bottle over the rose to soak it. Even with half the vodka landing in the sink, the rose was dripping wet. She didn't remember the baked Alaska quite this drenched.

"I hope this is safe," she said.

"Safe is for sissies, my angel."

Rules are for chumps and suckers, Nina thought. She pictured Gardner watching this scene unfold as if on a screen, taking note of Nina's shadow self. Then she pictured him in an empty theater, pining like David in *Endless Love.*

Frances closed her eyes and addressed the ceiling: "Mother. On this day of days, we send you a token of our love and devotion."

Nina clasped her hands at her chest. Not with love or devotion, but gratitude: *Thank you for giving her to me,* she told Pearl. She leaned against her mother. Frances's swaying bumped her around a little, though it was still more contact than they'd had in years. *My angel.* Her cheek felt damp. What a sap! But when she brushed away the tear it turned out to be blood, a cut from a thorn she'd been too high to notice.

Frances struck a match while Nina held the flower over the sink. The rose was quickly encircled in gold flames. "My God," Frances whispered as the flower quivered and the petals charred around the edges.

It really did feel holy. Nina watched in awe. The scent of bark and leather, the coils of smoke and the climbing blue fire. When a smoldering petal fell to her wrist, she just shook it off. It was nothing, nothing—she hardly felt a thing. The crackling of the petals continued even after the flames died, the rose immolating from the inside out.

"You think she got it?" she asked her mother.

Frances smiled and lifted her recorder to her mouth. "'We shall see,' said the deaf-mute."

Chapter Twelve

All the next week, Nina's temp jobs kept starting promisingly, then falling off a cliff. There was the art gallery with skylights and polished concrete floors, where she ended up shut away in an airless back room, addressing envelopes. The law firm with the kindly office manager and ultracool Dictaphone machine, foot pedals like a bumper car, except Nina confused the forward and rewind so often, she snapped a tape with a legal brief—and was not so kindly dismissed. The dermatologist's office where she transferred patient records from old file cabinets to new ones, an easy and mindless task that allowed her to zone out and daydream about Gardner, his fingers touching her cheek, warm breath, mouths getting closer . . . until she tripped and dropped a batch of folders, and revolting photographs spilled out. An eyeball overlaid with a gelatinous puddle. Bubbling black splotches eating into a collarbone. A torso caked in some raging rash that set her scratching the rest of the day.

By comparison, the burn on her wrist was nothing, just a red smudge that stung under hot water but was otherwise easy to forget, like the details of the dreamlike rose-burning ceremony.

Friday morning, for a one-day stint at a clothing manufacturer's office, she put on her new stirrup pants and neon-yellow top from

Saks, where she and her mother had gone to purchase Nina's "college trousseau," which Frances insisted also include a sequined beret, a leopard-print bra that clipped closed in the front, mesh fingerless gloves, and a satin blazer with massive shoulder pads. Plus a small mountain of jeweled barrettes for herself, "mother of the freshman."

In the kitchen, before he left for work, Ira asked Nina if Frances seemed a "little speedy." "Have you noticed how she keeps saying 'however'?"

She did keep saying "however," so much that it had wormed its way into Nina's brain.

"The swaying?" he added. "The chattiness?"

The late-night flower-and-vodka bonfire? However, why say anything when no harm had come of it, and in fact it had turned out to be a "wow"-upside-down, laughter-with-a-*d* bonding thing?

"You said yourself she's always been quirky."

Ira considered. "Well, I suppose. Did I ever tell you that a week after we got engaged, she kept a date with a boy from Amherst because she'd accepted months before?"

Interesting, but not necessarily what Nina would have categorized as quirky. Quirky was Frances in a pet store last weekend holding up a kitten and squeaking to the puzzled customers: "I regret that I have but nine lives to give to my country."

Quirky, and sweet: how, throughout that day, she kept stopping to beam at Nina, eyes shining like she couldn't believe this magical creature before her, saying, "You're so pretty," and "You're so smart," and "How did I get so lucky?"

A little speedy, maybe. But what was the alternative? Yank her back down to earth and bury her alive?

"Maybe all that time in bed," Nina said to her father, "she stored up extra energy that's now kind of spilling over."

Ira perked up. "You might be on to something. All that pent-up energy has to go somewhere."

At the clothing manufacturer's office, Nina sat behind the reception desk, mulling over her father's concerns while she answered phones and transferred calls. Not so long ago, it was Nina worrying about her mother's new high-octane energy, but now it had more than grown on her. Maybe her father just needed reassurance. On her way out the door to work, Nina had snuck a look at today's love note:

August 1, 1986

High 80, low 68

U.S. and Japan agree to settle semiconductor trade dispute. Nicholas Nickleby coming to Broadway. Our Exxon stock finally on the way back up.

My dearest hummingbird: good news all around! I'll call at lunchtime.

She'd been content at the reception desk the rest of the morning, thinking how nice it was to be the locus of power, but when she got back from lunch, the atmosphere had darkened. Everyone's office doors were shut. Soon a tall, tense woman emerged from behind a closed door to ask her if a Mr. Weber had called for Mr. Greer. A few minutes later, an older man with chunky onyx cufflinks came out of his office, to ask if Rita had asked if Mr. Weber had called for Mr. Greer. After he left, the tall woman came back and asked if Frank had been out to ask what she'd asked about. Then an older man came out of *his* office to ask if Rita and Frank were pestering her about each other's phone calls. Also, had Mr. Weber called for Mr. Greer?

"It's like one of those crazy SAT questions," Stephanie yelled over the jukebox at Flanagan's. Tonight was her first time here; she was still spending weekends in Hewlett, but she had to do inventory at Maison Rouge tomorrow, first thing in the morning. "If a train leaves Phoenix at four p.m. traveling two miles per hour, and another leaves New Orleans at eleven a.m. going thirty miles per hour, which conductor is vegetarian?"

"The radius times the hypotenuse," Nina said. "Obviously." She and Stephanie stood beneath an archway in the back, in a pocket of air, fanning themselves with their hands. You'd think people would be away on an August weekend, but the bar was packed. The only one not here was Gardner.

Or, thankfully, Rex or Walker.

"I just wish I'd given Gardner my number," Nina said. Those moments in the alcove last Friday night seemed like something she'd made up.

"Why not just call *him*?" Stephanie said.

"I don't want to seem pushy."

"Would he seem pushy if he called you?"

As if it were the same thing. She took out her coin purse, replenished by Stephanie via Damian, and they each did a quick hit. She wondered how she'd find a source in Nashville, and how she'd afford it without her temp jobs. She'd seen in the *Post* that some rich admirer had set up a trust fund for the model with the slashed face: $20,000 a year for life. In the cover spread, her expression was jaunty; she'd made a fresh start. She'd moved to a rental in Soho, far from her old building and its psychotic landlord, who was in jail awaiting trial. NEW LEASE! the headline said. There she was on her new bed, surrounded by the stuffed animals her fans had sent to the hospital.

Twenty thousand would buy a lot of cocaine. Nina imagined herself on her dorm room bed, surrounded by chubby teddy bears and floppy-eared bunnies stuffed with powder.

A girl in an eyelet camisole bumped Nina with a sharp, spindly shoulder. Her date, in a pink bow tie, crossed his arms when "Like a

Virgin" came on the jukebox. "Why does Madonna think anyone wants to hear her sing about what a slut she is?"

Nina glanced at Stephanie and pretended to stick a finger down her throat. She wasn't sure if she wanted her to like Flanagan's or to confirm that everyone here was awful.

"It's a preppy tidal wave in here," Stephanie snorted. "How have you managed not to get dragged under?"

"I think you rescued me in the nick of time." Nina pointed to her new stirrup pants and decidedly unpreppy Fiorucci shirt. She also had on a new purple lipstick, Violet Kiss, which she initially misread as Violent Kiss when she tried it on at Saks. "Although in my defense, when the girls at Bancroft used to make their *Top Ten Preppiest* lists, I was never on them."

"Ugh, Olympics for debutantes." Stephanie smiled, but her mood was low. She'd told her mother about her father's engagement to Mary Kay, and the call had gone exactly as expected: Stephanie to blame, as if she'd picked out the ring herself.

Now she looked toward the bar. "You think they can make a Slippery Nipple here?"

Behind them, Meredith said, "I didn't know anyone actually drank those."

Nina turned. Meredith and Leigh were studying Stephanie like a specimen, their gazes moving from her moussed-out hair to her cropped Run-D.M.C. T-shirt.

Stephanie gestured to herself and smiled sweetly at Meredith. "Hi. I'm Anyone."

Nina stepped in and introduced them. She started to describe how they'd met, but Meredith interrupted to tell Nina, "I played this in your honor." She pointed upward where "Like a Virgin" still clanged in the air.

Stephanie glanced at Nina then back to Meredith. "That's funny. I have a sudden urge to play 'The Bitch Is Back.'"

Nina tried not to look too pleased at Meredith's shock. No one ever called her out on anything. Although her shock was replaced with a smirk when Stephanie pulled a pack of Eves out of her bag. The arch of her eyebrows said, *Of course: bridge and tunnel.*

"I didn't know anyone actually smoked those."

"They light up and everything," Nina said.

Nina took hold of Stephanie to lead her to the bar, wishing she'd opted for Yorkville Debate Club tonight. Stained walls and colostomy bags were better than Meredith's scrutiny.

But Stephanie wasn't going anywhere. She stuck an Eve between her lips. "Speaking of which, got a light?" she asked Meredith, more of an order than a question.

Meredith hesitated. Nina started to reach for her own lighter. But then Meredith—frowning but wide-eyed as if caught in a trap, Stephanie's gaze trained on her—pulled hers out of her purse. She held it out for Stephanie, who deliberately dropped her hands to her sides and stood calmly waiting.

A prickling across Nina's skin, a jitter of excitement that was part cocaine and part the thrill of watching someone turn the tables on Meredith for once.

Sullenly, but as if mesmerized, Meredith thumbed the lighter, and the flame caught, a few inches from Stephanie's cigarette. Stephanie stood still, watching her. Meredith's eyes darted as she raised the flame to the tip of Steph's cig.

Stephanie inhaled, then blew out three perfect smoke rings. "Thanks," she said, in a voice that made clear she'd received an apology, whether Meredith intended one or not.

Nina hid her smile. Gloating was tacky, and anyway, Meredith looked not only dazed but also in some way diminished. It was hard not to feel a twinge of pity.

Leigh grabbed Nina's wrist. "Doesn't Meredith's skin look amazing?" she asked. She was practically pleading, her fingers squeezing hard, right on Nina's burn. "We got facials at Elizabeth Arden yesterday. Isn't she glowing?"

Like uranium, Nina thought. "Like the sun," she said aloud, although Meredith gave her a steely stare as if she'd read her mind. Nina grabbed Stephanie's hand. "Let's get you that Slippery Nipple," she said, steering her through the crowd to the bar, ready to tell off anyone who looked at her sideways. But people cleared a path without incident. The bartender looked pleased when they ordered Slippery Nipples—probably his first chance to make one at Flanagan's—and fetched them a clean ashtray. He even presented them with free shots of sambuca while he made their drinks. Nina held the cool glass to her burn while Stephanie, seemingly unfazed, downed her shot and studied the tin ceiling.

"People used to paint these white, to look like the fancy plasterwork in European mansions, but bare metal is so much cooler."

Nina nodded along, going for unfazed also, except she was too impressed by the Meredith takedown to maintain the pretense. "That thing with the lighter—did you come up with it on the spot?"

Stephanie shrugged. "When it comes to bullies, you can't flinch. Don't let them smell fear."

Meredith as a bully: Why hadn't Nina ever seen her that way?

"What's the story with the other chick," Stephanie said, "the one in love with the mean one?"

"Wait—what?" Nina felt her jaw drop while at the same time picturing Leigh's passionate pillow-sobbing last week. God, she was slow.

"Speaking of love." Stephanie was looking behind her. "Look what the cat dragged in."

She'd ponder Leigh later. Gardner was here, leaning against the wall beside the bar, beneath the Spanish bullfight poster, looking restlessly around the room. *Hey,* he mouthed when he saw her, and she casually mouthed it back, as if it didn't feel like that bull was goring her.

"Good to see a couple of friendly faces," he said when she and Stephanie made their way to him.

What face wasn't friendly to Gardner? All around them, people smiled and waved for his attention. Campbell Hughes had her eyes trained on him and her hands steepled at her heart, lips moving in what looked like a prayer.

Still, he looked grim. His jaw was clenched. "First time here?" he asked Stephanie.

Nina wished she didn't feel the need to study them for any hint of chemistry.

"Yup." Stephanie ground out her cigarette. "I like the decor anyway. Especially those." She gestured to the vintage photographs on the walls.

"That one's my favorite." Gardner pointed to a black-and-white photo of a crowd in the shadow of a brick building, staring up at a man in a straitjacket suspended upside down from a crane high above the street.

Nina squinted. "Houdini?"

"Greatest escape artist ever," Gardner said. He rolled his shoulders and stretched his arms. "God, I hate this scene," he said, surveying the room. "I don't know why I still come here."

"Where else would you go?" Nina said. How would she find him if he stopped coming here?

"I don't know. Palladium, Area. Meet some new people."

What new people?

"I hear Limelight's pretty cool," Stephanie said. "It was a church before they turned it into a club."

He stiffened. "You couldn't pay me to set foot in a church, even an ex-church." His eyes darted around the bar before settling back on Nina. "Hey." He grabbed her arm with surprising urgency. "You got any blow?"

"As a matter of fact—"

"Let's go to the park."

While he ordered a Heineken, Stephanie leaned closer to Nina and offered to beg off with an excuse about her early inventory at the store tomorrow.

Nina shook her head. "I didn't invite you here to ditch you." And, she was pleased to have noted, the energy between Steph and Gardner had dropped to an ordinary level. "But is the park safe at night? I mean, a kid shot a cop there like right at sunset last week."

Stephanie considered. "I've always wanted to go at night, but if it doesn't seem safe—"

Safe is for sissies, Nina reminded herself. Rules are for chumps and suckers. "Well, the policeman *was* questioning the kid about a stolen bike," she conceded. "It wasn't like the kid just walked up and shot him out of nowhere. I guess no one will bother us if we don't bother them."

Anyway, who would mess with Gardner? Beer bottle in hand, taller than almost everyone else, aloof, self-possessed, he started through the crowd, which unsurprisingly, parted for him, and for Nina and Stephanie in his wake. As they walked out together, half the girls' smiles collapsed. Campbell Hughes flinched like she'd been gut-punched. Minnie Potter grit her teeth in frustration. Alison Bloch followed them out, then jumped onto Gardner's back and locked her arms around his neck.

"Carry me!" she yelled.

Gardner wrenched her hands apart and shook her off. "Not to-night," he said brusquely, and kept walking. Nina shot her a consol-ing look—she'd warmed to her after seeing her call out Rex—but Alison eyed her with loathing.

"Ouch," Stephanie said as she and Nina started to follow Gard-ner down the block. "If looks could kill, you'd be on your way to the morgue."

"Let's hope she doesn't know where I live," Nina said, justified again in her dislike. She looked behind her in time to see Alison storm back inside, nearly slamming the door on Brian, who was on his way out. When he caught up to them, Nina hung an arm around his shoulder, like a sister or a buddy, trying not to be self-conscious after last week's awkward moment between them. He answered with a chummy elbow to her ribs.

"Coming to the park?" Gardner asked him.

"Seriously?" Brian said. "Now? Did you hear Bagley Adams got mugged at the boat pond the other day? Like three in the afternoon. They put a gash in his head with his own tennis racket."

Gardner laughed. "Bagley shuffles around like a guy who's asking to get mugged."

Brian turned to Nina with a look that said, *We're the prudent ones here.* Which felt a little too close to, *We're the prudes here.* She wasn't exactly thrilled about wandering around the park at night—she wasn't even thrilled about the possibility of grass stains on her new pants—but who wanted to be in that club?

They headed west on Eighty-Fourth Street. "Show no fear," Stephanie advised Nina. "The park zombies only fuck with you if you show fear." She looped her arm through Stephanie's as they walked a few steps behind Gardner and Brian, reminiscing about their first encounter, Stephanie's water gun and the "Ms. Bitch" guy, who apparently had gotten a strong whiff of Nina's fear. When they entered the park behind the Metropolitan Museum, she willed herself to not emit any apprehension atoms, although it was hard since the park was pitch-black, and the silence so absolute that if she didn't turn to look, she could convince herself the rest of the city had been obliterated by a nuclear warhead. In *The Easter Parade*, Emily had nighttime sex in Central Park with a soldier, but that was 1942 and the park was full of soldiers necking with girls on benches. There were no visible signs of life here tonight, necking or otherwise.

"How come no one says 'necking' anymore?" she whispered to Stephanie.

"Actually, Damian told me when the cartel slits a dealer's throat for stealing, it's called necking."

"Not exactly what I meant," she made herself say in her regular voice, "but thanks for creeping the hell out of me." The park's dead silence didn't seem to spook Stephanie at all: she spoke at normal volume, like they were back in Times Square at the sex shop, where, come to think of it, Nina had also whispered.

Gardner led them down a path past a row of benches, and for the first time, Nina understood what it meant to *penetrate* the dark: it seemed as tangible and alive as a physical entity.

"There's a spot I like up ahead," he said, but when they reached the lawn behind the Met, next to the glowing Temple of Dendur, Nina slowed. At least from here they could still see a sliver of street.

"Mind if we stop for a sec?" she asked Gardner. "It's so pretty."

"Getting a little spooked?" he said good-naturedly. He sat on the lawn and smiled up at her. "Here's fine for now."

She sat beside him. Stephanie lay down on Nina's other side and fluttered her arms and legs like she was making snow angels in the grass. "Why would anyone call their kid Bagley?" she asked no one in particular.

"Mother's maiden name," Brian said.

"In that case," Stephanie said, "call me Abruzzo from now on."

Nina took out her coin purse. She wanted to hand Gardner the baggie to lay out the coke, the way a woman hands a man a jar if the lid is stuck, or how at restaurants her father asked her and Frances what they wanted and then ordered for them when the waiter came. But she worried Brian might feel slighted, so instead she decided to just use her nail and then pass the bag around. Soon the dark felt inky and romantic, especially here beside the museum's glass wall and the incandescent pyramids inside. The sky curved over them like the domed lid of a cake platter.

Stephanie was talking with Brian about Flanagan's decor: "I was expecting chintz and duck prints."

Brian smiled. "We're not the Polo store, Abruzzo."

Gardner sat back on his elbows and stretched out his legs, and

Nina shifted an infinitesimal bit closer. He was staring up at the sky, so she stared with him. Under the vast void, no buildings to break up the expanse, she had a sudden revelation that she felt an urgent coke-fueled need to share with him. "When you recognize your minuteness and understand how inconsequential you are, anything you do is equivalent to the shiver of a flea—"

"What?"

She begged herself to zip it, but the coke made her blab on. "Nothing you do matters—it's minuscule, like when a flea shivers."

He smiled. "Sure."

"I mean, you're free," she said.

"Free to . . ." He flicked his gaze to her mouth, then back to her eyes. "What?"

She was aware of Brian leaning toward them, trying to eavesdrop, even while Stephanie grilled him about the pendant lights above the bar.

"I wanted to call you this week," Nina quietly told Gardner, "but I didn't have your number."

"I'm in the book. William Reed, Ninety-First Street." He drank from the Heineken.

"Oh," she said, as if this hadn't occurred to her and she had *no idea* he lived on Ninety-First Street. "Is William your dad?"

"If you can call him that."

"Fuck," Stephanie suddenly yelped, "does anyone have a tissue?" Her nose was dripping blood. She pulled up her T-shirt to blot it. As the white cotton hem went red, Gardner scooted behind her, pressed the palm of one hand against the crown of her head, and instructed her to tilt her head back. He pinched her nostrils shut with the other hand. Cradled like that, Stephanie looked like a wounded animal tended to by a careful, caring owner. Nina felt faint with envy. Stephanie noticed, moved her head away from Gardner's hands, and said: "I think *Nina* has a nosebleed."

Nina laughed, embarrassed but pleased as Gardner moved behind her. Of course, her nose wasn't bleeding, but "I do have a little headache," she hinted. Brian looked away and scooted himself just out of the circle. Gardner's fingers pressed into her scalp and she leaned back into them, tingling behind her eyes.

Stephanie worked on reengaging Brian while Nina pointed out a hill across the park to Gardner and couldn't stop herself from describing the first time she saw him, when she was eleven. "It was sixth grade, and there was a huge snowstorm and all the cars were buried and even the buses stopped running. A pack of us met up with you and your Buckley friends, and we walked across Seventy-Ninth Street to sled down that hill. You had on a green down jacket with a Killington lift ticket clipped to the zipper."

She pictured her sixth-grade self, pudgy cheeks and the limp, inch-long bangs she'd cut herself. *Look at us now,* she told that girl: *Gardner's fingers in our hair.*

Behind her, he lit a cigarette, tipped back his head, and blew smoke at the sky. She looked up to watch it swirl in the breeze and then evaporate. The lights of an airplane blinked near the moon.

"I miss that jacket," he said.

"You were carrying a stick. Every time we passed a buried car, you drew a, um, penis on it in the snow. We all thought you were the coolest."

"You sure that's what I drew? Not—?" His hand came around her hip, moved across her thigh. A sensation of heat, and thickening, between her legs as his fingers came closer. She was too twitchy to sit. She jumped to her feet, unsure what to do standing there, looming over the others, and looked up again at the airplane. A wave of propulsion rocked her as if she were flying with it. The plane was miles above, but she imagined the passengers looking out their windows and seeing her below.

Without thinking, she pulled up her T-shirt and unclipped her leopard-print bra.

"Hey!" Brian said behind her, sounding startled.

"Let us see!" Gardner shouted.

She would if she had real guts, but she didn't. Not yet. Maybe soon. Still, the air on her breasts felt cool and sweet. She arched her neck and threw back her arms. This body was *hers*, every bone and organ and drop of blood. In the airplane, a hundred pairs of invisible eyes ranged up and down her fluorescent skin, just able to make her out from the night sky.

"Nice tits," a voice called from the darkness . . . Oh! Oh, shit. The voice—hoarse, male—came from behind a clump of bushes a few yards ahead. Nina yanked down her top and squinted into the darkness. Someone was out there, moving.

Stephanie got up and flung her arm around Nina. "Nicer than your dick, you dick!" she called back at the guy.

With Stephanie beside her, Nina's alarm turned to giddiness. "Yeah," she yelled, "let's see your little baby weenie!" She whooped like a fan at a football game. "Whip it out if you can find it!"

"Guys, shh." Brian got to his feet. "I see him, right over there." He sounded nervous. Why hadn't he stayed back at the bar? He pointed to a shape popping up and down behind the bushes like a jack-in-the-box. "I think it's just a homeless guy. We should leave him alone."

Gardner stood now, gripping the neck of his Heineken in his fist like a club. He walked to the edge of the lawn and smacked the bottle against a rock, the sharp crack puncturing the silence. The bottom sheared off, leaving the edges of the neck jagged. He held it up.

"You guys want to see his dick? I'll get it for you."

Nina froze. Stephanie sucked in her breath.

"Come on out, asshole," Gardner called, "or I'm coming in."

"Let's just *go*," Brian said.

Nina was so ignited with coke and adrenaline that her vision was breaking up. She could hardly tell what she was looking at. There was the guy across the path, bobbing up again from behind the bushes, lifting his arms—but they looked like wings, with something webbing them. There was Gardner starting across the path, white shirt, summer tan . . . but also *not*-Gardner, slitted eyes and tensed shoulders, and the bottle's severed neck, its sharp points glinting where the moonlight hit.

"Stop!" Brian called after him.

But he kept walking toward the bushes. Then out of the blackness flew something large and dark, a flapping sound like a giant bird. Nina grabbed Stephanie's arm before she saw it was just a blanket, landing at Gardner's feet. The homeless guy's blanket. She could just make out someone running off into the night.

Gardner turned and saw them all staring at him, although it was Brian he addressed. "For fuck's sake. I wasn't really going to cut the guy's dick off."

"What *were* you going to do?" Brian asked quietly.

"I was kidding," Gardner said with an angry laugh.

"Obviously," Nina said, even if it hadn't been so obvious to her racing heart. That not-Gardner had seemed so real, a version who could charge into the bushes with a broken bottle. But now he was fading as the actual Gardner looked at the broken bottle in his hand with a kind of wonder, like someone else had put it there. "I can't believe that even worked."

Brian drifted closer as if to protect her. She walked a few steps away. We're both so easily rattled, she thought with irritation. We ought to be baby rattles.

"Impressive Heineken shiv," Stephanie said to Gardner.

Nina hoped to one day possess an ounce of her cool.

"I'm lucky I didn't slice off half my hand." Gardner laughed, but when he glanced back at Brian's pinched look of disapproval, the anger returned. He launched the broken bottle at the boulder. Nina willed herself to not flinch as the glass smashed.

Following him out of the park, walking past the museum the way they'd come in, she found herself stroking the burn on her wrist. Everything felt eerily primeval, the burn, and the sprinkle of glass, like an offering, in the shadow of the ancient temple.

———

On the way back to Flanagan's, she and Brian wound up walking behind Stephanie and Gardner. Hunched and scowling, Brian kicked bits of trash into the street. He stopped abruptly on the corner of Madison, even though the light was green.

"So listen," he said urgently to Nina.

Nina reluctantly stopped with him, even as she watched Stephanie and Gardner pull farther away, Gardner leaping to smack the hems of building awnings as they walked underneath.

Brian paused for a long moment, looking down at the sidewalk. He was clicking his teeth and Nina realized she was doing the same, like they were in a duet, and bit her tongue to stop it.

"I'm listening," she said tersely. Her rudeness embarrassed her, and she even disliked Brian a little for provoking it, but she couldn't seem to contain herself.

He clutched his hands together, rubbing one thumb with the other like a worried old man. "I just want you to be careful."

"About what?"

"Let's just say, people are kind of concerned about Gardner."

"What people?" Nina snorted, remembering Holland's Marmee voice.

"Holland says he stole her mother's credit card."

"Oh, please." Her irritation increased as she saw Stephanie and Gardner stop and turn in concert, like a couple, scanning the block. Would Gardner think Nina was purposely lingering behind with Brian—that she might even like him better? "Holland will say anything to make Gardner look bad and herself look good. Anything to justify ditching him for Rex."

"She said he tried to use the card at Mortimer's."

"I rest my case!" Nina practically shouted. Mortimer's was a restaurant known for ladies who lunched—a few blocks from her apartment building, so Nina always saw them outside, frail stalks in bouclé suits and Gucci bags that her mother both mocked and emulated. "As if Gardner would ever set foot in that place."

Brian looked at her in disbelief: "That was after he bought sunglasses, sneakers, and a stereo with it. Do you even know why he was kicked out of BU?" His habit of lowering himself to her eye level by standing with his legs apart suddenly struck her as highly unmasculine.

"He wasn't kicked out. He transferred."

Gardner and Stephanie had made a U-turn back up Eighty-Fourth Street and were yelling, "Come on, you two!" as if Brian and Nina were now the second couple.

Brian pointedly turned his back on Nina and rushed ahead. "Wait up, Abruzzo," he called to Stephanie. Nina made a face at his back, the receding dingy gray shirt. Gardner waited in the middle of the block for her to catch up, his white shirt a spot of light in the dark street. He had a loose-limbed way of standing as if he were slouching against a wall, even when there was only air behind him. His smile was both knowing and playful. No way he'd bother to take someone's credit card: it was too banal. His transgressions—the Spence bomb scare, the Tavern on the Green break-in—were so much more creative.

Walking beside him, her head barely reaching his shoulder, she wondered how couples held hands when they weren't even close to the same height, and worried that the unevenness signified a deeper mismatch. After a while, he said, "I like how you flashed that guy." She'd flashed an airplane, the homeless guy the unintended beneficiary, not that she corrected him. He jumped to tap another awning, his shirt rising as he raised his arms above his head. The hard little muscles at his waist, the slash of hair—her hands practically shook with the desire to touch.

As they neared Second Avenue and Flanagan's came into view, her stomach tightened: once they got inside, he'd be swallowed up by the crowd. Already she could see Alison Bloch peering through the window. They reached the row of tenement buildings down the block from the bar, the iron gate and the steps down to the alcove where they'd almost kissed. At this rate, she'd be a virgin at her college graduation. She had to do something. She grabbed his arm, probably too hard, and shouted, "Our spot!"

He met her eyes. "You guys go ahead," he called to Brian and Stephanie. "We'll meet you inside."

Behind Brian, Stephanie gave Nina a thumbs-up.

Gardner pulled her down the steps to the alcove. There, among some paint cans and a dumpster and a broken barbecue grill, he finally kissed her. His whole mouth on hers, his teeth and tongue. Violent Kiss. She hadn't known he'd involve so *much* of himself. If she didn't have her arms around his shoulders, she might have fallen down. Or floated up. She tasted beer and got a quick image of the broken bottle and its sharp, gleaming edges, and a thrill of danger corkscrewed through her. At the same time, she tasted a clean, pure quality that she understood to be *him*, his essence, like the fresh taste of water after a night of drinking. Then she entered a state of mindlessness, aware only that he was breathing hard, which meant she must be doing something right.

He stepped her backward against the side of the building. The corner of a brick dug into her spine and she tried to subtly twist away without interrupting anything. He pressed harder until she worried the corner would puncture her skin. She arched her back, inadvertently grinding her breasts into his chest. *Signal malfunction,* as she'd heard the conductor say on the subway this morning, because suddenly his hand was up her skirt, clutching between her legs.

Alarmed, electrified—she flinched and pulled back by instinct. He dropped his hand. Come on, she told herself. This is what you've dreamed of. Close your eyes and jump.

"I'm sorry," she stammered. "I'm not, um, I mean—"

He looked confused and a little impatient, which she couldn't exactly blame him for after that cogent explanation. She steeled herself as he cleared his throat.

"You're really sexy," he said.

"No, *you*." She was so relieved, it came out as a sigh. She put her face forward, eyes closed, to resuscitate the make-out.

But he'd already recalibrated. "To be continued," he said teasingly. "Let's get inside."

She'd been the one to put a stop to things, but she still felt horribly rebuffed. "I thought you hate it in there." She tried not to sound whiny.

He shrugged. "Where else am I going to go?"

A group of guys in ties and suspenders were crowded around the jukebox. Nina would bet they were investment bankers at one of the fancy uptown firms. They had jutting chins and tortoiseshell glasses. They were downing Woo Woo shots and singing along at the top of their lungs to "Surfin' Safari." Rex Parrish was right in the center of them, also in a tie and suspenders. It was after midnight. As if none of them had time to change before they came here.

Gardner saw them, too, and muttered "Fuck me" as he pushed through the crowd to the back of the bar, leaving Nina behind. Still, she had the sense of a dotted line running between them that lengthened or contracted to keep them connected. She found Stephanie leaning against a column, blowing smoke rings.

"I suck," Nina said. "I'm so sorry. I said I wouldn't ditch you."

"Are you kidding? That's exactly what I wanted to happen. Speaking of which, *did* it?"

"Depends on what you mean by *it*." She was a little delirious: Had she really just made out with Gardner Reed? Her lips felt swollen. Her mouth tasted like his mouth. "I mean, we kissed, but I kind of freaked out, right as things were amping up."

"Totally natural," Stephanie assured her. "I'm sure you did amazing."

Nina took a drag of Stephanie's Eve. What was wrong with her, thinking Stephanie might like Gardner? She'd finally found a true-blue kindred spirit and she couldn't put aside her jealousy. Coke paranoia: she had to watch out for that.

Stephanie exhaled a stream of smoke as her face clouded. "Hey, what's with Brian? He was all weird about Gardner. I thought they were close."

"Did he say something to you?"

"Just that Gardner's going through a hard time, and we should pay attention."

"Pay attention to what?"

"Who knows." Stephanie laughed. "Poor Brian might be a tiny bit jealous." She sang the chorus of the Pat Benatar song at Nina: *"You're a heartbreaker, dream maker, love taker—"*

"Yeah, right." She felt herself blush. "Did he tell you about the thing with the credit card?"

Stephanie shook her head. When Nina filled her in, she said, "I don't know, Gardner seems too smart for that. He knows he'd get caught, so why bother? There's enough legit ways to get money. Like, Patrick's friend Danny donates sperm three times a week, forty dollars a pop. The downside is, Danny's a moron so there could be a hundred little morons running around Woodmere."

Nina had managed to forget about Patrick for the past couple of hours. With his name now hanging in the air, it seemed awkward not to acknowledge his existence. She came up with the most innocuous thing she could think of: "I bet you'll miss him this weekend."

Stephanie shrugged. "We've been fighting a lot." She clenched her jaw and sniffed so hard it had to have hurt. "He'd hate this anyway." She pointed at the suspendered bankers, throwing back shots and high-fiving each other. "If only we could move Paddy McGee's to the city."

"Maybe we could find something like it," Nina said.

Stephanie brightened.

"Let's scout it out sometime," Nina added, wondering what

Gardner would think of Patrick. They had a similar watchfulness, the way they scoped a room and seemed to position themselves in it, although she couldn't imagine them being friends. Maybe Gardner could at least smooth Patrick's edges a little.

A couple of the bankers bumped chests midair and roared like they'd trounced a pack of wolves. She spotted Gardner leaning against the wall under the Houdini photo, watching them. She pictured that spot by the Oyster Bar in Grand Central, where you could whisper something into one end of the archway, and someone at the other end could hear it, the sound waves rippling along the arch. "You're so much better than them," she whispered now.

Rex bellowed "Rock Lobster!" at the jukebox like it should perform for him on command. Nina pointed him out to Stephanie.

"*That's* Herr Rex?" Stephanie asked.

Nina nodded, a clot of repulsion in her throat.

"God, those loafers," Stephanie said. "Those pleated pants. Those everything."

Gardner's mouth was set in a sneer. He pushed off the wall and started toward the bankers.

"Uh-oh," Stephanie said.

Inexplicably, Nina checked his hand for the Heineken shiv, even though she'd seen him smash it to pieces in the park. Brian, outside the men's room, looked uneasy too. She couldn't help but resent him for planting questions in her head.

Rex turned when Gardner tapped him on the shoulder: smarmy eyebrows, striped suspenders, deserving the same fate as Craig Bishop, in Nina's opinion. If only someone other than Gardner could dispense it. He was already in enough trouble.

"Don't," she whispered.

Gardner leaned in and said something. Rex said something back, and then Gardner calmly turned and headed out the door. That was it. No yanking or twisting arms, no face-slamming into the bar. Rex's expression was a mix of relief, confusion, and wariness. Considering

Rex's loathsomeness, Nina was impressed by Gardner's restraint. And, as if he'd heeded her whisper, proud of her own small, imaginary part in protecting him from disaster.

But as the minutes passed with no sign of his return, pain jabbed her stomach. Stephanie must have noticed her wince. "You okay?" she asked as she took out her coin purse and dipped her pinkie nail inside.

Nina nodded, remembering what time of month it was. "Must be my mittelschmerz."

Stephanie followed Nina's gaze to the door. She smiled sweetly. "Or maybe it's love. What's that guy with the mullet sing? Love hurts."

"I thought it stinks."

"Different mullet."

Nina laughed and clutched her stomach. Out of the corner of her eye, she saw Leigh stagger out the door with a skeevy-looking guy who looked familiar. It was the ponytail that jogged her memory, the fried yellow strands. Victor, the guy from the bandshell she'd seen Gardner arguing with at the Palladium. Though by the time she placed him, he and Leigh were gone.

A little while later, when Nina went into the ladies' room, she recognized Meredith's Bermuda bag and red Ferragamos under the closed stall door.

"I wish you'd keep an eye on Leigh," Nina said. It was just the two of them in the restroom, the drug-using outer-borough skanks apparently gone for the night. "Did you know she left with that creepy ponytail guy?"

"Why don't *you* keep an eye on her?" Meredith's voice sounded pinched. "Mine are kind of busy right now."

"Your eyes?" Nina asked as the stall door opened and Meredith emerged. Busy or not, her eyes were noticeably red, and her nose running. Had she been crying? Over Stephanie and the lighter? Since when was Meredith so sensitive? Nina felt a pinch of guilt over how she'd reveled in Meredith's defeat, along with a soft spot for her surprising vulnerability.

"I'm sorry about before, with my friend."

Meredith impatiently waved that away as she moved past Nina to the sink. She turned on the water and glanced at the mirror above it, then froze as she scrutinized her reflection. She brought her wet fingers to her cheekbones, digging into the hollows beneath.

"Do I look like I've lost weight?"

"You look great," Nina said reflexively. Not true. Meredith's face was tight with anxiety, her eyes tearing up.

Nina watched her with growing uneasiness. "What is it? What's going on? Please tell me."

She blew her nose in a piece of tissue, then spoke to Nina's reflection in the mirror: "I might have AIDS."

The water was still running in the sink, its level rising, threatening to overflow and flood the counter. "What?" Nina saw her own face in the mirror go flat with shock, even as she quickly twisted the faucet shut.

"I got a letter from the Health Department a couple of weeks ago," Meredith said. "It said someone I slept with tested positive."

"Who?"

"I've only been with Andrew, that one time." At Nina's blank look, she said, "The Hypnotist." She still faced the mirror, her eyes puffy and one shrimp earring hanging crooked off her earlobe. "The letter didn't say who it was, but it could only be him."

Nina scrambled for something to say. "Most of these things are false alarms, you know." Was that true? She had no idea. "Did you get tested?"

Meredith groaned. "I know I'm being stupid, but I really don't want to. The letter said 'strongly advise,' which makes me want to go even less." She balled up the tissue in her fist and Nina saw how scared she was, her knuckles white.

"Maybe just do it so you can put it behind you?" Nina said. "I'll go with you."

"That's okay." She gave Nina a grateful look, her eyes still wet. "Leigh said she would. But thanks."

She seemed suddenly small and childlike, the girl Nina had sat next to in Mrs. Adler's fifth-grade homeroom. "You're going to be fine," Nina said, and reached out with affection to fix her earring, although Meredith tightened up again and pulled away, then fixed the earring herself before heading out the door.

Nina was left staring at her face in the mirror. At least virginity couldn't kill her, and she was grateful to not have to worry about the terrifying consequence of even one sexual encounter. But she still couldn't shake the feeling that she'd been singled out somehow, protected against her will, uniquely incompetent to grapple with adulthood and everyone knew it. Especially her.

Chapter Thirteen

Last winter, Nina's grandmother Ruth had fallen and broken her hip in the St. Louis house where Ira and his sister Cathy grew up. Aunt Cathy still lived there, less than a mile away, but Ruth's care had become too much. Ira was flying out tomorrow to move his mother to a nursing home.

Today he'd joined Nina and Seymour on their Sunday walk. They were headed to Sam Goody so Ira could buy his first Walkman and the newest recording of *Aida* for the plane. Frances was at home, packing his clothes and toiletries. She wasn't going with him; he'd be completely tied up out there, trying to get everything done. Not to mention her antipathy to *the hinterlands,* as she referred to St. Louis, or St. Louis's antipathy to *her,* as Cathy and Ruth referred to Frances. Nina wasn't sure she'd ever heard them use her name.

It was the third of August, and the air was sticky with humidity. Ira walked beside Seymour with a tight grip on his arm; he had to have broken hips on the brain. Nina trudged behind them. She'd run out of cocaine Friday night and felt dismal since, a flat tire on the side of the road that even Vivarin couldn't reinflate. A cokeover, Stephanie called it, Nina's first, worse than a hangover because in addition to a hangover's headache and exhaustion, there was the sharp pain inside your nose, like it had been scraped with steel wool, along with a stinging shame.

Of course Gardner hadn't called. How could she have expected him to? He'd never even come back to Flanagan's to say good night after his encounter with Rex. No doubt he'd gone to see some girl who didn't jerk away from his touch.

And now Brian was annoyed with her for taking Gardner's side in the park, not to mention a homeless guy had lost his blanket thanks to her, probably his only possession, and Leigh had gotten so drunk on her watch that she'd left Flanagan's with Victor, of all people, and woken up outside her front door with a carton of orange juice in her hand and no memory of how she'd gotten there.

And Meredith. Nina had left three messages on her answering machine but hadn't heard back. Her mind refused to imagine Meredith sick, let alone terminally ill. Could girls even get AIDS? The stories were always about men: a wasted Rock Hudson on the cover of the *Enquirer;* Aidan Quinn as the stricken lawyer in *An Early Frost;* even Ryan White, that poor kid in Indiana who was barred from attending his middle school. But the health department didn't send out "strongly advise" letters for no reason.

"You hanging in there, kid?" Ira asked her over his shoulder.

"Sure," Nina said, not wanting to give him more to worry about. But the thought of this next week filled her with weariness. All she wanted to do was lie in bed under the covers and sleep away the few remaining weeks until college, but with Ira out of the way, Frances could carry out her plan to "freshen up" the entire apartment, and Nina would be drafted to paint the hallway or wallpaper the kitchen or handwash all the pillows. Worse, she'd be the sole audience to her mother's ceaseless chatter, which was fun and engaging if you were in the mood, but overwhelming if you weren't. Well, not *sole,* since the tape recorder would be there, too, to capture the tale about the time Frances got stung by a jellyfish in Boca Raton, or waved to Ann-

Margret at the airport in Vancouver. At this rate, her mother's auto-biography would take longer to read than to live.

They stopped at the corner, waiting for the light to change. She noticed her grandfather was sweating, made worse by the heavy wool cardigan he wore over his long-sleeve shirt.

"Let's get this off," Nina said.

He shrugged.

"Arms up." She was too enervated to navigate buttons. Seymour raised his arms. She pulled the sweater over his head and balanced it in the crook of her elbow. Old age was so brutal, turning you into a helpless child, your brain cells popping like soap bubbles. He'd already asked three times this morning where Pearl was. Nina wanted to fall onto the sidewalk and weep.

On the other hand, at least he'd *been* loved for most of his life.

"Better?" Ira asked Seymour.

"What can I tell you."

Ira gave Nina's back an appreciative pat as they continued walking. "Bet I'm the only one on the flight with Verdi in my ears," he said. He meant as opposed to the Rust Belt rubes tapping a foot to a polka. Ira liked to pretend he'd been hatched the day he landed in New York for law school. Although the few times Nina went home with him (*It's not home!* he exploded whenever she called it that), it was obvious it wasn't bratwurst or polkas that made his skin crawl. It was Ruth and Cathy, who'd sit there on the pleather couch, the same cloud of auburn hair, the same thick-lensed glasses that magnified their eyes to wounded saucers, and recount the innumerable ways they'd been rejected and abandoned. Old friends who didn't call or visit, cousins who didn't answer their letters, neighbors (and the cantor's wife, and the new nurse at the hospital where Aunt Cathy worked in Accounts) who turned down their invitations to tea. Ira, who'd left them for *that woman*.

Nina's father would sit stone silent in the matching pleather armchair, his face blank, fists clenched, until the conversation edged toward their second favorite topic: the shvartzes moving in and ruining the neighborhood. Then he'd jump up and suggest a drive downtown, during which Aunt Cathy would sit beside Nina in the backseat, all defensive saucer eyes, and mutter things like, "Sorry it's not the Empire State Building," when they drove by the Arch.

"You should have seen Aunt Cathy's face that time I played *Rigoletto* for her. She looked like I'd made her eat liver and onions." Ira wiped the sweat off his face with his forearm.

Nina had heard this anecdote at least a dozen times. She sided with her aunt on this one, picturing Ira bludgeoning her with his refinement. Another unkind vision, but she was drained of any goodness today. She was the guy on death row in her *Closing Remarks* book, whose last words in the electric chair were "Hurry up. I want to get to hell in time for dinner."

The stores on Third Avenue appeared blanched in the harsh sunshine, wilted clothes in their windows drooping off the mannequins. Heat rippled inside her body, wilting her also. She was so dispirited, she barely had the strength to carry Seymour's sweater. But when she looked up the block, there were Maison Rouge's windows, shimmering like Oz. Steph had said Damian might deliver more waffle irons today, although she probably hadn't meant for Nina to bring along half her family.

"I need to use the restroom," she announced. She handed Seymour's cardigan to her father.

Ira looked perplexed. "Can't it wait?"

She took off running. "Two seconds!" she called over her shoulder, invigorated by the thought of reinvigoration. "Keep going. I'll catch up."

"You have excellent radar," Stephanie said when they reached the supply room. They exchanged the coke for Nina's temp money, then Stephanie cut two lines of her own.

Nina's mouth watered, though the tray of brownies on the table did nothing for her.

Stephanie caught her glance. "I got them at Greenberg's. It's Beverly's birthday today." She handed Nina a dollar bill.

"Brownie points," Nina said.

"Yeah, well, she's not exactly my biggest fan."

"I'm your biggest fan," Nina said. She sniffed her line, then rubbed the residue over her gums.

Stephanie smiled. "If you pass her on your way out, don't wipe your nose or anything. She's been giving me major stink-eye lately."

"Better?" Ira asked when Nina caught up with them on Seventy-First Street.

"Heaps."

He studied her. Her pulse jumped. She worried there might be powder ringing the edges of her nostrils. She clenched her hands at her waist to stop herself from trying to wipe it away. But then Ira said, "You know, you're very pretty. You look more and more like Mom."

"Thanks." Her affection for him rekindled, heightened by the relief of not getting caught. They continued walking downtown, now three abreast with Nina in the center, taking up most of the sidewalk, and it was lovely to be the pretty girl that people had to make way for. She retrieved Seymour's cardigan from her father. She hadn't noticed earlier what a saturated red it was, the ferocity of ripe cherries; his shirt, she now saw, was the vibrant pink of carnations. He was still here, flesh and bone and pumping heart.

"Should we get something to eat?" she asked him. "Tuna melts at Skyline?"

He nodded. "Very good."

"You two have fun," Ira said, handing Seymour's cardigan to her.

"I've got tons to do before I leave." He turned to go, then hesitated, as if hearing himself say "leave" had reminded him what he was leaving. "Listen," he said, turning back, "you'll watch over Mom while I'm away?"

"Of course." Redecorating the apartment didn't sound so bad, now that her coin purse was restocked.

But her father continued to linger. He glanced at Seymour, then said in a low voice to Nina: "Vlad saw her yesterday and thinks he might need to adjust her medication. Reduce the dosage, or maybe stop it altogether. He's concerned she might be having an adverse reaction."

"Adverse? She's finally happy." Just yesterday, Nina had found her mother's latest note—elegant script on plain white typing paper, no little graph paper squares. *Evolution, revolution, innovation, transmogrification,* it said. Actually, she hadn't even "found" the note: it was right out in the open on the dining-room table as if inviting a public reading, not stashed away in a drawer or a crevice like the tortured scrawlings of the past. It made Nina think of how she'd flashed her breasts in Central Park the other night, the exhilaration you couldn't keep to yourself.

Ira blinked. "He thinks she might be getting a little . . . *too* happy."

Was there such a thing? "Isn't it good she's got so much more energy?"

"Well . . ." Uncertainty flickered over his face. "The way Vlad put it, there's energetic, and there's frenetic."

Nina rolled her eyes. "He's a poet and he doesn't even know it."

Her father looked a little startled. "I'll call you every day that I'm away."

Nina nodded solemnly and bit her lip to stop herself from repeating the poet-who-doesn't-know-it joke. She grabbed her grandfather's hand and led him back uptown.

———

"Soak for twenty minutes to soften skin, then scrub away calluses with a loofah," Frances read from the *McCall's* article "Beauty Is Only Kitchen Deep," a dozen at-home beauty recipes you could whip up with ingredients from your pantry. With Ira in St. Louis, Nina and Frances spent the evenings coating each other's hair with mashed bananas and their faces with avocados and olive oil. Nina had played along to keep an eye on Frances, and also to feel her mother's fingers on her scalp and cheeks. Tonight was vinegar-and-Listerine pedicures, their feet submerged in plastic buckets and Frances splashing Nina's shins with the puce-colored liquid.

"'After the scrub,'" Nina read, "'pamper your tootsies with loads of lotion.' Why can't they just say toes?"

"*Toot-toot Tootsie, goodbye,*" her mother sang.

They were in Nina's bathroom, half the size of her mother's, but Frances had packed hers with the overflow of the week's shopping extravaganzas, leaving her hardly enough room to squeeze in, despite her increasing thinness. She sat on the lid of Nina's toilet and Nina on the rim of the tub, their knees almost touching. Nina had a close-up view of her mother's clavicle poking out over the collar of her shirt, and the hollows beneath her cheekbones. Frances was mostly eating pumpkin seeds and chicken broth these days, as if anything thick or gunky was too reminiscent of the thick, gunky months of depression. Nina admired her angularity—she herself had lost more weight, her breasts happily diminished a whole cup size—but would Vlad consider it "adverse"?

"Can I make you a sandwich?" she asked Frances, even though it was close to ten p.m.

Her mother sniffed and made a face. "I don't have much appetite for a bite tonight."

"All right," Nina said, and flashed a quick poet-who-doesn't-know-it smile. The air in the small bathroom was so thick with vinegar and Listerine fumes, who could think about eating anyway? "You sure red vinegar's the right kind?" she asked. "I thought it was for salads."

"Relax, chipmunk. Vinegar is vinegar." Frances propped her tape recorder on the edge of the sink and pressed Record. "During the Depression, my mother made pies with vinegar when lemons were too expensive. They were called desperation pies. Anyway, white vinegar isn't even white, it's clear. False advertising. Call the attorney general!"

Energetic or *frenetic*? Semantics, Nina assured herself. Happy is happy. Vinegar is vinegar. "We're great!" she'd told her father each time he called from St. Louis. She didn't say, *Mom's sketching plans to turn my bedroom into a ballet studio once I'm at school, with a barre and a piano.* Or, *She's started calling you* Buzz, as in buzzkill, *for saying no to a trip to Reykjavík next week.* Nina wouldn't sound the alarm over some silliness. Let Vlad worry if he wanted to, but with all her father was dealing with—Medicaid, movers, realtors, Ruth's decline, Aunt Cathy's resentment—why pile on with a barrage of Frances reports over nothing? So Vlad could *adjust* her mother's newfound joy, or stop it altogether?

While they dried their feet and applied lotion, Nina told her mother about the temp job she'd be starting Monday at *Harvest Moon,* an agriculture almanac. Anything to distract herself from the fact that Gardner still hadn't called.

Frances pressed Record again. "What do you call a farm where none of the cows give milk?" she asked, then answered herself: "An udder disaster."

Nina tried to smile but instead her eyes teared. *She* was an udder disaster. She was back in a miserable mood that even cocaine couldn't lift her out of, the silent phone unbearable. Although she did have a few scraps of pride left. She wouldn't show up where she wasn't wanted. So, even though Frances had tried to shoo her out earlier— "Go have fun: I don't need a babysitter"—here Nina was, home with her mother on a Friday night, up to her shins in a bucket of vinegar and mouthwash.

Frances gave her a sympathetic look. "Life can be hard at your age." She had on her shirt with the winking eye, and she stroked the yarn lashes like a man stroking his beard, deep in thought. "Are you getting enough rest, chicken? As the inventor of the ant farm once said, 'The best bridge between despair and hope is a good night's sleep.'"

"Ant farm?"

"Speaking of farms—" Frances pushed Record again. "What time do farmers wake up? At the quack of dawn."

Nina didn't want to bring her mother down. She racked her slowed brain for a farm pun but all she came up with was some trivia about eggs from her *Book of Lists*. "Did you know Alfred Hitchcock was deathly afraid of eggs? It's called ovophobia. He was terrified of what he called 'that white, round thing without any holes.'"

The second the words left her mouth, she was struck with the horrid thought that this was how Gardner saw her. A pale, round, impenetrable *thing*.

"Are the fumes too much?" Frances asked.

Nina shook her head, shocked at her continued tears. She couldn't remember the last time she cried in front of her mother, but here she was, spilling over.

"Aw," Frances said. "*Toot-toot Tootsie, don't cry.*" She looked as though she might start crying herself.

"There's this guy," Nina started.

"Naturally. Boys must be dropping like flies at your feet."

"The opposite. He doesn't like me." She was surprised to be so open with her mother. She'd never mentioned a boy to her before, much less cried over one.

Frances pointed to the astonished-looking eye on her shirt. "Impossible," she said. "You're a showstopper."

Even if Nina didn't believe her, the maternal sweetness felt breathtakingly soothing. She grabbed a few sheets of toilet paper and blew her nose.

The phone rang in Nina's bedroom. It must be Ira; he hadn't called yet tonight. Nina lifted her feet from the bucket, reached for a towel, and started out the bathroom door, but she wasn't fast enough, and the call went to the answering machine.

A few seconds of honks and sirens. Then: "Hey, it's Gardner." His voice sounded urgent. "Where are you?"

Frances squealed with girlish delight. "Is that the boy? Run!" As if Nina weren't already, his voice jumper cables for her body's dead battery. Her still-dripping feet made her slip on a patch of bedroom floor and bang her hip into her dresser. But she made herself answer calmly.

"I thought you'd be here," he said.

"Gardner?" As if he hadn't once popped into her mind this past week. "Are you at Flanagan's?"

He was silent so long, she worried she'd overplayed it. "You know the Carlyle?" he finally asked.

"The hotel?"

"Meet me there in twenty minutes."

He hung up and she was left listening to the dial tone.

A hotel meant a hotel room, which meant a bed. She put down the phone and told herself to get a grip. Go brush your teeth and wash your feet. You've been wanting this for months. *I am not afraid. I was born to do this,* as either Joan of Arc or the woman in *Fear of Flying* had said.

She quickly applied some Violent Kiss lipstick, stuck one of Frances's rhinestone barrettes in her hair, and pulled on one of her new skirts, the black one that barely came to the tops of her thighs, and sheared into flappy strips of fabric in the manner of a car wash.

She peeked into the bathroom. "You okay if I go out?"

"More than okay." Frances pushed Record: "Why was the gardener embarrassed? He wet his plants."

"Oh my God, Mom."

Frances laughed. She and her shirt winked at Nina. "Go get him, chicken."

Meredith lived around the corner from the Carlyle, so Nina had walked by a million times, and while she had no idea what it looked like inside, the entrance always struck her as a little fussy: THE CARLYLE in calligraphy on the gold-edged awning, a swirly *C* embedded in the pavement outside the front doors. Four potted topiaries marked off a square on the sidewalk, ivy twists that stretched several yards high. It was all very elegant and debonair, which was not the setting Nina would have picked for her first time—the sex she'd imagined always occurred somewhere dark and covert, even a little seamy. Not Times Square seamy, but more Times Square than Fred Astaire.

Then she spotted him slouching in a doorway next to the hotel, smoking a cigarette. All that complexity in his eyes, the knotty tension in his shoulders. Here was dark and covert. It didn't matter where they were.

"Glad you made it," he said.

"You rescued me from a salad-dressing foot soak." Was her voice too eager? Her skirt definitely was: the flaps kept flying open as she walked. But as Gardner's eyes flicked hungrily up and down her legs, she relaxed. She was allowed to be eager. She was supposed to be. He'd invited her to a hotel—what was that, if not a declaration of desire?

"You look hot," he said.

"I wore the skirt for you."

He looked at her.

"Because you like car washes," she added.

"Right," he said, although she couldn't tell if he had any clue what she was talking about. He led her to the door and she stopped herself from asking if you were allowed to just stroll inside a place like this. She stopped herself from looking to the white-gloved doorman for permission. Of course you were allowed. Of course the doorman opened the door the second they walked up. Gardner didn't hesitate. No trace of nerves. He went in as if he lived here.

The lobby had gold velvet couches, giant urns of lilies, and a brilliant black marble floor that reflected the chandeliers overhead. The woman behind the onyx reception desk looked up when they came in, her nose twitching as if she'd caught a whiff of something—or someone—unfamiliar, not the usual Shalimar or cigar smoke but a vinegar-and-Listerine bouquet. The rooms here must cost a fortune. Concerns flashed through Nina's mind about how Gardner might pay for theirs—another of Holland's mother's credit cards? She considered suggesting someplace less fancy. But then she decided it was none of her business. He'd chosen this place for a reason; and for all she knew, he'd saved up for a room. How insulting to imply he couldn't afford it. Maybe there was a special summer rate.

And anyway, instead of going to the elevators, he veered off to the hallway that led to Bemelmans Bar.

Inside, the walls were covered in hand-drawn rabbits and sheep, bears with balloons, an elephant reading a book under a tree. A waiter in a white jacket seated them at a banquette beneath a sketch of the schoolgirls from the *Madeline* books. The lighting was dim and the low ceiling leafed in gold. A man in a tuxedo played "Anything Goes" on the piano. Silver caddies on every table held nuts and potato chips. The old-fashioned charm made her feel like a kid in a French storybook. Was that how Gardner saw her?

"Do you come here a lot?" she asked.

"Rex's dad lives here. He bought an apartment upstairs when he and Rex's mom split up a few years back." He smiled lightly, leaning back and tapping the table to the music. It was nice to see him so relaxed. "We used to spend a lot of time here."

Oh. "What if we run into him?"

"He's in Tangier right now."

She was too flustered to remember what country that was. "Cool."

She had more questions, like how did Gardner know that? Was the job with Mr. Parrish back on? But who was she, Curious George?

A waiter arrived with coasters, set them down carefully, then nervously rotated each a millimeter while Gardner eyed him.

"You're new?" Gardner asked.

"Yes, sir. Is it obvious?" he answered sheepishly. He had thick hair and a pug nose and might not have been much older than them.

Gardner shook his head. "I just haven't seen you before. My father's got a place here."

Nina worked to keep a straight face, while she also tried to work out what was happening. The waiter looked impressed. "Drinks, sir?"

"A bottle of Perrier-Jouët." Gardner stretched his arms across the back of the banquette. His hand brushed Nina's shoulder and she felt the reverberation down to her fingertips.

With an apologetic smile, the waiter asked to see their IDs.

It was her first time trying out her Playland ID. She worried the sky-blue backdrop would give her away, but he just glanced at it and said, "Welcome, Miss Grossberg."

He looked at Gardner's and nodded. "Thank you, Mr. Parrish. I'll be right back with the champagne."

She waited until he was out of hearing range. "Mr. Parrish?"

"His name, my address. My name's on his. We switched names when we got them, so they couldn't be traced if we got busted."

"Smart."

"Miss Grossberg?" he asked with a slight wince.

"I know," Nina said. It did hang a little coarsely in the tinkly, delicate atmosphere. "It's my mother's maiden name."

"She must have gotten a ton of shit at school." He pulled out a pack of cigarettes. "What's your real last name?"

"Jacobs."

"Lucky for you," he said.

"Remember the grandmother I thought I killed?" Nina said. "The one who hated smoking? She was the Grossberg, my mother's mother."

"Well, then, apologies to Grandma Grossberg for this." He placed a cigarette between his lips then handed one to Nina. He lit both with a match then blew out the flame with a stream of smoke. It still made her knees weak.

"I can't believe that's the first thing I told you when we met." Now she described the bizarre rose-burning ceremony in their kitchen for Pearl's birthday, then held out her wrist to display the remains of her burn, down to a small red patch.

"Nice," he said. He brushed it lightly with his thumb, then pressed a little harder, his eyes on hers. "Does it hurt?"

"Nope," she said, enjoying the tiny pinch of pain. "Now show me something on you."

He lifted his hair and pointed to an inch-long crease at the top of his forehead. She grazed the scar with her finger, and he closed his eyes for a second, which she interpreted as pleasure at her soothing touch.

"Hockey party for my tenth birthday. I got nailed by a puck. At first I thought someone had spilled cherry Kool-Aid on the ice. Tom had to carry me to Mount Sinai to get the gash stitched up."

"I thought your dad's name is William."

Gardner's face froze. "He wasn't there. If he had been, he'd probably have been too drunk to do anything, anyway."

"Oh, Tom," she realized. "Parrish."

Gardner nodded, his mouth tight. Good job, Curious George. Way to maintain a seductive atmosphere.

The waiter returned with their champagne. His inexperience seemed to loosen up Gardner, who told him things about the Carlyle he might not know, like Bobby Short's good-luck charm was a yo-yo, and guests' pillows were embroidered with their monogram, and JFK had kept an apartment here when he was president. Gardner played with the flaps of Nina's skirt under the table as he expanded on the details. "The Secret Service kept an apartment, too, but mainly for Kennedy's girlfriends." He rolled one skirt-flap up to her bikini line. "They used to smuggle Marilyn Monroe in through a secret passageway." He tugged up another flap, just as the waiter was glancing down to pour the champagne.

The waiter's face remained neutral, although Nina saw him sneak a look. Nina moved Gardner's hand away, smiling coyly to show him she wasn't offended. She rearranged her skirt and announced, "JFK's last words were 'No, you certainly can't.'" *Ugh. Nicely done, Miss Morbid.* Who else but her would leap from sex talk to death talk? But now Gardner and the waiter were waiting for an explanation. "In the car that day," she said, "Governor Connolly said to him, 'You can't say Dallas doesn't love you,' and JFK said, 'No, you certainly can't.' Right before, you know."

"Well," the waiter said, "I'll be back to check on you," then quickly retreated to another table.

"I think this might be *his* last day," Gardner teased.

"Sorry about that," Nina said.

"He'll get over it when he sees the tip."

They drained their glasses. Being alone with Gardner here, somewhere that wasn't Flanagan's, reminded her that the Flanagan's world was just a blip in an enormous city. "Did I tell you about my trip to Times Square?" she asked.

She'd caught his interest. He refilled their glasses, watching her closely. "What, to a peep show?"

"A sex shop. Le Sex Shoppe, as a matter of fact."

He paused mid-pour. "You and Brian?"

Was he jealous? She wished she were a good enough flirt to draw it out. "Me and Stephanie. It was nuts." A good flirt would hint at her wildness, describe the various sex toys they saw, the scenes in the poolside porno, yet she found herself launching into a description of the skeevy guy behind the counter, his leather vest and silver skull rings. "The whole time, he was reading a magazine called *Beaver Hunt*."

"My father's girlfriend was in *Beaver Hunt*," Gardner said.

"What?"

He broke into laughter. "Okay, not *Beaver Hunt*, but last time I saw him, he opened up a *Playboy* to show me this babe spread across the hood of a Camaro. He goes, 'What do you think: stepmother material?'" A shadow of uneasiness fell across his face, but Nina saw also a sliver of pride.

They finished the champagne. When the check came, Gardner added a $50 tip, signed Rex's name, and said to put it on his father's tab.

"Ready to go?" he asked Nina.

"Sure." She tried to keep the despondency out of her voice as she lurched to her feet, light-headed from all the champagne. She guessed they were headed to Flanagan's, where he'd as usual be torn away by a dozen girls. Or maybe she'd just go home, where she'd get ambushed with an avocado facial and then spend half the night awake, fevered with yearning.

He brought his closed hand up from beneath the table and held it out to her, then slowly opened his fingers. Resting in his palm, a filigreed medallion, an ornate gold *C* in its center, with a key attached.

Even drunk, her eyesight misty, she quickly realized that Gardner hadn't reserved this room, which wasn't a guest room but an actual apartment. Tom Parrish's apartment. They walked through a foyer with a small kitchen off one side and a large living room off the other: dove-gray walls, oriental rug, charcoal armchairs, a glossy black piano in the corner topped with framed photographs. One picture was Rex and an older man with the same severe black eyebrows, presumably Tom, both in down jackets on a snow-covered mountain, skis propped in the snow beside them and tinted goggles pushed up in their hair. Another was them in safari jackets, side by side, big grins, big rifles, with a dead leopard draped around Tom Parrish's shoulders. Literal blood on their hands.

"Did Rex lend you his key?" Somewhere along the way she'd missed a step. "I saw you talking last week at Flanagan's. Are you guys friends again?" If she wound up spending more time with Gardner, would she have to put up with Rex?

"I told him I wanted to talk to his dad, so he'd clue me in when he'd be away—which he did." Gardner smiled. "I took the spare key months ago. Figured I might need it one day."

"So we're, uh, breaking and entering?"

"Just entering." He looked pleased with himself. "I mean, Tom *did* always say, 'Mi casa es su casa.'"

Between her fizzed-up cerebral cortex and the repulsive leopard execution, she couldn't summon up much concern.

He sniffed and gave her the look she'd begun to recognize. She smiled, dug out her coin purse from her bag, and handed it to him. He set the ski photo flat on the piano top, then laid out a line across Rex's eyes, and another across his father's neck. He sniffed the line from Tom's throat through a rolled-up matchbook, then handed it to Nina. She did hers off of Rex's smarmy face. Once cleared of powder, Rex's eyes squinted at her, like, *I'd advise you to depart the premises, Miss Grossberg.* But too bad, he was trapped behind the glass and there was nothing he could do. She gave him the finger.

"You can tell he's a dick by the way he sticks out his chest," she said. "His father does it too."

Gardner wiped the powder remains off Tom's neck. "I took that picture outside their condo in Stowe. I'd beaten their asses down Goat, but they're still trying to look like hotshots." He sat on the velvet chair behind the desk and surveyed the room. She followed his gaze to the wall behind the couch, where two framed paintings hung, abstract faces in brusque black strokes.

"Tom calls those Amos and Andy," he said.

"What a surprise. I heard Rex refer to a Jewish girl in his building as a spoiled kike."

Gardner shrugged. "Rex and his father think they're hilarious."

She leaned awkwardly against the piano as he stared down at the oriental rug. Had she misread the situation? Was she just here as company? Maybe he'd downgraded her to *pal* after her flinch in the alley. Sit on his lap, she told herself. Plunk down like you're not even thinking twice. But while she was giving herself this mental pep talk, he crossed his ankle over his knee, so the best she could do was half-sit on the corner of the desk, facing him. She organized the flaps of her skirt to show more skin.

"Bobby Short taught me 'Fly Me to the Moon' on that fucking piano." He shook his head and yanked open the desk's middle drawer.

"Do you want to play it for me?"

He rummaged through the drawer's contents, a jumble of expensive fountain pens, cuff links, and cigar lighters. A dagger-sharp letter opener with an ornate gold handle. A tray of fancy watches, gold with slick sapphire crystals, Roman numerals, imposing crowns. "Second son to scum of the earth," he muttered.

He ran his finger over the various watches, his face tight with a longing that pierced her. Fuck the Parrishes for their arrogance, for their gleeful slaughter of innocent creatures. She brushed her knee against his leg. "You're worth a hundred of them."

"Which one's your favorite?" he asked.

"They're not exactly my style." She showed him her Swatch with the transparent face and pink plastic band. But he held out the tray to her, waiting, so she pointed to the least flashy, a black face that said HUBLOT in gold, with no numbers and a matte-gold case.

"Try it on," he said.

She took off her watch and held out her arm. Chills ran through her as he fastened it, his thumb brushing her veins. "Goes well with that burn," he joked as she admired her wrist, how fragile it looked encircled by the man-sized strap. Then he picked out an expensive-looking watch with an alligator band and an iridescent face.

"Patek Philippe. Sixty fucking thousand dollars. Tom had this on the day he offered me a summer job." He curled his lip as he buckled the band around his wrist. "And probably the day he pulled it, too, although he had his secretary call. Two-faced, chickenshit cocksucker."

Nina leaned forward and put her hands on his shoulders, which were hard as stone. "Shh," she whispered in his ear. "They're assholes. Forget them." She kissed his neck, hoping to bring him back to the present. He looked her right in the eye. Finally, he was focused on her. She felt herself start to float, the shimmering swirl of feeling between them.

"I need to fuck this place up," he said.

"What?"

He smiled tightly as he pulled back from her hands. He took a cigarette out of the pack he'd tossed on the desk. Her eyes were still half-closed and her head in an embarrassing please-kiss-me tilt. She jerked upright as he struck the match, her dismay so distracting she almost missed him move his leg and drive the lit cigarette into the chair's velvet seat cushion.

"What are you doing?" she said. Pale batting showed through the charred hole in the velvet.

He grabbed the ski photo and slammed Rex and his father face-first against the corner of the desk, shattering the frame's glass. He dropped his cigarette to the rug and ground it out under his heel.

"Hold on," she said. "Is this a good idea?" Meaning, *This is obviously a bad idea*. On the other hand, why shouldn't Gardner exact a little revenge on some Parrish keepsakes. He'd certainly earned the right. Who was she to interfere?

"Tom will think it was Rex," Gardner assured her. "They had a huge fight before Tom left on his trip."

"How do you know?"

"How do you think?"

"Holland?"

"Amazing what you can find out when you pretend to forgive."

He seized a marble obelisk off the desk and crossed the room to the piano. He pressed the hard pointed tip against the piano's side, next to the keyboard, then walked the length of the piano with it, digging a linear gash through the shiny black lacquer, like keying the side of a car. He glanced back at her. She expected to see a light in his eyes, the thrill of revenge, but was startled by the look of frustration. Or was it loss? There had to be something she could offer.

Her coin purse. He laid out more lines, thick as fingers, this time on the leopard photo. She tried to keep her eyes averted as she sniffed hers but she couldn't help catching sight of Tom's and Rex's preening grins and the gorgeous snuffed-out leopard worn as casually as a scarf. She noticed the leopard-skin rug beneath the piano and made the connection. Her mind went to lampshades made from the skin of Buchenwald victims adorning the homes of Third Reich officers.

"They ought to be in jail," she told Gardner. Her adrenaline surged and something came loose inside her. She opened the desk drawer and rummaged around. Pens, paper clips, rubber bands. Her hand closed on the letter opener.

She stuck its point in the hole that Gardner had made with his cigarette, and then it wasn't so hard to push through to the ornately scrolled hilt, and from there thrust up. The ripping sound was exhilarating. What else could she stab? She tore a jagged gash in a couch pillow and feathers spilled out. She thought of the gulls dive-bombing Tippi Hedren in *The Birds*. Then imagined them turning their fury on Rex at her command, pecking at his face and drawing blood. *Spoiled kike*, she heard him scream, even as he begged her to call them off.

Gardner laughed angrily. "I knew you had it in you."

I do! her brain on cocaine hyperdrive exulted. She shoved a jade bowl off the table beside the couch, thrilled at the sound of it shattering. And then, magically, her brain emptied. Carried away by the

sheer joy of destruction, she even momentarily forgot Gardner. There
was only a vase to overturn, a piano bench to topple, a crystal apple to
kick across the room.

A tearing sound startled her, Gardner pulling one of the gold
curtains off its rail. He yanked and it puddled to the floor. Through
one bare window came the navy sky; a sea of treetops; a hundred
buildings' glimmering lights on the other side of Central Park.

He turned and gazed down at the curtain for a few seconds, then
back up at Nina with a small smile. He was breathing hard. "Come
here," he said.

She picked her way through broken porcelain, her blood pounding. When she reached him, he pulled her down to the floor, on the
cloud of gold silk. In the wash of moonlight through the window, his
face was alabaster. She lay back and waited for his weight, already
arching up against the anticipation of him, her mouth open, enjoying
how he straddled and observed her. Had she ever in her life been
looked at so intensely? She was a fish at the end of his line, squirming
and helpless. Then he was on top of her and she heard herself make a
lovesick, keening sound, but her brain was so scrambled, she wasn't
even embarrassed. He put his hands under her head to cushion it
from the ground, and her heart cracked open.

"You have no idea," she said, "how much—"

A knock at the front door.

Gardner jerked up. Nina's head banged to the ground.

Tom, home early?

Another knock.

"Sir?" a man's voice asked. "Is everything all right in there?"

Gardner let out a breath and got to his feet. "Everything's fine," he
called. Someone must have heard the commotion and rung the front
desk. Nina was impressed with Gardner's composure, considering
whoever was on the other side of that door might have a key. She sat
up and rolled herself into a ball, trying to look like an errant cushion.

"Sorry about that," Gardner continued. "A shelf in the kitchen came down and all the dishes fell out. Trying to clean everything up now. Tell the neighbors apologies from Rex for the disturbance."

There was silence. Suspicion? "Very good, sir," the man said finally. Still that hesitation, but at last he retreated. They waited, stock-still, until the final discernible footstep.

"Let's go," Gardner whispered.

She was already up, turning the couch cushions to hide the holes.

"Leave it." He opened the door and checked the hallway, gave her an *all-clear* gesture. They crept down one corridor and then another until they reached a staircase. He ran down ahead, rounding the corners in a blur. Nina followed so fast she barely touched the steps, her skirt rippling behind her. *Don't get caught. Just don't get caught.* Her mother's menacing face from the bad old days hovered over her shoulder.

They came out through a service door onto Seventy-Seventh Street and ran up the block to a brownstone's shadowed doorway. They caught their breath, grinning at each other. No one had followed them. They'd gotten away with it, jabbed a few holes in the Parrishes' perfect life.

"Did I really just hack up a couch?" She lifted her arms to his shoulders and rubbed against him.

She felt his laugh reverberate in his chest. He said, "I won't tell if you don't."

"Where do we go next to continue our reign of destruction? The Stanhope? Plaza?"

He squeezed her ass, then stepped back from her embrace. "Can't. The Wicked Witch is threatening to kick me out again if I'm not home by two."

"She'd do that?"

"She's done it before. Once she even changed the locks. Since my dad left, all the fun lands on me." He glanced out into the street in a worried way as if he'd spotted her there. Nina remembered the day she and Stephanie had spied on Gardner's apartment building. *Nurse*

Ratched, Stephanie had called Mrs. Reed as they watched her abuse the maintenance man. No wonder Gardner's voice was weighted with dread. Tenderness blazed through her.

"Besides," he said, "Benji's picking me up first thing in the morning."

She smiled to hide her disappointment. "Where are you guys going?"

"Bridgehampton. His parents got a new place on Surfside Drive."

"How great." She hoped she sounded like she meant it. "How long?"

"Just a few days."

"You going to miss me?" she asked.

He closed the space between them and cupped her between her legs. This time she didn't jerk back. "You going to let anyone else in there?"

She shook her head. She was as happy as she'd ever been.

"We'll talk," he said, and kissed her quickly.

As he went one direction and she the other, she noticed DeeDee Elkin from her building walking her dog across the street, in Chanel ballet slippers, gold satin jacket and matching shorts, the dog on a gold leather leash. A flare of alarm as she looked over at Nina, who imagined her hearing about a Carlyle break-in and remembering the sight of Nina and Gardner racing out the service door. But her alarm receded when she realized that DeeDee probably had no idea who she was, considering she never seemed to recognize her even when they took the same elevator.

All along her block, lobby doors were propped open and the doormen standing outside to take in the huge and startlingly bright moon. Nina walked past, stride locomotive, skirt swishing around her thighs, basking in their discreet scrutiny. As if her eyes were bigger and her vision sharper, she saw blinking red and green traffic lights for miles, an endless stretch of silvery pavement. The hot, bright moon belonged to her.

Her building's doors, on the other hand, were closed, which no doubt meant Freddie was still on duty, shut up inside like a creepy dark secret. She'd managed to elude him earlier by shadowing the nice widower brothers from the seventh floor off the elevator and out the front door. But now as she neared her building, she wondered if she'd been worrying over nothing. Would her parents—so much happier now, so much less thin-skinned and irritable—even care about anything Freddie might say about her?

He opened the door and she strolled past him into the lobby, just a slight nod of her head. The door fell closed and the traffic sounds vanished, replaced by the sound of Freddie shuffling behind her. Who cared? She walked straight to the elevator and pressed the call button before she turned to face him, narrowing her eyes. *Don't even try it.*

He smiled with his lips together. "Miss Nina having pretty new watch."

She glanced at her wrist and saw Tom Parrish's Hublot still fastened to it. She'd forgotten to take it off. Under the lobby lights, the gold case gleamed.

"Is so expensive, no?" Freddie said.

She shook her head, trying to look casual, to ignore her heart's acceleration. He couldn't have known anything, but Nina covered it with her other hand anyway.

But where was her Swatch? She must have left it on Tom Parrish's black lacquer desk.

Freddie's smile lingered. She told herself to calm down. She was just coke paranoid. But when he held out his arms, she let his fat, blunt fingers encircle her.

Chapter Fourteen

When Ira called Sunday night, he sounded beleaguered. Things were a mess in St. Louis. His mother was threatening to sue him for forcing her out of her home. Aunt Cathy was threatening to sue *her* if she left anything to Ira in her will.

"Nothing there I need to worry about, right?" he said to Nina with a rueful laugh. "You've got things under control?"

Nina wound the phone cord around her hand and watched the skin turn various shades of blush and vermillion. "Absolutely," she said, leaving out the fact that, over the weekend, Frances had bought out Zitomer's entire stock of tortoiseshell headbands; spent two hours on the phone with some long-lost cousin in California recounting the graphic details of Pearl's death; and left plates of cupcakes on all the neighbors' doorsteps that she'd stayed up half the night baking. Not to mention Nina's multiple felonies at the Carlyle and the Swatch she'd left behind as evidence, while Frances was home alone, unsupervised.

"I don't know what I'd do without you," Ira said, sighing.

To be honest, she'd been too wrapped up in the Gardner helix to pay proper attention to Frances. When she wasn't reliving the rampage at the Carlyle, she was worrying about her Swatch, or the fingerprints they'd left everywhere, or Gardner's parting words to her. *We'll talk* had sounded like a promise at the time but now struck her as cruelly vague. *How* would they talk? *When?* Only twenty-one days until she left for Vanderbilt and she was as much a virgin as she'd been in June.

Ira would be home in less than a week. Nina promised herself to do better, be more responsible, make sure Frances ate and slept. Monday morning, before she left for her first day at *Harvest Moon,* she got up early and ran out for bagels, melon, and pistachio cookies. She came back and made a tray for Frances and quietly placed it on the floor beside her bed. Frances was on her side with her legs curled up and her head resting on her outstretched arm, eyes open.

"Say hi to the chickens for me, chicken," she said.

Everything else was falling apart, but at least for today Frances was all right.

Nina had pictured the homespun charm of the almanac's office: antique maps, rooster weather vanes, and chandeliers made from old wheelbarrows. But she'd misunderstood the job. It was actually *Harvest Moon*'s marketing firm, in a skyscraper on Seventh Avenue, the office filled with glass brick and a neon outline of a skyline on the wall behind the reception desk. A guy in a skinny tie and square glasses led her through a labyrinth of cubicles to one in the back. He deposited her with a timesheet, stacks of unopened reader mail, and, not that she believed in karma or anything, a letter opener.

Her job was to sort the mail backlog into two piles: "Fan or Pan." The guy with the square glasses told her that *Harvest Moon* hadn't predicted this past spring's deep freeze in the southern states, and people there were still outraged. Nina chose a random envelope and slit it open with a quick tug of the blade. Its hilt was completely unadorned, nothing like the one at the Carlyle; she pushed away thoughts of cops and fingerprint dust and jail cells and focused on the photograph of an orange tree encased in ice that slid from the envelope onto her desk. Scrawled across the back of the photo: *Please use softer paper so I can wipe my ass with it.* Not a Fan. A bride in Charleston said *Harvest Moon* had ruined her spring wedding and enclosed a receipt for the nonrefundable outdoor venue along with her address for reimbursement. A farmer in Mississippi sent a bill for a new henhouse roof to replace the one that collapsed in a blizzard: *Ida got a better forecast if Ida flipped a coin.*

Every half hour or so, she was distracted by snide conversations on the other side of her cubicle's wall about a woman in HR they called Plumpty Dumpty. Nina became desperate for a boost of pleasantness. She picked up the phone on her desk and dialed Stephanie's number at Mary Kay's apartment, not to talk—Stephanie would be at work—but to hear her cheery recorded message, and to leave a message herself. They did this sometimes, a quick anecdote or complaint as a placeholder for a later conversation. After the beep, she started to describe the frozen orange tree. Then Stephanie unexpectedly picked up.

"If you want orange, come over."

Nina instantly felt lighter, hearing her voice. She pictured Stephanie lounging on her zebra-striped bedspread, surrounded by her spider sketches and magenta bulletin board. "What are you doing home?"

"I called in sick today." Her nose was stuffed up, although her voice fizzed with energy. "Come watch *Divorce Court* with me. It's on right now."

"I wish." Nina cradled the phone on her shoulder while she opened another envelope. This letter, signed Mildred Wackernagel, blamed *Harvest Moon* for her tractor's frozen transmission.

"This lawyer's hair looks like marzipan," Stephanie said, followed by a prolonged sniff.

"That's some cold you've got."

Stephanie laughed. "Simmer down, Keith." When Nina called her Saturday morning to tell her about the Carlyle, Stephanie had buoyed her with stories about Keith Moon's hotel antics, the chairs he'd hacked to pieces with a hatchet and a toilet he'd blown up with dynamite. "Nothing's more rock 'n' roll than trashing a hotel room," she'd said, which Nina couldn't wait to repeat to Gardner. (*How? When?*)

Stephanie sniffed again. Nina felt an answering twinge in her own nose. She'd never done coke at work, mainly because it seemed like a waste of a high. Why be all gregarious for people she couldn't care less about? But Stephanie's energy, compared to her own lethargy, made it hard to resist. She told her she'd call her right back and reached into the inside pocket of her handbag, where she'd also stashed the Hublot so no one would discover it at home. She gave it a quick squeeze, like a good-luck charm, then headed to the ladies' room with her coin purse, nearly empty after Friday night at the Carlyle.

Back at her desk, the next letter was a compliment for an article about hiccup remedies. This was more like it, as if her pick-me-up had even affected the mail. She sat up straighter than she had all morning and dialed Stephanie again.

"Did you know you can stop hiccups by holding a dime against the roof of your mouth?"

"But then how would you cure the tetanus?"

Nina heard Stephanie flick her lighter. What she'd give to be there instead of here, inhaling flat office air. She started a "Fan" pile with the hiccup letter.

"Want to go play video games with me and Patrick Friday night?" Stephanie asked. "It's his birthday. Damian said he can rig the coin slots at Station Break."

"Is that still the only place Patrick will go here?"

Stephanie made a frustrated sound. "Let me ask you something. If I described the empathy between a napkin and a dinner plate, would you call me pretentious?"

Evidently, Patrick had been grumbling again about the city's bad influence. How best to avoid stepping in it once again? Nina decided on a succinct "Nope."

"If I said a door handle is a room's handshake, would you say I was certifiable?"

"Never." Nina picked up an envelope with a Santa Claus decal on the back.

"What if I said, 'The day is coming when a single carrot, freshly observed, will set off a revolution'?"

Nina paused mid-slit. "*You* said that?"

"Cézanne. I bet Gardner wouldn't roll his eyes if you talked about the things you love."

What did Nina love? Gardner. She laughed to herself as she imagined talking to Gardner about the empathy between Gardner and Gardner, with a door handle and a carrot revolution thrown in. But Stephanie was grinding her teeth and Nina's impulse was to comfort her, even if that meant choking out a half-hearted defense of Patrick.

"I'm sure he doesn't mean to be a dick," she said, although she had no basis for this assurance. "I bet he's just worried he can't keep up." The letter from the Santa Claus envelope said, *How do you cure chilblains? Just kidding. You are useless.*

"Something's going on with him. And that something better not have a girl's name."

Stephanie's worries about Patrick's fidelity had been escalating lately, but they were all based on such nebulous things—more call-waiting-click evasions, a Salem cigarette in his glove compartment, a meaningful look a girl gave him at Cartoons—that Nina couldn't tell if they were grounded in reality.

"I know you don't think he's appealing," Stephanie added, "but a lot of girls actually do."

"Who said I don't think he's appealing," Nina said, wincing. To change the subject, she read the chilblains letter out loud.

"Speaking of chilblains," Stephanie said, "let me get a sweater. It's freezing in here."

Nina slit open another envelope while she waited for Stephanie to come back. Work was so much livelier enhanced with cocaine: maybe this was the lesson she'd end up taking away from summer temping.

"I need to get rid of my mirror," Stephanie said when she returned. "My face is Mount Vesuvius."

"Don't be ridiculous. You have the skin of a milkmaid."

Stephanie sniffed again. "By the way, no presents on Friday."

"Too late. I already got him an empathetic dinner plate." Nina snuck the coin purse onto her lap and did a quick nailful. Why trudge all the way out to the ladies' room when there was no one else in sight?

"Wait," Stephanie said, "did you hear that? The humming?"

"Where?"

"Listen."

All Nina heard was the clatter of a copy machine on the other side of her partition.

"I seriously think Mary Kay bugged the phone in my room."

"Better watch what we say about Tennessee, then." Nina slit open another envelope. A photo of a bonfire with a note on the back that she read to Stephanie: *We're burning stacks of Harvest Moons to keep warm.*

A long sniff on Stephanie's end. Nina dipped into her coin purse. After a while, it felt like just the two of them, sharing a buzz. *Divorce Court* ended, and Robin Leach's unctuous voice filled Stephanie's bedroom.

"Caviar dreams!" Nina called. She was about to open another letter when she noticed a glob of blood on the envelope. "Ew," she yelped, when another landed beside it and she realized it was hers.

"Holy shit," she told Stephanie. "My first nosebleed."

"Aw, sweetie. We'll have to celebrate."

She was about to get up to go look for a tissue, when the guy with the square glasses appeared at her cubicle.

"This is a workplace," he sneered, glancing from her nose to her open coin purse. "You do that sort of thing on your own time. Your day is done."

She opened her mouth to say something, but what was there to say?

"Two minutes to clear out," he said as he stormed away.

Nina didn't remember she was still holding the phone until she heard Stephanie's voice. "Now you can come over. Take a cab. Robin says you don't want to miss Malcolm Forbes's private island."

The next morning, Nina found Frances on her hands and knees, buffing the parquet floor with a dishrag. "I'm tired of wood," she said. "It's so *knock, knock, who's there.*"

"I get it," Stephanie said when Nina told her. "Bring her to Maison Rouge tomorrow. Come a few minutes before ten and I can let you in before the store opens. We have tons of nice area rugs in the basement."

Frances was thrilled to be a VIP. "Have I met Stephanie?"

Nina had mentioned her a few times but hadn't had her over. She rarely brought friends home, at least not since tenth grade, when her mother roused herself from bed to yell at Leigh for smelling like cigarettes. Even with Frances feeling better now, Nina worried that Stephanie's brashness could rub her the wrong way and trigger an eruption—or Stephanie's energy would spike Frances's, and she'd be off to the races with her punning and rhyming. Nina was sort of becoming used to it, but others might find it an acquired taste. What if Stephanie found it so off-putting, it scared her off Nina?

But the second Steph met them at the door to Maison Rouge, she and Frances fell for each other. Frances smiled at Stephanie's hair, pulled up in a spout with a gold scrunchie.

"You couldn't be more adorable," she said.

"And you couldn't be more chic," Stephanie said, smiling back at Frances's tortoiseshell headband and new pearl-embroidered handbag.

Even if Nina felt like a dowdy stepsister watching two Cinderellas dance at the ball—dowdy with a side of cokeover—there was nothing like the rush of introducing people who instantly appreciated each other, creating an equation in which you were the common denominator.

"How about we start downstairs?" Stephanie asked Frances. "Nina told me you're interested in rugs."

"For floors, not heads," Frances said.

Stephanie laughed. "First stop, toupees for floors."

The rugs were piled waist-high and hanging on every wall. Stephanie fired questions at Frances: What pattern was the parquet? What color were the walls? Foot traffic? Furniture? "I love a Jijim runner in a hallway." She held up a sample for Frances to feel. "I know people are into Berbers right now, but they snag like shag."

"You're a poet and you didn't even know it."

"*You're* too cool for school," Stephanie said.

Caught up in color and texture, they chattered loudly and unselfconsciously, the picture of merriment. They were also both thin as string, hollow around the collarbones, black circles under their eyes. ("I'll sleep when I'm dead," Frances kept saying.) But still Nina yearned for their looseness, the way they'd forgotten themselves, like she had when Gardner kissed her, and when she'd plunged the letter opener into the velvet chair at the Carlyle. Imagine living in that space of just letting yourself be—or not even letting yourself. Just being. Up ahead, Frances and Stephanie lovingly stroked a turquoise and gold Persian rug, exclaiming over its nap. Nina bent to stroke a butter-yellow rug at her feet, but here she still was, locked in her head.

Her mother stopped beside a rolled-up rug stood on end, which had blue and green squares on a black background, with three red apples in each square. "I love it!" she said as she threw her arms around it.

"That's one of my favorites!" Stephanie said. "It's from the 1920s. People used to look down on hooked rugs because they were hand-made, for people who couldn't afford expensive machine-made rugs. Can you believe it? This one's wool, but a lot of them were made from old clothes and burlap feed sacks and worn-out curtains."

Frances beamed at her. "You are sharp as a tack."

Stephanie beamed back. "And you have first-rate taste." She noticed Nina hanging back and came to get her. "Your mom is awesome."

Nina laughed. "That might be the first time anyone's said that to me." She hadn't realized how good it could make you feel, to have one of those mothers other people enjoyed.

Stephanie pulled on her hair spout to revive its buoyancy. She clicked a tuneless song with her tongue that sounded a little like "Billie Jean."

"Have you heard from Gardner?" she asked.

"No."

"Not yet," Stephanie corrected. "Is he still in Bridgehampton?"

"I guess so?" Nina pictured him emerging from the ocean, his chest glittering with water droplets and specks of salt. You didn't think about sitting inside a house making phone calls when there was a beach to lounge on and sunshine to bask in.

She groaned. "I hate this."

"Next time you see him," Stephanie said, "try to look super-confident. Fill your brain with sexy words. It'll make your eyes shine."

Salacious, Nina thought. Feline.

Stephanie looked at her eyes and laughed. "Holy shit, it works!"

She stopped to even out a stack of felt rug pads. "How's your friend doing, the one who's worried she might have AIDS?"

Nina had told her what Meredith was going through. "Leigh finally convinced her to make the appointment," she said. "The test is tomorrow. I know she's not always the nicest, but I've known her forever, and if she's positive . . ." She shook her head. "It's too horrible to think about."

"I promise to stop calling her 'the mean one' if it's bad news," Stephanie said. "How long until she finds out?"

"They said it takes two weeks."

They caught up with Frances, who was searching for more fruit-themed rugs. Nina noticed a woman by the sheepskins a few yards away who seemed to be studying them. Maison Rouge red blouse, frizzy black hair, and cat-eye glasses, lips in a thin line. This had to be Beverly, Stephanie's boss.

Stephanie noticed her too. She squatted to flatten an errant strand of a braided rug and motioned Nina down to join her. "She went through my locker last week."

Was this more coke paranoia? In Stephanie's bedroom the other day, after the *Harvest Moon* fiasco, Nina had noticed a new butterfly sticker on the wall above the bulletin board.

I found a little hole there, Stephanie had said, *just the right size for Kay to hide one of those little spy cameras. She'd love to find a way to get my dad to kick me out.*

Frances reappeared and squatted to join them. She narrowed her eyes in the direction they were looking. "Who's the woman with the absurd glasses?"

"My boss," Stephanie said. "Beverly. She hates me."

Frances shook her head indignantly. "*Hates* you? She should be thanking her lucky stars for you."

"I only got this job because she's friends with my father's girl-friend. She flat-out told me she'd never have hired me otherwise."

How unnecessarily mean, especially considering Stephanie's zeal for interior design. "Bitch," Nina said—or whispered, because even though Beverly was now talking with a customer, her shoulders strained backward, as if trying to hear them.

"*Bitch* is right," Frances agreed at top volume, and Beverly's shoulders tightened.

Nina tried to shush her while Stephanie laughed. Frances stood up straight and rifled through her new bag. This morning, Nina had taken out the recorder and stuck it under a cushion on the living-room couch. It was one thing in private, the onslaught of puns and autobiographical anecdotes, her mother's broad, cheap-seats theatricality, but in public, the side-looks were hard to withstand.

But then Nina had put it back in her mother's bag, scared what Frances might do if she found herself without it. Now she held her breath, hoping a lipstick or a tissue would emerge.

But here came the recorder. Stephanie met Nina's eyes with a look of nostalgia, and for a moment Nina was back with her at the Palladium, interviewing the drunken pirate.

Then Frances pressed Record.

"Not now," Nina pleaded.

"I decided to confront the boss," Frances said, gripping the machine like a microphone, "tell the dimwit how ignorant she was for grinding this exceptional talent underfoot." Before Nina could stop her, she marched over to Beverly.

Stephanie's face lit up with gratitude.

"This is not a good idea," Nina said aloud, more for posterity since neither her mother nor Stephanie seemed to be listening. It was way too early in the morning for a scene, and Beverly didn't look like she'd welcome constructive criticism from some keyed-up stranger with a tape recorder. But Frances had planted herself directly behind her, even though she was still talking with her customer, a blond woman in a tennis skirt, who noticed Frances first, peering over Beverly's shoulder. Beverly turned her head and recoiled with surprise, seeing Frances there hovering, arms crossed.

"Can I help you?" she asked, although her tone said she doubted it.

"Can I help *you*, is the question," Frances said.

"I'm with a customer," Beverly said, right as the blonde hurried away.

"I presume you're the manager, and I wanted you to know that Stephanie is one of the best salesgirls I've ever met. But I get the distinct impression her efforts are underappreciated. What do you intend to do about that?"

"Wow," Stephanie said, eyes wide, and Nina tried to swallow back her envy. She couldn't remember a time Frances had spoken up for her this way.

"I was with a customer, ma'am," Beverly said.

"*I'm* a customer," Frances said, "and a very happy one, thanks to that kaleidoscopically knowledgeable young woman." She pointed to Stephanie, who got busy straightening a pile of braided area rugs. Nina went to the other side of the pile to make some assisting motions, while keeping her mother in her sights.

"I'm glad to hear Stephanie was helpful," Beverly said through clenched teeth.

Frances tilted her head. "You don't sound glad." She was doing that swaying thing again, and declaiming into the tape recorder: "I gave the dimwit a piece of my mind, but it remained to be seen if it would have the desired effect."

"Mom!" Nina said loudly, starting toward her. But Frances threw up her hand to stop her and Nina obeyed, hoping she would lose steam on her own, or at least wind it up quickly. Forcing the issue could ignite the opposite effect.

Beverly pushed up her glasses. "Did you just call me a dimwit?"

"I wasn't talking to you," Frances snapped.

"Ma'am." Beverly crossed her arms. "I have to ask you to lower your voice."

"My voice is fine," Frances yelled.

Stephanie giggled, at the same time digging into a pimple on her chin so hard, blood spurted down her fingernail.

Nina took another tentative step. "Mom," she wheedled, "we should go."

"I've been shopping at this store for a hundred years," Frances said. Her swaying made her look like a skinny tree caught in a windstorm. "I've never been treated this shabbily. When did you change your name to Maison Rude?"

"Ma'am, you're going to have to calm down." Beverly's voice was slimy with contempt.

Frances suddenly raised the recorder over her head as if to hit her with it. Nina grabbed her forearm, but her mother shook her off with a withering look and lowered her arm as if she'd just been stretching. "I intend to send this tape to your CEO," she told Beverly. "You'll be lucky to have a job tomorrow."

Beverly looked furious, and—gratifyingly—a little scared.

"Your glasses are ridiculous," Frances said. "I hate them."

"Ma'am," Beverly said sharply. "If I have to, I will call security."

"*Ma'am, lamb, pam, scram,*" Frances singsonged, but she let Nina steer her across the floor to the Exit sign, bypassing Stephanie so she wouldn't get in even more trouble by association, as if she weren't already thoroughly implicated.

Stephanie took the hint, giving just a small, discreet wave. Out on the street, Frances continued ranting. "I've been shopping there for a thousand years. She's not getting away with this."

They started walking home. Charged atoms swirled around them like a cloud of gnats. It was Wednesday; Ira was due home Sunday. Three days to get her mother brought back to some semblance of normal. They turned onto Seventy-Sixth Street. Nina tried to slow Frances down, but she was going top speed. People walking toward them veered to the edge of the sidewalk so they wouldn't get mowed down. Halfway down the block, a maroon Volvo backed into a parking space but ended up sticking halfway out into the street.

Frances stopped abruptly.

"Mom, no," Nina said. "It's none of our business."

Too late. Frances was knocking on the driver's-side window.

Dad, she'd tell her father when he called tonight, *maybe you want to think about coming home early.*

The driver's window rolled down and a bald head emerged.

"You're cutting the wheel too soon," Frances told the man in a voice that said he'd personally offended her with his subpar parking efforts.

"What are you, the parking police?"

"Am I going to have to park this thing myself?" Frances shouted.

"Get away from my car," the guy shouted back.

Frances yanked on the handle of the car door, thankfully locked. "Mom, come on!"

Frances's eyes bulged, white on all sides, like the irises were floating loose. Nina felt herself floating loose also. *Today,* she would tell her father. *Come home today.* She managed to pull Frances away from the car and the traffic whizzing by to the safety of the sidewalk. Just then, the Volvo settled into the parking space.

"You did it!" Frances said. Now she was grinning. She turned to Nina as if the guy and his car no longer existed; she'd provided a service and now she was done. "Let's get omelets at Yellowfingers. We can figure out what to do about that apple rug."

She turned and started walking up the block, leaving Nina and the driver to stare at each other in confusion. His gaze was a mix of pity and concern. Shut up, Nina thought. Then she turned to follow her mother.

She was glad she hadn't had a chance to call her father. Frances had calmed down, and they'd have a lovely lunch at Yellowfingers. Anyway, it was an hour earlier in St. Louis; none of this had happened yet.

———

When they got home from lunch, there was a message from Stephanie on Nina's answering machine: "Fucking Beverly couldn't stand hearing a dot of praise for me. She's been at me all day." A pause to take a drag off her cigarette. "If anyone's a *wackjob*, it's her."

Which Nina took to mean that Beverly had called Frances a wackjob after they'd left the store. Nina flinched at the thought of Beverly—*fuck* fucking Beverly—talking about her mother that way, even as she replayed the parallel-parking episode in her head, and later, walking home from lunch, when Frances noticed a discarded child-sized rocking chair and torn purple kite in a pile of trash, and started crying. *They look so lonely,* she'd wailed, squeezing herself into the little chair and crying even harder when she couldn't make it rock.

The trick, Nina decided, was to buffer Frances from outside irritants—let her recuperate until Ira got home. For the rest of the week, she volunteered for every errand and stuck by Frances's side for trips to the dry cleaner and Alexander's for new socks. She intercepted an invitation from a few of Frances's old Amity Club friends to join them for dinner at the super-chic and super-pricey Quilted Giraffe, the first time they'd been in touch in ages. The Amity women were mostly indifferent to anyone but themselves and hardly noticed when someone else spoke, but Frances narrating their dinner into a tape recorder would be enough of an oddity to catch their attention and undoubtedly get back to Ira.

"Quilts for giraffes?" Patrick asked.

Nina had just finished telling Stephanie about the Quilted Giraffe situation, wondering if she'd done the right thing.

"I'd love to go one day," Stephanie called from her bathroom. "I've heard it's amazing."

They'd decided to meet at Mary Kay's Friday night instead of Station Break, after Kay and Stephanie's father got a last-minute invite to *Me and My Girl*.

"The Quilted Giraffe," Stephanie said, "has crêpes filled with caviar and topped with real gold leaf." She peed with the door open while, out in her bedroom, Nina eyed Patrick on the edge of the bed—a spot he'd never left, in her memory—cutting lines on the night table. It was her first time seeing him since the Fourth of July party. She was even jumpier than she'd expected. She futzed with the things on Stephanie's dresser, looking anywhere but at him. She could still smell the stale tang of sweat mixed with Juicy Fruit gum, even more pungent than last time. She lined up the bottles of nail polish and studied the bud vases like there might be a test. She lit a Marlboro and hunted around for an ashtray.

"Do they also serve giraffe?" Patrick laughed like it was the funniest thing anyone had ever said.

Nina got a sudden, sickening image of the dead leopard slung around Tom Parrish's shoulders, but also a little thrill at the thought of Gardner that came with it. Picturing him made her body almost levitate, although she'd only have time tonight to stop by Flanagan's for a quick drink, since she'd have to get home to check on her mother.

She was pleased with her reflection in the mirror over Stephanie's dresser, her frayed denim cutoffs and Stephanie's Run-D.M.C. shirt knotted at the bottom to show a little skin. She felt the imprint of Gardner's hand cupped between her legs. She hadn't *let anyone else in there* since he'd been gone, obviously, but she looked like she could have if she'd wanted to.

She found an ashtray on the bookshelf, a sleek cast-iron oval grooved at the lip to hold a cigarette.

"You have the best taste," she called to Stephanie.

"That's why she's with me," Patrick said.

"Right." She wasn't here to make waves, not on his birthday. And tonight she was even a little sorry for Patrick, his hungry eyes tracking Stephanie and his blissful look when she came near. If he was cheating on her, it was only to wall off his heart for when she inevitably dumped him.

He held out a straw to Nina that he'd clipped to a couple of inches. There was dirt under his nails and a swarm of zits on his forehead. He'd drawn a lopsided skull on his arm with fangs and some ball-point dots that she guessed represented dripping saliva. It looked like he hadn't bathed since July.

But feeling sorry for him didn't mean she'd kneel at his feet again. She shook her head *No thanks*, fetched the coin purse from her handbag, and stood against the wall across the room. She filled her pinkie nail and braced herself; in addition to the nosebleeds, the coke had started to feel like a stabbing blade up there. She sniffed and forced herself not to flinch, since Patrick was already smirking at her.

"Fancy," he said, pointing at the silky coin purse.

Stephanie came out of the bathroom in Nina's pink tank top, unprissified by purple mascara and big black rubber hoop earrings. "Don't be a jerk, Patrick. I have the same one—you've seen it a million times. They were five bucks from a guy on Canal Street." She rolled her eyes apologetically at Nina. "Everything here is too *fancy* for him. We stopped at Popcorn Planet today and he was like, What's wrong with Jiffy Pop?"

Well, that Nina could understand. "I have to admit," she said, "flavored popcorn does kind of make me nauseous." At least she and Patrick agreed on something. "It seems so contrived. And what's the point, when the original is so perfectly good?"

"Like menthol cigarettes," Patrick said. "Why?"

"Sparkling water," Nina agreed.

"You two philistines," Stephanie said, and Patrick gave Nina a genuine smile.

Stephanie took the straw from him and bent over the table, sniffing hard with no apparent discomfort. "Some upgrades make everyday things better. Checker cabs. Blinis."

"She's never liked Jiffy Pop," Patrick told Nina.

"You have to turn it in a circle," Nina said. Maybe she and Patrick *could* forge some kind of peace. "It burns if you shake it back and forth."

"The Guggenheim's staircase," Stephanie said. "Mica in the sidewalks. Bendel's Lalique windows."

"Leaky windows?" Patrick said.

"Hot dog carts." Stephanie picked through the bowl of Starbursts on the dresser until she found a lemon. "The Puerto Rican Day Parade. The Brooklyn Bridge. The lobby of the Woolworth Building."

Nina had lost the thread. What were these upgrades of?

"The Chelsea flea market. Central fucking Park. The Palladium." She smiled at Nina and added, "Le Sex Shoppe." *Need I say more?* her tone said.

Nina got it: the city itself was the upgrade. Stephanie was never going back to Hewlett. She glanced around the room to avoid Patrick's pained expression. To change the subject, she said to Stephanie, "Ma'am? I'm going to have to ask you to calm down."

"Don't make me call security, ma'am," Stephanie said, laughing as she picked the wrapper off the Starburst.

"I'm so sorry again," Nina said. "I told you how she gets, um, carried away sometimes. She just really, really liked you."

"I really, really liked her too!" Stephanie put the Starburst in her mouth and suddenly Nina was dying for one too. She went for a cherry, unwrapped it, and bit. When she looked up, she and Stephanie were framed in the mirror, chewing. Behind them was the magenta board and the butterfly sticker covering the real or imagined camera lens.

"Would it be weird if I called her sometime?" Stephanie asked.

They looked completely different—Stephanie's wide mouth and green eyes, Nina's dark hair and thinner eyebrows—but also, somehow, like family.

"She'd love it." If Mary Kay really was listening in right now, imagine how peeved she'd be. "You could even stay in my room while I'm at school if things here get too shitty."

Patrick's head snapped up. So he had been listening. Stephanie whooped and leaped onto the bed beside him while Patrick caught Nina's eye in the mirror, his expression stony. She wasn't sure she'd ever been on the receiving end of a look like that, dead eyes wishing she were dead. Her heart was already beating too fast from the coke, so her joke to try to placate him came out in a babble: "Be sure to move my mom in a circle so she doesn't burn." Patrick's eyes flashed white-hot with dislike. *Don't even try,* they said.

At Penn Station, down in the LIRR passageway, the hall was filled with synthesized bells and beeps coming from the arcade. Inside, people leaned into the game consoles, shifting their weight from foot to foot, mouths slack, eyes huge and unblinking like they'd been stuck in place for days.

"Look who it is," said a tall guy in a short-sleeved button-down shirt. "The fucking birthday boy." A patch above his pocket said STATION BREAK. This must be Damian.

"Got a present for me, you ugly piece of shit?" Patrick said.

They hugged with self-conscious affection that might have been sweet if Patrick weren't such a dipshit. Damian looked pretty unremarkable for a coke dealer, no trace of Al Pacino's oily *Scarface* menace. He did look like a coke *user,* though, dime-sized pupils ringed in hazel.

Stephanie tilted her head toward him, then widened her eyes at

Nina. Oh, that was why she'd been invited: a setup, in case things with Gardner didn't work out. Nina saw why Stephanie thought she might like him. He was a good-looking guy, with Gardner's build and blue eyes and dark hair. But his face was rounder and his lips thinner. His hunch was a distant cousin to Gardner's sexy slouch.

"How's the action?" Patrick asked.

"Bunch of Jersey pussies hogging *Tempest* all night," he said. Like Patrick, he laughed at his own jokes, but then kept staring at everyone with a weird insistence until they joined in.

"Who gives a shit," Patrick said. "I'm here for *Robotron.*"

Was Gardner already at Flanagan's, wondering if she were coming? Were Alison Bloch and Minnie Potter wrangling over who'd buy his drink or rub his shoulders? Maybe she ought to show up with Damian, make Gardner realize he wasn't the only guy interested in her. Although that fantasy crumbled when Damian turned to Stephanie and the longing in his eyes was fierce enough to power a missile.

"How about you, Steph? *Ms. Pac-Man?*"

Stephanie obliged with an amused snort. "Have you forgotten who creamed who in *Joust* last time?" She absentmindedly picked at a pimple. "Tonight's Patrick's turn to get taught a lesson. Come take your medicine, babe." With a last pointed head-tilt toward Damian, she smiled at Nina, then pulled Patrick down the aisle to a screen of robots shooting multicolored gunfire.

"So you're the city friend," Damian said to Nina. He could barely tear his eyes from Stephanie's tight-skirted ass.

"Is that what Patrick calls me?"

"Wouldn't you like to know." More laughter and aggressive eye contact. "Want to see *Howard the Duck* sometime?"

"Um, maybe? I'm going to college soon, but maybe when I'm home for Thanksgiving?"

His face reddened. Well, at least she'd managed to pull the plug on the creepy eye assault. She tried to brush away a pang of guilt. She *was* going to college soon. And hadn't she just watched him drool over Stephanie's behind?

"Sure thing, princess," he said, then stomped over to the air hockey table to yell at some kid for sitting on it. *Princess?* She visited the ladies' room for a quick nail scoop from her *fancy* coin purse, then wandered around for a while until she found an unoccupied pinball machine. Its artwork was a leering centaur—half man, half motorcycle—and a woman dressed in a tight leather corset and a thigh-length boa straddling his seat. Nina inserted a quarter, red lights began to flash, and a deep, distorted voice intoned, *"Destroy Centaur."* She worked the flippers a little awkwardly, her bag on her shoulder so no one could walk off with it, but she kept the ball in motion, striking the red bumpers and setting off a legion of dings and thwacks and clacks and clangs.

If cocaine were music, she imagined telling Gardner, *this is how it would sound.*

The ball finished ricocheting and whizzed straight between the flippers down the drain. *"Bad move, human,"* boomed the centaur.

"Haven't you ever played pinball?" Patrick said. He'd come up behind her. "Don't push both flippers at the same time. It gives the ball too much room to fall between."

He was standing too close for comfort, his chest grazing her back. Another ball popped up and she considered purposely bungling it to end the game, but why give him the satisfaction?

"Where's Steph?" she asked.

He sniffed flamboyantly.

"She's going to wreck her beautiful nose if she doesn't slow down."

"Thanks, Mom. Why do you think we've started smoking it?"

They had? Nina didn't have time to absorb this information before yet another ball popped up—there were two zipping around now, then suddenly a third. The bumpers flashed faster when the balls collided with them, more frantic bells and thumps. *"No class, human!"* the reverberating voice scolded when Nina accidentally tilted the machine. Patrick still hovered behind her. She rolled her shoulders, like, *Give me some space.* His teeth clicked close to her ear, like, *Nope.* A ball passed through the flippers, down the drain.

"Why so clumsy, princess?" Patrick said.

So yeah, that was where Damian got it. *Didn't Stephanie tell you I trashed a hotel room?* she felt like saying but didn't, out of worry it could still come back to bite her and Gardner on the ass. She tried to ward off the onslaught of paranoia, but it was hard not to picture Patrick and Damian snickering about her. *Princess. Prig. Prude.* She stepped in closer to the machine, the metal edge digging into her bare stomach. She hadn't noticed the game board was covered in ghouls and snakes. The bumpers glowed topaz and crimson, like dragon eyes on fire. Another ball down the drain.

"You gotta put your body into it," Patrick said, and then he was pressing into her, hands covering hers, knees against the backs of her legs, crotch prodding the small of her back. Hot, smoky breath on her scalp. The flippers thrashed as he pressed her fingers. She jerked away and the machine tipped again. *"No class, human."*

She whirled around and glared at him. He gave her an innocent look as he stepped back, like nothing had happened. She was a bug he'd flicked off his arm. Fury filled her. Not the exhilarating kind that made you brave. The concrete kind that paralyzed. She could hardly move her mouth, much less form words or thoughts. She just stood there, trying to catch her breath, until she saw that Stephanie was stalking toward them, furious, too, but ignited by it, shoulders thrown back and hips swinging. Nina roused herself. She needed her nerve to explain how Patrick had ground into her; she couldn't let him grab control with lies. She felt a mix of shame that she hadn't extracted herself sooner combined with relief that Stephanie had finally seen his fuckery for herself. At least now Nina wouldn't have to describe it from scratch.

But Stephanie's anger wasn't for them. It was aimed at a girl in the restroom who'd somehow splashed her at the sink.

"I'm standing there washing my hands, and then, *motherfucker*, I'm drenched!" There was a wet patch in the middle of the pink tank top she'd borrowed from Nina, but she was as wild-eyed as if she'd been blasted with a garden hose. "Bitch took off before I could catch her. Have you seen her? Red hair, stupid dress covered with Space Invaders." She jabbed her index finger around her chest and torso about fifty times as she looked around for the girl.

One day Nina would tell her about Patrick. But not this day. She couldn't bear those dagger eyes turned on her.

"Does the newsstand have Coke?" Stephanie asked. "Will one of you go see?"

"If they do I'll have an eight ball," Patrick chortled.

Stephanie scowled. "I'm gonna throw it in her face when I find her."

"I'll get it," Nina volunteered, happy to escape Patrick's presence, that vile smirk and his nicotine-yellowed teeth. And, admittedly, Stephanie, too, the menacing energy not currently aimed at Nina but seeming volatile enough that it could swing her way at any moment. She grabbed her bag and went out to the station.

As she searched for a newsstand, her clenched jaw sent up a flare of pain. She could still feel Patrick hemming her in from behind, his hands trapping hers, his hot breath on her scalp. But he'd been just careful enough to profess innocence, make Nina seem paranoid and vengeful. What would she say—he stood too close while giving pinball tips?

Where else would he stand, across the arcade?

Typical city princess. Drama queen. Easily offended.

But she knew he'd done it on purpose, to make his point, the same one he'd made in Stephanie's bedroom at the July Fourth party: *You can't have her.*

She passed a guy with no legs playing "Let's Go Crazy" on the saxophone and remembered the night Gardner sang it at Flanagan's after his breakup with Holland, his bright white shirt, supernova energy, and the slice of tan flesh when he'd raised his arms. Her longing to touch him was making her fingers twitch. She walked by a bank of pay phones and ordered herself to keep going, but the chance to hear his voice was impossible to resist. She had to know if he'd come back from the Hamptons, that he hadn't fallen for some girl out there and stayed. Maybe he'd even tried to call *her* and she'd missed it—she hadn't been home for hours!

She punched in his number.

An exasperated female voice: "Hel-*lo?*" His mother.

Nina hesitated, her finger hovering over the hang-up lever as she conjured Mrs. Reed's bitter face.

"You goddamn girls!" Her voice was so furious, it trembled. "Why can't you leave Gardner alone?"

"What?" Nina blurted, then stuck her hand over the receiver, regretting that her voice had in any way entered Gardner's home.

"I am so sick of you girls throwing yourselves at him," Mrs. Reed said. "Are *you* the tramp who sent those disgusting Polaroids? Stop hounding him, for Christ's sake."

Nina slammed down the phone. "Polaroids?" she said as she backed away. A guy in a cropped Mickey Mouse shirt smiled as if she'd started up a conversation with him, so she walked faster. *Disgusting,* Mrs. Reed had said, so they must have been dirty. Nina pictured breasts, smiles, open legs. Had Gardner asked for them? From whom? Which *tramp?*

She found a can of Coke at a pretzel cart and headed back to the arcade. Just how many girls were hounding him? Was one of them at the Carlyle right now? She wrapped her fingers around the cold can and, to distract herself, tried to think of other animals that were verbs for things humans did: ape, crow, badger, bug, carp.

Back at the arcade, Stephanie wasn't upset anymore about the *Space Invaders* girl—in fact, she and Patrick were now *playing* it, their faces leached of color in the monitor's gray light. Nina handed her the Coke and she chugged half of it.

"Thank you. And sorry about that. When that girl splashed me, my heart was just like: *boom.*" She whacked her palms together.

The game's deep banging bass quickened as the aliens descended. Patrick, his dumb *Star Wars* T-shirt reflected in the game screen, thumped his laser button like a chimp releasing treats in a lab experiment.

"Fudge-packing assfaces," he yelled when his guy got smashed. Stephanie rolled her eyes, but at least she was laughing again, which meant she was okay, and that Nina could leave without worrying about her. She promised herself: tomorrow she would tell her about Patrick. For now she just said she had to go.

"Remember," Stephanie whispered. "Sex eyes when you see him."

Nina hugged her hard, inhaling the scent of Eves in her hair, the burnt-sugar scent she had grown to love.

If she went to Flanagan's, would she be just one more hounding (bugging, badgering) tramp? Maybe the only thing that could make her stand out was to *not* show up.

It was only ten thirty. She'd stop at home to check on Frances, pick up a Xanax and an Actifed, and then decide. When the cab dropped her off at her building, she waited a moment for Freddie to open the door—usually he was standing right there, peeking out through a gap in the thick brass scrollwork that covered the glass— but it stayed closed. She reached for the handle, catching sight of a swirl of cream fabric, a flash of a woman's satin slipper. Most of the residents left on the summer weekends; maybe Freddie had snuck in a girlfriend and wouldn't notice Nina go by.

She pulled open the door and heard the transistor radio playing his sitar music with the flutes and bells. The woman was in the center of the lobby, swiveling her hips in a kind of belly dance. Nina froze as she recognized those bony hips.

"Hello, dear. Bonsoir!" Frances greeted her. She turned to Freddie. "How do you say 'hello' in your language?"

"Salam," he said, smiling. He was standing at his console, shuffling his feet and snapping his fingers to the music.

"Salam," Frances echoed. She gave Nina a stagy wink. Her dress swished around her calves—no, not a dress, but one of her new nightgowns, girlish with a lace-edged collar and tiny buttons but still gauzy enough for Nina to see the shadow of her underwear.

"What are you doing?" The heat in Nina's voice made Freddie pause, but her mother just laughed.

"Having fun. You ought to try it." A burst of tambourines hit the air. She raised her hands to her eyes with her elbows bent to the sides, peeking through spread fingers. "This is how Vera-Ellen danced with Gene Kelly in *On the Town*."

Freddie pointed to a plate on the console with a single cupcake in the center, frosted in pink icing. "She bring for me. Then she hear music."

Anyone could come in that front door, or down the elevator. For all Nina knew, someone already had. She could only hope Freddie would have put a stop to the dancing if there were a witness. Although *Nina* was a witness, and that hadn't stopped anything.

"They called it the cooch dance in the movie." Frances held her hands aloft, tapping her fingers to the rhythm of the tambourines.

"Mom, that's enough," Nina said, as if even a little might have been okay. "Let's go upstairs."

"Freddie, what is it with this girl of mine?" Frances sighed flamboyantly. "Can you believe I gave birth to such a stiff?"

She heard Freddie snicker behind her. What a fitting climax to this perfect evening. "You're a terrible dancer," she said angrily to Frances.

"Says who?" Frances lifted her arms and clasped her hands as if around an imaginary partner's neck. She swayed foot-to-foot to what must have been a tune in her head, since her steps had nothing to do with the fast-paced percussion. Her eyes had a glassy shine.

"Come dance with me." She beckoned to Nina.

"Yes," Freddie said. "Miss Nina dance with mother."

A new tune started up, with an overwrought violin and twangy harp. "Salam," Frances said to Freddie. "I dance in your ancestors' mother tongue." Her nightgown slipped off one shoulder. The harp accelerated, joined by aggressive cymbals. The music had the same relentlessness as the soundtrack to the centaur game at the arcade.

"Turn it off!" Nina said to Freddie. He gripped the edge of the console, bobbing to the music as if he hadn't heard her.

A trumpet roared and Frances still swung her hips, but her face had gone even paler and sweat pooled in the hollow of her throat. She was starting to wobble, frowning as she tried to keep her balance, gripping handfuls of nightgown in her fists.

Nina saw a flash of fear in her eyes as if she wanted to stop dancing but couldn't. An engine inside her was combusting and she didn't know how to switch it off. For a second, Nina was helpless also, stricken with her mother's fear. Then she yelled at Freddie, "Turn the goddamn radio off!" She pushed him aside and did it herself. Silence fell over the lobby, although Frances continued to swivel her hips. Freddie stared openmouthed.

Nina was both in her body and far outside. She felt her lips move, coaxing, "Mom, Mama," and she watched herself slither toward Frances, the snake charming the charmer. Because she was a snake, already planning to betray her to her father.

But for now her mother allowed herself to be led to the elevator, her hips slowing and her shoulders going still. Behind her back, Nina caught Freddie's gape-mouthed stare—his eyes were wide, unnerved; he was backed against the wall beside the intercom, hands up as if to plead innocence. *I'd say we're even,* she did her best to convey with a searing look. He nodded, she presumed with understanding, as the door to the elevator closed.

All the lights were on in Frances's bedroom, including the bedside lamps, and a new tall, squiggly-bodied floor lamp the size of a ficus, aimed at the ceiling. The shades were raised, too, with that bright moon flooding in.

"No wonder you never sleep," Nina said. It felt good to put a little wryness in her voice, after the frightened yelling in the lobby.

Frances's brow creased, a puzzled look edged with suspicion.

Probably better not to put anything in her voice, Nina decided, or in fact voice anything at all. Silently, with a careful, nurse-like smile, she led her mother to the bed, settled her on her back, and pulled off her slippers. Frances's expression stayed the same as she gazed around the room at the array of crap that had accumulated in Ira's absence— hatboxes, stacks of blank *Congratulations!* cards, picture frames, L'Eggs eggs—as if she had no idea how it had gotten there. Nina reminded herself to clean it all out before her father got home the day after tomorrow. It was one thing to describe what had happened while he was away, but another to clobber him with the evidence.

She found a half-empty glass of water on the nightstand and a bottle of Halcion. Frances desperately needed to sleep. Nina remembered learning in a European history class that in the 1600s, women accused of being witches would be forced to stay awake until they finally started to hallucinate and spout inanities that sounded like sorcery. She gave Frances a Halcion and swallowed one herself. She turned off all the lights and then, obeying some filial instinct, lay down next to her mother on her father's side of the bed.

"Did we miss the flight?" Frances asked after a minute. She sounded vague and mercifully close to conking out. "Where's the scissors?"

The Halcion was pulling Nina under too. Freddie's face darted by behind her eyes, then Patrick's, then both imploded and sprinkled to the ground in shards of terra-cotta, like broken planters. From outside the window came the distant howl of a siren.

"My ride's here," Frances mumbled.

The next thing Nina knew, the room was swarmed with sunlight and her father was at the foot of the bed, demanding to know where her mother was.

Chapter Fifteen

If you didn't sleep enough to sleep it off, Halcion left you irritable and nauseated, with a throbbing headache. The opposite of halcyon, Nina thought as she trailed her father to the living room, where he looked around in utter confusion, blinking and blinking.

"You need to tell me what the hell is going on."

What day was it? What was he doing home? What time was it? Why was the sun blazing through the windows, directly into her brain?

"What do you mean?" she said groggily.

"What do you *mean* what do I mean?" He spread his arms to indicate the chaos that hadn't been there when he left for St. Louis: dozens of new embroidered pillows, tags still attached, piled on the couch. A herd of jade elephants on the coffee table. A life-size plaster bust of Beethoven. The gargantuan Think Big harmonica propped against the fireplace mantel beside the mammoth Think Big hairbrush with black bristles the size of a porcupine's quills. Stacks of waterlogged *Vogue*s on the windowsill. Baskets overflowing with napkin rings, silverware, and packets of mini cassettes. A torn box of encyclopedias. The lonely child's rocking chair and torn purple kite that Frances must have retrieved from the street. An old red rotary phone on its side on the floor, in a puddle of sunshine.

Saturday, she remembered. Today was Saturday.

"You weren't supposed to be back until tomorrow," she said to her father, trying to keep the accusation out of it. Funny how just a few days ago, she'd thought she wanted him home early.

"Grandma's settled, so I got an earlier flight. What difference does that make? What is all this? You said she was fine."

"I would have cleaned up." She turned away guiltily from the mess—it was as if her mother had cut herself open on Nina's watch and here they were, gawking at her entrails.

"Are you telling me this is all *your* stuff?"

She shook her head. No use lying when he must have known the truth the instant he walked in.

"You should have told me things had gotten this dire."

She swept her arm around the room and said, "It looks a lot worse than it is." *Uh . . . really?* the little rocking chair piped up. "She's not that bad. You'll see."

He stalked to the window where the moldy *Vogue*s were strewn over the sill, models on the covers in various stages of disfigurement, one with a jagged rip across her face, another with sun-bleached eyes that made them look bulbous, as if the scarf around her neck was pulled too tight. Even from across the room, Nina could smell the mildew, unless maybe the odor was coming off her: stale mouth, smoky hair, some noxious crud inside her that seemed to soil every part of her life.

"Well, where is she?" her father asked.

"What do you mean?"

"Jesus Christ!" Ira shoved the magazines to the floor. "Where'd she go?"

"I don't know! I can't watch her every second."

"You apparently don't watch her *any* second."

You talked to her every night! she wanted to scream. *Why weren't you paying attention? You're the one who married her.* You *chose her. I'm just an innocent bystander.* But his clenched jaw made the words stick in her throat.

The door to the apartment opened and Nina heard two women talking.

"What a lovely 'ome," one said in a Cockney accent.

"We're quite 'appy 'ere," Frances answered in the same accent.

Ira met Nina's eyes. The two of them went quickly around the corner to the foyer, where the British woman, or at least the one who wasn't Nina's mother, was gazing wide-eyed at the carved mahogany bench and bronze wall sconces. Although she looked the age of a grandmother, she had on a ruffled dress printed with strawberries, Keds sneakers, and a flowered sunhat tied beneath her chin; and even though it wasn't yet noon, Frances was outfitted in a sequined blouse and more than a few rhinestone barrettes in her hair. She swayed from foot to foot, all gleeful energy, no trace of a Halcion hangover.

Ira cleared his throat.

Frances turned and beamed. "Welcome 'ome, dearest!" She kissed him on both cheeks, two loud smooches that left crimson imprints. Her eyes were bright and darting.

"Fran," he said. A muscle jumped below one of the kiss marks, but now he spoke softly. "Where have you been?"

She raised her arms over her head in a wide V. "When I sees the sunrise I says to meself, 'Self, what a glorious day for an 'orse-and-carriage roid frew Central Park.'" Any minute she'd start singing about the rine in Spine. Nina couldn't tell if the accent was unconscious or a put-on, but after last night's belly dance in the lobby, she wasn't sure there was much these days her mother was in control of. And while Nina didn't see any fear in her mother's eyes now, they still glittered in the same combustive way.

Nina turned to the British woman. "Are you the carriage driver?" It seemed to make as much sense as anything.

She snorted. "In town from Whitechapel, ain't I? Me mum's 'ere in 'ospital."

"Poor fing's got a 'ole in 'er 'art," Frances added.

"So's I'm in the park, dragging me arse up the fountain steps when I 'ears this nice lady in a carriage calling to me, *Yoo-hoo!* She invites me in 'er carriage, she does."

"Plenty a' room," Frances said. "Just meself and Gypsy."

Ira looked utterly bewildered. "You're Gypsy?" he asked the British woman.

She and Frances broke into uproarious laughter.

"Gypsy was our 'orse!" the woman gasped. "Old nag dropped a giant shite in front of Bethesda Fountain!" She planted her sneakers a foot apart, squatted, and neighed as if to demonstrate.

Ira blinked a hundred times, watching Frances's gaunt shoulders shake with hilarity while a stranger squatted and whinnied in his foyer. Nina had never seen him so flummoxed.

The woman maneuvered herself back to her feet. "Clara's *me* name," she said in an oddly insistent way, as if it were crucial they remember. Now Nina noticed a dilapidated suitcase by the front door, patched with duct tape. Frances had progressed from bringing home abandoned junk to people; soon there'd be a collection of them lounging around the living room.

"Let me show you to your room," Frances said to her.

This roused Ira from his daze. "Clara, will you excuse us? Fran," he said, motioning her farther into the foyer, a few feet away. Nina strained to listen while keeping one eye on Clara and the other on the Baccarat vase on the console that her parents had gotten as a wedding gift. Clara had the look of an operator, the cartoonish clothing and too-innocent gaze around the room that was probably her casing the joint. What was her mother thinking? By morning their place would be picked clean, probably just the kite and the rocking chair left behind. The distaste must have shown on her face because Clara shot her an insulted look as she retied the ribbon of her bonnet beneath her chin.

"What room?" Ira asked Frances.

Clara was straining to hear too.

"The guest room," Frances said, like it was obvious.

"What guest room?"

Clara glared in their direction. "Don't let 'im bully you, Francine," she called.

Ira flushed, pushed past her to the front door, and flung it open. He grabbed the grungy suitcase and stuck it out in the hallway. Holding the door open, he pointed down the hall toward the elevator. "You. Out. Now."

The woman looked to Frances to intervene.

"Sarah," Frances said, her voice low, accent gone.

"Clara," she said sullenly.

"It appears you'll have to find someplace else to stay."

Clara set her mouth in a thin line. For a moment, Nina feared she wouldn't go, and imagined having to shove and kick her into submission. But then Clara muttered, "Bloody 'ell. So much for Yankee 'ospitality," and stormed out of the apartment, slamming the door so hard, the vase on the console table quivered. Nina steeled herself for shattered crystal.

Her mother stood still, watching the vase as it righted itself, her face frozen. Then suddenly, as if her eyebrows itched, she smoothed both several times with the tips of her fingers.

"I've missed you so much," she told Ira, back to her regular voice.

He stared at her. "Who was that woman? What were you thinking?"

Frances laughed and flicked her wrist, as if at inconsequential old news. "Just some kook," she said. "How was your flight?" She put her hands on his shoulders and smiled. "Why didn't you tell me you were coming back early? I would have gotten you lox and a brownie."

Were they going to pretend her mother wasn't just speaking in a Cockney accent? Hadn't brought some neighing stranger into their home? Offered her a bedroom and free roam of the apartment?

As if remembering what he'd come home to, Ira gently brought Frances's hands down to her side and gripped them there. "Are you taking the Norpramin? Have you spoken with Vlad?"

She flicked her wrist again as if none of that mattered. "I just need to rest a bit. I don't sleep well when you're not here."

From the tenderness in his eyes, Nina guessed that Frances was already managing to convince him . . . maybe not that she was *all right*, but that things weren't as wrong as they looked.

And apparently, Nina was the only one still concerned about Clara, if that was even her real name. "Would you like me to call downstairs and tell them not to let anyone up, no matter what they say?"

Ira looked at Nina, angry again. Why was she the bad guy here? "What I'd *like* is for someone to clean up that mess," he said, pointing at the living room.

Someone meaning Nina. While he and her mother went into their room and closed the door, Nina cleared out the street junk and carted it down the hall to the incinerator room. Next were the Think Big hairbrush (coat closet) and harmonica (behind the sofa). She stashed Beethoven and as many embroidered pillows as she could fit under the draped side table. Then she went to her room and got into bed with the *Book of Lists*, hoping to be lulled into a nap, except she happened to open it to "20 Wonderful Boners." Not erections, it turned out, but infamous mistakes—the Leaning Tower of Pisa; U.S. coins stamped "In Gold We Trust." Speaking of mistakes, *was* it a mistake to not tell Stephanie what Patrick had done at the arcade or her father about Frances's late-night belly dance? She decided to call Stephanie, unburden herself of at least one secret.

When she picked up the phone to dial, Stephanie was already on the line. They were trying to reach each other at the exact same time.

It had to mean something, didn't it? Synchronicity, or telepathy, or the empathy between a napkin and a dinner plate . . .

Stop stalling, Nina told herself. Just say it: When I was playing pinball—

"Guess what?" Stephanie said.

Nina's heart jumped. But before she had a chance to ask, Stephanie galloped ahead: "Beverly called today and fired my ass."

"Oh my God."

"She said they had to *Let me go*, like they were dropping me into a ditch. I was like, They should let *your* ass go; *I* sold a four-thousand-fucking-dollar chandelier last week."

"Please tell me this isn't because of my mother."

Stephanie barked out a laugh. "Shit no. That was just her latest complaint. Beverly's been circling me for weeks, building a file on me, apparently. She starts reading off crap like *tardiness, shiftiness, extended lunch breaks*—"

"Shiftiness?"

"*Erratic behavior, insubordination.*" Stephanie paused and then inhaled sharply, and Nina wondered if it was cigarette or cocaine smoke she was sucking in.

"I'm so, so sorry," Nina said as her grip on the phone loosened a little. She *was* sorry, even if a small, shameful part of her was relieved that her own confession could now be postponed. "Let's go somewhere," she said. "How about the park? I'll bring wine and Starburst."

Stephanie didn't seem to hear her. She was talking so fast, Nina could hardly follow: Beverly had also called Kay, who'd then searched Stephanie's bedroom and found a pint of vodka and a hand mirror smeared with coke.

"What pissed off Mary Kay most was how it reflected on *her*. She was so mad, she was literally shaking. I mean, who's the injured party here? You're not even my mother and you're searching my room? She goes, 'From now on, you're living under *my* rules. Your door stays wide open. Midnight curfew. No drinking, no smoking, no drugs.'"

"No boys, either!" Patrick yelled in the background.

Nina jumped. What an unpleasant surprise, although she should have known Stephanie would go to his house after the blow-up with Kay.

"What did your father say?"

"Nothing," Stephanie said flatly. "It's Kay's apartment. Plus, he already bought her that hideous engagement ring."

Nina thought of Stephanie's exuberantly detailed rug tour at Maison Rouge. She'd loved working there among the beautiful objects, even under Beverly's tyranny. "Maybe if you follow Kay's rules for a little while," Nina said, "you could get your job back? They'll never find anyone as good as you. Beverly knows that."

"Are you kidding? I will never set foot in that place again. Or Kay's, for that matter. No way. But listen, remember how you said I could stay in your room when you leave for school? You think I still could? If it's okay with you! I won't touch anything, just sleep and study, and I'll even eat my meals in there if your parents want, I'll keep it neat, I can pay rent or help around the house, I'll move out when you're home on vacation . . ."

Nina held the phone so tight the pain shot down her forearm. It would be so nice to give Stephanie hope in this moment, but with her mother off the rails, it was impossible. And what if Stephanie brought Patrick over, into Nina's bed? She tried to tap the brakes to slow things down: "I can see once my mom's a little—"

"Do I *look* like I want to pet Zeppelin?" Stephanie shouted. Nina heard the phone clatter to the ground. When Stephanie came back, she was even more agitated. "Sorry. Patrick decided this was the perfect time to sic his demon cat on me. She just scratched the crap out of my chin. Will you talk to your mother? I'll call you back later."

She hung up. Nina listened to the dial tone until it climbed to an urgent beeping. Since she was already holding the phone, she ought to call Meredith to see how she was doing as she waited for her test results—twelve excruciating days to go. But she found herself dialing Gardner's number instead.

Her finger hovered over the hang-up lever in case his mother answered again. She just wanted to hear his voice. She wanted them to make plans. She wanted to lie beneath him, with his body pressing into hers. She wanted to look up into his burning-blue eyes—

"What?" His voice was snarled with aggravation.

She didn't say a word, but she was sure he could tell it was her, her desperation whooshing through the wires. She slammed down the phone. Although at least she knew he was back.

But not back at Flanagan's, not the next stifling, damp Friday night anyway. Nina shifted on her chair, her skin soggy everywhere, even the backs of her thighs. It had rained most of the week and the place was steamy with accumulated humidity. Her hair was frizzed, her face glazed with oil—maybe it was a good thing Gardner wasn't here after all. When she saw her wounded, craving eyes in the mirror behind the bar, she knew she shouldn't be here either.

Meredith ordered Brian to check on the air conditioners. She was tense and imperious, gesturing with a cigarette clamped between two rigid fingers. Six more days until she found out her results—"so please stop asking," she admonished Nina, who hadn't actually asked.

Only Leigh was upbeat. "Our apartment got robbed," she breathlessly told Nina. She and her parents had been out of town all week for a cousin's wedding in Bar Harbor and didn't discover the burglary until this morning. They'd taken TVs, stereos, jewelry, and Leigh's mother's fur. Police said there'd been a rash of robberies on the Upper East Side with the same MO—doormen distracted or on break; owners not at home; burglars able to get in and out quickly, sometimes with the security code.

"We can't figure out how they knew we'd be away." She banged the pitcher of sangria with her elbow and some of it sloshed out. Nina mopped it with her napkin.

"Speaking of break-ins," Meredith told Nina, "did you hear about Rex's father's place at the Carlyle? Somebody got in and trashed the place. Holland said whoever did it got interrupted and all they took were some cuff links and watches."

"How funny a coincidence is that?" Leigh asked.

"So funny," Nina said, as casually as she could manage with the Hublot ticking in her handbag. She mopped the table harder, even though it was now bone dry. "Do the police think it's the same guy?"

Meredith poured herself a glass. "This is the crazy part," she said. "Mr. Parrish blamed Rex. Apparently, they'd been in a huge fight over money. Rex says he hadn't been anywhere near the place in weeks, but he'd signed for drinks, and he had to have used his key to get in."

Good.

"But now," Meredith said, "his father's not so sure. Rex swears someone framed him."

Leigh, already tipsy, lit the back end of a cigarette, which Meredith yanked out of her mouth and crushed in the ashtray.

"It sounds a little far-fletched," Leigh said. "Far-*fetched*."

"I agree!" Nina said at top volume, to muffle the watch's ticking, which now sounded loud as a school clock. She thought of "The Tell-Tale Heart" and imagined the cops showing up at Flanagan's, pulling up chairs to her table, interrogating her as the stolen watch beat louder and louder. Until she couldn't take it anymore and confessed. *Here here! It is the ticking of his hideous watch!*

———

Alison Bloch had been happily screeching along to the music all night, but when Nina ran into her in the ladies' room, she was complaining to her friend Jill about the lack of Journey on the jukebox.

"Who do I have to blow around here for 'Girl Can't Help It'?"

She and Jill stood at the mirror, squirting mousse into their palms and molding their bangs skyward. Jill threw her head back and sang, "*The girl can't help it, she needs more.*"

"I'm not blowing *you*," Alison said, then joined in, in a loud, off-pitch falsetto. Nina noticed that Alison's earrings were big white plastic hoops and that Jill had slightly smaller white discs, as if they'd excised the insides of one for the other. Nina's chest went hollow as she thought back to last Friday night, she and Stephanie wearing each other's clothes. She'd loved being one of a pair this summer; now it seemed she was back to just herself. Stephanie hadn't called all week or answered the phone—Nina tried not to picture her on Patrick's couch, sucking in clouds of cocaine smoke and laughing when his answering machine picked up with its stupid recording: "Wait for the beep, douchebag."

Alison caught Nina's eye in the mirror. "Do you even know who Steve Perry is?"

Nina wasn't in the mood. "The one with the sideburns growing into his mouth."

For some reason, this sent them into hysterics. Alison grabbed the counter for balance while Nina went into a stall and slammed the door. Soon she heard footsteps going out the door, their laughter finally receding. She lifted the lid of the toilet and peed, then brought her handbag to her lap and fished out the watch from the inside pocket. She studied its matte black face and remembered how plain—almost forgettable—it had looked next to all the shiny jeweled and gold ones in Tom Parrish's desk drawer. Would he even notice it was missing? And anyway, how many watches did one person need? It wasn't like he had a hundred wrists.

At least Meredith hadn't mentioned a Swatch. Unless that was one of those details intentionally left out of news reports, so police would know when they'd found the real culprit. Her scalp began to sweat. She considered flushing the Hublot down the toilet, but what if it resurfaced and whoever found it in the bowl went around asking people if they'd lost a watch. And when nobody claimed it, some-one got suspicious, linked it to the Carlyle story, put two and two together . . .

The door to the ladies' room opened and a gust of music and bar chatter blew in, jolting her back to the present. She shoved the watch back inside her bag, then stepped out of her stall, surprised to find Alison still at the mirror, bag open, makeup scattered around the counter.

"Did you fall in?" she asked Nina's reflection. She started drawing wings at the outer corners of her eyes with a teal pencil.

"Good one," Nina said, noticing how plain and forgettable her own eyes were in the mirror. She looked down at the sink as she washed her hands, wishing she had on some crazy chartreuse eye shadow, while also trying to ignore Alison. Although it was nearly impossible with her leaning back and forth to survey her handiwork from different angles, scrunching up her face, grunting when she messed up a line. She was desperate to be paid attention, and it was so enormously satisfying not to pay it. Nina dried her hands with a paper towel, looking anywhere but the mirror. She tossed the paper in the trash can and started for the door.

"Hold on a second," Alison said. "I have something for you." She rustled through her Sportsac.

"Me?"

"A going-away present." She held out her fist and Nina obliged by opening her hand and allowing Alison to deposit some small item wrapped in layers of tissue paper.

Nina felt herself relent. Maybe she'd read Alison wrong. Maybe her catty, sneering outsides were a front for a softer inside. Maybe she'd wanted to be friends with Nina all along but hadn't known how. "I've been meaning to tell you," Nina said truthfully, "how impressed I was, the way you called out Rex and Walker for that spoiled-kike thing."

"Frigging Nazis." Alison rolled her eyes. "You'd think no one in this place ever ate a bagel." She gave Nina a glistening, gloppy, flamingo-pink smile and pointed to the tissue paper in her palm. "Are you going to unwrap that, or what?"

Inside layers of paper was a metal button backed by a pin, like the ones Alison wore on her jackets and the straps of her bags (tonight's two, fixed to her shirt collar: a brooding Don Johnson with the caption I'D GET IT ON WITH DON, and John Belushi in a toga). Nina turned hers over to see what was on it. A cartoon finger radiated red lines of pain, and in capital letters: BEWARE OF SPLINTERS FROM THE STICK UP MY ASS.

Nina's skin burned. God, she was a sucker. In the mirror, her reflection had the pursed lips and raised eyebrows of a shocked schoolteacher, which was especially annoying because she wasn't offended but annoyed.

Alison howled with laughter. "Don't you get it? It's so you, it's funny."

"You are just so pathetically childish," Nina said.

"Spoken like a true stick-up-her-ass!" They stared at each other in the mirror. "Which is why," Alison added, "Gardner's never going to fuck you."

"What? Like he'd ever fuck *you*."

"Who said he hasn't?"

Nina banged open the bathroom door and wove through the crowd to her table. That hyena laugh and Triscuit-colored tan. That uncooked-spaghetti hair. No way, no way, had Gardner slept with her.

Holland was now sitting where Nina had been, leaving Nina to hover awkwardly behind the chair. She blotted sweat off her forehead with the back of her hand.

"Are you okay?" Leigh asked.

"Just some weird stuff in the bathroom."

"Bathrooms are like that," Leigh said, clearly drunk, and preoccupied with distributing pens and napkins for a new personality test. At least she'd moved on from talking about burglaries. "Draw a triangle, square, circle, and a squiggle," she said.

"There is nothing I'll miss less than this," Meredith said, then stabbed through her napkin with the tip of her pen.

Leigh gave her a compassionate smile, but it was strained, and her eyes dark with hurt. Nina could see it now, thanks to Stephanie pointing it out, the longing all over her face, the pain of unrequited love in her quivering lips.

"Squiggle?" asked Brian, who'd come to the table and now stood beside Nina.

Leigh recovered herself, taking a sheet of instructions out of her handbag: "Choose one of the shapes to draw again. Don't overthink it, just pick."

Brian leaned in closer to Nina. "I've been meaning to apologize," he said quietly. "That night in the park, what I said on the street about Gardner . . ." He trailed off, studying her.

She wished she could tell him everything, what had happened at the Carlyle and the watch in her bag.

"I'm sorry I snapped at you," he added. "You were totally right. He's one of my best friends. I should give him the benefit of the doubt."

"I'm sorry too," she said. She cringed as she remembered yelling *I rest my case!* "That was a strange night."

Brian sighed. "This whole summer's been so strange. Like disjointed, if that makes sense. Dis something."

Disturbing, she thought. Especially tonight: something jangly in the air, atoms knocking around in a fitful way. But maybe it was just the sticky heat, or Gardner's absence, or Alison now at the bar, shouting, "Who do I have to blow around here for a piña colada?"

"Well, it's almost over," Nina said. "At least we made it through okay."

"So you're not mad?" Brian asked. "Because I haven't seen you for a while, and I got a little worried."

"I could never be mad at you."

"True tangles," Leigh said to Holland, then corrected herself: "Two *triangles* means your favorite dance is the tango, the dance of power. You like ambitious risk-takers like Margaret Thatcher and Ivan Boesky."

"Ivan is old friends with Tom!" Holland chirped. "He took Rex and I out on his yacht in the Vineyard."

"Rex and me," Nina muttered.

"Oh, it was *I*," Holland assured her.

Brian laughed, but hearing "Tom" and "Rex" made Nina's stomach cramp. She wanted to talk to Stephanie.

Holland fanned herself with her napkin. "Grand-Mère said it's been tropical in Paris too: 35 Celsius." Holland smiled. "That's 95 Fahrenheit for les Américains."

"I'm a little dizzy," Nina told Brian. "I'm going outside for a sec." She'd go to the pay phone on the corner, where it was cooler and quieter, call Patrick's house, and talk to his machine until Stephanie picked up.

The rain had stopped, but the night air was still heavy and wet. Nina felt it pushing down on her, as if to say, *Get out of this city; you don't belong here anymore—go home and get your shit together for Vanderbilt.* Which was what she ought to do, considering she was leaving in a week and had barely filled a single packing box. But the thought of going home right now and dealing with her mother—rhyming, punning, belly dancing, Cockney, or some new iteration of bonkers—made it hard to breathe. At the pay phone, she found herself unable to dial Stephanie and instead transfixed by the cars rushing by, contemplating the phrase *she could stop traffic.* As in, she supposed, a girl so captivating, drivers would screech to a halt to gawk. Holland Nichols, she thought sourly, could stop traffic. Nina would just get mowed down.

A guy was walking up Second Avenue in her direction: sexy loose-jointed walk, slight lean forward, a worn Lacoste the color of moss. *Now?* she screamed silently as Gardner came into focus. When she already felt so deflated? She grabbed the phone and said, "I agree," into the receiver, so at least she wouldn't look as alone as she felt, before hanging up and greeting him casually, as if he were some Joe Shmo she'd never spared a second thought.

Close up, his skin was sallow, with a cluster of pimples on his chin like Stephanie's. The whites of his eyes had a grayish tint, although maybe that was the strange light from the humidity.

"The dream is over," he announced, "and the insect is awake."

"What?"

"You haven't seen *The Fly?*" He tilted his head and looked at her in that way she couldn't seem to resist, that made the rest of the world crumble to dust.

She shook her head, staring into his eyes. Lush, she thought, trying to slick hers with sex as per Stephanie's instructions. Lascivious. Carnal. He stared at her mouth like her lips had formed the words, then stepped in closer, his chest brushing her breasts.

With all the hounders and harassers, he still wanted her. She felt a wave of pure joy. It surged even higher when she saw Alison and her friend Jill at the window staring out at them.

"Coming inside?" Gardner asked Nina as he reached for the door.

She crashed back down to earth. "I don't think you should go in. People are talking about Tom Parrish's apartment, and Rex is saying someone must have framed him."

Gardner stepped back abruptly. "You didn't say anything, did you?"

"Are you kidding?" She tried not to be insulted. "Of course not. I would never in a million years."

"Nobody can prove it anyway."

"But I've still got—" She thought better of saying it out loud, so she only tapped her handbag. His eyes widened a little like he could read her mind, which she didn't disbelieve, considering he lived in there twenty-four hours a day.

He gazed at her for a moment with a small smile, then asked if anyone was home at her place.

"My parents." She swallowed and tried to keep her voice calm. "You?"

His smile turned bitter. "The evil witch. She wants me out by the time school starts."

"Ouch," Nina said. "You want to go to Carl Schurz Park?" It was closer than Central Park, and probably just as empty this time of night.

"Sure." They headed east, then through the park to the East River esplanade. Gardner chivalrously swatted puddles of rain off a bench so they could sit. They faced the river but the wrought-iron fence that served as a railing was so high, the view was prison-like, black bars with slices of water through them. Besides one old man a few benches down, they were the only ones here.

There were small hazy lights in some factory windows across the river, but on this side, in the dark, it was eerie and desolate. She moved closer to Gardner. "Me and my friends used to come here after school," she said. "We'd chug wine on the swings, then worry the mayor was watching us through a telescope from Gracie Mansion."

"Mayor Crotch," Gardner said with disgust. He looked through the iron bars at the water. "Ever been here for the spring harvest?"

She shook her head. "Never even heard of it."

"Bodies dumped in the river in winter stay at the bottom, but when the water warms up in the spring, the gases in them expand and they come bobbing up."

"How delightful."

He shrugged. "If you end up in the river with a bullet in your brain, you've definitely fucked over the wrong people." He made a gun with his fingers and held it to his temple. "Rex and I used to come every spring to try and spot a floater, but we never got lucky."

Even through the grisliness, she heard a melancholy that pierced her. He missed Rex, probably the same way she missed Stephanie. Actually, it was even sadder, since Rex had so resoundingly screwed him over, yet Gardner couldn't help the longing. She put her arms around his neck and spoke into his ear.

"I'll come here with you next spring." She stroked the hockey-puck scar on his forehead. "We'll make sure we see a floater."

"Deal," he said. "In the meantime, let's do a bump."

"A what?"

He pointed to her handbag. "Your coin thing."

Oh. "I don't have it with me. I ran out last weekend."

"Uh-huh." He raised his eyebrows in mock suspicion, trailing his fingers up her inner thigh. Behind them a barge churned the water. "Do I have to torture you for it?"

She laughed and gasped at the same time, pressing her mouth to his. He moved one hand up under her shirt, into her bra. A melting sensation in the pit of her stomach. She swung her leg around him, her bare ankle scraping the damp wooden bench.

He pulled back again, looking in her eyes. "You smile when you kiss."

"Because you make me happy."

"You're a nice person. You remind me of that girl on *That Girl*." He placed his hand over hers. "How about just one line each."

"You could have twenty if I had it." She was still half-dazed, riding waves of lust. Or maybe it was love. Some velvety mix of the two. "But really, I'm out."

He frowned. "Fuck."

It finally dawned on her that he hadn't read her mind outside Flanagan's. When she'd tapped her bag, he'd thought she meant she had coke. How mortifying to have led him here under false pretenses.

"I'm really sorry," she said. He was turned away from her, staring off into the distance, while she was still awkwardly splayed across his lap like some wannabe sexpot. The barge belched a guttural blast from its horn. She removed herself with as much grace as she could muster.

"I'm sure I can get more tomorrow," she said, trying not to sound beseeching. If Stephanie still wasn't answering the phone, Nina would camp out at Station Break until Damian showed up.

Gardner took a joint out of his pocket and lit it. He inhaled and held the smoke in his lungs as he said, "Okay." With a grunt he exhaled the smoke, handing the joint to her. She almost sighed her relief out loud. He'd just gotten his hopes up. She knew how that kind of disappointment felt. She inhaled hard, holding the smoke in her lungs as he had, staring through the bars at the river. The corpses at the bottom, waiting for spring.

"I wonder if people swim in there." Her voice sounded funny without breath, strangulated. She passed the joint back to him.

"Only if they like wading around in sewage." His face was glum, and Nina sensed that the Parrishes—speaking of sewage—were inhabiting his mind. Tom Parrish's watch in her handbag continued its condemning tick. Certainly that deserved to wade around in sewage. And Alison's obnoxious button too.

She stood up unsteadily, already stoned, and opened her handbag. She took out the button and sailed it over the railing like a Frisbee, into the river.

"What the hell was that?" Gardner asked.

"Just some shit that needed to be among its kind."

He laughed, and she was pleased to be cheering him up. Wait until he saw what came next. She reached into her bag again and came out with her fist up, then slowly opened it to reveal the watch, brandishing it like a magic trick—"Now you see it"—before flinging it over the railing into the water. "Now you don't."

"What was that?"

She smiled. "Incriminating evidence."

He stared at her for a moment, then jumped to his feet and grabbed her wrist. "Was that Tom's *watch*?"

She nodded.

"Why the fuck did you do that?"

"I don't know—I—"

He squeezed her wrist. "I could've sold it." He was shouting. "What a fucking waste. Why would you do that?"

Shame burned through her, for being so ignorant, blithely destroying a valuable object when he'd been cut off by everyone who could help him. At the same time, she felt a pinprick of alarm. He was squeezing her wrist so hard, the bone hurt.

"It was evidence against us," she stammered. "And I hate them! I hate Rex and his stupid leopard-murdering father. I hate what they did to you."

He took a deep breath and dropped her arm. "Sorry," he said. He was looking at his hand with the same wonder as that night in Central Park, when he'd beheld the broken Heineken bottle there. "I'm just in a really shit mood. I should go." He turned and walked away so fast, she had to run to catch up or be left here in the dark. Alison's John Belushi button flashed through her mind and Nina remembered his last words from *Closing Remarks* book: *Just don't leave me alone.*

As they came out of the park onto East End, Gardner slowed to light a cigarette and she caught up. He walked with his head bowed, barely speaking to her, but at the same time furiously exhaling gusts of smoke as if in angry response to some conversation in his head. When they got to Flanagan's, Nina saw Alison still stationed at the window, like she hadn't moved since they left, which might in fact be true. Then she spotted Leigh still at their table, teetering on the edge of her chair, head bent, hair brushing the mess of napkins on the table covered in squares and triangles and squiggles.

"I meant to ask you about your friend Victor," Nina said to Gardner. "He left here with Leigh a few weeks back and she woke up on her doorstep with no idea what happened."

Gardner stiffened. "Who?"

"Victor. He was at the Palladium on Bastille Day. With the ponytail?"

"He's not my friend. I barely know that guy." Had Victor screwed him over too?

She stopped on the corner outside the bar. "Let's not go in there. Let's go see *The Fly*."

"I already saw it."

"I know, but—"

"We'll talk," he said. He looked so defeated, she thought her heart might split. He walked down Eighty-Fourth Street without looking back.

Chapter Sixteen

Sunday was meant to be Nina's last walk with her grandfather before she left for Vanderbilt, but since it was raining again, they stayed in and watched TV at his apartment. Or rather, while he dozed in his worn leather armchair, she sat through a movie on cable called *Private Hell 36,* mainly to find out what thirty-five private hells had preceded it. But 36 turned out to be the address of the trailer where a couple of corrupt cops stashed the money they'd taken off a dead crook. One of the cops falls for a lounge singer played by Ida Lupino, and at the end of the film, stares at her with a lovesick look and says, "I've never wanted anything like I want you." Nina felt it like a punch. Would anyone, even a corrupt cop, ever look at her that way, like he would die without her?

She relived the kissing by the East River, Gardner's clean-water taste and warm breath. She imagined them back in Carl Schurz, this time with her packed coin purse, finding a spot on the lawn to do bumps and then, as Stephanie liked to call it, the deed. Speaking of Stephanie: already today Nina had left two messages for her on Patrick's machine, beating back the fear that Patrick wasn't passing them along, or worse, that she was just tired of Nina. *Emergency! I need Damian's number!* she'd said in her second message. It *was* an emergency: Gardner was in pain and she needed to ease it. If she didn't hear back from Stephanie by dinner, she'd head to Penn Station to deal with Damian herself.

Once *Private Hell 36* was over, she flipped through the channels. *Blonde Bait* on USA, *Bad Blonde* on Cinemax, *My Favorite Blonde* on A&E. Maybe she should dye her hair. Her grandfather's was the pure, snowy white of swan feathers. Tears came to her eyes as she watched him sleep, chin to his chest, snores whistling through his nose. Her parents were so preoccupied: Would they remember to take him out for Sunday walks? Would he remember why Nina wasn't around? Or that she'd ever been?

The phone rang and he jerked awake. "Pearl?" he asked.

"I'll see," she answered automatically. Seymour's ancient telephone rang with an old-fashioned clang, and for a moment it felt possible that her grandmother was calling from the afterlife to rebuke her. *You stink of cigarettes. Are you trying to kill me again? Where are your Dynamints?* Or maybe it was just Frances, reminding her to buy another pair of tweezers from Drug Loft. "Have you ever noticed," she'd asked Nina last night with a meaningful stare, "that eyebrows are miniature antennas?"

The phone rang a second time and Nina picked it up.

"Nina," Stephanie said.

"Stephanie! My favorite blonde!"

Of course she wasn't avoiding her. But how did she know to call her here?

"Your mother gave me this number," Stephanie said in an odd monotone.

"You sound tired. Late night at Paddy McGee's?"

A long pause that got sharper and blacker as it went on, and on.

"Steph?"

"Did you think I wouldn't find out?" she said in the same cold voice. "What am I, a fucking idiot?"

Nina's lips, still stretched in a dumb-ass smile, went slack. She hadn't let herself imagine this moment, had decided that what had happened with Patrick at the arcade simply hadn't happened, and erased it from her memory. Now it came flooding back. His knees against the backs of her legs, his crotch pressing into the top of her ass. But a small, gutless part of her still hoped Stephanie meant something else: "Find out what?" she asked.

"You . . . *traitor.*" Stephanie's voice picked up speed. "Damian saw you and Patrick at Station Break, *gyrating.*"

Panic splintered Nina's brain, and for a second, she couldn't remember what *gyrate* meant. Gyro? Hydrate? Stay here, she told herself. She gripped the phone. "I swear, that's not what happened."

"How could you?"

Stephanie's misery was piercing. Even so unfairly accused, Nina wanted to wrap her in a blanket and soothe her. "I would never do that to you, I would never—"

"Patrick said it's not the first time you've hit on him."

"What?"

"My Fourth of July party? In my fucking bedroom."

The only thing that stifled Nina's scream was her grandfather, now roused and struggling to push himself out of his chair. "I can't tell you how not true that is," she whispered into the phone as she pulled him by his wrist to his feet and walked him to the bathroom, careful not to trip either of them on the extra-long and tangled phone cord, then closed the door.

"I would never hit on Patrick." She was glad Stephanie couldn't see her revulsion as she pictured Patrick's greasy skin and Bic pen tattoos.

"Are you saying *he* hit on *you?*" Now Stephanie sounded even angrier.

"No one hit on anyone," she said, emphasizing every word to ensure Stephanie heard her. She made herself describe what Patrick had done at the pinball machine. "He was trying to intimidate me. That's all it was. He just wants me out of the way."

Stephanie was silent. Nina studied the man-high mahogany cabinet in the corner of the living room, noticing its resemblance to a coffin standing on end. She heard a lighter spark on the other end of the line and pictured an Eve cigarette, which morphed into a glass pipe, and suddenly knew without a doubt whose idea it had been to smoke cocaine in the first place. You couldn't exactly be out and about, doing it in public. He'd made it a leash around her neck.

"He's never letting you out of that house," she told Stephanie.

"Don't be so dramatic," Stephanie said. "I just got back from the mall."

"I mean metaphorically."

"So now Damian's a liar too?"

Nina remembered his eyes stuck to Stephanie's ass. "You know Damian's into you, right? He'd say anything to break up you and Patrick." As she said this, her grandfather opened the bathroom door, and Nina reached in to grab his hand.

"Oh, really? So then why do you want his number?" Stephanie asked.

"I can't say it out loud right now."

"What the hell is going on? Why is everyone always lying to me?"

Nina steered Seymour back to the couch. "I'm with my grandfather." She sniffed loudly into the phone, like a game of charades, but Stephanie seemed not to hear.

"This fucking world is so full of liars," she said.

"I need to refill my coin purse," Nina mumbled into the phone, "by tomorrow night."

There was silence on the other end, until finally Stephanie said, "If I find out you're lying, I'll never speak to you again."

"I swear I'm not."

"Damian starts work at seven tomorrow. I'll tell him you're coming by. That's the best I can do."

"Can we please get together this week?" With her free hand, Nina tried to maneuver Seymour down to the couch without pushing him.

"I'll come to Hewlett, whatever you want." Face-to-face, maybe she could convince Stephanie to come back to the city and free herself from Patrick's hold. "I swear I'll ask my parents about you staying in my room."

Stephanie lowered her voice. "I don't know. This is all really messed up."

"Please," Nina said, and she must have sounded so plaintive, Seymour squeezed her hand.

The silence on the line was unbearable, but she forced herself to wait it out.

"Fine," Stephanie said finally, grudgingly. "I need to get all my shit from Mary Kay's anyway. I'll meet you at Martell's tomorrow night at eight."

"Thank you," Nina said to Stephanie, and also to her grandfather, who'd finally sat.

More silence. Had Stephanie hung up? But then she said, "You should have told me. We could have dealt with it. I could have cleared things up. But now I don't know. I want to believe you, but I have to believe Patrick, too, you know? I wish you'd just told me."

Nina sat on the couch beside Seymour. "I'm sorry. I wanted to pretend it didn't happen."

"But it did happen. You don't get to decide what's true." Stephanie sighed. "We'll talk about it tomorrow."

You should have told me. The same thing her father said when he got home from St. Louis and saw the condition Frances was in. Fine, Nina thought as she hung up the phone. Her cheeks pulsed with heat, the embarrassment of being called out. No more secrets or half-truths or omissions to spare people's feelings, or pretending, or lying—

"Where's Pearl?" asked her grandfather.

She hadn't expected to be tested quite this soon.

For what might have been the first time since he'd been asking that question, she looked at him closely. He was leaning back on the couch with his legs crossed, looking more into space than at Nina. Maybe it was a reflexive question, not really meant to be answered. And some part of him had to know. He was at the funeral, and Pearl hadn't appeared since. But still, at his age, how much pain should he (or could he) withstand?

On the other hand, the truth was the truth. She had to stop denying everyone their right to reality.

Seymour wiped his mouth on the back of his hand, still not looking at her.

Very gently, she said, "Grandpa, you remember what happened with Grandma back in April? You haven't spoken to her since."

Now he did look at her.

"It's because she's dea—"

He sat up straight, his mouth open, his eyes terrified.

"Deaf!" Nina shouted. "Remember? She went to the doctor to get her ears checked." Her heart was hammering so loud *she* could hardly hear. "She's fine, totally fine! Just a little hearing loss."

Seymour peered at her. She smiled as convincingly as she could, trying to breathe evenly. Then something clicked off in his brain and he sat back.

"Very good," he said.

"Yes." She put her hand over his.

It wasn't so easy, she'd explain to Stephanie tomorrow night, to tell someone something you knew would smash their world into pieces.

At dinner the next night, Frances couldn't stop talking about Graceland, which she wanted to visit the minute they got to Tennessee to take Nina to college. "There's a built-in waterfall in the Jungle Room," she said, and then, into her tape recorder: "Elvis would shoot the TV if Robert Goulet came on the screen." She was gaunt and garrulous and missing half her eyebrows. Vlad had prescribed a new medication to help her sleep, but it seemed instead to have catapulted her into some new ether. Ira kept squinting at her, as if trying to bring the real Frances into focus. Nina tried it, but she couldn't look too long before her eyes started to sting.

"Vanderbilt's in Nashville, Fran, not Memphis," Ira said. "I can't imagine we'll have time for any side trips." Nina nodded, although she'd hardly thought that far ahead. Not much existed beyond tonight: Station Break after dinner, for Gardner, and then Martell's with Stephanie, where they'd hopefully fall back into their easy friendship. And Flanagan's after. For Gardner.

The drive to Nashville might as well be a magic carpet ride for how real it felt. "I'm not that into Elvis anyway," Nina said. "I only know, like, two of his songs." She winced as she remembered kneeling at Patrick's feet in Stephanie's bedroom at her Fourth of July party, laughing over Elvis's last words and hoping she and Patrick would be friends.

"He had a pet turkey named Bowtie," Frances said. She twirled her fork through a serving bowl of applesauce, the Bakelite bangle she was wearing—it had been Pearl's—too loose on her skinny wrist and clanking against the rim of the bowl. Nina had noticed that over the summer, more and more of Pearl's things had migrated from Seymour's apartment to theirs. A worn suitcase with a broken zipper, a pair of reading glasses in a needlepoint case, an emerald-green crocheted blanket folded across a chair in her parents' bedroom. Hooked over the coat closet doorknob, the ebony cane Pearl used after she broke her hip.

"We're not going to Memphis," Ira said.

Frances ignored him and spoke pointedly to Nina. "Elvis is buried in the backyard with his parents." Throughout the week, her affections had swung back and forth between Nina and her father. One night she'd complain to Nina about Ira's stinginess, and the next she'd cry to Ira about Nina's selfishness. Tonight Nina was in favor again. She couldn't help feeling some relief, since it was no fun getting raked over the coals by your mother for your many, many failings.

"Since when do you care about Elvis Presley?" Ira said. "I've never once heard you mention him."

Frances addressed the tape recorder again: "Mention, prevention, suspension, detention." She looked at him with loathing. "He pays no attention to my comprehension because he is all condescension."

Her father's hurt was painful to witness. He was so beleaguered, his face sagging, his belt missing two of his pant loops. He listlessly peppered a plate of string beans with the pepper mill Nina got him at Maison Rouge, which seemed so long ago it made her wonder if pepper could go stale. She recalled the *season's greetings* joke her mother had made. Those early, rosy days of what they thought was a miraculous recovery.

Nina stabbed a piece of meat. It tasted like pork on her fork, or was it stork? Good thing she was leaving for college soon, before her mother completely colonized her brain.

"Frances, if we go that far out of our way, it'll take all day," Ira said.

Did he know his brain had been colonized too?

"Everything's out of the way for him," Frances hissed into the tape recorder.

Nina kept her face blank and speared another piece of chicken. She didn't want her mother's attention anymore. "Let's go in October, during parents' weekend," she said to her plate, emphasizing *parents'*. She needed them united so she could leave with a semi-clear conscience.

Frances picked up the salad bowl in both hands. "Everything's iceberg," she said to Nina, "like your father." She dumped the bowl upside down. Soggy clumps of lettuce fell to the table. Frozen, Nina watched the salad dressing seep into the tablecloth. Her mother grabbed the roll from her plate. "Everything's goddamned white bread, like your father." She threw the roll across the table at Ira. It smacked him in the cheek.

He jumped to his feet. "Frances!" Then he didn't seem to know what else to say.

"Don't patronize me! I'm not a flea!" she shouted back. She raked the string beans off their serving plate into the bowl of applesauce.

He was blinking a mile a minute. "What the hell are you talking about?"

She shoved her plate off the table to the floor, where it shattered. Then her face crumpled, and she covered it with her hands. "Shut up, shut up, shut up!"

She ran out of the room and Ira ran after her. Nina heard them arguing but told herself it was okay to stay where she was, just to clear her head for a few seconds, and while she was at it clear the table so no one would have to look at this mess later when things calmed down. If they did. But they had to; they couldn't stay like this. First, though, she crawled under the table to collect the remains of her mother's plate. She thought of the porcelain lamp she'd wrecked in Tom Parrish's Carlyle apartment, the sharp, flying shards when it hit the floor that could have sliced her eye. She remembered the exhilaration of leaving herself, and realized, now, how lucky she was to have come back.

"Nina!" her father bellowed from the foyer. She banged her head on the corner of the table and dropped the pieces of broken plate, then crawled out to follow his voice. He was standing at their open front door.

"Go find your mother."

"What do you mean? Where is she?"

"I don't know." His face was the color of chalk. "She went downstairs. I couldn't stop her." There were three deep scratches across his forearm, sprouting beads of blood. For a second Nina thought maybe he'd cut himself on the broken plate, except he hadn't been anywhere near it.

"This can't go on." Ira stared at his arm. "You find her while I call Vlad."

Nina hesitated.

"Go get her. It's okay, she won't come at *you* right now."

That he even had to say that made Nina queasy. She ran down the hall and stabbed at the elevator call button, waiting for the numbers to reach the lobby and reverse themselves. She imagined her mother bursting out into the street, chirping about Elvis and Bowtie, her thoughts spinning out in a thousand directions.

When the elevator finally came, *This can't go on* sank in: he meant a mental hospital, barred windows, straitjackets, sadistic orderlies. Electroshock. But maybe there was still time to get her back. Nina would find her and grab her from the sky like a balloon, reel her in, tie her string to a chair before it was too late. She urged the elevator to go faster. She remembered reading that if the cable broke and your elevator went into free fall, you could maybe save yourself by jumping upward an instant before it hit the ground. She had that sensation in her stomach, of trying to outjump a crashing elevator.

"Miss Nina!" Freddie pulled the lobby door open as soon as he saw her, peering at her with worried eyes.

Nina had avoided looking at him, much less talking to him, since the belly-dancing debacle, but this wasn't the time to worry about that. She looked him full in the face and said, "Not now!" It felt good to explode for a second, but the fear blew back at her when she got out to the sidewalk. Her mother was across the street, talking to a guy who was swinging around a leather dog collar on the end of a chain leash like a lasso. His hair was matted, his skin sunburnt and grimy, lips pinched around gums with just a couple of teeth. He had the feral-eyed look of a Charles Manson mugshot. A woman on roll-

erblades came around the corner and the guy stomped in her direction, shrieking that she'd stolen his dog and swinging the collar at
her. As Nina got closer, she saw it was studded with rows of steel
spikes. The woman on rollerblades screamed and ducked as she
swooshed past.

He pointed at Nina as she crossed the street. "You're the bitch
who stole my dog!" His voice was guttural. "Give me back my fucking
dog."

Frances frowned at Nina. "Did you take his dog?"

"Mom, please." Nina reached for her hand. *Grab her string, tie her
around your finger.* "Come back upstairs."

"But he's lost his dog!" Frances cried. She yanked her hand away
and held out the recorder to the guy as if this were an interview.
"How big is your pup? Would he fit in a cup?"

He hocked up a glob of phlegm and let it loose at their feet. It
had the slimy shine of an oyster.

Nina swallowed back bile. "Mom, there's no dog." She tried not to
focus on the empty dog collar, the spikes sharp as daggers.

"Fuck you and fuck your accusations, you bitch thief," the guy
snarled. His body jerked all over like it was being pierced by invisible
arrows. His filthy pants hung off his waist, tied loosely there with
rope, and for a second Nina worried they might slip down and expose
god-knew-what.

"*I* believe you," Frances told him. "No one lies about a lost dog.
Or dies about a lost log, for that matter."

Nina put her arm around her mother's shoulder, attempting to
maneuver her back across the street, but Frances was immovable as a
fire hydrant embedded in concrete. Instead she flung her arm around
Nina's waist as if they were buddies, enjoying a warm late-August
evening as they shot the shit with their new psychotic pal.

"What's your puppy look like?" Frances asked him.

He swung the collar in a wide arc. "Every dog is a hairy bitch."

Frances nodded. She'd started her swaying, one foot to the other. "Merry witch," she said into the recorder. "Scary glitch."

Across the street, DeeDee and Kassidy Elkin came out of the lobby. They stopped and gawked for a second, then shook their heads and kept walking.

"Mom, please, can we go upstairs?"

"Hairy bitch," the guy growled at Nina. White crud bunched in the corners of his mouth. He glared at her like she'd performed some unholy act in his twisted imagination.

"Mom, come on." The edges of things were starting to blur in the twilight. Her head felt riddled with holes, with the wind rushing through. "Let's go upstairs and plan our trip to Graceland. I want to see the Jungle Room."

"Everything's *I want* with her," Frances chided. To the guy and into the recorder, she said, "She's very selfish. She has no idea what it's like to lose someone you love."

Which wasn't true. She was losing her mother, right now, right in front of her.

The guy shoved the dog collar in Nina's direction. "Put it on."

"Please—just leave us alone." She grabbed hold of Frances's arm, cold even in the heat. "Mom, if you keep this up, they're going to take you away in a straitjacket." Her voice was high with panic. "They're going to put you in a hospital and fry your brain. I'm not kidding. Vlad said so. Is that what you want?"

But her mother still wouldn't move. Instead, she raised a cupped hand to her ear. "I hear barking," she said, although there was nothing but the guy's rattling breath. She cocked her head. "Your dog misses you. He wishes he could kiss you."

"Put it on," he ordered Nina again. He held the collar around his fist with the spikes pointed at her throat. She had no doubt they could puncture flesh.

Her mother looked on with a vaguely amused expression. She held up the recorder to capture the event. "Come on, party pooper," she scoffed, like they were at Bloomingdale's and Nina wouldn't try on a dress.

Pain filled Nina's throat as if the guy had already gored her.

"Your dog must be hot. Hot dog," Frances said into the recorder. She was swaying faster. She sniffed the air. "I smell mustard. Do you smell roses? That's my mother."

The guy ignored her and remained fixed on Nina. He bared his teeth, broken yellow chunks in black gums. He crouched, every muscle tensed. "I will carve the skin off your bones," he said, then lunged at her.

She reared back. Shrieks hit the air—her shrieks—although she had no sense of making a sound. Suddenly the guy stopped and stared over Nina's shoulder at something approaching. It was Freddie, running toward them with a baseball bat raised over his shoulder.

The guy erupted in laughter and scuttled down the block.

"Help him find his dog, goddammit!" Frances yelled at Freddie. She pointed as if Freddie should follow the guy, who'd disappeared into the darkening shadows.

"Leave him be," Nina said to Freddie. Relief and shame rolled through her as she watched him watch Frances, who was swaying so fast it was almost dancing.

"*He lost his dog,*" she sang. "*He crossed his bog. He flossed his frog.*" She shot Nina an exasperated look. "What's with the waterworks, Wilhelmina?"

Ira came running out of the building. He stopped short as he took it all in—Frances and her recorder, Freddie and his bat, Nina and her tears—then resolutely crossed the street to where they stood. The pain on his face made Nina dizzy. But at least her father would take care of things now. She wasn't in charge, or to blame, anymore.

"Enough, Fran," he said. He put his arm around her and pulled her close, even as she kept swaying. "It's done. Let's go."

Vlad met them at the entrance to the psych ER, wearing a ten-gallon hat and a bolo tie like he'd wandered over from a cattle ranch. He and Ira went to talk to the intake nurse while Nina was left in charge of getting Frances to settle into one of the brown plastic chairs. An impossible task, since she kept leaping up to pace the waiting room and stick her tape recorder in people's faces. *Where you're from, do robots drive? Do newlyweds on the moon honeyearth?* Not that anyone was paying her much attention. The friends or families of the other patients were too freaked out about their own situations to do more than shoo her away. The patients themselves were too busy moaning or cursing or screaming at the walls.

Frances surveyed the room with the same detached tourist expression as when she'd interviewed the guy with the dog collar. "What a bunch of head cases," she sniffed. She glanced at Pearl's bracelet on her wrist over and over, as if it were a watch and she was late for an appointment.

Nina couldn't tell if she minded being here, or even knew exactly where she was. She led her mother back to the chair, curbing her impulse to shove her down into it. Worse had come to worst—Frances now on the literal threshold of the psych ward—but instead of feeling sorrow and sympathy, Nina was bristling with anger, and not because her mother had stood by while a crazed man nearly stabbed her in the throat, but for the pettiest of reasons: Frances's disdain for her tears, that old irritation that shrunk Nina down to an annoying gnat. She tried to shove away the feeling. What a child, she thought, focused on my own petty grievances when my brain-sick, helpless mother has fallen into the abyss. But another part of her wished she could sit on Frances and suffocate her. She envied the woman who'd just been wheeled in on a gurney, handcuffed to the rails, shouting, "Fucking cockroaches!"—the freedom to let yourself scream your head off.

Well, she didn't envy the holes in her shoes and open sores on her face. But the screaming.

She kept hold of her mother with one hand and held the other over her nose to block out the smell of pee and sweat and what had to be some dead rodent trapped in the walls. Behind them, a girl was scraping her bare legs with a Brillo pad. At the end of their row, a guy scribbled all over his arms with a black Sharpie, *father, heaven, deliver us from evil*—Nina was reading them when Frances broke free from her grip and leaped up again, this time heading to the woman on the gurney and shoving the tape recorder in her face.

"Why are they called handcuffs? Shouldn't they be called wrist-cuffs?" Frances asked her.

The woman looked at her in disbelief. "Get out of my ass, you filthy cunt."

Frances's eyes narrowed to slits. She whipped back her arm as if she were going to throw the recorder at the woman's face. Nina raced to reach her, but a nurse got there first and snatched the recorder from her mother's hand.

Frances wheeled around, screeching. "Give that back! It's mine! Give it! Dirty birdy cunt-grunt. Give it back, or I'll beat the crap out of you!"

Unfazed, the nurse gestured to the gurney. "We have more of these if you don't quiet down," she said. She locked arms with Frances and led her back to her chair.

Nina's anger at her mother vanished. Seeing her humiliated, here of all places, made her want to beat the crap out of someone too. "We're not supposed to take the recorder away," she told the nurse.

The nurse ignored her as Vlad approached. "Does she need re-straints?" she asked him.

Frances went suddenly still, as though hearing "restraints" had immobilized her with fear. It definitely had Nina. She sat down be-side her mother, stiff as a plastic doll.

Vlad responded in a low voice. Nina caught the word "break." Give her a break? Then she realized he meant break with reality. As in, psychotic break. "It's time for the intake," he added, and Nina pushed down a bubble of hysterics over Vlad's brain having been colonized too. The nurse gave the recorder back to Frances, who stared at it in her palm like she suddenly didn't know what it was.

"Where is everyone?" Frances asked.

"Right here," Nina said, trying to sound comforting, as if *here* were a fine place to be.

A few minutes later, Vlad and Ira came to get her, each grasping an elbow to lift her from the chair and walk her down the hall to thick wooden double doors. Nina stood and hoped her mother might look back before she went through them, but she didn't, and the doors fell heavily behind her.

Nina stood there, unsure what to do now. The woman on the gurney muttered, "Crazy cunt," and Nina snapped back, "At least she isn't handcuffed to a bed." It didn't make her feel any better, and the nurse gave her a stern look, like Nina better watch it or she'd get marched through those doors herself. Then she handed Nina a sheaf of mimeographed pages. "You can drop off her suitcase tomorrow morning."

Nina sat back down in her chair, glad at least for some direction, although the pages turned out to be a long list of prohibited items and only a short list of what was allowed: socks and underwear, casual shirts and slacks, flat comfortable shoes (no laces). It sank in, then, that Frances wouldn't be coming home anytime soon.

A scared-looking man and woman came in with a teenage girl who was yelling that they were elephants in disguise. The guy with the Sharpie had colored his lips and teeth. He caught Nina's eye and smiled, showing her a gaping black hole. She stared down at the pages the nurse had given her and mentally organized the prohibited items into categories, *things that burn* (curling irons, heating pads); *things that choke* (yarn, dental floss, tube socks); *things that cut* (mirrors, razors); *things that provoke* (sheer nightgowns). She made a little poem out of it—*burn, choke, cut, provoke.* You're a poet and you didn't even know it. She recited it to herself at various tempos until Ira finally emerged through the heavy doors.

He sat beside her, shoulders slumped. "She was hearing voices through her eyebrows," he said. "They gave her an injection of Haldol."

"Will that make her better?" How childish she sounded. But she couldn't stop herself from asking.

He shook his head. The scratches on his arm had dried to ruddy stripes. "Vlad says it should quiet the hallucinations so maybe she can sleep. We were lucky they had a bed for the night."

"Then she can come home?" Why couldn't she stop herself?

"This is going to take time. We'll see tomorrow if we can't find her a nicer long-term facility."

How long-term? But she'd already asked enough questions that didn't have answers. Ira told her he had paperwork to fill out and that she should go ahead home. She wanted to say she'd wait for him, but she couldn't force out the words.

Back home, yearning for blankness, Nina took the last Halcion in her jewelry box. But even in her bedroom, curtains closed and eyes shut tight, things kept glinting behind her lids like flashes of lightning: the dog collar's spikes, the snaps on Vlad's western shirt, the Brillo pad's steel filaments. The needle she hadn't seen but now imagined, jabbing her mother with Haldol.

Her mother had lost her mind. She was locked up with a bunch of crazy people. She *was* a crazy person. Behind the heavy doors, were people moaning and screaming in the halls? Was the crazy woman on the gurney in the room next to Frances, rattling her wrist-cuffs?

Nina's room was warm, but she was still shivering. She went to her parents' room for Pearl's emerald blanket and wrapped it around herself. Back in bed, she turned restlessly onto her side, wondering if the Halcion was ever going to take hold. Halcion, Haldol. *Hal,* she remembered from Latin class, meant to breathe, as in inhale, exhale. She pictured her mother awake in her hospital bed, curled up, afraid, maybe not even sure where she was. She pictured the birthmark on her finger and her crooked bottom teeth. She pictured herself in the bed beside her. *I'm here,* she told her mother. *Breathe with me.* Inhale. Exhale. Inhale. Exhale. The bedlam receded and they finally fell asleep.

Chapter Seventeen

In the psych-ward waiting room, still sitting in the molded brown chair, Nina slowly pushed the pin of Alison's STICK UP MY ASS button into her arm. Haldol flooded her veins.

Stephanie watched from a gurney, handcuffed to the railing. *Isn't that painful?* she asked.

It's supposed to hurt, Gardner said. He was in doctors' scrubs, kneeling by Nina's chair. *That means it's working.*

Nina bolted awake in her bed, dizzy, thirsty, head throbbing.

Stephanie.

She'd forgotten to meet Stephanie last night.

She lurched out of bed, almost tripping over a plastic milk crate half-filled with books for college. What day was it? She squinted at the calendar hanging on her bedroom door: August 26. As if she could possibly flit off to school in five days with her mother's sanity hanging in the balance. The room spun, and for a moment she was back in the psych ward—Frances on the loose in some mad, chaotic terrain where eyebrows talked—but Nina made herself push away the dream and stay on course to the phone. Before she contended with everything else, she needed to let Stephanie know she hadn't blown her off.

She'd been too exhausted last night to look at her answering machine. Now she saw there were six messages. She couldn't bear hearing Stephanie yell at her. Maybe try her at Patrick's first, cut her off at the pass. She dialed his number, steeling herself for his grating recorded message. But worse, he picked up.

"Stephanie, please," she said icily.

He was silent for a while, leaving her to twist in the wind. "Not here," he said finally.

"Do you know where she is?" Another long silence. "Hello?" she said.

An impatient sigh. "She was gonna stay with her dad last night after she saw you."

"Really?" Nina was surprised that Stephanie had been allowed back at Kay's after the blowup.

"Yeah, *really*."

She could practically smell stale Juicy Fruit through the phone line. "Just tell her we had to take my mom to the hospital last night and to please call me, okay?"

He laughed. "I'm not telling her shit for you. Bitch been fucked up since the day she met you."

Oh, was that right? Bitch been fucked up? "You know what? Fuck *you* for fucking her up. Fuck you for telling her I came on to you. Fuck you for *ensnaring* her."

Silence on the other end of the line.

"That means trapping her, birdbrain."

She heard scornful laughter as she banged down the phone. So she hadn't reduced him to tears. At least she hadn't backed down.

She tried Stephanie's number at Kay's, but there was no answer. She must have taken her answering machine when she moved out to Patrick's.

She finally forced herself to press Play on hers. "I'm here," Stephanie said in the first message, calling from Martell's. There was loud chatter in the background, a Fleetwood Mac song, the clink of silver-ware against dinner plates. "It's eight thirty," she said. "You're half an hour late."

Then a ten-second message, just the silverware and now a Sade song, setting off an almost unbearable longing to press Rewind and somehow live out the sane version of the night.

The third message: "Seriously? Are you standing me up? Jesus, Nina, this was your idea."

She stopped the machine and dialed Stephanie again. Eight thirty must have been when they were waiting in the psych ER. Once she had a chance to explain, Stephanie would have to understand. And maybe, despite the tension between them, even offer Nina a little comfort?

Stephanie's phone just rang and rang.

Message number four was car horns and ambulance sirens raging in the background, then, "Hey, where are you?" Gardner! Wondering where she was, the same urgent tone as the night she'd met him at the Carlyle. But then he just hung up.

She was about to dial his number when the fifth message began to play: Stephanie, saying she was on the pay phone outside Flana-gan's. The same pay phone Gardner must have called from. The same one Nina had grabbed the other night to look occupied as he'd ap-proached. Funny to think of that same chunk of plastic in all their hands.

"I figured you blew me off to stalk Gardner here," Stephanie said.

That stung. Not the stalking part, since Nina couldn't exactly disagree, but the idea that she'd so blithely abandon Stephanie, even for him.

Stephanie sniffed hard—making do, Nina figured, since she couldn't exactly whip out a glass pipe in the middle of Second Ave-nue. Nina glanced at her pinky nail, still longer than the others but starting to tear. The sound of Stephanie snorting coke, which all summer had set off such intense craving, now made her a little nauseated. Last night's wildfire energy had left her unmoored and depleted. Now all she wanted was to sit in a silent, dark room, her mind quiet and rooted.

Stephanie sniffed again. "Patrick's right: city girls think their shit doesn't stink." The coke seemed to hit at that instant. "How could you, Nina? Where are you? What am I supposed to think? You should have told me. I would never do that to you. Friends don't do that! I would never—" She abruptly stopped. Then she said, "Oh. Well, look who it is," with a note of satisfaction in her voice. "Karma's a bitch, huh? Let's see if *someone* wants to buy me a drink."

Nina knew instantly: *someone* was Gardner. The throbbing in her head started up again. She pictured his pleased smile when he saw Stephanie. She pictured that night in Central Park when he'd cradled Steph's head to stop her nosebleed. *Fuck with me and I'll fuck you back harder,* she remembered Stephanie saying at her July Fourth party. Did she really believe Damian's inane *gyration* lie? Enough to gyrate with Gardner?

The next message was a hang-up, the dial tone's flat drone.

Still no answer at Kay's, just endless ringing.

At Gardner's, his mother's brusque "Reed residence." Nina hung up.

Ira had left a note for Nina on the kitchen counter, saying he'd gone to his office since they weren't allowed to see Frances on her first day, anyway, and asking Nina to drop off her mother's suitcase at the hospital. Beside the note was a small stack of cash for any last-minute purchases for college, and in the doorway the black suitcase. Already, thankfully, packed: Nina didn't think she could stand reading through four pages of hazardous items again. Just thinking about it detonated the *burn-choke-cut-provoke* rhyme in her head.

But it was good to have a task. To not sit home brooding about Stephanie and Gardner. (Had he bought her a Slippery Nipple? Had they sat at the bar with their knees touching? Had he pulled an errant thread from the hem of her shorts, then balled it up and put it in his pocket?) She picked up the suitcase, thought for a second, then put it down and went to get Pearl's emerald blanket.

In the lobby, Freddie ducked his head as soon as he spotted her. Why did she suddenly feel insulted, rejected even, when all this time she'd just wanted him to leave her alone? Did a crazy, belly-dancing mother who conversed with street people about imaginary dogs make Nina less appealing? Like she might also morph into a lunatic at any second?

"You hear about girl?" He pointed to his radio.

"What girl?" She stopped and the suitcase swung back hard against her knee. Hopefully her father hadn't packed an illicit Walkman or hair dryer.

"Central Park dead girl."

"A dead girl in Central Park? Who?"

Freddie shrugged. "They just say girl dead in park. Kill there last night."

She could see she wouldn't get much more from him. He studied the floor, back stiff. She was about to stalk out the door when she remembered how he'd intervened last night with the baseball bat, the look on his face as Frances babbled away about the guy's lost dog—alarm, but edged with empathy and even sorrow, like maybe crazy wasn't completely foreign to him. Maybe Nina was more of a real person to him now, kind of the way he was to her.

She was suddenly shy. "Thanks for your help last night. It was, um, weird, and would have gotten weirder if you hadn't come along." For some reason—she hardly believed it herself—she placed the suitcase on the ground and opened her arms.

"You are nice girl, Miss Nina," he said as he stepped into her embrace. She let him snake his hand up the back of her shirt, just a little, a couple of inches, before she pushed him away.

The hospital was only a few blocks uptown, so she decided to walk, squinting in the sunlight. You could see the end of summer in the sky, which was no longer powder blue but a more vigorous azure; summer verging on fall, with the air already smelling like turning leaves. In one of Leigh's personality tests, if you heard "fall" and autumn came to mind, you were an optimist; down or plummet, you were a pessimist. "Rocky road" a flavor of ice cream, you were an optimist; a tough time, you were a pessimist. "Stroke" a caress—optimist; your grandmother's intracerebral hemorrhage that led to despair, catatonia, rose bonfires, and wild-eyed insanity—pessimist.

She was still shocked how wrong she'd been about her mother's feelings for Pearl, that her grief was actually so intense it had unhinged her. She pictured Pearl shaking her head at all the angst. But her absence was a crater that Frances had fallen into. As Nina came up to the hospital, she was surprised by a vision of her and her grandmother at the edge of the crater, trying together to haul Frances out.

She'd figured she'd leave the suitcase and blanket with the guard at the front desk, but he told her she had to take them upstairs herself, to the psychiatric unit on the fifth floor. She considered dumping them at his feet and running out. She pictured filthy walls and patients crawling on the ground, grabbing her ankles. She pictured her mother's strange blank face from last night: Would she recognize her own daughter?

But *upstairs* turned out to be just a long desk behind a glass partition, beside a tall door with a buzzer beside it and a window so tiny and scratched you couldn't see through it even if you wanted to. An older nurse in navy scrubs sat behind the desk, reading *People*.

"These are for Frances Jacobs," Nina told her.

"We'll see that she gets them, dear."

"Please." She was unexpectedly choking up. "Take care of her."

"Just leave them there, dear," the nurse said, pointing to the corner, business as usual, before returning to an article about Vanna White's exercise routine.

She needed something, a Xanax or a shot of vodka, but she'd settle for a cigarette. She found a deli a couple of blocks away. Next to a tip jar on the counter was a sign that said, WE'RE COMMITTED TO SERVICE WITH A SMILE. If you heard "committed" and thought *psychotic break,* you might be a pessimist. Down another block was an electronics store with a sign in its window: TRY BEFORE YOU BUY. NO COMMITMENT. A cheerier offer anyway. Also in the window, a dozen television sets of various sizes, all running at once and tuned to the same channel: a grim-faced anchorman with a BREAKING NEWS graphic over his head, white letters outlined in scarlet. Nina paused to look, although she couldn't hear anything through the glass. The picture flashed to a live view of Central Park, a large tree with a bunch of police milling around. This must be about the dead girl Freddie had mentioned.

Two women stood next to Nina, also watching the televisions. One was in her twenties, the other looked late-forties. Both had on red blazers with linebacker shoulders and carried gold-monogrammed briefcases, "A.M.H." on the older woman's and "L.S.H." on the younger's. Boss and assistant, Nina figured. Or a mother-daughter real estate team.

A.M.H. curled her lip. "God. This city." She had on huge sunglasses, and a razor-edged haircut.

L.S.H. wrinkled her nose. "It's a cesspool. Why do we keep living here?"

Feeling like part of the problem, since her cigarette smoke was wafting right into their faces, Nina dropped the butt to the pavement and stamped it out. But it was just her paranoia: they ignored her and went on staring at the TV sets. She thought of the night at the Palladium when Stephanie and Gardner gleefully described their coke-induced paranoia. Two beautiful people who probably belonged together. The obvious spark between them. Again, she imagined them at Flanagan's last night, leaning closer, mouths about to touch, murmuring *We shouldn't do this,* which of course meant, *Let's absolutely.* They'd both be in the city this fall, while Nina was stuck down in Nashville eating grits at the Grand Ole Opry.

On the TV sets, the camera pulled back to a shot of the Temple of Dendur. The night they'd been there, the pyramids behind the glass had glowed, the way she'd felt her skin shine when she lifted her shirt to flash the airplane. But now, in daylight, the sun reflected off the windows and made them opaque and a little eerie.

"The radio said she was only eighteen," L.S.H. said to A.M.H.

Nina was startled. *Girl* had made her think *child.*

A.M.H. seemed enraged. "What was she thinking, traipsing around the park in the middle of the night? Who does that?"

"I have no idea," the younger woman said. "I would never do that."

Nina was about to walk away when the TV screens switched to a shot of a restaurant with a familiar green awning. Hanging plants in the windows, wrought-iron lanterns, red-and-white checked tablecloths inside.

"Hey, that's Flanagan's," L.S.H. said, a second before Nina placed it.

Why were they showing Flanagan's? There was the somber-looking anchorman again, the BREAKING NEWS banner still gleaming over his head. Nina tried to read his lips. She ought to go inside and find a TV she could hear, but she felt strangely stuck in place.

"I bet the girl was there last night," said A.M.H.

"I wouldn't be caught dead in that place," L.S.H. assured her. Hearing the words "eighteen" and "dead" and "Flanagan's" and "last night" shattered whatever spell had immobilized Nina. She had to hear Stephanie's voice, to know she was okay. She ran to the phone booth on the corner, but again Stephanie's phone just rang and rang. Nina tried not to picture her at the base of that tree, or in the terrifying moments before, in the dark, running into the guy with the hair dye she'd shot with her water gun the day they met. Or the coked-up music nut from the Palladium. Or the slashed model's attackers. Nina's brain was a panicked scramble. She ordered herself to calm down. Of course Stephanie hadn't gone to the park. Alone? Why would she?

Although *some* girl had.

She wished she had her sunglasses, the ones that turned the sky silver, that Stephanie gave her the day they met. This glut of blue made her vision skip in little spasms. She imagined Stephanie at the foot of the tree in a pool of blood, then started walking to Flanagan's so fast it was basically running, but the terrified part of her stopped her at every corner, even when the light was green. She noticed Missing Cat signs taped on nearly every crosswalk pole: *Sassy, Luna, Duchess, Gidget, Sheba.* Black cats, orange ones, green eyes, torn ear. So many lost cats! Or had they run away? What were they out here looking for?

At the entrance to Flanagan's, Brian and his father huddled with two policemen. A Channel 7 News truck was pulling out from the curb into traffic. Nina still felt as if she were watching TV through a window, everything incomprehensible.

When Brian saw her, he said something to the policemen and came to meet her mid-block. Her legs almost gave way, like when she'd watched the *Challenger* take off on live TV a few months ago, the announcer saying *T minus fifteen seconds, T minus ten, nine, eight* . . . before it exploded midair.

"You heard?" Brian asked. His face was drained of color.

Nina nodded, slow-motion, heavy-headed. Dread stopped up her throat. She heard Stephanie's jangly bracelets and elaborate rug lectures. She saw her sweet green eyes and her perfect smoke rings.

Brian held her shoulders as if to prop her up. He seemed taken aback as he peered into her face. "Are you okay?"

"Please." It was unbearable. "Just tell me who it was."

"I thought you knew," he said. His eyes bore into hers until she couldn't take it and stared at his neck instead.

T minus three, minus two, minus one—

"Alison," he said. "Alison Bloch."

In the street beside them, a guy on a bicycle jangled his bell at a taxi about to cut him off. Two men argued as they hauled a blanket-wrapped couch into a moving van. Nina came back to herself with a long, deep breath. It wasn't Stephanie. But the heaviness stayed in her chest, the shift from the terror of the unspeakable to the horror of reality.

"*Alison?*"

"You knew her, right?"

She nodded, now picturing Alison's moussed hair and gleaming lip gloss, her loudmouth energy and X-rated buttons. It was impossible to imagine her not in motion, much less not . . . alive, lying at the base of that tree. How enraging it must have been, to be overwhelmed by some cold-blooded killer in the dark.

"Are they sure it's her?" Nina asked.

"She had her driver's license on her. And one of our matchbooks in her pocket. The cops are asking if she was here last night."

"Was she?"

He nodded. "At least till one, when I left."

Now Nina pictured Alison as she'd always known her, sniffing around after Gardner. She shivered. Good thing Brian couldn't read her petty thoughts. He was staring at the ground, grinding down some piece of trash with his sneaker.

"This must be terrible for you," she said.

"It wasn't like I was so close with her, but she was funny. Those buttons." He laughed lightly. "She was always after me to put Billy Idol on the jukebox." He glanced over his shoulder and his face went slack. Mr. Flanagan was still in the doorway, talking with the police. "I should go. You'll be okay?"

She'd never seen him look so miserable. She gave him an awkward sideways hug and said, "Go."

The sky had gone even more vibrant now, an adrenalized blue—the blue of police cars and uniforms. She walked back down Lexington in a daze. Alison, of all people, dead. Of all the loud, aggravating people. You could want to kill someone, but you obviously didn't want them actually dead. But someone had.

She imagined Alison and her friend Jill last night, drunk and silly, deciding to walk to the bandshell after Flanagan's to belt out Journey on the stage. And when they parted ways to go home, Alison taking the path behind the museum, belting "Girl Can't Help It," unable to hear the guy creeping up behind her. Ghastly. Sickening. A horror movie come to life.

She checked every newsstand she passed for more information, but all the headlines were about last night's Mets victory. Although the *Post* had another story about the model: she'd fired her agent and was now auditioning for movies. "She's a manipulative little girl," the ex-agent was quoted as saying. "See where that gets her."

At the corner with the sign for the missing *Duchess*, a man stopped beside Nina, near enough so their shoulders practically touched. She was so jumpy, she almost screamed. He crossed the street when the light turned, but her heart kept pounding. Imagine actual terror, how it felt knowing you were about to die.

Had Gardner heard about Alison? She'd been at least as crazy about him as Nina was. Maybe they'd even gotten together one night . . . he must feel so strange, a girl who'd worshipped him, who he might even have slept with, murdered.

She called him from the pay phone on Seventy-Ninth Street but hung up when there was no answer.

There were three new messages on her answering machine when she got home. Leigh: "Did you hear about Alison Bloch? Can you believe it?" and Meredith: "I saw her last night at Flanagan's—she was telling everyone she made out with Simon Le Bon behind the Nassau Coliseum."

The third message was from Stephanie: "I just got back to Hewlett. I've been worried sick about you! Alison Bloch: oh my God. Patrick told me you called, after I threatened to cut his dick off. Your mom's in the hospital? Is she okay? Are you? I met these Brazilians at Flanagan's and ended up crashing at their hotel. Anyway, I know you wouldn't come on to Patrick. He's just crazy jealous and possessive. Also a douche rocket. Call me the second you get this."

Nina picked up the phone, allowing herself a moment of relief before she dialed Stephanie, then a jab of guilt for feeling relieved not just that Stephanie was safe, and had forgiven her, but also that she hadn't been with Gardner.

For dinner, her father picked up cheese blintzes at Three Guys, Nina's favorite, which felt a little self-indulgent considering the people in her life who weren't well enough—or alive enough—to enjoy fried dough and ricotta cheese. But tonight's were undercooked and watery, like chewing wet sponge, so she went ahead and ate them.

"You might not get to visit Mom before you leave for school," Ira said. He absently cut his blintz into halves then fourths then eighths as he told her that Frances was still too "unsettled" for visitors, according to Vlad. Nina tried not to imagine what *too unsettled* looked like in the context of a psych ward.

"She's exhausted but still fighting sleep," her father added, continuing to hack at the blintz until it was practically mush. He kept glancing at Frances's chair and opening his mouth as if he wanted to say something to it, maybe reassure it that its usual occupant would be back soon, but then he'd close his mouth and toy with his blintz again.

"I could defer Vanderbilt until January," Nina said. She saw herself at the hospital every morning, reading to Frances, the nurses praising her devotion. In the afternoons, she'd shop for ingredients at neighborhood markets to make dinners she'd learn to cook for her father. At night she'd stay with Gardner in the Hunter dorm room she imagined for him: lofted bed, picture window with a view onto Lexington Avenue, plants on the sill he'd be surprisingly good at nurturing.

She tried not to sound too eager. "A lot of freshmen do it. They're called *j-frosh*. January freshmen." She heard her mother's gleeful voice, pre-Haldol anyway, saying, *That means next year you'll be a j-soph, then a j-jun, although I hope not a jejune j-jun for the tuition we're paying.*

"Out of the question," her father said. Clearly not the time to press; she'd work on him a little more this week. For now, they cleared the dishes and settled on the living-room couch to watch *Last Days of Mussolini,* her father's pick, but Central Park and SPECIAL REPORT were on every channel, video of the Temple of Dendur and the giant elm tree surrounded by crime-scene tape, which Nina had seen at least thirty times by now. She still had trouble believing that Alison was dead—strangled to death was the working theory, according to a police briefing. The guy had killed her and then left her there on the ground. Nina remembered how small she'd felt under the endless black sky the night she and Stephanie went with Gardner and Brian to the park. Unbelievable to think that Alison had been made even smaller, stamped out until she disappeared.

"There are still more questions than answers," said a fluffy-haired reporter with dangly silver earrings.

Ira sighed. "I always thought Mom would have made a great reporter. She's got the beauty and smarts of a Diane Sawyer." He frowned at the screen. "This gal's got no gravitas."

"Her earrings sure don't," Nina said. They blew around in the wind, festive as tinsel.

The reporter gestured toward the tree: "The young woman's lifeless body was found beneath this elm tree by a jogger on her early morning run through the park." Cut to video of a woman in nylon shorts talking to police earlier in the day. Cut to a photo of Alison, what looked like her yearbook picture with a velvety blue background, chin high, hair teased almost to the top of the frame.

"Attractive and popular, Alison Blotch would have started college next week," said the reporter.

"*Bloch*, you dingbat," Nina said, unexpectedly furious.

"Oh," Ira asked, "did you know her?"

The screen switched to the outside of Flanagan's, the video footage Nina had seen earlier, then back to Alison's yearbook picture. "Not very well, but I talked to her there a few times."

"Nice girl?"

Alison's gaze was so direct, Nina could swear she was looking right at her, daring her to tell the truth. "I guess so," she hedged, picturing Alison and Jill laughing at her in the bathroom.

Another photo of Alison appeared on the screen, orange lipstick, braces, sweatshirt pulled down one shoulder à la *Flashdance*, and then video of her parents, identified as EVAN AND SHELLY BLOCH, hands covering bleak faces as they pushed through a horde of photographers into a tall gray apartment building. "Police continue to search for clues," the fluffy-haired reporter said, "but what we do know is that while the city slept, the life of an eighteen-year-old girl, bright with promise, was extinguished here in Central Park." The wind blew her hair in her face, and her earrings thrashed her cheeks. "More on this story as it develops."

Nina hadn't been out since this morning. "Was it that windy when you left your office?" she asked her father. "It's like a hurricane made landfall right where she's standing."

When he didn't answer, she turned to look at him. He was crying, which she couldn't remember ever seeing.

"Are you thinking about Mom?" she asked, although it wasn't really a question. Nina would bet the air in the apartment smelled wrong to him without Frances's carbon dioxide. "You're right," she said, "she'd be an excellent reporter. No way she'd mispronounce Alison's last name."

He looked at her through reddened eyes and squeezed her shoulder. "I'm thinking about that poor girl's father. The hell I'd be in if anything like that happened to you."

The surprise of this and the tenderness in his voice made her throat close. Tears came to her eyes. Then she did something she'd never imagined: she leaned against her father and wept. Just for half a minute while he patted her back, just until the Mussolini movie started, at which point they traded self-conscious smiles and sat back to watch, although they only got as far as the Munich Agreement, before, both weary, they called it a night.

The next morning, Ira left *The New York Times* on the kitchen counter, open to the Metropolitan page, along with a note: *Do you know him?*
SUSPECT SEIZED IN CENTRAL PARK SLAYING, said the headline.

Next to the story, a photograph of two cops leading the guy to a van. He had on a light-colored, well-worn Lacoste shirt. His arms were cuffed behind his back, dark hair falling in his eyes, scratches down the side of his face. The caption beneath the photo said, "Suspected Central Park assailant, Gardner Reed."

Chapter Eighteen

Of course it was an accident. A horrible, unthinkable accident. 'A TRAGIC ACCIDENT,' CLAIMS PREPPY SLAYER'S LAWYER was the headline in the *Daily News*. So why were they charging Gardner with murder? He was a regular guy, not some murderous psycho.

"One of us," Clayton Chase said that night at Flanagan's. Reminiscences about Gardner filled every corner of the bar, bordering on eulogies, Nina thought. "Remember that time he bombed down Ajax Mountain on one ski? The epic all-night backgammon game in Palm Beach?"

"We were both born at New York–Presbyterian, one day apart," said Dean Ehrenkranz, one of Gardner's poker buddies. "Literally, twenty-four hours!"

Nina shifted on her barstool, self-conscious about sitting by herself, but Leigh was already at Princeton, Meredith at home packing for Penn, and Stephanie in Hewlett. She crossed her legs and stared down at her knee. She'd packed most of her clothes already and had on the plain black tank dress she'd worn to Stephanie's Fourth of July party a million years ago. Her skin stuck to the leather and burned when it came unstuck. She was so hungry for any new information, she'd been unable to stay away, but every time she heard Gardner's name, she wanted to kick out a window. She knew Alison's death was an accident. There was no reason for Gardner to kill her. But knowing that barely put a dent in her fury. If Gardner had shown better judgment, Alison would still be annoying but alive, prancing around the bar wearing her FET's LUCK button, and he and Nina would be making plans for fall break. He'd called her from here Monday night. Why give in to Alison just because Nina hadn't shown up? He couldn't wait one night?

"One time we drove my parents' Jeep into Georgica Pond," Diana Sloan said, laughing. "I had to tell my parents the brakes had failed." Nina recognized her as a friend of Holland's, with a grating, openmouthed laugh she'd bet drove Gardner up the wall, no matter how much she tried to play up their closeness. It would be nice if Nina could publicly claim her own closeness to him, but her stories were filled with land mines: the Carlyle rampage, their shared love of cocaine, the homeless guy in the park. Brian was outside trying to fend off reporters, but it wasn't hard to imagine that a few had slipped inside. Out of context, anything could be misconstrued. Best to keep her trap shut. Rabid reporters weren't interested in nuance.

"It's all so ludicrous, charging him with murder," Clayton said.

"Absurd," agreed Polly Jessup, who Nina knew for a fact hadn't seen Gardner since June, when she and her family had left for the Amalfi Coast.

"I will absolutely testify for him," Diana said.

There was a commotion at the door. Chris Armstrong had come in with a late edition of the *Post*. A reporter had managed to get an interview with Gardner at Rikers. Chris planted himself at the end of the bar where Nina sat, and a dozen people gathered around him while he read aloud from the article. Gardner said that Alison went crazy when they got to the park, when he told her he wasn't in the mood for sex—hit him and scratched his face. They'd been sitting at the base of a tree behind the museum; he started to get up, but she'd apologized and begged him to stay, then took off her underwear and tied his wrists behind his back, trying to be sexy: *You're cute, but you'd look cuter tied up,* she'd said. She'd straddled his chest, facing his feet, and pushed his pants down. When he said again that he wanted to leave, she got rough, squeezing and slapping his balls, even hitting them with a stick. He'd yelled at her to stop but she wouldn't. That's when he pulled his hand loose from behind his back and hooked his arm around her chest, or maybe it was her neck—it all happened so fast; he just wanted her to stop hurting him—and yanked her off him. She'd landed at the base of the tree, not moving. He thought she was kidding at first, but when he saw she was dead, he panicked and went across the road to sit on the stone wall, waiting for someone to find her and the police to come take her away.

A shocked silence as everyone stared at each other. "It makes sense," Erin Ward finally said. "You can't make up a story like that."

Brooke Limbocker nodded. "I can totally see it."

Nina saw it, too, the giant elm tree, the crazy glowing August moon, Alison's underwear phosphorescent as a wedding dove. Her rage when Gardner said he wanted to go.

"I can't say I'm surprised," Campbell Hughes said. "That girl *was* really aggressive."

"Not to speak ill of the dead," Brooke said, "but she was always throwing herself at him."

Kate Wells said she'd heard Alison kept handcuffs in her bedside drawer. That she'd once let a guy stick a live, wriggling zebra fish inside her. That her nickname in high school was Maxwell House, since she was *good to the last drop.*

Nina was no fan of Alison's, but this was getting personal, and ugly. As if she'd not only provoked her own death but deserved it. Shouldn't Nina say something? Except, to what end? It wasn't like she'd change anyone's mind.

"You should have heard the messages she'd leave for Gardner on his machine," Benji Peterson said. "He played them for me once: *Hey, dickhead, why haven't you called me back? Call me back, you prick, you fuck!*"

Chip Wainwright said he saw the naked Polaroids Alison had sent. Jesus.

"When's her funeral?" Holland asked. "Should we go?"

"I heard it's this Friday," Brooke said.

"In two days? Why so soon?"

"She was Jewish. That's how they do it."

"Oh," Holland said. "There must be a discount."

Tossed off so matter-of-factly, it took Nina a moment to register the insult. She tasted blood. She'd bit her lip so hard, she'd split it. *Spoiled kike* banged through her brain. *Aggressive. Pushy.* Alison was dead, unable to defend herself. What was Nina's excuse? But she couldn't make herself say a word.

That night, she dreamed she was walking in Central Park. She came to the clearing under the elm tree. The sky was dark, but the moon cast light on an open cottage beneath the tree limbs, just the insides, like a stage set for a play: an iron stove, a pine table and chairs, a round, braided rug. They'd just finished dinner. Alison dried dishes and placed them in a hutch while Gardner sat at the table with his legs stretched out, relaxing in front of a TV.

He gave Nina a private smile. Oh, she missed that smile. She missed his eyes, his breath in her ear, his tongue moving in her mouth like he wanted to swallow her.

But it was Alison she spoke to: *You should come back. No one knows where you are.*

The air rippled with the wild wind that had battered the TV reporter's earrings, although Alison's hair was moussed solid. *We live here now,* she said with a smug laugh that made Nina want to reach under the tree and haul her out. But when she tried to get closer, she bumped against an invisible wall. Their existence was a diorama, no one going in or out. Alison and Gardner would live here forever, outside of time. Nina stood watching them, a sickening envy clotting in her veins.

Their telephone rang, but neither of them got up to answer it. Alison slithered over to Gardner, twirling her underwear as she straddled him in his chair. The phone rang again and Nina was startled awake. She sat up in bed, her brain cloudy and her spine in flames, and picked up the receiver.

"It's me. Did I wake you up?"

It took her a minute: Meredith. Nina cleared the sleep from her throat. "I'm good. Just a little hungover."

"I wanted to let you know, I got my test results."

Nina blinked hard to reset her brain. AIDS test. Today was results day. She tightened her fist around the receiver and dug her knuckles in her cheek, bracing herself. With everything else gone to hell, this had to be bad news too.

"Hello?" Meredith said. "Are you there?"

She tried to push away the image from the news the other day, a skeletal guy in a wheelchair on the St. Vincent's AIDS ward, lesions up and down his bare arms, but now it was Meredith's face on his body, terror in her cratered-out eyes. "I'm here," she whispered, unable to breathe any volume into her voice.

An interminable pause.

"Negative!" Meredith finally shouted.

Nina fell back in bed. "God, I'm so relieved."

Meredith laughed. "You and me both."

"I knew you'd be okay, but it's still so good to hear."

"Listen. I'm sorry if I've been a bitch lately." Meredith sounded lighter than she had all summer.

"You've been fine." Why spoil anyone's happiness this week?

"Hey, guess what the nurse said when she found out I know Gardner?"

"How'd she know?" Even fully awake now, Nina couldn't shake the image of Alison and Gardner in the clearing, eternally linked.

"She saw my address and asked me," Meredith said. "Isn't everyone asking you?"

Nina's father had, last night when she got home. He'd shown her the *Times* cover story, with the headline DARKNESS BENEATH THE GLITTER, which mentioned Gardner's "unemployment" and "academic futility" (who had they interviewed, Rex and Holland?). "Just how well did you know this boy?" Ira had asked her, with a sharpness in his voice that felt like a warning: *Don't tell me something else I need to worry about right now.*

She'd been more than happy to comply. If her father knew her part in this mess, he'd forever view her with suspicion and maybe even a little repulsion, no matter how much she tried to explain. She wasn't sure how interested he was in nuance either.

"Anyway," Meredith said, "the nurse's theory was that maybe Gardner had too much to drink and couldn't get it up, and Alison teased him and, I don't know, flipped a switch."

"That's insane." Also, Nina thought but didn't say, she knew firsthand that Gardner *could* get it up when he was drinking, remembering him pressed against her in the alcove outside Flanagan's. "Besides, Gardner said it was an accident. No switch was flipped."

"Well, I know that," Meredith said. "It's just interesting what people who don't know him are saying."

"If I want their opinion, I'll ask them," Nina said, inadvertently repeating one of Pearl's mottos.

"Anyway, the nurse was so nice," Meredith said. "She had a map of Martha's Vineyard on her wall. She gave me so many condoms I could practically open my own store. If you were to ever need a test, definitely go to the clinic on Seventy-Fifth Street and Lexington."

If you were to ever. It was too vague to qualify as an intentional dig at Nina's virginity, but it still felt like a slight.

Getting dressed Friday morning in the same clothes she'd worn to her grandmother's funeral, Nina thought back to that day, how she'd sat there dry-eyed through the eulogy that described someone other than the Pearl she knew. Mortified by her lack of tears, she'd tried to call up loving thoughts but could only remember reprimands: *Stop talking so much, laughing so loud, walking so fast, eating me out of house and home.* She'd finally managed to cry by mentally replaying that agonizing scene in *The Champ* when Ricky Schroder sobs over his dead father's body, pleading, "Wake up, Champ!"

Nothing made you feel more monstrous than a frozen heart at a funeral. She wouldn't be going to Alison's if Ira hadn't pressed her to. "It's a mitzvah," he said. "It will be a comfort to her parents, seeing how many friends she had."

At least she didn't have to go alone: Stephanie wanted to go too. The night she'd gone to Flanagan's to try to find Nina, she'd wound up sitting with Alison for an hour—it turned out they'd lived just a few miles apart on Long Island until Alison's family moved to Manhattan when she was in seventh grade. They'd even had the same sadistic orthodontist, whose office walls were covered with photos featuring hideously cockeyed teeth, to show patients what would happen if they disobeyed instructions.

"She was funny," Stephanie said on the phone, "and she *really* liked attention. She'd want a crowd at her funeral."

They arranged to meet before at a diner on Amsterdam a few blocks from the chapel. Nina got there first and chose a table far in the back so they could smoke and talk in private, without having to deal with testy customers waving smoke away, or nosy ones leaning closer if they heard Gardner's name. Which was on the cover of every newspaper again today, along with his and Alison's photos and headlines like: SEX PLAY GOT ROUGH! and PARK SEX ROMP ENDS IN TRAGEDY! She might not have been Alison's biggest admirer, but even she was offended by *play* and *romp*, like the night in the park had been some mischievous frolic.

She was already tense anyway, back muscles screaming, mittelschmerz cramping her abdomen. This morning, she'd made what now seemed like a questionable decision to forego a Xanax, so as not to risk conking out at the funeral. She ordered a Diet Coke and massaged her side.

Had only two weeks passed since she last saw Stephanie? When she came in the door, Nina had to hide her surprise at how worn-out she looked. She'd lost even more weight and her gray dress hung loose. Her face was dotted with scabs poking through a blanket of makeup, her beautiful pond-green eyes a dull olive. An image of a gaunt, terrified Frances in the emergency room flashed through Nina's mind. Then she refocused and it was *Stephanie,* silver moons and stars up her ears, a rhinestone bracelet on each wrist. Nina stood to hug her, careful not to crush her thin shoulders. They sat down and smiled awkwardly across the table, a funny shyness between them.

"It's amazing how you look the same as always," Stephanie said, "when inside you must feel so strange."

She'd almost forgotten what a relief it was to be so thoroughly understood. "I'm mainly in complete shock. I feel really far away from myself."

"I bet."

"Like everything's too big to get my head around."

Stephanie nodded and Nina relaxed. Today would be all right.

She took a long sip of her soda, glad for its familiar bittersweet tang. But then Stephanie asked: "Did the police call you?" and the Diet Coke went down the wrong pipe.

"What?" She couldn't quite catch her breath. Had someone found out about the Carlyle? "Why?"

"Well, we do know the killer."

"He didn't kill her."

Stephanie's eyebrows shot up.

"I mean, yes, she was killed. But 'killer' makes it sound like he did it on purpose. And he didn't. He couldn't have. There was no reason."

"A lot of people do bad things for no reason."

"Did you know he waited on the stone wall across the road from the elm tree until the jogger found her body and the police came? He wouldn't have done that if he didn't care."

"Maybe he was admiring his handiwork."

"Stop it: it's Gardner! Remember how nice he was to you in the park when your nose was bleeding?"

"I remember he almost cut a guy's dick off with a broken bottle. I can't believe we were with him that close to where he killed Alison."

Where she died, Nina was about to say, but got distracted by another thought: Why *hadn't* the police called her? The thing between her and Gardner was apparently so insignificant, it might as well not have existed. How many other Alisons—and Ninas—had there been this summer?

"What did you tell the police?" Nina asked.

"I didn't call back." Stephanie shrugged. "I don't talk to cops unless I have to. And I'm sure it was a routine call to everyone who was at Flanagan's Monday night, to see if anyone noticed anything."

"Did you?"

"Same as everyone else. Alison hitting on Gardner and him brushing her off."

"She was obsessed with him."

Stephanie tilted her head and gave her a look.

"*I* never jumped on his back and yelled *Carry me*. *I* didn't send naked Polaroids to his house."

"Good thing. Nothing says *Go ahead and kill me* like a piggyback ride and a few pictures."

Nina bristled. "You know that's not what I mean."

Stephanie looked at her for a second, then flicked her hand, meaning agree to disagree. "I'm just glad it wasn't you—"

Nina crossed her arms. "*Me?*"

"'Cause if they'd found your cock ring, I'd have to tell the whole world you thought it was a bracelet."

Nina allowed herself to laugh and her arms to drop. She reminded herself that Stephanie had only met Gardner a couple of times. She didn't know him the way Nina did, the tenderness in his hands and his clean-water taste. The waiter came for their order, and she was tempted to not eat, to hold that remembered taste in her mouth, but her stomach needed something to chew on besides carbonation. She asked for blueberry pancakes. Stephanie scrutinized the menu, then just ordered coffee.

"Won't you be hungry?"

"Patrick made eggs this morning."

Nina nodded blandly, as if she believed her, and also as if Patrick's name didn't feel like a splinter in her eye. Agree to disagree.

Stephanie took two cigarettes out of her pack and passed one to Nina. "How's your mom doing?"

"Mostly sleeping, from what I hear." Ira had gone to see her last night, but he wanted Nina to hold off until Frances was more alert and Nina had gotten settled in at school. She could come back to visit Frances in a few weeks. "When she woke up last night, she asked for ice cream, which was apparently a good sign."

"Sounds it." Stephanie dug her nails into the side of her face, scratching hard. Not a good sign. Was that smear on the collar of her dress dried blood? The pancakes came, and she eyed them avidly.

"Help yourself." Nina stamped out her cigarette.

Stephanie continued to ogle the pancakes. Nina couldn't figure out why, until she saw the resemblance of the powdered sugar to cocaine. Their eyes met, that old illicit spark leaping between them until Nina looked away and reached for the syrup.

"I stopped," she said, surprised at how abashed she felt. She was the lightweight she'd always feared, unable to keep up. "Seeing my mother so crazy"—she'd told Stephanie over the phone about the dog-collar episode—"and now with school starting . . ." She trailed off. Abashed, and also oddly guilty.

Stephanie nodded vigorously. "I'm going to stop too."

"Oh, good!" Nina smiled as she obliterated the powdered sugar with syrup. "I can't imagine lusting after coke while I'm sitting in an eight a.m. class. Speaking of which, doesn't Pratt start next week?"

Steph looked at the table. "The other night after Flanagan's, I saw, like, an army of rats running down Eighty-Third Street. Then," she added vaguely, "I almost got mugged. And now this Alison thing."

"Mugged?"

"I'm going to lay low for a little while." Her hair hung in her face. "Take a break. School's not going anywhere."

"Wait." Nina was confused. "You mean you aren't going?"

"I'm so not into the city right now."

"Isn't Pratt in Brooklyn?"

Now Stephanie crossed her arms. "Please don't judge me," she said. "Do I judge your Gardner fixation?"

Nina flinched.

"I'm sorry." Stephanie stood up. "This is a really bad day. Everything's getting to me. I'll be right back." She walked fast in the direction of the restrooms, leaving Nina to stare at her soggy pancakes with their mushed-up blueberries leaking out, which had done nothing for her cramps. She wished she had the nerve or skill to browbeat Stephanie to college. It wasn't hard to guess what she'd do all day at Patrick's, until one day soon, her spark just fizzled out. But harping on it would only push Stephanie further away. Or maybe Nina was still too much of a coward to make waves, even after all that had happened this summer.

She signaled for the check and got out her coin purse, which these days contained only cash. On the next table was a newspaper someone had left behind, opened to an interview with some Upper East Side church pastor who was holding a prayer vigil for Gardner this weekend: "Let us pray for this young man in trouble," he said. She suddenly noticed how small the diner was, a low-ceilinged stucco box. Or maybe it had shrunk during the past hour. Claustrophobia, she remembered, could be brought on by the craziest things, even a turtleneck or a backpack or a cast on your leg.

She paid and went outside to avoid a stucco-induced episode, although it wasn't much better here: another too-blue sky, way too vibrant for a funeral. Offensive, actually. At least she had her sunglasses with her.

"Nice shades," Stephanie said when she joined Nina on the sidewalk.

"You gave them to me."

"Right! The day we met." They started up Amsterdam. She'd have liked to ask the name for the sky's gaudy blue, remind Stephanie who she was, except it would backfire if she drew a blank.

After a minute, Stephanie said, "It's so weird to think of us spying on Gardner that day at the bandshell."

"If he hadn't been doing community service," Nina said, "I probably wouldn't have even walked you there."

Stephanie sighed and linked her arm through Nina's. "I have to admit, it does make it a little harder for me to hate him."

They continued up the block, passing a flower shop with racks of potted plants and bags of topsoil out on the sidewalk. The funeral chapel, a plain, four-story-high brick building, came into view, and Nina fantasized about turning around and hiding under a bag of dirt.

A knot of weeping girls in black dresses came up alongside them. A man with red-rimmed eyes blew his nose in a handkerchief. Two men half-carried a sobbing woman with a veil over her face. An old lady's shoulders quaked so hard her shawl slipped off to the sidewalk. This was awful. This was misery, black and hot as the fumes from the Greyhound bus idling at the corner.

"Let's get on that instead," Nina said, "wherever it's going."

"I think I'm underdressed," Stephanie said, looking at her reflection in a shoe-repair shop's window.

"For a bus?" A dumb joke couldn't hurt right now.

Stephanie smiled at the effort.

"I'm *overdressed*." Nina pointed to her black skirt and blazer. "I didn't know her well enough to look this doleful."

As the chapel loomed closer, more and more mourners crowded the sidewalk. Nina briefly considered turning around, but then she pictured her father's disappointment. And there was Brian, standing with Alison's friend Jill and awkwardly patting her on the back as tears ran down her cheeks. As uncomfortable as he must feel, Gardner's friend and the face of Flanagan's, he'd shown up today. He'd even put on a yarmulke.

"I heard Alison was wearing Jill's clothes that night, down to her underwear," Nina told Stephanie. "Have you ever worn someone else's underwear?"

Stephanie shook her head distractedly.

"I'd let you wear mine," Nina said.

But Stephanie was suddenly veering left. "I'm going to run and get some Starburst."

"I'll come with you. There must be a deli nearby."

But Stephanie was already walking fast, headed around the corner. "Get us seats," she called over her shoulder. "I'll be right back."

"Don't make me go in there alone," Nina pleaded. Why hadn't she thought to bring one tiny, just-in-case Xanax?

"Brian's here. Five minutes, I promise!"

Great.

Come on, Nina assured herself, you can do this. She made her way over to Brian and Jill. Brian looked somber and kind and more than a little freaked out. When Nina reached him, Jill glanced at her and abruptly started to laugh. Out of politeness, Nina tried to join in.

"Alison hated you!" Jill said, and Nina was left with her mouth in a ridiculous grimace. "I mean, you know, because you both liked—" Jill's face crumpled. She stuck out her tongue and made gagging sounds, then turned and wedged herself into a group of crying girls. Nina imagined Gardner's dismay if he were able to observe all this grief, what he'd inadvertently caused. She stared down at the pavement, thankful for Stephanie's sunglasses so no one could see that thought in her eyes. Behind her, a guy with tightly crossed arms muttered, "That fucking bastard, that fucking murderer." She felt radioactive, emitting enemy vibes.

"This is horrendous," she said to Brian.

"And the service hasn't even started yet."

"Make a break for it?" she joked weakly. The air was a mix of rot from the garbage on the curb and a sickly-sweet room spray billowing out the chapel's open door. She tried to breathe as shallowly as possible.

"I guess we'll be glad we came?" he said.

They were pushed inside by the crowd pressing forward. Where was Stephanie? Nina was about to ask Brian if he'd heard from Gardner, if they could visit him in his cell, bring him cigarettes, but she was struck silent by a photograph of Alison in the entryway, blown up to the size of a poster and propped on an easel. She was around five years old, a beautiful kid in a gigantic felt hat, one side of the brim pinned back with some plastic grapes and a clump of blue feathers. She stared solemnly at the camera, cute contrast to the musketeer headpiece. You couldn't help but feel sick about this little girl's fate.

Then there was some sort of logjam, and for a minute Nina was trapped in place, people's chests and breath pushing in from behind, black suits smelling of mothballs. She couldn't stop looking at the photograph, and the longer she looked, the more she noticed that Alison's lips were pressed together as if she were holding back a smile. Her eyes shone with a kind of swagger.

I fill his head night and day, those eyes told Nina. *He'll never stop thinking about me.*

Congratulations, Nina thought back at them. *You won.* Self-disgust swept through her. Only she would have a silent fight with a dead girl at her funeral.

They filed into a pew close to the back. She tried to keep a space clear for Stephanie, but a white-haired man and his wife pressed in. Both smelled strongly of eucalyptus cough drops. The room was packed, the pews filling fast. She noticed the walls were painted with bucolic scenes of barefoot medieval villagers herding sheep, black birds flying in a V. The ceiling was indigo, pinpointed with white stars. So that if you were claustrophobic, you could imagine yourself outdoors? Now she remembered that claustrophobia, along with agoraphobia, could be traced back to your time in your mother's womb: either you were dying to get out or desperate to burrow back in. She wished she were at the hospital with Frances, burrowing in.

It was so crowded, she had to crane her neck to see to the front of the chapel: some tall plants, a couple more poster-size photographs of Alison on easels—toddler Alison kicking a soccer ball, teenage Alison in a turtleneck and pink pearl earrings—and the gleaming mahogany coffin, dead Alison inside. At Nina's sharp intake of breath, the white-haired woman seated next to her leaned closer.

"Were you there last night?" she asked through a cloud of eucalyptus.

Nina looked back at her, confused.

"The visitation," the woman said, "for family and close friends to say goodbye before they seal the casket. Even with all the makeup they put on her, you could still see the purple."

Nina was having a hard time focusing. "Purple?"

The woman peered at her. "The bruises. All around her throat. It was horrible." She jammed a tissue against her streaming eyes. "If I ever run into that boy, I'll strangle the life out of *him*."

Nina thought of the last time she saw Alison, in the Flanagan's bathroom mirror, and tried to envision her neck unmarked, but all she could see now was a dark purple flush, chin to clavicle. She reminded herself that this didn't prove Gardner had meant to hurt her. If Alison had gotten rough, like Gardner said, and he'd yanked her neck with the crook of his arm to pull her off, as he'd told the police, surely that would have left some pretty serious damage.

On Nina's other side, Brian stared fixedly into his lap.

"Are you okay?" she whispered. Stupid question.

"He was in such a shitty mood Monday night," he said quietly. "Everything with Holland and Rex, school, Tom, his mother kicking him out again . . . he just wanted to sit by himself, but Alison kept coming over and bugging him." He winced. "I should have said something to her."

"It wouldn't have mattered. She wanted to be with him."

He shook his head in frustration. "Why would you want to be with a guy who's rolling his eyes and making fun of you, who's like, 'Why won't this bitch leave me alone?'"

"He said that?"

Brian nodded, and Nina's mind automatically jumped to Gardner's defense: of course it sounded bad, in light of what had happened, but people said unkind things all the time when they were in a bad mood. That didn't make them murderers. Although she hoped that Alison's wrecked parents, now hobbling to their seats, and her brother and sister bent over in pain, never had to hear it.

The rabbi came to the podium and sighed. Did he do that at every funeral to demonstrate empathy? And yet his voice caught as he said good morning, which seemed hard to fake. He enumerated Alison's familial roles: cherished daughter and granddaughter; treasured niece; beloved sister of Shayna, David, and Pumpernickel. ("Their poodle," someone behind them whispered.) The woman with the cough drops laughed and sobbed at the same time. The rabbi instructed them to recite Psalm 23, which they could find in their programs. A rustling as everyone opened them. Nina hadn't seen programs being handed out, not that she would have taken one, since she knew she didn't really belong here, even draped in black. The part in the psalm about lying down in green pastures reminded her of Stephanie fluttering her arms and legs in the grass that night in the park with Gardner and Brian. She was right, they hadn't been far from the spot where Alison died.

Her mittelschmerz flared. She glanced behind her for Stephanie, but there was only a sea of damp-eyed strangers.

Jill and two other girls made their way to the podium, clutching each other and whimpering. One of the girls described the night she and Alison snuck out of the house to see *The Rocky Horror Picture Show* but got lost trying to find the theater, coincidentally the same thing that had once happened to Nina and Meredith. The other recited the lyrics to "I've Loved These Days" by Billy Joel, one of Alison's favorite songs, prudently skipping over the line about cocaine.

"I love that song," Brian whispered, and Nina nodded. It was one of her favorites too.

Pale and trembling, Jill stammered through a story about Alison making Shrinky Dinks and nearly burning down the kitchen. Nina thought again about how Alison was wearing Jill's clothes the night she died. Did Jill feel as if she'd been there too? That part of her would always be under the elm tree, in some way dead also? Suddenly Nina remembered a detail she'd heard on the news yesterday: that Alison had been left on the ground the way she'd fallen, with her clothes in disarray—shirt and bra bunched up near her shoulders, skirt hiked up around her waist. It seemed obscene, that she'd been left exposed like that. But Gardner must have been in shock. He'd told police it was all a blur; he'd never seen a dead body before. Maybe he'd been scared to touch her.

The temperature in the chapel had climbed several degrees. Perfume and deodorant couldn't mask the scent of perspiration. Grief infiltrated the air like pollution. On the other side of the room, there were gasps as someone fainted and had to be carried outside. The girls left the podium, and a tall, bearded man took their place, his face and shirt collar damp.

"Her uncle," someone behind Nina whispered.

He looked anguished. "Evan and Shelly have asked me to say a few words on their behalf," he said. Nina sang Billy Joel to herself to try to block him out. "Alison had a zest for life," he said, pushing past the song's barricade. "She was born bubbly. When she was a kid, she would go up to strangers at the movies or in the subway and hug them. I had to pry her off more than a few times." People laughed, although Nina was picturing Alison straddling Gardner on the ground beneath the elm tree, demanding too much, refusing to let go.

"She had a zany side, to be sure," her uncle continued, "with a fondness for silly buttons. And she could certainly be feisty, which was part of her strength and charm."

The air-conditioning must not be working. Why didn't someone at least open a door?

"I think it's safe to say that Alison liked people and parties more than she liked books," her uncle said, "but she was whip-smart and fiercely loyal to her friends, which is why people were drawn to her like moths to a flame. We will never understand why anyone would have wanted to harm this precious girl."

He *didn't* want to! He hadn't *meant* to! Nina wondered if she and Alison were the only ones here who knew this. She squeezed her eyes shut. Even her eyelashes were sweating.

Alison's uncle told a few more stories and read a poem. The rabbi returned to the podium for final prayers. Nina prayed that Stephanie really had gone to get Starburst, and not to meet Damian. Then the service was mercifully over. Brian's face was ashen. People leaving their pews to head back to the exit were soon bottlenecked in the center aisle. Nina didn't know how much longer she could wait for fresh air. She found Brian's hand and clutched it, pulling him through the crowd. She knew her palm was sweaty and she was squeezing hard enough to hurt, but he let her hold on.

They finally made it through the chapel doors into the hallway, but when they got to the exit, the rush of sky and sunshine gave her the spins, like altitude sickness.

She needed a small, quiet space to collect the pieces of herself and hold them together until they stuck.

"I'll meet you outside. Just a couple of minutes."

She stopped in the ladies' room. She remembered Frances studying her reflection after Pearl's funeral, squinting as she moved her head this way and that as if trying to find her mother in her face. Now Nina looked for Frances in the mirror and caught a glimpse of her in her eyes, that same walnut brown.

Two women stood together over a sink, wiping off runny mascara.

"I've never heard that story about the pregnant goldfish," one said. During the eulogy, Alison's uncle had told an anecdote about Alison, as a child, slicing open the dead fish to rescue the babies.

"He didn't tell the funniest part," the other one said. "The goldfish died because Alison thought pregnant fish needed milk, so she put it in her glass of Nestlé's Quik."

A woman in a black lace dress said, "I tried to give a goldfish a bubble bath when I was a kid, and it didn't go well either."

Once inside a stall, Nina pulled down her underwear, and for the thousandth time since hearing Gardner's account in the *Post* interview, imagined Alison dangling hers from her finger and telling Gardner he'd look cuter tied up. Nina could definitely see it: the exhilaration of taking charge, Alison in a trance of sexiness and power, going too far, unaware she was seriously hurting him.

She flashed back again to the night at the East River, his fury when she threw Tom's watch in the river. The painful twist of her wrist when he grabbed onto it. They'd been alone, an empty park, a pitch-black night, Gardner in a *shitty mood*. She brought her hand up to her throat and squeezed, tightened her grip until she couldn't breathe, until her face pounded with blood and fear.

She dropped her hand. He couldn't. Not the same person she'd lain on the floor with at the Carlyle, who'd cradled her head to cushion it. That person couldn't purposely cause a girl's death.

Outside her stall, a few more women had joined the childhood pet-snuffing conversation, turtles who escaped their aquariums, hamsters hugged too hard, gerbils overfed. Their voices were buoyant with post-funeral relief, their laughter almost feverish. Then everyone went suddenly silent.

"Is this how it goes from now on?" asked a new woman's voice. "I walk into a room and conversation stops?" She sounded both bitter and defeated.

"Oh, Shell," someone said. "Honey. We were just saying what a beautiful service it was."

Shelly Bloch, Nina guessed. Alison's mother.

"You didn't think the rabbi talked too fast?" she said. Her voice had a similar peevishness to Alison's, but you could tell it was to keep herself afloat, a piece of driftwood to grab on to while the ship went down.

Everyone murmured things like, "I heard every word," and "Such an awful day," and "I'm so sorry," and "Joel's eulogy was wonderful." The woman who'd called her *honey* asked, "Want us to wait with you?"

"That's okay. I'll be out in a minute."

The woman hesitated, then said, "We'll tell Evan you'll be out soon. Let's give her some space, ladies." A few moments later, the restroom was silent again. Nina breathed as quietly as possible, planning to leave her stall as soon as Mrs. Bloch either went into one or left. But every time she looked under her door, the black high heels were still out by the sinks, the black pantyhose with a tiny run at the ankle. Nina told herself to stop being ridiculous. Mrs. Bloch was a living adult, not Alison's ghost. She wasn't going to ridicule her for not recognizing a diaphragm case or hand her some snarky button.

When Nina finally emerged, Mrs. Bloch didn't seem surprised to see someone come out of a stall—in fact, she had the zombie affect of someone who'd never be surprised by anything again. She leaned on the counter with both hands, examining the contents of a small wicker basket that contained tampons, bobby pins, packets of Excedrin, a mini-bottle of Pepto-Bismol, and individually wrapped Life Savers. She picked out a Life Saver and sniffed it. Her mouth twisted in a grimace.

"Wintergreen," she said. "Alison's the only one I know who likes this flavor." She squeezed the mint out of its plastic wrapper and placed it reluctantly in her mouth, like a punishment.

"I like wintergreen too," Nina said. "It makes sparks when you chew it." She wondered if she and Alison might have been friends if they hadn't been battling over Gardner. "I wish I'd known her better," she said.

Mrs. Bloch nodded. Nina had never seen such extraordinarily

tired eyes. Her sadness was so vast, it was a galaxy. "I wish I had too," she said.

Outside the chapel, the hearse idled at the curb with limousines and cars lined up behind it. People were hugging goodbye and ignoring all the photographers gathered behind a barricade that must have been erected during the service. Except there was Stephanie, chatting to one of them, his camera pointed at the hearse.

Nina's spirits lifted, until she took in Stephanie's clenched jaw and clicking teeth, her hands drumming against her thighs. She'd definitely seen Damian. She gestured Nina over with a gregarious, cocktail-party wave. "I didn't want to come in late," she said when Nina reached her. She turned to the photographer, who leaned over the barricade. "Will you take our picture?"

"Sure." He aimed the camera right as Nina was saying, "No, that's okay," and praying Alison's mother didn't come out and see what looked like posing.

"Your mouth was twisted," Stephanie told Nina. "Can we take another one?"

"Come on," Nina hissed. "This is a funeral."

The photographer straightened up, like he'd caught a whiff of something in the air. "Hey. You girls know Garner?"

"*Gardner*," Nina corrected automatically.

"She does," Stephanie said.

"*Really.*" Everything about the guy went on high alert. He lifted the camera again. Nina grabbed Stephanie and pulled her down the block until they were behind a Pepsi truck. "What are you doing? I don't want anyone here to know that!"

"Sorry. You're right." Stephanie set her jaw and stared at the ground. Her hair was tangled, stringy at the roots.

Now Nina felt guilty. She'd sounded like Pearl. "It's okay. I'm sorry. I overreacted."

"It's fine."

She'd never seen Stephanie like this, refusing or maybe unable to meet her eye. "Can we get a drink or take a walk or something?"

Stephanie shook her head. "I should probably get home."

Now was the time to say something, tell Stephanie the truth, or at least what she believed to be true, if she could just summon the courage. That they weren't invincible, and there wasn't always a second chance. That life wasn't always long. That Patrick would drag her down and strangle her spirit. That the things that had hurt them weren't their fault, but that avoiding pain wasn't the same thing as happiness, and sometimes you had to hurt to know the difference.

In an instant, the doubts swooped in. *She doesn't care. She can't hear you.* Could anything have stopped Alison from going to the park with Gardner? Anyone who tried would have been crossed off her list of friends.

But didn't you have to try anyway?

Down the block, the hearse pulled away from the curb and into traffic, followed by a line of cars with their headlights on.

"I miss you," Nina finally said. "Please don't go to Hewlett."

"It's where I live." Stephanie's eyes darted in every direction. She lit a cigarette and blew three quivery smoke rings, then raised her hand to hail a cab. "I'll be in touch," she said as she got inside. "I promise."

Brian was waiting down the block, a discreet distance away. Nina noticed he was standing that way she'd once disparaged, his legs apart so his face would be level with hers. But now it was nice to not be loomed over, to be seen eye to eye.

"Is she okay?" he asked.

"I'm not sure." She told herself not to read anything into Stephanie's cab merging with the line of cars headed for the cemetery. "I hope so."

"You have time for lunch?" he said. "Or do you need to get home and pack?"

She still had half-filled boxes all over her room, shoes to sort through and books to select. A million things to do before Sunday.

"I have time," she said.

Chapter Nineteen

Friday night, her first time home from Vanderbilt for the short fall break, Nina stepped off the elevator into the lobby to find the doorman blocking the front door. Not Freddie, who Ira said was now working weekdays, but a new guy Nina didn't know, young and wiry with lank, long hair under the too-big uniform hat. Kassidy Elkin, the fifteen-year-old who lived on the eighth floor, was trying to lunge past him, although she seemed hardly able to balance on her red stiletto heels.

"I'm gonna be late," she said, half whine and half giggle.

The doorman shifted from side to side to thwart her attempts to get by. Nina cleared her throat. *She* needed to get by, away from the suffocating atmosphere upstairs, her father in bed by himself watching baseball, her mother's side still empty. Frances had been transferred to a private psychiatric hospital in Westchester for what Vlad said would be "an indeterminate stay," where Nina and Ira would visit tomorrow.

"Say the magic word," the doorman said to Kassidy.

"Please." She lunged again.

"Nope." He gave her a gloating smile as he flattened his palm against the door.

"Thank you?"

"That's two words."

"Come on," she pleaded. She had the look of someone being painfully tickled, laughing while also turning red. She tugged down the hem of her short Spandex dress.

"Still two words."

What made him think this was okay? Had he been trained at the Freddie school of door-manning? Nina refused to let another girl get caught inside this lobby again. "Jerk," she said loudly, startling them and herself. "That's one word."

The doorman shot her a wounded look and opened the door. Kassidy smiled triumphantly as she tottered forward.

"She's a kid," Nina told the doorman. "Leave her alone."

Kassidy stopped short, her smile turning sour. "Um, thanks, *Mom*," she said. She and the doorman snickered as Nina passed by them and went outside. Nina recalled the many times she'd shared the elevator with Kassidy, the petulance and over-it sighs, even when she was by herself, without her mother there to argue with. What had Nina expected, a genuine thank-you?

Outside it was dark, a cool mid-October night, pumpkins in every shop window and the sidewalk littered with dead brown leaves. Nina stopped at the newsstand for cigarettes. The model who'd been attacked in June was on the cover of *New York Magazine*. The headline said, RECOVER GIRL: SLASHED MODEL CAN SMILE AGAIN. In the corner was a tiny black-and-white photo taken right after the attack, the model's spooked, sliced-up face. In the larger cover photo, she was all blithe color, lavender blouse, honey hair, and berry lip gloss. The faded scar sloped gently down her cheek.

Nina flipped to the article. "I just want to get back to normal life," the model said. She'd signed up for an acting class. She'd soon appear in a Gimbels ad. Nina envied her ability to put the summer behind her. She wanted to get back to normal life, too, but she never didn't feel strange these days, especially now that she lived in a strange place. At first, the newness of Nashville was so absorbing, she'd barely missed Manhattan. Honky-tonks and fiddlers in cowboy boots on every corner. Hot chicken and Bushwackers and paddle boats. And just as she'd fantasized, Nina had caused a little stir at Vanderbilt, the glamorous New York girl in lace leggings and the rhinestone bracelets she'd copied from Stephanie. She smoked Marlboros. She had a bedspread from Conran's. She knew the Preppy Killer, as Gardner was now known throughout the country. Not that she walked around blabbing about him, but a girl in her dorm had asked her the first night, and word spread. Soon people were stopping her on campus to ask what he was like and why he'd killed that girl.

"If I come to New York over Christmas," they'd say, "can you take me to that bar where they met?" as if Flanagan's were a tourist spot like Rockefeller Center.

Dining out on tragedy, however accidental, was obviously immoral. She just wished it didn't make her feel so important.

But a couple of weeks ago, the night she heard Gardner was out of Rikers on bail, she'd slipped up. It was Sunday night in the dorm lounge, people lying around on couches, drinking whiskey. Patsy Cline on the boom box. She hadn't heard from Gardner since he'd been arrested, because of course he couldn't call from jail—but would he call now that he was out? Did he think about her? Did he know she was still on his side? *I've got your memory,* Patsy sang, *or has it got me?* Every guy on campus who looked nothing like Gardner still looked like Gardner, and Nina didn't see that changing anytime soon.

When people asked her about him, she'd been evasive, since everyone was already convinced he'd killed Alison on purpose. But that night, under the spell of whiskey and Patsy's melancholy prairie voice, Nina confessed what she knew to be true: It was an accident. And he'd be unfairly tarred with it the rest of his life.

Her dormmates sat up straighter and exchanged glances, although they kept their mouths clamped shut, polite freshmen who hadn't been there long enough to rock the boat. But since then, their faces emptied out when she met them in the hall, and either stayed that way or filled with false, hale friendliness.

"Have a good day!" they told her. "Have a good weekend!" But there were no more invitations to dinners at Daryl's or shopping at Hickory Hollow.

She left the newsstand and started the walk up to Flanagan's. She'd been looking forward to being back home, feeling restored to herself as she walked the streets, but even the city felt strange now. Streetlights were smashed out, glass sprinkled over the pavement. Pleading signs taped in every car window—NO STEREO, DO NOT BREAK IN—and a mess of wires sprouting from the empty dashboard space the stolen stereo had occupied. Everyone stepping over a homeless man stretched across the entrance to the 6 train staircase, as if he were just another stair.

It appeared that notoriety had made Flanagan's even more popular. The line to get in reached halfway down the block. Some of the crowd—acid-wash jeans and mustaches—were clearly rubbernecking, but it was mostly guys in suits and ties and women in cocktail dresses, as if Nina and everyone she knew were being supplanted by more mature and better-behaved versions of themselves.

Brian and one of his brothers were checking IDs at the door. He'd told her on the phone that, since Alison's death, police had been showing up unannounced at all the Upper East Side bars to make sure they weren't letting in underage drinkers. Nina dug her Playland ID out of her bag. The first time she'd used it in Nashville, she'd called Stephanie as soon as she got back to the dorm. She was always thinking of reasons to call: a *Who's the Boss?* rerun on TV, a girl at a frat party in a UTenn-orange tank top. But most of the time she restrained herself, because so far Stephanie hadn't answered the phone or returned any of her messages. One of these days, Nina would have to accept the Texas girls' invitation to go out with them for drinks, instead of waiting in her room for Stephanie to call back. One of these days, she'd have to accept that Stephanie was gone.

Brian waved her to the front of the line, then steered her to the vestibule of the building next door. He was handsomer than she remembered, in a forest-green corduroy blazer.

"I'm really happy to see you," he said.

"Me too." She meant it. Since she'd been away, they'd been talking on the phone, sometimes for hours. She would read to him from the *Book of Lists,* and he to her from his Intro to Ethics textbook for his class at John Jay. Phone sex for dorks, a girl on Nina's hall had called it, but when Nina closed her eyes to picture a mouth pressing hers, it was still Gardner's, even now.

She pointed to the crowd waiting to get inside the bar. "I can't believe how packed it is."

Brian frowned. "We're in the news all the time, especially since my father decided to put up our apartment as collateral for Gardner's bail. The *Post* hammered us: 'Flanagan's Shenanigans Bails Out Preppy Killer.'"

"Ouch." But she hoped this meant Mr. Flanagan also believed Gardner hadn't deliberately killed Alison. It was good to know that people in authority were on his side. Brian had told her that the archbishop of Newark, the friend of Gardner's mother there'd been that reception for back in July, had written a letter imploring the judge to grant Gardner bail and vouching for his trustworthiness. In fact, Gardner was now living at a rectory uptown, which for some reason Nina pictured as the great hall in *Beowulf,* with monks in robes milling around.

"Mrs. Reed called my father in hysterics. She and Gardner's dad couldn't afford the bail. He was trying to do a good deed." Brian shook his head. "He didn't see Alison . . . what that woman at the funeral said she saw at the visitation."

Nina looked down, recalling the cloud of eucalyptus. For all she knew, the woman could have imagined the bruises. It was all so murky and indefinite. Nina had even tried to do some research at the school library about neck injuries, but there were no clear-cut answers and she wound up distracted by stories of famous strangulations: Isadora Duncan, whose neck broke when the long scarf she was wearing got caught in the rear axle of her open car; and Thomas Midgley, the polio-stricken inventor of leaded gasoline, who got tangled up in a pulley system he'd devised to get out of bed and choked to death.

"Hey!" Brian's brother called out. "A little help here?"

Brian walked her back to the door and held it open for her. "I'm monopolizing you. Leigh and Meredith are inside. I'll be in soon."

"Come find me," she said.

She stopped just inside the door to steel herself. In her Vanderbilt dorm room, trying to fall asleep at night, she'd gotten unexpected comfort from taking mental walks through Flanagan's, corner to corner, over to the jukebox, down the hall to the restrooms. In these walks she was the only person there, moving freely through the space, cataloging the bar's brass footrail, the Marilyn poster, the Houdini photograph, the specific taupe of the fireplace brick. But now she saw that it was just a bar, filled with people she didn't know—she guessed the regulars had been deterred by the gawkers and tourists. Wood, brick, bone, flesh. Random shoes against the footrail, people hollering for drinks. It was never really hers, and it would carry on fine without her. Already there was a new Yankees banner over the bar, a new lacquered coat tree in the corner. Alison was a ghost and Gardner a gossip column. One day no one who came here would even recognize their names.

She found Leigh and Meredith crammed at a tiny table in the back. She hadn't spoken much with them these past weeks while they'd all been busy settling in at college. She was surprised how glad she was to see them, the pleasure of their familiarity, the pitcher of sangria on the table, the packs of Newports and Parliaments. Leigh in her pearls, chattering about the Cottage Club.

"I've been dying to know," Nina said as she wedged a chair at the table. "Are you an official Cottage Cheeser?"

Leigh smiled. "I'm not allowed to bicker until sophomore year, but my friend Alex is a member, so I get to eat dinner there all the time."

"Sounds like you're a shoo-in for next year."

"Fingers crossed." Leigh poured Nina a glass of sangria, while Meredith turned to Nina with one of her sly smiles.

"Speaking of shoo-ins," she said, "did you lose it yet?"

"Good one," Nina said, shading her voice with more irritation than she felt: she actually didn't mind bantering like this, especially if it meant skating on the surface of things instead of falling through the ice into a conversation about Gardner. She'd never told Meredith and Leigh about her connection with him, let alone the Carlyle rampage or the broken beer bottle in the park or his temper at the East River. They'd probably be insulted that she'd kept it all a secret.

Meredith peered at Nina. "I see you with someone older, like a professor. My poli-sci prof is *hot*. Half the class failed the first exam because no one could concentrate." Meredith raised a cigarette to her lips and Nina noticed a silver bracelet around her wrist, the Tiffany's one with the hook-and-eye fastener that every bat mitzvah girl got as a gift.

"He actually looks a little like Gardner," Meredith added. "It's kind of spooky."

"Where'd you get that bracelet?" Nina asked, to change the subject. She tried the sangria, which tasted like turpentine.

"It's my roommate's. She's Jewish, from Scarsdale. She came to Penn with satin sheets and a fur coat!" Meredith held out her arm to admire the bracelet. "On *her* it just looks Jappy."

Let it lie, Nina told herself. Why cause friction on their first night seeing each other in weeks?

"I used to think Gardner was so good-looking," Leigh said, "but Alex says he looks like Jack the Ripper."

"How would he know what Jack the Ripper looked like?" Now it was genuine irritation in Nina's voice.

"Did you hear that Polly Jessup wrote Gardner a character reference letter for the bail hearing?" Meredith asked. "She said she ran into him a few days before he killed Alison—"

Before Alison died, Nina thought.

"He was crying about a dog he'd just seen get hit by a car."

"Clea Glass wrote one too," Leigh said. "I heard it was five pages long."

"I heard Holland said no, but they got one from Marina Delafield."

Conversation and music thrashed the air. Was that "Let's Go Crazy" blasting from the jukebox? Nina remembered Gardner joyously singing along and playing air guitar to it after his breakup with Holland. She tried to recall her delight at his exhilaration, but her eardrums throbbed with anger. Why hadn't he asked *Nina* for a character letter? Was she that unimportant to him?

Or was "Nina Jacobs" too Jewish? It suddenly struck her that no one involved in the case was Jewish—no one alive, anyway, other than the lawyers. Not Gardner, not the judge, none of the character witnesses she'd heard about. Did her name disqualify her from the list? She was probably being hypersensitive, but then she remembered the night at the Carlyle, before they went up to Tom Parrish's apartment, Gardner's grimace when she told him her mother's maiden name was *Grossberg*. His muted reaction to Rex and Walker's *spoiled kike* comment. Not that she was any better: she'd laughed along at Grossberg, said nothing during Rex's public trashing of his Jewish neighbors. And again just now, with Meredith.

Nazi dickweeds—what Alison had called Rex and Walker that night—was too strong for Meredith, obviously, but Nina still felt compelled to say *something*. She held her breath, heart racing, and leaned forward.

"Listen," she said to Meredith, and had to force herself to keep going. "You know I'm Jewish, right?"

Meredith laughed uneasily. "I actually forget sometimes. You're so not Jappy."

Nina exhaled. Not the point. "*Jappy* probably doesn't seem like a big deal. But it makes being Jewish sound like something bad." Why had something so simple always seemed so hard to say?

"Huh." At least Meredith had the decency to look a little embarrassed. "I didn't realize. Okay."

Who knew if she really got it, or if the insight would last. But Nina felt suddenly . . . *present*, surprisingly calm without any pills or alcohol, save one sip of rancid sangria. She'd told the truth about how she felt and she hadn't burst into flames. Maybe she'd always feel like an outsider in one way or another—wasn't everyone an outsider, somewhere?—but for now she was just herself, here at the table.

Leigh lit a Newport, then held it away from her face and studied it. "I've got to stop smoking these."

"Cigarettes?" Nina asked.

"These menthol ones," she said, and Nina noticed that she was surprisingly calm, too, not to mention sober: she'd barely sipped her drink either.

"Alex says menthol crystallizes in your lungs," Leigh said.

"Alex, Alex, Alex." Meredith perked up, obviously relieved to be off the subject of ethnic slurs. "I barely know anything about him. What's he like? Is he cute?"

Leigh blushed and coughed out a mouthful of smoke.

Meredith laughed. "I knew it. Tell us about him."

Leigh squared her shoulders. Even not knowing what she had to say, Nina sensed she'd been readying herself for this moment for weeks, if not months—if not, maybe, forever.

"Her," Leigh said. "Alexandra."

Nina felt her mouth drop open and saw Meredith's do the same, although neither of them had a chance to say anything before Leigh calmly added, "And yeah, it's what you think." She took a handful of pens out of her bag and passed one each to Nina and Meredith.

"Now write down your favorite condiment," she said, "and three adjectives to describe it."

Nina didn't hear anyone around them mention Gardner or Alison for the next hour, as if it would be gauche to bring up their names, or maybe uncool, like acknowledging a geeky thrill in a celebrity's vicinity. But around midnight, she wasn't the only one to notice the songs some joker had played on the jukebox—"Sex Crime," "I Didn't Mean to Turn You On," "Don't Leave Me This Way." People paused conversations to point to the air and laugh, and then, as if unleashed, started shouting opinions and rumors at top decibel with what felt like bloodthirsty glee.

"I heard she kept a sex diary ranking all the guys she'd fucked," a girl with a mean red mouth yelled over the music.

"I heard he strangled her with her bra."

"I heard she liked to be choked," said a guy in a polka-dotted tie.

"I heard he took her diamond earrings off her dead body."

At first, Nina shared little scoffing looks with Leigh and Meredith—*they'd* been here all summer and actually knew the people being gossiped about, its own sort of insider status. But was that really something to feel so superior about? "Her Last Fling" played. "Accidents Will Happen." Nina smoked a cigarette, her throat burning, purple bruises floating before her eyes. Then she pictured Gardner standing over Alison's body, scared out of his mind. She couldn't imagine being alone with a person who'd just passed from life to death, a space occupied by two now suddenly, solely, one. She couldn't imagine there existed a silence as loud.

Brian had been in and out of the bar all night, but when Nina went outside, he was there again, dealing with the still-unruly line. She told him she was heading home.

"What time do you leave for Westchester tomorrow?" he asked.

"I think early," she said, soothed by his thoughtfulness and glad she'd told him about Frances's condition during their phone calls. But as she walked to Lexington, she still felt too weird and restless to be boxed in again, even inside her own room. She continued to Fifth, imagining Gardner and Alison walking down these blocks, exchanging—as one of the detectives was quoted as calling it—"boy-girl talk," whatever that meant. She walked past the Met and stood for a moment at the entrance to the park. She pictured Gardner cracking his Heineken bottle against the rock and starting toward the homeless guy in the bushes.

Want to see his dick? I'll get it for you.

But she wouldn't have put that in a character reference! Was that why Gardner hadn't asked her? She'd have described his charisma and intensity, his depth, his contempt for arrogance personified by the abhorrent Rex and Tom Parrish. The vulnerability she'd gotten glimpses of: his absent selfish father, his coldhearted mother whose egregious condescension Nina had witnessed herself—

Speaking of which. Here she was on Ninety-First Street, *his* street, where, she realized, some instinct had been leading her since she left Flanagan's. The block was quiet with a glowing half-moon and the faint scent of gasoline. Trash blew around in the chilly wind. Behind her, a bus chugged down the avenue in a distant, desultory way. She walked to a shadowed vestibule across from Gardner's building. She thought of that day she'd stood here with Stephanie practicing smoke rings, trying to guess which house Gardner lived in. And the next night, at Flanagan's, when he'd sniffed behind her ear and said she smelled juicy. The loss was so strong, she crossed her arms around her rib cage, to hold herself together so her organs couldn't spill out.

Then her eye fell on a glint of gold in the street, the foil border of a sheet of graph paper. The gold was overlaid with green and purple, *Hello* in bubbly white script across the top. There were more of the same scattered on the sidewalk, and then the graph-paper notepad itself, as if her mother had bought one for Nina and deliberately placed it here for her. What, she chided herself, you believe in signs now? On the other hand, as signs went, this was pretty hard to ignore.

She picked up the notepad and dug Leigh's pen out of her bag. She'd remind Gardner that she existed, that she believed in him. She'd add her phone number to the note, along with an urgent message for Mrs. Reed to bring it to him at the rectory, and slide it under the building's front door.

Dear Gardner, she wrote, before she got stuck.

She lit a cigarette. Across the street, the light in a third-floor window switched on and the shadow of a face appeared. For a second, she saw her grandmother, watching Nina smoke on the street before dropping dead from a stroke. Get a grip. It was probably Mrs. Reed, which might actually be worse.

She squinted in the dark until she recognized the face framed in the window, pressed against it to peer back at her. It was Gardner, waving for her to come up.

He stood in the doorway of his apartment in jeans and a faded blue oxford shirt.

"I knew you'd come through." He kissed her sweetly on the cheek, letting his lips linger, as if to acknowledge their special and tender connection. Her breathing was heavy from the climb up the stairs. She hoped it didn't make him think she'd come here for sex. What had happened with Alison was still too big and unsettling. It would take a lot to entice Nina anywhere near a bed. She had to admit, though, that being the object of pursuit instead of the pursuer for once, with the power to extend or withhold, had its appeal.

He led her through the dark apartment. It was more cramped than she'd expected, with almost no windows, and the walls were covered with dozens of framed photographs: smiling babies, boys playing various sports, young men graduating and driving a car. Oh, they were all Gardner. Every photo. Gardner, Gardner, Gardner.

"Is your mom home?" she asked, suddenly terrified of running into her. No wonder Mrs. Reed wanted everyone to *stop hounding* Gardner; no mother with a shrine like this could bear the competition. Nina crumpled the unfinished graph-paper note still in her hand, glad she hadn't had to rely on Mrs. Reed to deliver it.

He pointed vaguely in the direction of the front door. "She's staying out in Sayville with my aunt. Things are a little crazy here."

His room was small and square, navy walls, Pink Floyd poster, striped blanket on the bed, a dark wood desk beneath the small window overlooking the street, the one he must have seen her from. A floor lamp aimed at the ceiling cast a fuzzy circle there, leaving the rest of the space dim, except for a spotlight over a wall shelf illuminating a row of figurines constructed of nuts and bolts. One strummed a guitar made from a washer and a spring. Another balanced a tiny model rifle. To Nina they looked eerily skeletal, souls in limbo, waiting their turn for the afterlife.

Gardner sat on the bed. She went to the chair at his desk. In the near-dark, she could just make out its surface, covered in a mess of papers, notebooks, folders, and videotapes. She swiveled the chair to face him.

"Have you been watching a lot of videos? I still haven't seen *The Fly*. Although it's probably not out on tape yet, right?" She was talking too fast, nervously twisting the chair back and forth.

He smiled. "Producers keep sending them over. They want to make a movie about me. One guy even told my lawyer I could star as myself."

Of course he could. That face, that jaw, the singular and extraordinary cobalt of his eyes. He leaned back against the wall with his long legs extended. She realized she'd never seen his bare feet before, which were also perfect: tan and narrow. Nina felt a little feverish, staring at his naked toes. Not to mention the hectic swiveling that was starting to make her motion sick.

She pointed at his wrinkled sheets. "I thought you had to live at a rectory."

"Fuck those priests, and fuck that judge for making me stay there." He pulled his legs up and hugged his knees. "Hey, what did the altar boy say to the priest?"

"What?"

"Nothing. His mouth was full."

It took her a moment to get it. "Ew," she said, and tried to laugh, while some vague, dark recognition buzzed through her brain, just out of reach. Then she wondered if the joke was a hint about what he'd like Nina to do for him. She became aware how dry her own mouth was. Why hadn't she brought her Dynamints?

He looked at her closed hand. "So. What have you got?"

She stared back blankly, until she remembered the balled-up note. "Oh. It's nothing. I just wanted to make sure you had my number. I thought you might want to talk sometime, or maybe I could write you a character letter."

He looked confused. "You didn't bring coke?"

She turned the chair around so her back was to him, ashamed of the dumb hurt that must be all over her face. Was that all she was to him? A coke-delivery service. A nuts-and-bolts figurine with a coin purse on a silver platter.

"It's okay," he said. She felt him reading the hurt in her hunched shoulders. "Fucking weekly drug tests. You've probably saved me a shit-ton of trouble."

She still couldn't look at him, but the reminder softened her: he was already in a shit-ton of trouble, for an accident.

"Come here," he said. The bed made a muffled thud where he patted it.

She swallowed, urging herself to get up—*quick, before he changes his mind*—but her mouth was still arid from nerves. It would taste like dirty sand if they kissed. She spotted a bottle of Heineken on the edge of the cluttered desk, resting on a shiny square coaster. Just reaching for it made her feel more fluid, ready for what was about to happen.

She lifted the bottle. The coaster turned out to be a Polaroid—damp, warped by the condensation, a wormy ridge bisecting a naked girl's stomach. Nina looked closer. It was Alison, walnut-tanned with stark white breasts and bikini lines, standing in a doorway with her arms stretched out to either side, fingers gripping the doorframe.

This must be one of the photos she'd sent him over the summer, the *disgusting* ones Mrs. Reed had referred to on the phone, that Chip Wainwright had seen. Why did Gardner still have it? Why was he using it as a coaster?

Nina set the bottle on a small patch of clear space in the midst of the mess. As she did, the desk was illuminated by the lights of a passing truck and she saw there were other Polaroids strewn around, all Alison, naked and blazingly alive. Nina wanted to turn away, but it was as if she were being directed to look. One was wedged in a stapler's jaw: Alison holding a cherry to her lips, tongue poking out, her face scrawled over with ballpoint pen, staples through her eyes. Another stuck out from the pages of a notebook like a bookmark: a close-up of her breast, a cigarette hole burned through the nipple. Under a leather pen cup holding a single brown Sharpie: Alison lying on a bed in nothing but white knee socks, legs rolled back, ankles up by her ears. He'd drawn brown blobs tumbling out of her ass onto the flowered comforter beneath her.

Nina blinked, staring at the ground for a patch of empty floor, but here was yet another photo, Alison squeezing her breasts together in her hands, pushing the flesh forward in a coy, hopeful offering—this one shoved under a leg of the desk, like a matchbook to still a restaurant table's irksome wobble.

Nausea splashed through her chest. She saw, as if it were happening right in front of her, Gardner and Alison at the base of the elm tree; maybe she *had* tied his wrists with her underwear like he'd said, but trying to be playful, teasing him, misreading his mood. She saw her straddling him, then Gardner's hands come suddenly around her throat, tightening his grip as Alison clawed at his face, her disbelief turning to terror, bright lights exploding behind her eyes. She saw him squeeze even harder until the cartilage gave way, until Alison was silent and limp. She saw him fling her lifeless body to the ground and shake the cramps out of his fingers.

She started to reach for a Polaroid of Alison in a sheer red bra, where you could see from her smile that she'd loved him—he shouldn't get to keep that picture—she'd loved him and he'd left her lying in the dirt then sat on a low stone wall across the road and waited for someone else to find her body. Watched with the other onlookers until the ambulance came and carted Alison away in a bag. Went home and took a nap, like nothing important had happened.

Nina heard the bed squeak behind her, then felt his breath on the back of her neck. She was stuck to the swivel chair, her muscles so tight it was motionless.

"I told her to leave me alone," he said. His voice cracked with self-pity and indignation.

She pulled her hand back from the photo. "I should go," she said carefully. Did he notice her voice was shaking, the terrified lurch in her breathing? "I have so much to do tomorrow." She stood as casually as she could, pausing only for a theatrical stretch and fake yawn before pushing past him with a cursory "See you later," then quickly out the door and down the stairs until she was back on the street. She started to run, already regretting that she hadn't grabbed the Polaroid of Alison in her red bra, that she'd left her behind with him. But she couldn't stop running until she made it home.

Chapter Twenty

The next morning, she and her father drove to Westchester to visit
Frances in the hospital. Nina hadn't slept and she welcomed the exhaustion, her brain mercifully dulled as if encased in a rubber membrane. Her father was chattering away, but he barely registered. She
sensed thoughts orbiting around her, Alison's scorched breast, her
own aching lungs as she sprinted home from Gardner's—little jabs as
they bounced off the membrane, though so far it was keeping them
from sinking in their teeth.

"Wait till you see the garden and the courtyard," Ira said. He
changed lanes to get ahead of a slow-moving Datsun. "The grounds
are just lovely." She was grateful for his focus on the hospital's land-
scaping; it kept him from looking too closely at her or asking any
questions. Not that she would have told him where she'd been last
night. He'd have a conniption, horrified at her recklessness. Although
she'd have countered that it wasn't so much recklessness as a pro-
foundly arrogant failure of imagination: *she* hadn't believed Gardner
was a murderer, so it must not have been true. But this analysis
wouldn't much interest her father, especially after the news that broke
this morning, booming from the radio behind the Hertz counter as
they waited for the guy to bring around their rental car.

"Gardner Reed, the so-called Preppy Slayer," the announcer had intoned over the jaunty lead-in music, "is expected to be indicted this week for burglary. He and a partner, Victor Grimshaw, are accused of burglarizing several Upper East Side penthouses. Reed is currently out on bail for the alleged murder of Alison Bloch in Central Park last month, a tragedy he blames on rough sex."

Had anyone's imagination ever failed them worse? Victor with the fried ponytail. *He's not my friend,* Gardner had said. *I barely know that guy.* The same guy who'd left Flanagan's with Leigh the night of her drunken blackout, a week before her parents' apartment was burglarized. Leigh must have let slip that she and her parents would be out of town.

Ira had shaken his head. "What a nasty piece of work." And he hadn't even seen Alison's stapled eyes.

As they drove up the Hutchinson, he drummed his fingers on the steering wheel. He'd spent the past half hour describing the hospital, called Whisper Lake, which didn't seem like a great name if you were trying to put paranoid patients at ease. This would be his fifth visit. "The garden has trees and benches," he said. "They hold exercise classes in the gazebo."

"Nice," Nina said for the dozenth time.

"Mom did a bunch of jumping jacks last Sunday."

"Nice," she repeated, although this was hard to imagine, considering how frail Frances had looked last time Nina saw her, in the psych ER. A jumping jack would have shaken her bones loose.

"And she's been eating, and mostly sleeping through the night. I think you'll be pleasantly surprised."

Nina did her best to return his upbeat smile. Of course she was glad Frances had come down from the mania, that she no longer belly danced in public or thought her eyebrows quivered with invisible transmissions or chattered into a tape recorder about desperation pies. Though Nina still couldn't bring herself to ask her father *how* she'd gotten better.

The last time Nina spoke with her, a week after she got to college, Frances had sounded spacy and slow and thick-tongued. That night Nina had dreamed about the human warehouse in the movie *Coma*, the comatose victims suspended from the ceiling with wires through their bones until their organs could be harvested. And maybe the call wasn't so great for her mother, either, because afterward, Ira said Nina should focus on school: in other words, no mother–daughter communication for the time being. "We don't want you to have any unnecessary distractions," he said—they were *we* again, and Nina *you*, making her feel both relieved and excluded, that mix she'd inhabited before this summer and had now, apparently, reinhabited, with no trace of the wild intermission in between.

A low-slung red sports car came roaring past their rental. Ira glanced over and gave an admiring whistle. "Look at that Ferrari. Your grandfather called Ferrari drivers *shmegegges*."

"How is he? He never answers the phone."

Ira fiddled with the rearview mirror. "Not good, I'm afraid. He's been diagnosed with Alzheimer's. He's moving to a nursing home. I've been meaning to tell you."

Nina's stomach dropped. "Why didn't you?"

"You've had enough to worry about, with school and your mom."

"Why can't he just stay at home with, like, another aide?"

"He's having trouble eating. He forgets to swallow."

"You can forget that?" Nina swallowed. It did take an effort to kick her esophagus into gear. "Do you mean he forgets *to* swallow, or forgets *how* to swallow?"

Ira shook his head, impatient. "I don't know. We can talk more about it later."

"Mom must be so upset."

"Well—" He pushed the air vent closed and the car went instantly musty. "I haven't exactly told her yet. We need to keep her as calm as possible right now."

As if Frances were a child. *This* "we," she assumed, meant him and

Vlad, the old dynamic duo. "Doesn't she have the right to know what's going on with her own father?" She thought he might at least have the decency to look chagrined at the deception. If one day he forgot to swallow, should she be kept in the dark?

"Why are you taking that tone with me?" He got in the right lane at the exit for Underhill Road. "I'll tell your mother when I think it's time."

"Underhill Road sounds like *undertaker*," Nina said as they got off the highway, wanting to fire her anger at an available target that couldn't answer back. "It's creepy."

He shot her a look as he turned into a small lot and parked the car. "There's nothing to be nervous about."

"I'm not." Her mother's brain was sick, the way someone else's mother might have cancer or gout: Would she be scared to visit a gout hospital? Anyway, it was Ira who seemed jittery, the rapid blinking and staccato throat-clearing as they got out of the car. Although maybe this was more excitement than nerves since he was already craning his neck toward the cluster of brick buildings they'd parked behind.

"If anyone approaches you," he added, "just say, 'Nice to meet you, but I'm here to see my mother.'"

"What do you mean, approaches *me*? Where will you be?"

"Approaches us." He briefly laid his hand against the small of her back, either to comfort her or push her along. They walked up a stone path to the front lawn, passing the jumping-jacks gazebo, along with picnic tables and a few wooden lounge chairs painted white, a summer-camp feel. But once they were inside, there was no mistaking the pea-green hallway and institutional stench of ammonia. Not to mention the locked steel door. Ira peered through its little square window, then pressed the buzzer beside it. After a minute he glanced at his watch and said, "We're a little early." Nina automatically checked her watch, too, a Timex she'd bought to replace the Swatch she'd left at the Carlyle. How trivial her fears seemed now, that Gardner could have gotten in trouble if someone found her watch there. How was murder for trouble? And burglary? And his constellation of other crimes, from whatever he'd done to get kicked out of BU to stealing Holland's mother's credit card and, come to think of it, Grand-Mère's frigging Nembutals.

Ira buzzed again. A little plastic plaque next to the door said, HIGH ELOPEMENT RISK: PLEASE MAKE SURE THE DOOR IS CLOSED & LOCKED BEHIND YOU. Were patients sneaking out to get married? The door opened and a young nurse in glossy purple eye shadow emerged and directed them to a wall of lockers where Nina could leave her bag. Mrs. Jacobs would be right out, she said, and led them to the waiting room. Nina was glad they didn't have to go back to the bedrooms, where there might be padded walls or sinks chained to the floor or patients strapped into straitjackets, all of which would undoubtedly also burrow their way into her dreams.

She and Ira sat across the room from the only other visitors, a man and woman perched stiffly at the edge of their cane chairs, staring at the fuzzy carpeting. The man wore sunglasses and the woman a straw hat with a brim so wide, half her face was concealed. Nina wished she'd thought to bring Stephanie's sunglasses: how nice to be able to hide in plain sight. But she guessed exhaustion made her eyes pretty flat anyway. They probably didn't contain more than a neutral *Good to see you. I hope you're feeling better.* No neediness or expectation.

But when her mother appeared in the doorway, a sudden wave of feeling broke over her. She might even have rushed into Frances's arms, if she'd held them out. But her mother hovered in the doorway with her arms at her sides, and her eyes might as well have been hidden behind sunglasses for all they revealed, a coolness that could almost pass as indifference. For increasingly awkward seconds, Frances continued to hang back as though she didn't know what to do with her body. The crazy summer energy was gone. Her eyebrows had grown back in, and she'd gained a few pounds. Her face was pinker, no longer the hue of cement.

Nina got to her feet, *no big deal.* Frances finally hugged her, hardly an over-the-top, crushing embrace. She'd had more enthusiastic hugs from Freddie.

"This seems like a nice place," Nina said. "I like the lawn and the gazebo."

Frances smiled. "There's a pretty garden with roses."

"Grandma's favorite flower," Nina said. Where had that come from?

Ira kissed Frances on the forehead. See? Nina thought. Like a child. "Why don't we show Nina around?" he said. "Then we can sit outside and catch up."

"How is it out?" Frances asked.

They walked out of the waiting room, discussing the weather like acquaintances in an elevator.

"Sunny," Nina said. "Cool but not cold."

"This is my favorite time of year," Frances said, "when it's crisp in the mornings and then gets warmer."

"It *was* crisp this morning," Nina said, "but now it's probably sixty degrees." Would they talk this way all day? For the rest of their lives?

Frances led them down the pea-green hallway. A barefoot woman in a caftan approached them. She was eating a doughnut, globs of jelly all over her cheeks and chin.

Unfazed, Frances said, "Good morning, B . . ."

"Bettina." The woman stuck her tongue out at them, coated with powdered sugar.

"She has a new name every day," Frances explained to Nina. "It always starts with a *B.* Yesterday was Bianca."

The woman flicked jelly off her cheeks into her open mouth and looked Nina up and down. "Who are you?"

Frances introduced them, "Bettina, Nina," and Nina waited for the rhyme torrent—*Gina, Lena, Sabrina*—but her mother just smiled agreeably. Nina chastised herself for her pinch of disappointment.

At the end of the hall was a room with a black-and-white checkerboard floor, scatter of chairs and tables, a TV at one end playing *American Bandstand,* and a table with snacks, sodas, and coffee on the other. Ira went to get coffee, and a Diet Coke for Nina, while Frances brought her over to meet a woman working on a jigsaw puzzle of a Monet painting. The woman looked to be in her eighties and had a sweet round face, pink cheeks, and silver hair.

"Dolores is my roommate," Frances said. "She sleeps turned around, with her feet on the pillow."

Dolores jerked her neck and grimaced. "Fuck! Fuck off, asshole," she barked. Then, "Nice to meet you, dear."

Nina stared at her mother, who just stood there with a serene smile.

Dolores whistled sharply and gave them the finger.

"Tourette's," Ira whispered in Nina's ear, annoyingly blasé, like he was the mayor of Whisper Lake. He'd come back with coffee and doughnuts and Nina's soda.

"You might have given me a heads-up," she whispered back.

They walked by a woman in a wooden chair who had tied herself to it with a blue-and-coral argyle cardigan that Nina was sure she'd seen before.

"Frances," she called, "your sweater's working wonders."

Right, it was her mother's cardigan, the one she'd worn to Nina's Bancroft graduation.

"Therese, this is Nina," Frances said.

"I'm supposed to sit still for ten minutes every hour," Therese told Nina, clutching the knotted sleeves around her waist. "But my impulses can be overwhelming. Frances came to the rescue."

"Careful you don't stretch it out too much," Frances said. "That's good cashmere, from Scotland."

Her mother introduced Nina to a few other people—as *Nina,* she couldn't help but notice, not as *my daughter.* As if she were a neighbor. It was a subtle thing, but Nina's tension rose with each omission. Was there some protocol against introducing visiting family to other patients, like it could be seen as gloating? Whatever the reason, it didn't feel great to be renounced by your own mother.

She and her parents sat at a small table to eat their doughnuts.

"I like these," Frances said. "They taste like the glazed ones from Dean & Deluca."

"Remember when we ate all the sausage and mozzarella off the sample tray there?" Nina regretted saying it before she even finished the question—a reminder of the joyful midsummer tear through Soho, the mania that clearly no one wanted to remember. *Nina* didn't want to remember. She'd brought the gargantuan Think Big hairbrush to school and set it in a corner of her dorm room, the air sparkling with memories of that day, her mother's effervescence as they buzzed from street to street, sunlight bouncing off the buildings' windows, iridescent objects in every store. But then Nina had the phone call with her mother. That kind of joy wouldn't be coming around again. She'd wound up stowing the hairbrush under her bed.

And yet, she seemed unable to stop: "Remember we took the train to Spring Street? The German shepherd?" Was this her new tic, her version of Dolores's whistle? As if that subway ride were a happy memory. The dog had sniffed out the cocaine in Nina's handbag and nearly gotten her arrested.

Her mother shook her head, looking confused.

"Since when are dogs allowed on the subway?" Ira asked, then suggested they go outside to the garden.

———

Down another hallway off the dayroom, around a corner, up a set of stairs, through a door propped open with a rubber doorstop—Frances knew her way around here a lot better than Nina did Vanderbilt, where she was forever finding herself on a bus going in the wrong direction, or at the door to the library when she'd been aiming for the cafeteria.

They sat inside the gazebo, Nina on one small wicker bench and her parents on the other. Frances asked about school and she described a Western civ essay due this week—religious cults of ancient Egypt—which made her think of that night beside the Temple of Dendur, Gardner's hands in her hair, those same hands closing around Alison's throat—

"Vanderbilt sounds like a great place for you," Frances said.

"Yes. It's going well."

The sun was high and bright, but it was cool in the gazebo's shade and her arms prickled with goose bumps. She wished she'd brought a sweater. She wished she could go back to the dayroom and unravel Therese. *Mine*, she'd say as she draped the cardigan around herself while Therese toppled off her chair.

"How's Dad?" Frances asked Ira.

He cocked his head in a stagy way, as if Seymour had been nowhere on his radar. "Fine," he said. "Good."

It was the head-cock that made Nina blurt: "He has to go into a nursing home. He has Alzheimer's."

Her mother sat silent for a moment while Ira shot Nina a reproving look. Then Frances sighed. "I can't say I'm surprised. Poor Dad."

See? Nina's look back at Ira said. *Not a child.*

He repeated what he'd told Nina: "He's having trouble eating. He forgets to swallow. It's more than an aide can handle."

Frances took that in. "He forgets to, or he's forgotten how?"

"That's what I said!" Nina's spirits lifted a little. Then she remembered the book she'd brought with her. "I have a present for you," she told Frances. "*Take My Word for It.*"

"I believe you," her mother said.

"The new William Safire book, I mean." But where was it? Oh, right: in her handbag, which she'd had to leave in a locker when they came in. She got to her feet. She'd run in and retrieve it. She could use a Diet Coke refill anyway.

"Be right back!" she called as she headed toward the door they'd come out of.

She went down one hall and then another, searching for the route they'd taken to get outside so she could follow it back to the day-room, but of course she was lost. Down another hall: she'd somehow landed in a completely different wing. Instead of pea green, the walls were the resigned beige of oatmeal, and she was sure she hadn't seen that blue-speckled linoleum floor before. She kept walking down the dingy hallway until she reached—a dead end. Only she could manage to trap herself inside a mental hospital.

She turned around to retrace her steps, but when she looked up, an older man in a stained gray sweatshirt was standing outside his room, eyeing her, thick wet lips like he'd just eaten something dripping with grease. He started toward her. Her back was to the wall, so she stepped to her right, hoping he'd let her pass. But he stepped in the same direction, and when she went left, he did, too. She was back in Central Park at the start of the summer, the crazy guy with the dyed hair calling her *Ms. Bitch.*

"Shut up," he said, although she hadn't uttered a word.

She was so tired of all this. The unhinged guy with the dog collar, Walker and Rex, Freddie and the new doorman, the model's land-lord, the roped-up girl in *Beaver Hunt.* Those sickening, savage Pola-roids at Gardner's.

"Why are you still talking?" he said.

She was also so tired of cowering. She didn't have Stephanie's water gun, but she had her cup of half-melted ice. She jerked the cup toward him, splashing his sweatshirt with watery soda.

Except instead of retreating, he kept coming toward her. "They can hear you," he hissed. "Don't move. Don't even breathe. If they find us, we're dead."

He was less than a foot away, hemming her in. If he reached up, he could close his hands around her throat. She could almost feel them, crushing her windpipe—then it was Gardner's hands. Her vision went blurry. *I told you to leave me alone.*

"Leonard, stop that this instant!" The voice was her mother's. Frances wedged herself between him and Nina and turned to face him, arms spread as a shield. "This is my daughter," she said. "Now, stop causing trouble and get back to your room."

Leonard's face went lax, his head lolling to the side. "Sorry, Fran," he said, and shuffled away.

Her mother's room wasn't so chilling after all: white walls, two narrow beds with navy bedspreads, one with Pearl's emerald blanket folded at its foot, and a pair of blocky wooden dressers. On one of the dressers was a silver-framed photograph of Nina, Frances, and Ira all dolled up at an Amity Club New Year's Eve party. On the other a heap of clothes that Dolores was in the process of folding and stacking.

"Don't mind the mess," she said. "The bottom drawers get stuck halfway, so everything has to live on top."

"Sounds like they've come off the track," Ira said.

"Cunt Jew hello!" she erupted, and gave him the finger.

He smiled pleasantly and went over to take a look.

Nina and her mother sat on the edge of Frances's bed, side by side. Nina looked down at her lap, hands clenched together, thumbs hidden inside like they were also embarrassed to show their faces.

"I'm sure Leonard wouldn't have hurt you," Frances said, "but that had to be scary. I'm sorry."

"Will he get in trouble?" Nina asked. It was somehow still hard to admit how scared she'd been, the fear of a man's hands around her throat. She wondered if she'd be expecting it the rest of her life.

Frances laughed lightly. "That's not how things work here. They'll adjust his medication and limit his hall pass until he settles down."

Ira had managed to pull the drawers out of the dresser. He was squatting, fidgeting with the drawer tracks, and Nina was glad he had something he could fix.

Frances cleared her throat, then was silent, rubbing the birthmark on her pinkie with her thumb. Nina now saw that she wasn't indifferent, but nervous and uncertain, and probably had been since she heard Nina was coming. She remembered her mother telling her, years ago, "When you were born, I looked in your eyes and said, 'I hope you'll like me.'"

"That boy who killed the girl in the park," her mother said finally. "Gardner. I saw it on the news."

Nina nodded. There was nothing to say.

"He called you, the night we were soaking our feet in vinegar. That was him?"

"I didn't think you remembered anything about the summer."

"I remember enough." Her mother's face was bunched in a wince and Nina understood how painful each memory must be considering what she'd gone through, the battle to hold on to her mind while it soared and plunged against her will. A battle that took a kind of courage Nina could hardly imagine, that didn't make noise or ask for applause, no BITE ME swagger or Carlyle Hotel bravado, but the slog of hacking through a thicket of hopelessness and joylessness day after day, just for a glimpse of a clearing.

"I'm glad you're all right," Frances said shyly, still rubbing her birthmark.

Nina remembered the despair she'd seen in Alison's mother's eyes in the ladies' room after the funeral. She'd never have the chance to really know her daughter, and Alison would never get to be known in just that way.

Did Nina want to be known in that way? She put her hand over her face. She wasn't sure she had even a speck of Frances's courage. But maybe courage also meant just letting someone see you. She dropped her hand and looked at her mother.

"I'm not sure I am," she said. "All right, I mean. I didn't know if I should tell you."

Her mother looked back at her. She brushed a piece of hair out of Nina's eyes.

"Tell me," she said.

Acknowledgments

My deepest gratitude to my agent, Lisa Bankoff, for her confidence in my work and impeccable guidance, and to my editor, the peerless Amy Einhorn, for her belief in this story and invaluable insights, and to the entire team at Crown for their skill and support, most especially Lori Kusatzky, Mary Moates, Josie McRoberts, Terry Deal, and Rachelle Mandik. And special thanks to Chris Allen and Christopher Brand for the cover of my dreams.

To the Writers Studio community, which I feel endlessly lucky to have been a part of all these years, and especially to Philip Schultz and Monica Banks, for their enduring friendship. *A Gorgeous Excitement* originated as a short story in one of Phil's legendary workshops, and revealed itself, over many Pain Quotidien conversations, to deserve a larger canvas.

Huge appreciation to Heather Sellers, book doula and font of talent, wisdom, and kindness, for her exceptional feedback and assistance in shepherding this book to its conclusion.

Thank you to Steve Adams, Marcy Dermansky, Jack Livings, and Margarita Montimore, for their excellent input and advice during the writing of this book. Special thanks to Renee Landau for her thoughts on the ending.

To Lesley Dormen, Elizabeth England, Lucinda Holt, Andrée Lockwood, Joanne Naiman, and the late Isabelle Deconinck, for their friendship and our many conversations about books, clothes, life, and writing during these past years, which would have been a lot duller and less fun without them.

To Emily Colas and Jean Murley, for helping me keep things in perspective.

To my brothers, Jeff and Michael Weiner, with apologies for making Nina an only child, and to all the Weiners and Liftons, for generously sharing their family memories.

To my Chapin girls, for the '80s adventures that made it into the book (and for those that didn't).

And last but most, to the brilliant and beloved Gary Weinstein, without whom this book would not exist.

ABOUT THE AUTHOR

Cynthia Weiner's writing has appeared in *Ploughshares, The Sun,* and *Pushcart Prize,* among other places. She is the assistant director of the Writers Studio in New York City and currently resides in New York's Hudson Valley. *A Gorgeous Excitement* is her first novel.